Love, Scribbles

&

Other Things

JOAN EMBOLA

LOVE, SCRIBBLES & OTHER THINGS

LOVE & OTHER THINGS
BOOK 1

JOAN EMBOLA

LOVE, SCRIBBLES & OTHER THINGS

Copyright 2025 by Joan Embola

Love Qualified Press

All rights reserved.

This novel is a work of fiction. Although the settings and locations are based on fact, the characters, dialogues, and incidences portrayed are either the work of the author's imagination, or used fictitiously. Any resemblance to actual persons, living or dead, are entirely coincidental.

No part of this book may be reproduced in any form or by any electronic or mechanical means, including information storage and retrieval systems, without written permission from the author, except for the use of brief quotations in a book review.

No AI training: Any use of this publication to "train" generative artificial intelligence (AI) technologies to generate text or audiobook is expressly prohibited. The author reserves all rights to license uses of this work for generative AI training and development of machine learning language models.

No AI was used in the creation of this story or cover design.

Scriptures used in this book whether quoted or paraphrased are taken from;

New International Version, copyright © 1984 by Zondervan Publishing House. All rights reserved.

Blurb and manuscript edited by Michaela Bush

Cover designed and illustrated by Carelle N'guessan

For more information, contact;

www.joanembola.co.uk

ALSO BY JOAN EMBOLA

<u>Sovereign Love Series</u>

The One Who Knows Me (Book 1)

The One Who Loves Me (Book 2)

The One Who Sees Me (Book 3)

The One Who Holds Me (Book 4)

Sovereign Love Ebook Boxset (Books 1-4)

<u>Devotionals</u>

Outpourings Of A Beloved Heart: A 30-Day Poetry Devotional About God's Love

The God Who Knows Me: A Companion Devotional & Journal

Trigger Warning: This story addresses sensitive topics such as the death of a loved one, sexual assault and self-harm. I have done my best to treat these issues with the care they deserve. However, if these topics are triggers for you, I suggest you please pray before going any further, knowing that my intentions for choosing to address these topics are not to plunge readers into darkness, but to point them to the light and hope we have in our Lord and Saviour—Jesus Christ.

To my Heavenly Father, the One who made this possible.

To the one who has been hurt and feels like there's no way out of the darkness, I hope this story is an encouragement that there's no pain God's love can't heal.

"Forget the former things; do not dwell on the past. See, I am doing a new thing! Now it springs up, do you not perceive it? I am making a way in the wilderness and streams in the wasteland."

— ISAIAH 43:18-19

NAME PRONUNCIATION GUIDE

Ayuk (A-y-oh-k)- A Cameroonian name, often from the Bamileke tribe.

Chidimma (Chi-dee-mah)- A name originating from the Igbo people of Nigeria which means "God is good" or "God is great." Another variation of the name is Chidinma.

Oben (Oh-ben)- A Cameroonian name which can be used as a forename or surname. Can be associated with a group of related ethnic groups in Cameroon that speak various dialects of the Beti language.

Ayomide (A-y-or-mi-day)- A gender-neutral Nigerian name of Yoruba origin which means "my joy has arrived" or "my joy has come home."

Bankole (Bang-k-or-lay)- A Nigerian name of the Yoruba tribe, which translates to "build me a house."

Molua (M-oh-lu-wa)- A Cameroonian name which can be associated with particular ethnic groups like the Bakweri.

Enjema (En-j-ay-m-ah)- A popular female name in Cameroon associated with the Bakweri tribe.

1

BEX

"Hey, *Lexi*. How do you spell the word *puzzle*?" I lean back in my chair as my phone chimes.

"*Puzzle...*" The voice-activated digital assistant responds. "P-U-Z-Z-L-E."

"*Aha!*" The excitement in my voice catches me off guard as I point at the highlighted word on my computer screen. "In your face, *Scribbles.*" My writing software, *Scribbles*, tried to convince me I spelled the word wrong, so it brings me joy to click the "ignore" button instead of letting this artificial intelligence question my literacy.

But my moment of victory is short-lived because I'm back to staring at the blinking cursor on the blank page. It must be mocking me, I'm sure. Why does it keep blinking when it knows I have no idea what to write?

You would think that after four years of perfecting my story outline, crafting the perfect characters, spending hours making mood boards, and watching countless videos online in the name of "research," I'd at least know what the first sentence of this book is. But here I am, back at my desk again, for the fifth day in a row, with nothing to show for my hard work, except the word *puzzle.*

Puzzle? Seriously? That word has absolutely nothing to do with this story and that was the first thing my brain could spit out? *Lord, please, have mercy on me.*

I let out a groan and rub my eyes before deleting the word and pushing myself away from my desk. The pain that rushes through my head and down the back of my neck reminds me I've been sitting at this desk for way too long, or maybe it's a sign that I should stop wearing my hair in a high puff every day.

It's no secret that I love wearing my natural hair out, but I'm what you call a *lazy natural* because I can't be bothered to keep experimenting with different hairstyles. If my hair is not in chunky twists, then it'll be in a high puff with an *Ankara*[1] head-band and my high puffs always bang—if I do say so myself. But I think it's time to switch up the hairstyle unless I want to keep dealing with headaches every day.

After filling my mouth with the last bits of my cheese and onion crisps, I toss the empty packet in the bin before closing my window to stop the early September draught from coming in. Then I take a big gulp of water from my bottle, just in case dehydration has contributed to this headache I have—which I'm sure it has, since it's evening and my bottle is still three-quarters full.

After pacing the length of my room, I sit on the edge of my bed and let my head fall into my hands. I take deep breaths in and out, trying to drown out the siren noises in the distance, which could either be from an ambulance or a police car.

I like to always think it's the former, since the hospital is only a ten-minute drive from our house. But you can never be too sure about what these kids are up to these days. My parents bought a decent three-bed, one bath house in Croydon because it has affordable housing and good transport links into Central London.

The location makes it perfect for commuting to my investment banking job in Canary Wharf. But even though it's only a thirty-minute train journey, my introverted self always feels like I've run a marathon every time I get back home from work.

I promised my sisters I'd start writing this novel this week, but here I am, on Friday night, with nothing to show for it. How do these author vloggers find the time to write with a full-time job and a family? They make it look so easy, but I'm already failing before I've even started. Surely there's something I'm missing because this cannot be it.

My phone vibrates at my desk, pulling me away from the spiral of my thoughts. Rhoda—my youngest sister's name—flashes on my screen and I swipe left to answer.

"Sissy, we're on our way. Are you ready?"

I frown and stare at the watch on my wrist. It's six-thirty PM. Wow, I can't believe I've been sitting in this room for an hour. I haven't even changed out of my work clothes yet. "Ready for what?"

"*Ugh*, I knew you'd forget. You haven't seen our messages on the group chat yet, have you?" Rachel, my other sister, responds this time.

I gasp before opening my messaging app, panicking about missing a special birthday or anniversary or something. My sisters and I make a big deal about celebrating each other, so I would never want to be the one to forget.

"Oh." A sigh of relief escapes my lips as I bring the phone back to my ear. "I actually forgot the worship event was tonight. Soz[2]."

"Yeah, you wouldn't have if you had read your messages. Now get ready, coz we're two minutes away." Rhoda ends the call before I can put in another word and I roll my eyes.

Ugh, can you imagine the audacity? She better apologise when she gets here or else I'm not going.

The three of us have completely different personalities, Rhoda being the sharp-mouthed one, even though she's the youngest. As I've already established, I'm the introverted and more reserved one, while Rachel sits in between like the perfect middle child she is.

We were all born in Cameroon, but our parents moved to the UK when we were eight, six, and four years old. In secondary school, they used to call us *the three sister-teers* because we were always together and even though we've individually made friends through university and our jobs, we've always been each other's best friends.

As much as our personalities are different, so are our personal styles. Rachel loves wearing make-up every time she goes out because she has been practising for years and she's basically a master at it. Even though she wears prescription glasses, you would never know because she has different glasses with different frames to match her outfit. She also changes her hairstyle every four to six weeks because she does her hair herself and if she wasn't also my personal hairstylist, I would envy her.

Rhoda is much more laid back than me. She always wears her type 4a natural hair in a *wash-and-go* hairstyle, her gorgeous curls popping every time, no matter the season. Rhoda also doesn't joke with her comfort. The girl doesn't like stress, so flats and warm clothes are her go-to—especially when the cold weather rolls in.

Rhoda flings herself on me, almost knocking my tired self to the ground when I open the door for them. "I've missed you, Sissy." She squeezes me into a tight hug, barely leaving me with enough energy to hug Rachel. The entire speech I planned to scold Rhoda for hanging up on me flies out the window because she gives the best hugs.

"Wow, I didn't know I was that loved." I smirk as Rhoda gives me a side eye. I only missed one of our weekly catch up sessions and now she's acting like I disappeared for a year.

"You can't miss our next outing," Rhoda says as we follow her lead up the stairs and into my room, which used to be our hang out spot when we all lived at home with our parents. The room is bigger and doesn't have a bunk bed like Rachel and Rhoda's old room, so we used to lie on my bed for hours talking about everything and anything.

When Rachel got her job as a secondary school science teacher, she moved out and got a two-bedroom flat in Mitcham. She didn't need to, as the commute from Croydon to Mitcham is not too bad, but Rachel loves her independence and her own space.

Rhoda also joined her and they both share the rent, so we've moved our weekly meetups to their flat, which has given us the freedom to catch up without worrying about our parents eaves-dropping on us.

Last Saturday, the plan was to go see a movie together at the cinema. Rhoda bought the tickets and everything, but work was so busy and I just wanted one evening to do nothing, so I cancelled. My sisters understand that sometimes I need days to recuperate when my physical and emotional energy is drained. That's why they gave me space.

They never give me too much space though, because before I blink, they're back knocking at the door, invading my space and bugging me as always. With Mum and Dad away on their yearly trip to Cameroon, we have our privacy today.

"So, how's your writing going?" Rhoda asks as she throws herself on my bed, messing up my perfectly-laid sheets.

I avert my gaze and open my built-in wardrobe, staring at my row of blouses and pretending I didn't hear her.

"Bex?" They both call out and I turn around before laying out a black-and-white striped blouse on the bed.

"Well, I was in the zone until you girls showed up and ruined my flow."

"Really?" Rachel taps the space key on my laptop, turning it on and exposing my lies. "There's nothing on the page, Bex. Just a blinking cursor."

"*Urgh.* You girls can't let me get away with anything, can you?" I plop down on the edge of my bed and my sisters sit on either side of me.

"What's going on, Bex?" Rachel asks, pushing her glasses close to her face.

"Yeah, talk to us, Sissy," Rhoda places her arm around my shoulder and I lean my head on hers before sighing.

"I just..." My words falter as I fight the tears blurring my vision. It wouldn't be the first time I've bawled in front of my sisters, but I fear they would think me silly for crying over a book. The thing is, it's more than just a book and I don't know if I can ever make them understand why it's so important that I write this story.

"I just can't bring myself to start." My words come out in a whisper as one tear escapes. "I've spent so long preparing for this moment and now that it's here, I can't find the words. How am I going to write the story if I can't find the words?"

"Hey, hey." Rachel wipes the tears sliding down my cheeks. "The words will come. Maybe you're just afraid of making it perfect from the beginning, so you're putting pressure on yourself."

"Yeah, but you have to push through that fear and just start writing," Rhoda adds.

"I did. I sat here for an hour today and do you know what my first word was?"

The girls both give me blank stares.

"Puzzle. How can my first word be *puzzle*? What has that got to do with anything?"

"I guess that's a puzzle we need to solve," Rhoda says, and we all laugh. "Come on, Sissy. Remember when you first told us about this story idea four years ago? You said God was the One who gave you the story, right?"

I nod and sniffle.

"So if He gave you the story, don't you think He'll help you write it too?"

"He sure will," Rachel answers for me.

"Yeah, but sometimes I wish I didn't have so many distractions around me. My job is a blessing, but it physically drains me and I barely have any energy left at the end of the day. When I can't write, I watch other author vloggers online and end up feeling sorry for myself because I can't be as productive as them."

"Okay, you need to stop watching those vloggers." Rachel wags her finger in my face. "You know most of them only show you the hills of their journey and never the valleys, right?" She refers to one of our favourite songs by Tauren Wells.

"Yeah, stop comparing your journey with them," Rhoda chimes in. "You don't work weekends, so maybe you can leave the writing until then? Remember, you used to go to coffee shops to work on your outline on Saturdays?"

"Oh yeah. I was so proud of myself for leaving the house every Saturday." I smile, remembering my initial excitement about the story when God first gave me the idea.

"If coffee shops worked for you before, why don't you try them again? I'm sure there are so many in central you haven't explored yet."

I pause for a moment, thinking about Rhoda's suggestion. Even though the idea of leaving the house and interacting with people gives me palpitations, I can't deny the fact that I was more productive at coffee shops. Plus, if God helped me do it before, then He can surely help me do it again. "I guess I can try one out next week."

"Yay. That's what we like to hear." Rhoda pushes herself up from the bed and claps her hands. "Well, now that the crisis has been averted, it's time to hit the road or we'll be late." She taps on her watch and then rushes out of the room and down the stairs to the kitchen. Of course, she needs a snack for the journey, even if it's only a fifteen-minute drive. The girl is such a foodie.

I wipe my tear-stained face and put on my clothes before walking to the bathroom to do my quick ten-minute makeup routine. After sliding my feet into my ankle boots, I spray on my fruity and aromatic perfume combo, which always gets me a lot of compliments. I may not always enjoy interacting with people, but I like to smell good when I do.

"I'm ready." I pop back into the room.

"Finally." Rachel picks up her handbag and we both troop downstairs to meet Rhoda, coming out of the kitchen, a half-eaten bag of plantain chips in her hand.

"What?" Rhoda asks with wide eyes, crunching the chips in her mouth as we both stare at her. "A girl has to eat."

"We didn't say otherwise, Madam." I chuckle. "Just wipe the crumbs from your mouth, please. If anyone sees you at church looking like this, Mum and Dad will hear of it. Don't disgrace us, oh." I pull my ears, mimicking what our mum would say, and we all laugh as we get into Rachel's car.

"I can't wait for Mum and Dad to return on Monday. We need those authentic Cameroonian treats before my stomach withers."

"Did someone ever tell you you're so dramatic?" I turn to Rhoda in the backseat as we put on our seatbelts.

"What's so dramatic about loving food?"

"Don't worry, tell me what you want to eat and I'll make it next week," Rachel says as she turns the key in the ignition.

"Ooh, *poulet DJ*, please." Rhoda's face lights up as she mentions her favourite Cameroonian meal. "Give me that and I'll make dessert."

"I'll buy drinks, then," I add, and just like that, our date is planned. That's the benefit of having sisters who have mad cooking and baking skills. I just have to do the bare minimum and I end up having the best food, the best dessert, and the best company. God knew spending time with my sisters was exactly what I needed today after the hectic week I've had. I can't wait to get over this hurdle and finally start writing this story.

2

——————

JEVAUN

Time, they say, heals all wounds, but what they never tell you is that it only works that way in an ideal world. My experience so far has been nothing but the opposite. We all wish it got easier with time, so we comfort ourselves to believe that's all we need.

But healing takes more than just letting time pass. Mum knew that too, as she looked into my eyes on her deathbed. She tried her best to force a smile during that final moment, but we all knew as we surrounded her that the sparkle had disappeared from her beautiful brown eyes. Her response to me was that healing is not a destination, but a journey.

As my dad, my younger brother Tréjon and I watched her take her last breath, I hoped she was wrong and that the pain would eventually fade away. But I quickly learnt that she was right.

The pain doesn't just go away. It stays right there, lurking, and waiting for the right opportunity to rear its ugly head again. All it takes is one word, one memory, one encounter or one confrontation for those wounds to open up again, oozing and bleeding as fresh as the original, with no sign of healing at all.

I thought the pain would've eased off by now, given how much my life has changed in the last five years. Not only have I had to adjust to living in a world without Mum, but I've been actively living the dream life God gave me. That dream life that led me away from my parent's home and to London while still trying to keep the relationship between myself, Tré and Dad—just like I promised Mum.

Tré's not the problem because not only is he my brother, but my best friend. The real problem here is Dad. I wish I was strong enough not to carry the burden of that promise every day. Every time I want to walk away, the chains of my own words pull me back to where I started.

All the self-help books and the so-called experts have lied to me so far. It hasn't gotten easier. I don't know if it'll ever do. But what I know is that only God helped me get through all those sleepless nights.

I know I didn't get here by just 'letting time pass' and hoping for the best. It was me realising that I couldn't do life without God. I wish Dad and Tré believed that too, but again, that is not my current reality. I don't know if it'll ever be, but that's a worry for another day. Today's focus is to spend time with Tré.

After over an hour-long journey on the coach, I'm finally standing in front of the house in Dartford—the same house Tré and I grew up in. The same house Mom died in. These days I only refer to it as Dad's house because it's hard to remember the times when we used to call it a home, given all the unpleasant events that have taken place in it in the last five years.

It would've been a lot easier if Tré had come over to my flat in Shoreditch, but I didn't dare suggest that to him unless I was prepared to receive the total unleash of Dad's wrath on me. It's bad enough that Mum isn't here with us. The last thing I want to do is create an unstable family environment for Tré.

"Jevaun?" Tré's voice pulls me out of my thoughts as he

opens the front door and walks across the damp path in the front garden. Even though we're approaching the end of summer, I still expect us to have decent sunshine to enjoy, but no. You could have all four seasons in one day. The UK weather is confused like that. It's no wonder my vitamin D levels are always deficient whenever I do a blood test.

"Hey, bro." I smile and pull him in for a hug as he towers over me. "Feels like I haven't seen you in ages." I take a step back and give him a once-over from head to toe. "Being a doctor is looking good on you, though." I point to his clean-shaven beard, which makes him look younger than his age of twenty-four.

Tré started the first year of his junior doctor foundation programme in Nottingham a month ago. We all hoped he would have an easy start, but they threw him into the deep end with his first rotation in the accident and emergency department.

"Come on, you're just saying that to make me feel better. It's only been a month and I've lost weight, can't you see?" He raises his arms up to show me the evidence. "All the work you and I did at the gym over the summer is gone."

"Ah, don't worry about it. Once you're settled, you'll find time to go back to the gym." I adjust my backpack strap on my shoulder.

"I hope so."

"Is Dad around?" I ask as we both walk to the front door, my chest already tightening at the possibility of seeing Dad sitting in the living room.

"No, he stepped out ten minutes ago. Said he'll be back in time for dinner."

"That's fine with me." I'll treasure every moment with Tré that doesn't include Dad's presence.

Taking off my shoes, I place them on the shoe rack in the hallway before walking into the spacious living room Tré and I used to run around in as children. The sofa, TV, chandelier, and side tables are still in the same place, but the walls that were once decorated with photos of our then-happy life are now just plain, white and boring.

At first I thought Dad took down the photos because it helped him grieve Mum, but I quickly learnt that he had other reasons. Reasons I hope I won't have to bring up again tonight for the millionth time. *Lord, please give me strength.*

"So, what are we cooking tonight?" I place my backpack on a sofa before joining Tré in the kitchen. I could take my backpack upstairs to my old room, but that means I'll have to walk past the room Mum died in. Sometimes I think I can still smell her perfume and the coconut oil she always had in her hair. But olfactory hallucinations are real. Grief can do that to you.

"Well, we'll be having some rice and peas, jerk chicken, and plantains." Tré's voice breaks into my thoughts as he shows me his display of the ingredients on the kitchen island. Cooking is one thing we have always enjoyed doing together. When Mum noticed we had an interest, she handed over her kitchen to us and made us in charge of dinner one weekend a month.

We used it as our time to show our culinary skills and tried so many recipes, including orange chicken, pasta bake, lasagnes, fried rice, chilli, and so many others. Today, we're taking it back to our Jamaican roots, so it has to be delicious.

"I know I've only been working as a doctor for a month, but I can see why you quit and pursued entrepreneurship instead," Tré says as he chops up onions.

"Really?" My brows furrow. "Why do you think I did it?" I ask before peeling a plantain and cutting it into pieces.

Tré and I did everything together as kids even though we are six years apart. I started asking my parents for a sibling when I turned five, so when Tré came a year later, my excitement knew no bounds. We've grown closer over the years and I'd say we definitely have some sort of 'brother telepathy' going on, so I'm interested to hear his response to my question.

Tré shrugs before looking at me. "It's simple. Medicine is a stressful career and not everyone is built for that kind of pressure."

"Well, that's true, but entrepreneurship is also stressful. It has its own disadvantages too. It's not all rosy out here. I can tell you that for sure."

"But you are your own boss. You work on your own terms and you're doing brilliantly for yourself. Mate, you earn way more than I do."

"Yes, but I've been doing this for five years, remember? Didn't I tell you that after my first month as a full-time entrepreneur, I earned less than a hundred pounds? I had to rely on my savings for the first six months before my income became decent enough to pay for my life expenses. Trust me, it's a hard alternative to a stable nine-to-five job." I pick up another plantain and start peeling it before continuing.

"Contrary to popular belief, entrepreneurship is not the easy way out and not everyone will be successful in the business endeavours after quitting their day job. If God has made you a light at your workplace and you enjoy what you do or find it rewarding, then definitely stay there. It's easy for people to look at things the way you are, but what you don't see is that I work round the clock, my income is unpredictable every month, and I still haven't published my first novel even though I'm an experienced writer."

Tré nods as he drains out the kidney beans he soaked overnight. "Yeah, I see what you mean. That sounds tough and anxiety-inducing. I definitely like the idea of a stable income every month. But I'd still like to have some sort of side hustle, though."

"Yeah, diversifying your income streams is a great idea. I'm always here for you to pick my brain."

"Cool. How's your querying journey going?"

I put down the knife and let out a deep sigh as Tré laughs because he knows I'm about to go into full ranting mode. "Listen, don't even get me started about how tough the publishing industry is. I have now sent a query letter to almost a hundred agents and none of them see the potential in my book."

"Ah, don't worry about it. You only need 'the one,' right?"

"Of course. Just the one. I haven't given up. I know God will bring that one agent at the right time."

"Amen to that." Even though Tré says those words casually, it warms my heart to hear them come out of his mouth.

When I first announced to my family that I had chosen to become a Christian, Tré and Dad made it very clear that they are atheists and they didn't want me trying to convert them. Tré has even made fun of the fact that I chose to write "Christian fantasy" books as he doesn't think a genre like that makes sense.

But even though talking about my faith with Tré can sometimes feel like walking on eggshells, he has never condemned me because of it. That's the complete opposite of what Dad did.

I never want Tré to feel like I'm forcing my beliefs on him, but every morning, I pray for God to provide opportunities for Tré to see Jesus in me and that his heart will be receptive to God's word. It has been five years and even though there's nothing much to show for it, little moments like this are reminders that I shouldn't stop praying.

After putting the marinated chicken in the oven, Tré starts cooking the rice and peas while I fry the plantains and our conversations, even though they shift to everything and anything, keep coming back to entrepreneurship. Of course, I use that as an opportunity to share how God has been helping me along the journey.

"Honestly, I think it's so cool that you can just work on your own terms and do whatever you want," Tré says as he stirs the pot of the cooked rice and peas before closing it again. "The freedom of it all is very appealing."

"But you dare not do that, though." Dad walks into the kitchen and the silence that passes between us is so intense that I imagine they can hear my racing thoughts and my pounding heartbeat.

"Welcome back, Dad. Dinner will be ready in about ten minutes." Tré breaks the silence as the older man approaches me.

He stops on the opposite side of the kitchen island, staring deep into my soul with the usual anger in his brown eyes. With Dad's clean-shaven face and barely noticeable grey hairs, you could say he is the pure definition of 'black don't crack' and he uses that to his advantage given the trail of female companions he has had over the last six years.

Judging from his youthful attire, gold wristwatch, and the feminine perfume that follows his trail, I know exactly where he's coming from. For him, it has always been about impressing the ladies and it doesn't matter who he hurts along the way.

"What makes you think you can come in here and start spreading all your ignorant ideas?" He spits out the words like venom and my heart bleeds from the pain they inflict.

Tré clears his throat and turns off the hob so the last batch of plantains doesn't get burned. "Dad, we were just chatting about—"

"You think you were just chatting," Dad turns his head sharply to Tré, "but your brother here has an agenda. He always does." He turns to look at me again as I grit my teeth and try to slow down my breathing.

"You want to lure him into following your footsteps, don't you? It starts with you encouraging him to leave his job just like you did and soon you'll be coercing him to believe in your so-called God, isn't that right?"

And there it is. The real reason for the outburst. It has always boiled down to me choosing God over everything and everyone else.

"How dare you mention God in this house?" He flares his nostrils and raises his voice as his gaze intensifies. "Haven't I told you never to utter such rubbish in front of Tré?"

"Dad, my beliefs are my beliefs. My relationship with God is important to me. The events in my life over the last five years are evidence that He's real. I can't force you to believe in Him, but you also can't force me to stop talking about the God who has literally been with me through thick and thin."

"Oh, really?" He shakes his head and laughs. "The same way He was with your mum as the cancer sucked the life out of her, right? The same way He tricked us into believing the cancer was gone and that she was healed, only for it to come back a few years later with a vengeance that claimed her life, right?"

"Dad, stop!" Tré raises his voice and drops the silicon ladle on the kitchen countertop. "I didn't travel three hours down here to watch you two reach for each other's throats. I came here to spend time with my family, so if you're not ready to be in the same room as each other, then tell me and I'll make my way back," he says, before stomping out of the kitchen and leaving me alone with Dad.

Even though we continue staring at each other, our nostrils still flaring, we don't exchange any more words until he finally walks out of the kitchen. We've had this argument several times before and every time his words get more bitter and his frustration higher.

He used to tell me he couldn't wait for God to fail me, so I'd realise all along that he was right. I guess every time I come back with more testimonies to share, he gets more antsy. And he'll continue to be that way because the God I serve never fails.

I made a promise to Mum that I won't give up on my family, so I'm not letting Dad's sour mood rub off on me. I set up the table and call Tré to come down so we can eat. If Dad is hungry, he can come down too. If not, we'll be more than happy to have his share.

3

BEX

Despite Rachel's pathetic attempt to get us to church before the start of the programme, we still arrived fifteen minutes late. I'm not surprised because Rachel refuses to drive above the speed limit even when there are no cameras or no other cars on the road.

Unfortunately, today, we also had the annoying road works to contend with, so we spent a lot of time in traffic. They've been working on that road for almost three months and I'm still struggling to see what exactly they're building or fixing.

The usual fifteen-minute journey took us almost double the time, getting us to church just after the first praise session. We slipped in before the worship session started and just before the doors closed.

We walk across the red-carpeted floor as we follow the usher's directions to the back row of seats, and I'm able to catch a glimpse of the worship team on the mounted stage at the front of the auditorium.

The drummer, Keith, is playing behind the drum shield with headphones over his ears. The guitarist, Samuel, is on the opposite end of the stage, in his element as always. The lead singer,

Mirabelle, is behind the pulpit, eyes closed and hand stretched out, while the backup singers, Léonie, Chidimma, and Joshua, are standing on either side of her.

At Living Hope Church, the ushers close the doors during the worship session to prevent any distraction from people walking in and out of the auditorium. Anyone who comes after the praise session gets to worship the Lord from behind the closed front doors, as the two ushers stationed at the front always make sure this rule is observed.

I've had to wait outside once or twice before. It wasn't too bad, but the only problem is that once the doors open and we all flood in, the auditorium is usually quiet with everyone seated and I'm not a fan of the attention it draws on me. It definitely is a motivating factor to get to church on time.

"*Phew*, that was close," Rhoda whispers as we take our seats on the soft red chairs in our usual order, me seated closest to the wall, Rhoda in the middle, and Rachel closest to the aisle.

"Yes, thank God for that," Rachel responds while Rhoda shakes her head at her.

"That's no thanks to you. A snail drives faster than you." Rhoda rolls her eyes and the two girls bicker at each other.

"Shh! We are in the house of God, so can you two please show some respect?" I send both of them my death glare and they stop talking immediately as we focus on the slow worship music filling the auditorium.

Thank God I can still use my firstborn privileges on these two.

There was a time when I didn't understand what it meant to worship God through songs. My head would swell and my heart would beat so fast whenever I heard my favourite worship song, but it was always about how I was feeling and never about Who I was singing the songs to. Now I know better. It's not about the song or me or the person who is singing. It's about focusing on who God is—period.

The fact that I'm still here, declaring that God is good, is a testimony I won't take for granted. Maybe someday, God will finally give me the courage to open up about my traumatic university experience. But until then, I'm taking it one step at a time, worshipping God as I go.

At the end of the worship session, Pastor David takes to the stage and leads us in prayer before going into the announcements and the various events the church has lined up for the month.

Being the family church that it is, LHC comprises one hundred percent Africans, most of whom are Nigerians. Our family and the Oben family make up the only two Cameroonian families in the church—the rest is made up of Ghanaians, Zimbabweans, Congolese, and some Jamaicans.

But apart from the diversity, the sound Biblical teachings, wonderful music, and kind people are all reasons I love being part of this community. But just like it is in every community, you won't always have fond memories with every single person. The one person I wouldn't mind not coming across today is Ayo —my ex-boyfriend, who is also one of the pianists.

"Look who's playing the piano today," Rhoda whispers in my ear and although I know exactly who she's talking about, I keep my head down, refusing to look in his direction.

Who would've thought that just looking at someone could immediately trigger so many unpleasant memories? Memories of the time when I didn't know who I was and when I set my standards so low because I let my past trauma define me.

I saw all the red flags, but chose to become colour blind against the advice of my well-meaning sisters, because I thought I would never find love with the baggage I carried. Ayo was only a Christian with his lips and I knew that, but again, I ignored the signs God was showing me that Ayo's heart was very far away from Him.

I thought I knew better. I thought the reason God brought him into my life was so I could change him. But thank God for God, who held me back from adding another mistake to my already long list.

It was not a shock when Rachel and Rhoda found out that Ayo was cheating on me. God had already warned me about him and He helped me muster up the courage to end the relationship. It was through that experience that I learnt to trust God, no matter the cost.

The Bex of six years ago, who was fresh out of university, would've given in to any man who looked her way. That's how I ended up with Ayo in the first place—falling for all his empty promises and sweet nothings. But experience, they say, is the best teacher, and God taught me a valuable lesson—to sit tight and wait for the man He has planned for me. That man, I've learnt, is *definitely* not Ayomide Bankole.

After two hours of enjoying a variety of worship ministrations from guest ministers such as singing, praise dancing, and a saxophone worship, the event finally ends and we pick up our bags and make our way towards the door, greeting everyone who stops us on the way.

"Good to see you, Rebecca." Aunty Vivian Oben, one of the children's church teachers, stops us at the door. "Are your parents back from Cameroon yet?" she asks with a warm smile.

I shake my head. "No, Aunty. They'll be back on Monday."

"Okay," she says, before turning to Rachel. "My dear, I'm still waiting for your response about joining the children's teachers' department. I think the children need you."

"Yes, Aunty, I'm still praying about it." Rachel smiles, but Rhoda and I both know that her hesitancy is because she's currently overwhelmed with everything on her plate.

"Okay, thank you girls so much. God bless you and have a good night."

When we get to the church car park, a familiar voice shouts out my name and I stop in my tracks before turning around.

"Ayo?" My brows furrow as he runs towards us.

"Sorry for bothering you, but do you have a minute? I'd like to speak to you, please." He says, catching his breath as his eyes stare deep into mine. Those brown eyes used to make my cheeks warm up every time he sent a long gaze my way, but not anymore.

"Me?" I ask, before shooting a glance at my sisters.

He nods. "Yes, if that's okay with you." He scratches his high-top dreadlocks before sending me a sheepish smile that comes across as more of a plea. The Ayo I knew before was never this polite, so to say I'm shocked is an understatement.

"Sure." I turn to my sisters and Rachel drags Rhoda away.

When they're gone, Ayo steps forward and places his arms by his sides, before opening his mouth and closing it again. He looks like he has a war going on inside his mind, but instead of pressuring him to say what he has to say, I remain silent so he can get his thoughts together.

He fiddles with a button on his denim shirt, which was the uniform of the choir members and instrumentalists today. "You...erm...you look nice today," he finally says after clearing his throat and I lift my brows.

Seriously? Did he just ask me to wait behind, so he could tell me this?

"Thanks." I shift my weight to my right leg and smile at Joy, one of the ushers, as she walks past us on her way home.

Turning back to Ayo, I cross my arms against my chest and tilt my head, saying nothing, but I'm sure he's getting all the cues that he's wearing my patience thin.

"Listen, B. I know this is coming very late, but I wanted you to know that I'm very sorry for what I did," he starts. "A few months ago, God convicted me about my lifestyle choices and I realised it was time for me to stop playing around and take my relationship with Him seriously. I've been thinking a lot about my life and I've realised that I need to right my wrongs."

He pauses before taking a step forward, but I step back, letting him know he needs to stick to his boundaries.

"B, please, I'm sorry I treated you the way I did. You were nothing but good to me, and I took your kindness for granted. I wish I could go back and fix everything, but I can't. Please, would you be able to forgive me?" He rubs his palms together as he waits for my response.

To be honest, I was very bitter after the breakup and I had to stop myself many times from praying certain prayers about Ayo, whom I considered as my enemy. I wanted his actions exposed so he could be ridiculed and expelled from the church. But thank God for working on my heart and redirecting my prayer points.

I never would've thought that I would see the day when Ayo became remorseful. But God works in mysterious ways, and this is one mystery I'll never be able to wrap my head around.

I let out a sigh before saying, "Ayo, I've already forgiven you."

A bright smile appears on his face. "Really?"

I nod. "Yeah, I made my peace with it a long time ago. I've moved on and I'm happy that God has brought you to the same place as well." I smile at him, sending a prayer of thanks to God for the work He is doing in him.

"That's great. Thank you so much." He leans forward and hugs me briefly before stepping back again. "Erm…" He stumbles on his words. "Do you think you and I could grab dinner sometime? Or whatever you choose, really. It's been a while, and I just wanted us to catch up."

Wow, I know God is full of surprises, but this was one I never saw coming.

"Actually, Ayo, I'd like to remain friends," I say without hesitation. "Even though I've forgiven you, I don't think things can ever be the same again between us. I would love for you to please respect that."

The hurt that flashes across his facial features is unmistakable, but he doesn't push and he doesn't try to convince me otherwise. He nods and rubs his bearded face before saying, "I understand. I'm just grateful that you've forgiven me. I messed up my chance with you, but I'm sure the man you'll end up with will be blessed to have you."

"Thanks, Ayo. Your wife will be blessed too. Have a good night." I smile at him before taking retreating steps, so he waves at me and heads towards the church building.

Back in the car, my sisters squeeze out the details of our encounter by asking countless questions.

"So it took him five years to realise what he was missing?" Rhoda scoffs from the back seat as Rachel drives us out of the car park. "I hope you told him to get lost and go find someone else to deceive."

"*Ah-ahn*. Rhoda Ayuk." Rachel stares at our little sister through the rearview mirror. "I now see the reason you're still single. Your mouth is too sharp."

"And since you have a tamed mouth, where is your man?" Rhoda retorts.

"Look at this girl, *oh*. If I wasn't behind this wheel now, my left shoe would've landed on your face." Rachel kisses her teeth before we all burst out laughing. I just love how we always switch to our 'Cameroonian accents' when we're arguing.

"Girls, it's okay." I step in as usual to bring their attention back to the matter at hand. "You don't have to worry because I politely declined his request, but I believe God is truly working on him."

"Yes, and sometimes it can take a long time for God to work

on people's hearts." Rachel glares at Rhoda before turning the car left onto the main road.

"That's true," I concur. "I'm genuinely happy for him and it feels like a weight has been lifted off my shoulders, too."

"Aww, that's great," Rachel says.

"Yeah, you've come such a long way and it can only go up from here," Rhoda adds. "God has healed you from that heartbreak. You're finally writing your book and on Monday, you're going to get a promotion or a huge pay rise at your job."

I forgot about my appraisal with my manager on Monday, which Rhoda thinks is for a promotion, but I doubt it. Every year around this time, I hope and pray they'll give me a promotion, but it ends up being the same story of disappointment. Maybe it's time to move to another organisation who will appreciate the work I put in.

When the girls drop me off at home, I hug them goodbye and rush up to my room as a boost of inspiration sparks ideas in my brain. I'm not sure whether it's my encounter with Ayo or just the joy of worshipping God with other believers, but that mental block I had before is gone.

My plan for tomorrow is a solo writing date at a coffee shop I found online at Waterloo Station called The Buzz Café. Just imagining myself in the middle of the chaos of that station makes me want to change my mind, but I have to push myself to try new routines because my current one is clearly not working.

As for tonight, I can't let this motivation go to waste, so without changing out of my clothes, I plant myself at my desk and my fear of the blank page vanishes as I open my laptop.

Lord, please help me. I say a quick prayer before resting my fingers on the laptop keys. Letting out a deep sigh, I type the first word, which is not *puzzle*, and then the next word, and the next, typing well into the early hours of the morning, until the first chapter is done.

. . .

Nothing could've prepared Vanessa Molua for the months of turmoil that lay ahead of her. Like any other fresher arriving at university in London, away from Coventry where she grew up, the only worries on her mind were how she would survive alone, how she would make new friends, and of course, how she would manage the pressures of her busy medical degree.

Vanessa had joined a social media group chat during the summer break, and she connected with some of her course mates there because she was a planner, and she wanted to make sure she wasn't left in the dark. One of Vanessa's life mottos was to always be one step ahead of the game. She hated it when anything took her by surprise, so she never failed to plan, because she wasn't planning to fail.

Vanessa's mum Diana and her sixteen-year-old brother Victor helped her carry her suitcases to her university accommodation, and they spent two hours helping her with her pink and purple room decor. Of course, Diana couldn't leave without praying over her daughter and anointing every creak and corner of the ensuite single room Vanessa was going to stay in for the next year.

"God will be with you, my darling daughter," Diana said as tears rolled down her cheeks. "You will make the right friends. You will pass all your exams with flying colours, and you will finish well in Jesus' name," she added as she hugged her daughter, sobbing like there was no tomorrow.

When it was time to say goodbye, the tears Vanessa had been holding back finally burst forth as she waved at her mum's car disappearing from her sight. It was at that moment that she wished her dad was there.

But instead of embracing the self-destructing spirit of sadness that grief often tempted her with, Vanessa consoled herself with the fact that her dad would be proud of her as he celebrated his fifth heavenly birthday.

Back in her flat's communal kitchen, connections were made at the meet and greet session with her four flatmates and that's how she met Anne—the tall, soft-spoken Nigerian girl whose room was directly across from hers. Conversations with Anne were effortless and when Vanessa found out that Anne was also a Christian studying medicine, she knew right away that God had answered her mum's prayers.

The rest of the evening comprised eating pizza, icebreaker games, and lots of conversations with Anne about their hopes and fears of studying medicine. They planned out their week by looking through the freshers' programme, and they chose the events they were interested in. Out of all the events, they most looked forward to attending the Christian union meeting and also checking out the local churches in the area.

By the time Vanessa got back to her room that evening, her muscles ached from all the exciting activities of the day, but she couldn't deny the fact that her heart missed home. So she called her mum and spoke to her brother too for half an hour before saying a prayer and drifting off to sleep.

She had survived her first day of university and everything had gone to plan, just like she had anticipated. Even so, nothing could've prepared Vanessa for the months of turmoil that lay ahead of her.

4

JEVAUN

For the past five years, God has been the creative director and CEO of my business and I'm so grateful for all the blessings I've been enjoying. But some days, I struggle to motivate myself to keep going. Yesterday was definitely one of those days and it has everything to do with the altercation I had with Dad.

Tré always tells me to block out Dad's words and not let them get to me, but that is so much easier said than done. How can I not let them get to me when all the memories I now have of him are filled with accusations, arguments, and hurtful words?

If I could just wave a hand and unhear everything he said yesterday in front of Tré, then I would do just that. But here I am, back at home, staring at the wall in my living room, and replaying those words over again in my head.

This is exactly the reason I dread our family reunions and even though Mum would've been heartbroken to hear me say this, it's a truth I can't deny. How long can I keep exposing myself to such negativity?

It's been five years, and it hasn't gotten any easier. Every encounter with Dad leaves me feeling more discouraged than the last one. I used to wonder how some parents could become estranged from their children and I promised myself I would never be that child, but now I know better not to judge.

I'm slowly approaching the end of my tether and one of these days, all my bottled up emotions will all come bursting out of me, without me caring about the consequences of my words or actions.

I miss those days when I couldn't do wrong in Dad's eyes, not because I liked the attention he gave me, but because that was the last time we enjoyed peace as a family. If someone had told me that things would ever get this bad, then I would've laughed in their face.

But no matter how much my heart longs for things to be the way they were, I'll choose the peace I've found in Jesus over everything and everyone else. It's what's most important to me and I'm not looking back.

I take a deep breath and exhale as I bow my head over the open Bible in front of me, eyes closed but struggling to pray. I usually have my Bible study at the dining table in the living room, but today I chose to sit at my home office desk.

When I quit my job as a doctor and moved from Preston to London to pursue my career as a creative entrepreneur, I was conflicted about what part of London I wanted to live in. A nurse I used to work with at my old job mentioned Shoreditch in passing, as she had heard that it was a vibrant place filled with lots of young creatives.

After watching countless videos online, visiting the area, and praying about it for months, the answer to my prayer came when God helped me get a two-bedroom flat for a very affordable price. Now, five years down the line, I can confidently say I don't regret that decision and it could've only been the grace of God.

The sound of honking cars coming through my ajar window

fills my ears and brings me out of my reverie. This part of Shoreditch is usually quiet as it's away from the busy high street, but we occasionally get some traffic related noises, even from the second floor where my flat is.

The quiet environment works well for me as I don't have to bother about noise when I'm working. Saturdays are for content creation. It's the day when I batch record all the videos that will go live on my social media platforms during the week. It's eleven AM and I should've started recording my second video by now, but my motivation is all gone.

"Lord, please help me." Those are the only words I have the strength to say as I close my men's study Bible.

The scripture from Romans chapter eight verse twenty-six keeps ringing in my heart, reminding me about the fact that even when I don't know what to pray, the Holy Spirit intercedes for me. It's days like today that I hold on to those words tighter than ever before because as the months pass, I'm becoming more easily discouraged and I hate this for myself.

I ask *Lexi* to put on some worship music in the living room and, as it blasts through my speakers, I make myself some porridge for breakfast before taking a quick shower and changing into a pair of jeans and a jumper.

Walking back into my office, I scan through the to-do list pinned to the corkboard on my wall before sighing. I'm so behind on my schedule, and thinking about how much work I have to do to catch up makes me not want to even try. I need to finish recording a video for a brand that sent me some recording equipment, and I also haven't finished reading the book pick of the month for my online membership community.

This is the part of entrepreneurship nobody talks about. Working for myself is a blessing, but it can also be very dangerous when all the decisions are on me. I should probably revisit my decision not to hire a virtual assistant before everything blows up on me.

Today is not a good day, and if I'm not able to change my attitude quickly and get back into work mode, I'll regret it at the end of the month when my paycheck comes through.

"Lord, please help me," I repeat as my gaze sweeps through the room. The bookshelf behind me serves as the backdrop for my videos and I keep my ring light, camera, and tripod stand next to it, so I can grab them easily whenever I'm ready to set up. The monitor sitting on my desk is where I do all the video editing and livestreaming for my online membership community.

I also write on the monitor whenever I'm in the office, but any writing outside of the office is done on my laptop, which is currently sitting open next to me on the desk, the words to the outline of my new fantasy novel staring at me.

I knew this journey wouldn't be easy. That's why I often ask God to remind me of what truly matters when things become overwhelming. It's so easy for me to get bogged down with the running of the business that I forget about the foundation of it all—the books God wants me to write.

Even though my to-do list says I'm not supposed to write until seven PM, I'm taking an emergency detour today to find some hope again. I think getting out of the house will do me some good.

Placing my laptop into my backpack, I swing it over my shoulders and head out, walking the short fifteen minutes to Shoreditch High Street. After taking a bus to London Bridge, I change to the Jubilee line on the underground train to Britain's largest train station—Waterloo.

The Buzz Café is my favourite hang out spot on the upper level of the station. Like its name suggests, it has all the buzz I need to boost my creativity, and it's also the perfect place to grab a hot drink or food before you head on your journey.

But I love the extended seating area outside, which provides a panoramic view of the station below. There's a type of inspiration that comes with watching the world go by that I can't explain. The busy, chaotic view always sparks the creative side of my brain and makes the words burst out of me like water coming out of a failed dam. That's the energy I need for a day like this.

"Good morning, Jevaun." Jennifer, the barista, smiles at me when I get to the front of the queue. She usually works here on Saturdays and even though the other baristas are great, it was Jen's warm and welcoming smile that made it so easy to become her friend.

Jen's probably the only person in this café who knows I'm a writer and she's always so keen to listen to me talk about books when she's on her break. I love having deep and effortless conversations with people because they keep my creativity growing.

"Morning, Jen. You alright?" I adjust my backpack strap over my shoulder.

"Yeah, I'm good. You're early today. Are *you* alright?" She twirls a strand of her braids before tilting her head.

I shrug. "Yeah, it's just one of those days, you know? I needed to get out of the house."

"Yeah, I know that feeling all too well, so I don't blame you. Well, I'm glad you're here. What will you be having today?" She smoothes the hem of her burgundy apron.

My eyes scan through the menu of sandwiches, pastries, and salads before settling on my choice. "I'll have the roast chicken shawarma hot wrap and a caramel latte, please," I say, my mouth already watering as I read through the components of the shawarma.

"Okay. Eat in or take away?"

"You know I'm always eating in. Those books won't write themselves."

"That's true." Jen chuckles. "I see you're still on your quest to try something new every time you come here."

"I sure am. Life is too short to eat the same thing every day, right?" I tap my phone on the card reader.

"It sure is," she responds with an even brighter smile as I move to the side and she walks away to prepare my order. Five minutes later, Jen calls out my name and hands me a small basket with my hot wrap and my latte in their branded coffee cup.

"Thank you very much."

"You're welcome." She flashes me another smile as I walk over to my favourite table next to the balcony in the seating area.

My view of the station below comprises men, women, and children from all walks of life, backgrounds and ethnic groups, striving to get some place where they can make their day productive—well, at least that's what I'd like to think.

I also like facing the four-sided clock, an iconic landmark feature at the south side of the station above the main entrance and booking hall. It serves as my focal point when I'm deep in thought and there's something about looking at it that makes ideas form in my brain.

After turning on my laptop, I open up my writing software, *Scribbles,* before clicking on the completed and edited version of my fantasy novel *Parallels*. I received an email last night from one of the literary agents I queried, asking me to send the full manuscript for them to review.

This doesn't mean they'll give me an offer of representation, as they could still read my book and not like it, but it's a significant step in the right direction, so I have to make sure all my files are ready to send over to the agent today.

I bite into my shawarma, which is made of roast chicken mixed with grilled peppers, tomato, coriander, and spinach with hummus and chilli mayo all wrapped up in a seeded tortilla wrap. The blend of the spices does wonders for my taste buds, reaffirming my decision to go for this meal today.

My phone vibrates on the table as a text message notification from Tré flashes on the screen. I swallow my food before opening the message.

Tré: Hey, bro. I'm getting ready to leave soon. I have a row of night shifts this week starting tomorrow, so I need to rest before the chaos.

Me: Of course. Let me know when you get home. We'll catch up at the end of the week then, yeah?

Tré: Sure thing. 👍

As I place my phone back down and take a sip of my latte, a woman takes a seat two tables across from me. She pulls out her laptop from her backpack and places it on the table before removing her denim jacket, allowing me to read the words—*God's chosen*—written on her white t-shirt.

Those words alone are enough to pique my interest, so from my corner, as subtly as I can, I can't stop myself from staring as I read the words on the back of her laptop case which say, *"I trust the next chapter because I know the author."*

That's a paraphrasing of Jeremiah 29:11 and a great conversation starter. I wish I was sitting next to her, so I could ask her what she's working on. I don't know why I can't shake off the feeling that she's a writer too.

I'm about to walk up to her and introduce myself when her phone rings and she puts on her headphones before answering the call. So instead of getting answers directly from her, I have the pleasure of eavesdropping on her one-sided phone conversation. Well, not eavesdropping intentionally, though. Her voice is loud and I can't exactly close my ears because I'm so interested.

"Yes, I finally finished writing chapter one of the novel last night." She chuckles and her eyes light up as she stares at her phone screen. "Can you imagine I stayed up until two AM writing? It's crazy, but it's done. God finally did it."

Hearing the excitement in this stranger's voice as she talks about her achievement and how she gives all glory to God builds up a mound of gratitude in my heart for her, even though I have no idea who she is.

I didn't even know she existed until a few minutes ago, but I'm sitting here, smiling like a fool as I take in the sight of her. I'm not sure whether it's the honey-brown sparkle in her eyes, the soft glow of her brown skin, the coily strands on her head, which she is wearing up in a high puff, the gold hoop earrings dangling from her ears or her infectious laughter that keeps my eyes glued to her. Whatever it is, I have to speak to her.

"So, what do you think?" Jen interrupts my thoughts and partially blocks my view as she sits in the chair across my table.

"Huh?" I turn my attention swiftly to Jen, hoping she wouldn't figure out the reason for my distraction.

"How is it?" She nods at my half-eaten wrap on the table.

"Oh, it's absolutely amazing. I made the right decision." I pull the basket close to me. "Are you stepping out for your break?" I point to the jacket in her hand and her bag slung over her shoulder.

"No, I'm actually done for the day. My mum texted me to say my daughter has a fever, so mummy duty calls." Jen has a two-year-old daughter, which she has mentioned a few times. I know she lives with her mum and daughter, but she never mentioned the father of her daughter and I've never asked.

"Oh, I'm sorry. Yes, you should head home. I'm sure your daughter will be happy to see you."

"Thanks." Jen stands up, allowing me a full view again of the woman sitting across. "Actually, I've been thinking." Jen sits down again. "Since you enjoy trying out new food, I have a long list of places I've always wanted to go to. It'd be good to hang out outside of this place, you know? We could go out for lunch or dinner if you'd like."

"You mean like a date?"

She nods. "Yeah, a date. Is that okay?"

"Oh...erm." Jen's question catches me off guard and I scratch the back of my head, trying to choose my next words carefully. But even my lack of a coherent response doesn't stop a smile from tugging at her lips as she waits patiently for my answer.

For the past two years, I've enjoyed getting to know Jen and having all the deep conversations with her about life. She has also patiently listened to me talk about my faith in God, even though she made it clear from the beginning that she doesn't share my views. But this whole time, I thought we were just friends.

I clear my throat. "Jen...I don't think that would be a good idea because I'm not interested in you like that."

Her smile fades. "Oh, okay. Well, thanks for being honest." She stands.

"Jen...wait. I'm really sorry."

"No, that's okay." She forces a smile. "I'll let you be, then. Have a good writing session." With those words, she walks away, leaving me with the biggest heap of guilt on my chest.

"Jen. Jen," I call after her, but she doesn't stop.

I rub my hand over my face and let out a groan, before replaying all our encounters in my head and wondering whether

I might have ever suggested to Jen that I was interested in her romantically.

After a moment of reflection, I say a quick prayer for Jen, that God would help her overcome any disappointment. And for me, that I'll learn to be more vigilant and discerning about my encounters—especially with women. I can't keep passing on the wrong message every time.

Lifting my head, my gaze lands on the woman across from me, and this time, she's in her zone, with her pink headphones over her ears, a look of determination on her face, and her fingers typing away on her keyboard as she works on the story God has given her.

Watching her today has reminded me again about what truly matters—the stories we are writing. I haven't even spoken to her yet, but her excitement has already rubbed off on me. That's all the boost I needed to start working on my new novel again.

As much as I'd love to thank this stranger for what she doesn't know she has done, and find out more about the story she's writing, I don't want to be the one to interrupt her while she's in the zone and I certainly don't want to leave a bad first impression or pass on the wrong message.

I sigh as the guilt of Jen's disappointed smile pinches at my heart again. But I push those thoughts to the back of my mind and focus my attention on my laptop again.

5

BEX

I should take Rhoda's advice and feel more excited about today, because there was a time when getting a promotion at work was all I prayed for. It was what kept me working harder and striving to be better. I'm pretty sure at some point, I was so consumed by my pursuit for a promotion or a raise that I let it affect the way I did my work.

But thank God for the Holy Spirit, who convicted me about the reason He put me in this space. It didn't matter where I was or what I was doing—I needed to do my work for God's glory and use it as an opportunity to serve the customers that came my way.

I'm trying to be hopeful, but I can't shake the feeling that this current season is ending. I felt God press that into my heart as I read Isaiah 43:18-19 last night.

Even when I meditated on the passage on my commute to work this morning, the message that kept coming to me was that this job is only a waiting area and that God will launch a new thing in my life soon. But I have no idea what this new thing is— maybe it's in fact that promotion, so I better start practising how I'll dance in church when I give my testimony.

I glance at my watch and quicken my steps as I continue my ten-minute walk from Canary Wharf Station. I'll never get used to the stunning view of the skyscrapers all around me and my fascination with them is still as fresh as the first day I started working here.

"Good morning, hun." Neha's bright smile welcomes me as I close the door behind me, walking into the warm front office of the bank. I like being one of the first people to arrive, as I can still smell the freshly cleaned carpets and appreciate the quietness of the empty room before everyone else comes and I'm forced to engage in small talk.

"Morning." I give Neha a hug, catching a whiff of her rosy perfume, which always turns my gloomy Monday morning frown upside down. "How was your weekend?" I ask as we both settle behind our desks, which are next to each other, and she tells me all about her experience with her in-laws visiting from India.

Neha, my work bestie, as we both call ourselves, has worked with me since our summer internship six years ago at this bank. Although we studied at different universities, we were both offered full-time analyst positions after graduation and I've watched her go from a single woman to a wife and now a mother to an adorable little boy.

"Wow, sounds like you've got your work cut out for you, then." I chuckle as she nods.

"Sadly, I do. What about you? What did you get up to over the weekend?" Neha asks and I always struggle to answer these questions as my life seems so boring compared to everyone else's. How can I explain to anyone how exciting it is that I finally broke through my writer's block and started writing my first novel?

I shrug before spilling my usual answer. "Nothing much. My sisters and I went for a worship event at church on Friday evening and I spent the rest of the weekend resting and recuperating."

"Nice." Neha smiles before tucking a strand of her silky dark hair behind her ear as Sean, a fellow analyst, walks in.

"Morning, ladies. Do any of you fancy a cuppa? I'm about to put the kettle on." He points toward the kitchen and we both shake our heads.

"No, I already made one." Neha lifts her floral mug up to her lips and sips.

"I'm good, Sean. But thanks for offering." I try not to rely on caffeine to keep me awake in the mornings because I don't want to become addicted to it. Also, Rachel gets regular migraines and one of her triggers is caffeine, so that's a *no-no* for me. "My new goal this week is to drink at least two litres of water a day." I grin before sipping on the water from my bottle.

"Okay, then." Sean smiles at us. "Good luck with that." He runs his hands through his blonde hair before walking away.

"Thanks, Sean." Neha responds before wheeling her chair close to me and whispering. "So, are you ready for that pay rise?"

"Well, we can only hope, right?" I shrug.

"Right. We've worked so hard and this year has to be our year. Arjun and I are saving up to buy our house soon, so it has to be good news." Neha reaches over and squeezes my hands. "Congratulations in advance."

The hope in her voice makes me want to believe too, but again, I can't shake the feeling that something unexpected is looming around the corner. Neha and I started working in the middle office as first year analysts and in our third year, they moved us to the front office, which is the part of the bank that generates revenue.

We both thought we would get a significant pay rise with this move, but met our first disappointment when this wasn't the case. We were told this was because we only moved within the same bank, so it would take a few years to catch up with our peers in the same division.

We believed this lie until last week when Neha, who loves talking about salary with our colleagues, something I need to do more of, found out that Sean moved from the middle office to the front office and got a significant pay rise—much higher than what we were offered two years ago.

So we're both hoping that today, we would either get the good news of promotion to associates, or at least, finally get that significant pay rise we've been waiting for.

As more people troop into the office, I settle into my morning routine of responding to emails and bringing up my to-do list for the day on my colourful online calendar. Being the planner that I am, everything has to be mapped out in front of me, otherwise I won't be able to function.

Everything is structured in an investment bank and since I have to report to the associate who then reports to the managing director of my team, I have to constantly be on top of my work, so these calendars help me do just that.

At 8:30 AM, Neha and I join the team meeting as everyone gives a quick update on the different deals they are working on with clients. They usually give opportunities for interns and analysts to present at these meetings too, but today, Neha and I aren't presenting.

Back at our desks after the team meeting, I start working on a proposal for a new client. As an investment bank, we advise and help businesses on how to overcome their financial challenges, and the services we provide are vital to the company's growth and the growth of the economy.

Whenever I tell my friends from secondary school or university about what I do, they always mention how they envy the stable and lucrative nature of my job. It's truly a blessing to earn enough to support not just myself but my siblings and parents when needed.

But why do I also feel like I want more? Is it wrong that I want more? Does God care that I want more? Is it in His will for me to want more? Or is my flesh making me covet a life or dream that is not mine?

Lord, please help me. I exhale the breath I've been holding for the last thirty seconds as I focused on the rush of thoughts in my head rather than the tasks in front of me.

Whatever this new thing is You're doing, Lord. I'm ready. Please show me now and show me fast, because I could do with a change in my status quo.

Neha's ringing desk phone cuts my prayer short as she picks it up and brings the phone to her ear. "Hello?" She pauses, her eyebrows furrowing. "Right now?" She turns to look at me, a quizzical look on her face. "Okay, I'm coming." She drops the phone and stands.

"Everything okay?"

She shrugs. "I don't know. That was HR."

"HR? What do they want with you?" I ask rhetorically, because our unspoken silence tells us we're thinking the same thing.

Neha slowly sits back down, her eyes searching her desk, worried lines etching across her forehead as she shakes her head. "Bex, I can't lose this job."

"No, let's not jump to conclusions." I leave my desk and walk up to her, throwing my arm around her shoulder. "Maybe they just want to...clarify something." Even I don't believe that excuse myself, so of course Neha doesn't take comfort in it. "Take a deep breath, hun. Go and see what they want. I'm sure it'll be alright."

She takes my advice and practices her deep breaths. When she's calm, she hugs me tight before making her way down the open plan office, giving me one last look before she closes the door behind her.

As I return to my desk, the overwhelming feeling I had earlier this morning on the train takes over me again. I stare at my desk phone too, the surrounding noises fading away as the sound of my heartbeat increases.

Then, what I knew was going to happen, finally does. The phone rings and when I bring it up to my ear, it's Hannah from HR. She wants me to come up for a 'quick word,' as she puts it.

I don't remember leaving my desk, walking down the hallway, and up the stairs to the fourth floor. I don't even remember tapping my access card on the HR office door and entering, but when Neha rushes past me with tears in her eyes, everything becomes clear.

I start running after Neha, but stop in my tracks when Hannah calls out to me and asks me to come into her office and take a seat.

"Rebecca." Hannah fixes her brunette bangs before locking her fingers on the desk. "It's been a lovely five years working with you. We appreciate all the work you've put into this bank." She spills out the unnecessary sugarcoating before breaking the bad news. "But we've decided to make major structural changes around here, so I'm sorry. We're going to have to let you go."

She pauses, probably waiting for me to throw a rebuttal, to curse or scream at her or break down crying. But my God is not a God of surprises, and He prepared me for this moment.

"Your work with us has been outstanding," she continues. "That's why the managers have agreed to arrange a generous redundancy package for you. Brian will also be willing to write you a wonderful recommendation letter for your next job. This is your official six week notice as per your contract, but if you wish to leave earlier, then let me know and we can put that in writing." She finishes her speech and slides a white envelope across the table.

The Bex of five years ago would have definitely kicked and screamed and probably reached across the table to smack that look of pity off her face. But what the enemy meant for evil, God has already shown me how He will turn it around for my good.

"Thank you." I take the letter from her and walk out the door without another word. In the ladies' bathroom, I stare at myself in the mirror, taking a moment to reflect on what just happened. Out of all the scenarios I imagined about today, this was never one of them.

What surprises me more is that this is actually the best scenario and the best outcome. I've been complaining about my lack of time and how my day job drains all my energy, preventing me from writing. But here I am, with the answered prayer I never knew I needed. This can only be God.

A bright smile flashes across my face as joy floods my heart. I raise my hands in the air, ready to break into my praise dance, when the sound of sobbing in one of the stalls stops me, hands in mid-air.

Embarrassment washes over me at the thought of rejoicing out here when someone is having a not-so-great time in there. Work can get so stressful and because I've had my fair share of bathroom breakdowns in the past, I better let this person have their moment.

As I'm about to leave, I stop in my tracks when my gaze lands on the heeled boots peeking from underneath the stall door. "Neha?"

She stops crying and pulls her feet in, but her silent sniffles betray her once more.

"Oh, come on, hun. Please open the door. It's me. Bex." I check that the other stalls are empty before begging her to come out.

She takes her sweet time, but finally opens the door, revealing her swollen eyes and tear-stained face. "Arjun is going to struggle to pay the rent. We have a fast-growing two-year-old we need to care for. How will we cope? It's all over for me."

"No, it's not, hun. Come here." I pull her in for a hug as her sobbing continues. "You are one of the smartest people I know." I hold her face with both hands, tilting her chin up so she can look at me.

"You are hardworking and you've got great character. You are an amazing employee and you had so much to give them, so it's their loss. This can't be the end. There are so many better opportunities waiting for you outside of this building. You have to believe that, Neha. One day we'll look back and laugh at today because we would be in much better places."

Neha wipes her eyes and takes a step back from me, her eyebrows creasing. "We? What do you mean we? Did they fire you, too?"

I nod, and Neha exhales before shaking her head. "I'm so sorry, Bex. What are you going to do now?"

"Oh, don't worry about me. I'm still living with my parents, so I have time to figure things out. What are you going to do?"

She shrugs as we both walk to the sink. She opens the tap and washes her hands and face, then she pulls a few hand towels and dries her face before looking at me again. "I have to find another job, like, yesterday."

"Fine. You will." I cross my hands against my chest and she raises her brows at me.

"Why do I have the feeling you already figured everything out before today? You don't sound or look disappointed at all."

"Oh, trust me, I am *very* disappointed and I have nothing figured out." I place my arm around her shoulders as we walk out. "But I'm also holding onto my faith in God right now. He is already in my future, so I have nothing to worry about."

Nothing to worry about because now I don't have to wonder anymore. God promised He was going to do a new thing and I think He just did.

6

BEX

The stars of the show are back from Cameroon today, so of course we had to receive them from the airport like the king and queen they are. Mum and Dad's flight landed at Gatwick airport at six PM, and since I agreed with Hannah to terminate my contract immediately, I left the office when Neha confirmed her husband was on his way to pick her up.

I could have waited the full six weeks, but I didn't see the point and since they gave me an option to leave early, I took it without hesitation and I don't regret it. It's going to take me a while to process all the events of today, and it's going to take me even longer before I can bring myself to tell my parents about my next plan.

Rachel and Rhoda never asked about the outcome of my appraisal, probably because we've all been so busy with getting Mum and Dad from the airport to the house safely. I'll tell them when the topic comes up, or I'll tell them when we have our girls' night next week, so we can brainstorm on how I can break the news to Mum and Dad.

The thing about our African culture is that parents think they always know what's best for their children—especially when it comes to career paths. Anything, but the traditional way of doing things is seen as unserious or even worse—a failure. My hesitation to tell my parents is not because I'm scared of them. God has given me confirmation, and that is enough for me.

My hesitation stems from the fact that I know it'll take a lot of convincing before they can understand that there's nothing wrong with pursuing a career in writing, whether part time or full time, if God wills it for me someday.

"*Chai*[1], it's so good to be back," Dad says as he steps into the house, taking off his jacket to reveal his tracksuit top and bottom underneath. Like Rhoda, Dad loves his comfortable clothes, especially when he is travelling. He also loves exercising and keeping fit, and that's what he has in common with Rachel. As for me, I share all of Dad's facial features and everyone says I'm just a photocopy of him.

We catch Dad inspecting the floor as he walks into the living room and here's where I say a prayer of gratitude for Rachel and Rhoda, who came over last night to help me clean the house, so we don't get a lecture from Dad today.

"I've missed you, Daddy." Rhoda throws her arms around the old man, as if she didn't get her fair share of hugs at the airport. "You're looking so good. Cameroon really smiled on you."

Rachel rolls her eyes. "Why do you have to be such a Daddy's girl?"

"And a Mummy's girl too." Rhoda sticks her tongue out at Rachel.

"Please leave my baby alone. It's not her fault she's my *last coco*[2]." Mum smirks, but we can all see the tiredness on her face. She's only tired because instead of resting on the car journey from the airport, she called everyone in Cameroon to tell them she had landed safely and then complained about how horrible the plane food was. Rhoda shares not only Mum's facial features, but that's where she gets her sharp mouth from.

We take our parent's suitcases upstairs—all but the one which has the souvenirs they brought for us. After showering, changing their clothes, and eating the *jollof*[3] rice the girls and I cooked last night, Mum and Dad show us videos of the house they are building in Buea, in the South-West Region of Cameroon, where we used to live before our relocation to the UK.

They only bought the land a year ago, but the builders are eighty-percent done. Mum and Dad oversaw the roofing during their trip and in the next few months, we will have a house ready for us whenever we visit Cameroon, which is very exciting.

When my parents first embarked on this journey, all my aunties and uncles based in Cameroon discouraged them because apparently it can be difficult finding and working with trustworthy people to oversee projects for you in the motherland when you are abroad. But God directed Dad to an old school friend who owns a construction company, and he has been nothing short of amazing.

"It's *time*," Rhoda sings-songs, her excitement for the souvenirs making her reach for a Mariah Carey worthy note, but she misses and ends up in a coughing fit, so we all burst out laughing.

"Wait, *o*. So all this singing is for the food in this bag?" Mum asks as she opens the suitcase.

"Mum, that's what you get when you spoil your last child," Rachel says as she pinches Rhoda playfully, but instead of their usual bickering, everyone gasps when the contents of the suitcase are revealed.

"These are your *kabas*." Mum shares out two packets, each containing the free-flowing African print dresses popularly worn by Cameroonian women. Mum always buys us clothes whenever she visits Cameroon.

A few years ago, Mum used to get our measurements and get a tailor to make us different outfits from scratch, but the tailors never delivered on time and gave her way too much stress, so she just buys ready-made clothes now.

"Thank you, Mummy. I was just thinking about how I needed a new one, as my old one is really worn out." I tear open the first packet and place the yellow dress across my body.

"They're so beautiful," Rachel concurs.

"You're welcome, girls." Mum picks up another plastic bag and checks the content. "Ah, yes, this one's for you, my baby." She hands the bag over to Rhoda, who grabs it with no restraint.

When she opens the bag, her eyes sparkle like a child opening a bag of sweets—and it's literally the case as the bag in her hands contains a variety of Rhoda's favourite Cameroonian snacks, including chocolates, biscuits, and many more.

"Wow, *Mambo*." Rhoda pulls out the famous Cameroonian milk chocolate bar, ready to tear open the wrapper when Mum stops her with a raise of her hand.

"Remember, we agreed you would have it all in moderation," she says, the tone of her voice reminding us of all the times she has scolded us about eating too much sugar.

After Mum's dad died of a heart attack and her mum and three sisters were diagnosed with diabetes and hypertension, Mum has made it her mission not to let her lifestyle choices put her at risk of getting these diseases.

"It will end with my generation," she reminds Rhoda, who puts the chocolate away and nods.

"Amen," we all respond in unison.

"Okay, before I forget, here are your ingredients." Mum hands another bag over to Rachel, which has all the

Cameroonian spices Rachel requested for like *njangsang*[4], dried crayfish, country onions[5], and *Maggi* seasoning cubes.

"Yay, thank you so much, Mummy." Rachel's smile brightens. "I can't wait to cook up a storm in my kitchen."

"And I can't wait to taste the product of that storm." Rhoda grins. I bet her mouth is already watering just thinking about the food.

"Okay, that's all for now." Mum zips up the suitcase and I push myself up from the sofa, getting ready for an early night so I can start thinking about ways to break the news of my joblessness to my family, when Mum's voice stops me midway across the living room.

"Oh, that reminds me. Rebecca?"

"Hmm?" I turn around to look at her, my insides already sensing the question before it comes out of her mouth.

"How was your appraisal today? You promised you were going to update us on the family group chat, but I heard nothing from you."

Rachel, Rhoda, and Dad all turn their heads to look at me, all of them waiting, probably expecting me to tell them the good news about a pay rise or a promotion. But when my words don't come, Mum stands up and walks up to me.

"What's the matter? Did something happen?" She places her hand on my shoulder.

I could easily lie and tell them what they want to hear. That would buy me some time until I figure out how I want to pitch my plan to them. But that would only plunge me into a deeper hole that won't end well.

"Mum, please, can we talk about this in the morning when you've all rested?" I sigh, sending a prayer up to God for Mum to let it go. But of course, Mum's the queen of not letting things go.

"So, it's not good news?" she asks as the room goes dead silent. "Please, tell us what happened."

I stare into her brown eyes as I push my fear aside and just go for it. *Lord, please help me.* "No, it's not."

"*Weh, papa God*[6]. What happened, Rebecca?" Mum's eyebrows crease up with worry.

Dad, who was relaxed and scrolling through his phone the entire time we were gushing over the souvenirs, is now on his feet, hands crossed behind his back and his gaze pinned on me. "What exactly happened?" he asks and I spill out every single detail of what went down earlier today at the office.

"*Weh.* How could they just let you go like that without a warning?" Mum throws her arms up in the air when she can finally form her words.

"Yeah, is that even legal?" Rhoda frowns.

I shrug. "Well, they gave me a six-week notice. But they also said I could leave early if I wanted to without it affecting my redundancy pay. It sounds like they really just wanted to get rid of me, so I didn't see the point of staying."

Dad grunts. "Well, it's their loss. You don't need them. God has bigger plans for you, so it's not the end of the world, my dear." He squeezes my shoulder and I hope he'll still be this supportive when I tell him what God's plans actually are.

"Yes, I know that."

"Good. So you will start applying for jobs immediately, right?"

Rhoda and Rachel send knowing looks my way as I stumble on my words. "Erm...well..."

"Yes, you must start immediately," Mum cuts in. "I'm sure you'll get an interview in no time and you'll find a job without a problem. You're *hot cake.*"

I pause, staring at both of them as they go back and forth, throwing words at me about how quickly I need to get back into the job market and get things rolling. This is the reason I wanted to work on my pitch before telling them about me losing my job.

Lord, I have no plan right now, so you're going to have to help me because I'm totally winging it.

"Actually...I'd like to take a break." The words come out louder than I wanted them too, as both my parents stare at me, confusion written all over their faces.

I swallow to wet my dry mouth and glance at my sisters on the sofa. Rhoda gives me a thumbs up and Rachel nods, encouraging me to keep going.

"A break?" Dad's voice goes deeper. "What do you mean?"

"I mean, I don't want to jump back into working just yet and I have a good reason, but please, I need you to hear me out."

Dad places his hands into the pockets of his jeans before taking a seat next to Mum on the sofa. "Okay, then. Carry on."

Lord, please help me.

"Four years ago, God gave me an idea for a book, and I've been trying to write it since then, but work has been so busy. I've not had the motivation to write because after work I always feel so tired and exhausted. I prayed to God to give me an opportunity to finally write this story and this morning, He told me He was going to do a new thing."

Dad and Mum look at each other. "So are you saying that the new thing He promised was for you to lose your job? Not a promotion? Or a raise?" Dad's voice goes higher with each question.

Of course, this was part of His plan, but we're not getting into that today. "Dad, I'm saying that I've been waiting for this moment for four years. I didn't know it was what I needed, but now I do. I need to write this book and I only need to stay at home for one year and..."

"One year?" Dad jumps to his feet. "Why do you need to stay at home for that long? Do you want to waste your talents?"

Here's the point where I tell Dad he doesn't have to be this dramatic, but that'll do nothing to pacify the situation. "Dad,

God is building up a new talent and a new gift in me." I pace the length of the living room.

"This entire experience feels like I'm in labour and this story can't wait to come out. You can't stop the process of labour. If I don't give birth to this child, we could lose the child, lose me or, even worse, lose both of us."

"Ah, wait, wait, wait." Mum pushes herself up from the sofa. "I'm confused. Rebecca?" She shoots a glance at my abdomen before looking me in the eye again. "Are you sure we're still talking about a book?"

Rhoda suppresses a laugh, and Rachel drives an elbow into her side.

"Mum, Dad, come on." I place my hands on my head, my patience growing thin. "Could you please just reason with me? It's only a year. It's not a big deal."

"Yeah, it's not that deep." Rhoda chips in and she gets death glares from our parents. If looks were actions, they both would have twisted her mouth right about now.

"Mum, Dad, please. Bex is a great writer and God will use this story to impact so many lives," Rachel pleads my case.

Dad shakes his head as he groans. "I know writing for God is good. But all I'm saying is it doesn't pay the bills. It will never do."

Well, I know it can. The words leap to the tip of my tongue, but I hold them back. I'm choosing one battle at a time. Let me write the book first. Dad self-published a book a few years ago about his struggles as an immigrant in the UK and the decisions he made that helped him flourish. He still complains about how sometimes he forgets he's an author because of the lack of sales. But I'm not surprised about that because he never talks about the book.

Even though my main reason for writing this book is not the money, I hope that someday I'll prove to Dad that writing can be lucrative. The six- and seven-figure authors I follow online don't have two heads. If they can do it, then I can too. *I think.*

"This will not replace my job, Dad. I'm not quitting the corporate world. I just need a break to write this story. One year and I'll start applying for jobs again. I have enough money in my savings to last me that long." I bring both my palms together in a prayer pose.

"So, you really think squandering all your savings like this is worth it?" Dad raises his eyebrows.

"Please, Daddy." Rachel and Rhoda stand up too and join me in a prayer pose.

Even if Mum and Dad don't get on board, I'd still do it because I'm twenty-seven years old and thank God I can hear Him for myself. But it would be a lot easier if I can work on my story without worrying about negative talk or discouragement from my parents.

Dad and Mum look at each other one last time before responding. "Okay, fine."

"Yes," I squeal as the three of us hug our parents tight.

"*Abeg*[7], don't choke us here *o*," Mum says when we finally release them.

"We love you." I plant a kiss on their cheeks and after saying our good night, Rhoda and Rachel follow me up to my room, as we let Mum and Dad get some much-needed rest.

Later that night, when Rachel and Rhoda leave, I rush back to my desk, my heart full of inspiration and my hands itching to get the next chapter of my book done.

Freshers Week came and went with the blink of an eye. Vanessa and Anne couldn't go to every single event, but the highlights of their week included food, laughter, and a lot of freebie stationery items.

The planner in Vanessa screamed for joy every time she went home and stacked her shelves with new notebooks, pens, and colourful sticky notes. Only a fellow stationery lover like Anne knew how much fulfilment it brought her.

The first Christian union meeting was on the Tuesday of their second week. Vanessa still remembered how eager she was to find their table during the Freshers Fair. She had scribbled down her name and email address on their sign-up sheet so quickly she thought she would break the pen.

"Keep an eye out for our welcome email," the CU president had said, and that's exactly what she did. Throughout the following week, she constantly refreshed her inbox and spam folder to make sure she didn't miss that first email.

The day it finally came, Vanessa leaped from her bed and dashed across the hallway into Anne's room to share the good news.

"Whoa, calm down. What's so deep about the CU, anyway?" Anne asked as she styled her wig on her desk.

"Don't you get it?" Vanessa said in between breaths. "We're starting a new life and a new season here at uni. The friendships we make now could make or break us. My mum always says that finding the right community is important so that when things get hard, you'll have the right support system around you."

Anne paused as she reflected on Vanessa's words. "That sounds fair enough. Looks like there's going to be food, so count me in."

"Yay." Vanessa hooted before hugging her official uni bestie.

The small lecture theatre was already buzzing with people when the girls walked in for the first CU meeting. The smile of the tall brunette guy that greeted them at the door made it diffi-cult to walk past without coming in. Worship music played softly in the background and at the front of the room was a table with a variety of snacks.

Anne sent Vanessa a knowing glance as they both smiled at each other before walking over to the snacks table. There were already over a dozen students scattered across the room, some in groups and others in twos, talking, chatting, and laughing.

"You came," a familiar voice said to Vanessa, and she turned around, a chocolate biscuit in her mouth.

"Yes, I did." She smiled at the CU president, who introduced himself as Joshua.

"Please take a seat when you're ready. We'll be starting soon." He nodded before walking to another group to tell them the same information.

The girls poured themselves some pineapple juice and rushed off to the back of the room, carrying packets of crisps and grapes with them. The meeting started with an opening prayer from Joshua, followed by a session of worship led by two girls who introduced themselves as Sarah and Chloe.

Then Joshua led everyone into the first icebreaker session—human bingo. They each had a sheet of paper with boxes that had either a trait, a hobby, or a life experience. Each person had to walk around the room chatting with others to match descrip-tions to their cards until all the boxes were filled.

Anne and Vanessa went separate ways, trying to fill their boxes, and the first person Vanessa bumped into gave her a smile that would capture her heart like a fly caught in a spider's web.

Vanessa didn't know whether it was his coily strands that sat so perfectly on his crown, or the way he licked his lips to high-light their pink colour, or the deep husk of his voice as he said his name, or the softness of his hand as he stretched it forth and shook hers.

Whatever it was, it was working, and before she could even think of saying a prayer, her heartstrings were already being pulled with every passing second of their conversation. Little did Vanessa know that that same smile and those same hands would be the instruments of the tragedy that would befall her—the tragedy that would change her life forever.

7

———————

JEVAUN

I shake my head for the umpteenth time, holding my phone against my ear as I wait for Tré to stop laughing at the other end of the line. For someone who has just come back from a night shift, he sure has a lot of energy. "Mate, are you done making fun of me now?"

"No." Tré chokes on his words before going into a coughing fit and clearing his throat. "I mean, yes," he says, his laughter finally dying down. "I'm sorry, bro. I can't believe you keep getting yourself into situations like this."

I adjust in my seat as the bus comes to a halt at the stop before Waterloo Station. I usually change from the bus to the tube when I'm going to Waterloo, but I opted to take the bus the whole way today. It takes a little longer, but at least I won't have to worry about losing the signal on the underground train. "So you're saying it's my fault?"

"To put it simply, yes," Tré responds.

"So you're saying it's a crime to be nice?"

"No, I'm saying you're *too* nice sometimes, and especially with the ladies. Come on, you know they easily catch feelings, so why are you surprised?"

60

"But I didn't tell Jen I liked her or wanted to date her."

"Your actions speak louder than your words, bro." He chuckles. "If you don't learn from this experience, then you'll only have yourself to blame for all the women's hearts you break in the future."

I get Tré's point, but I don't think one can ever be *too nice.* Apart from the important fact that having deep conversations with people inspires my creativity, the Bible also encourages me to be kind to others, to be respectful, and to always have conversations that are full of grace.

I can't stop being kind. It's part of who I am and part of my new nature in Christ. Fighting that would mean fighting the Holy Spirit, and I can never win in a fight like that. But what I've learnt from this experience with Jen is that I definitely need to be aware of boundaries and what message I could be passing.

I guess I also need to learn how to read body languages, take cues, and rely on the Holy Spirit to teach me when it's time to retreat. *Ugh, nothing in this life is simple.*

"I hear you, bro. I appreciate it. Thanks for always looking out for me." I step out of the bus at Waterloo and walk across the busy street, with the rest of the crowd streaming into the station.

"You're welcome, but did you tell Jen you have a brother? If you don't want her, I might as well swoop in and take my chance. I'm sure she won't mind." Tré laughs again and I kiss my teeth before rolling my eyes.

"Listen, you need to get some sleep." I ignore his question. "Only two more night shifts to go and you can rest for a bit."

"Yeah, you're right." He yawns as the fatigue becomes clear in his voice. "Alright, talk to you later."

"Later." I end the call and walk up the escalator toward The Buzz Café. After ordering a caramel latte and a cheese toastie, I walk over to my favourite seat next to the balcony.

Five minutes later, the same girl from Saturday also walks

into the coffee shop. Today, she has her hair up in two afro puffs with single strand braids dangling on the sides of her face next to her hoop earrings. She orders a hot drink and a croissant before walking to the same seat she sat in three days ago.

Lord, are you trying to tell me something? I ask silently, before casting my mind back to what happened during my Bible study this morning. While I was praying, I had the sudden urge to pray for this same girl, even though I know nothing about her.

I even asked God to let me see her again if it was His will and I know that was cheeky of me, but I might as well get the chance to know her a bit more if God wants me to keep praying for her.

I didn't realise I was going to walk right into an answered prayer today. I want to know why she's here so early on a Tuesday morning. Is she a full-time author too? Is today her day off from work? Or does she work remotely and just likes working here? What's her novel about? Is she planning to query too, or will she self-publish it?

All these unanswered questions make me want to walk over there and end my misery, but my feet are still hesitant, my mind is still overthinking about boundaries and deep conversations and sending the wrong message after what happened with Jen.

But I'm certain God didn't ask me to pray about her this morning for no reason. Eventually, we'll find out, but I just have to wait for the right time. *Lord, please lead me.*

After the girl settles in her seat, she takes off her denim jacket, opens up her laptop, puts on her pink headphones, and gets to work immediately, only stopping to take bites of her croissant and sips of her beverage.

She had determination in her eyes before, but she looks a lot happier today as she bops her head and mouths the lyrics to the song she's listening to. Everything about her demeanour tells me we would be great friends. But again, I have to tread carefully from here on out.

Speaking of treading carefully, when I turn my head back towards the till, Jen emerges from behind it with her apron around her waist and a cloth and spray bottle in her hand. She locks eyes with me and I smile at her, but instead of her usual warm response, she keeps a straight face and walks to the table next to me, before spraying and wiping it down.

"Hey, Jen." I lean close to her, but she doesn't respond. *Wow, I didn't realise she was angry with me.* "Listen, can we talk about what happened on Saturday?"

"No," she says simply, before wiping down the table one more time.

"I'm really sorry if what I said offended you, but I just wanted to let you know it wasn't my intention at all."

"I know." She pauses, lets out a heavy sigh, and plops down on the chair next to me. Dropping her head in her hands, she takes a moment to breathe before looking at me. "I'm sorry for making it look like it's your fault. You never told me you liked me, but I just assumed that since we had such easy conversations, there was a spark there. I hope this won't ruin our friendship."

"No, of course not. You'll always be my friend. You know that."

She smiles, but only for a short while. "Jevaun, can I ask you a question?"

"Of course."

"Would you have agreed to go out with me if you didn't know I have a child?" she asks, and that's how I know we're treading on thin ice.

"Jen, my decision had nothing to do with your daughter." I squeeze her hand as her eyes become wet with tears. "I've never met her, but from the way you rave about her, I have no doubt that you're a wonderful mother. The most important factor in my decision is that we don't share the same faith in God. That's a deal breaker for me."

"Of course." She laughs and wipes the tears falling down her cheek. "I should've known from how passionately you talk about your God. I just didn't know He also dictates who you should be with."

"My whole life revolves around Him, Jen. I'm absolutely nothing without Him. If I can rely on Him daily to help me run my business, relate with others, and survive all my daily challenges, then wouldn't it be fair to also rely on Him when it comes to choosing who I want to spend the rest of my life with?"

"Whoa, no one's talking about marriage. I just wanted us to hang out and get to know each other more. That's it."

"Yeah, but I like to be intentional from the beginning."

"Of course." She draws in a breath and shakes her head. "You sound just like my mum. I'm not sure if I ever mentioned that she's a Christian as well. I still remember the disappointment in her eyes when I told her I was pregnant, and the father wanted nothing to do with the baby. But she never cast me out. She has made this journey of motherhood so easy for me and I don't know how I would've survived without her." She sniffles.

"But every day she keeps reminding me about making amends with God, giving my life to Him and surrendering, but I can't be bothered. Life's too short to stay bound by rules. I just want to save enough money so I can get my own place and leave my mum's house. Until then, I'm stuck there, with all her sermons and daily prayers."

"I hope you'll see one day that the situation you are in right now is God's way of showing you He's caring for you, protecting you, and leading you to where you need to be. There's someone out there for you, Jen. Someone who would love you and your daughter the way God has designed it."

"Yeah, whatever." She stands up. "Until that day, I have to

hustle, innit?" She chuckles, straightening her apron. "I'm glad we're back to being friends again. Let me head back to work before I lose my job."

"See you later, Jen." I wave at her as she walks back to the counter, in awe of what God has just done. I wasn't expecting her to open up to me like that and I can only imagine the guilt or the shame she must be carrying around with her.

Thank God for Jen's mom, who God has strategically placed in her life, and I pray that someday, Jen's heart will be soft enough to receive the good news that changes lives.

Opening up the notes app on my phone, I add Jen's name to my list of people to pray for alongside Tré, my dad, and the beautiful girl sitting across from me, whose name I'd love to know.

After reading through more rejection emails from agents, I send out another batch of query letters before outlining the story for my new ghostwriting client. My goal for today is to finish the outline, so I can send it over for approval.

Three hours later, I cross off the last thing on my to-do list and email my client before calling it a day. But coincidentally, the girl across from me is also packing up her bag, still bobbing her head to the music from her headphones.

I let her make a head start before following a few paces behind. Down the escalator, she turns right and walks toward the main entrance of the station while I walk in the opposite direction towards the underground.

But when I catch a glimpse of the pouring rain outside, I pause in my tracks before watching the girl join the crowd of people waiting at the station's entrance. One thing I've learnt about the UK weather is that you need to have trust issues with it to avoid any kind of embarrassment. That's why I always carry an umbrella with me no matter what season we're in.

But hang on a minute. She doesn't have an umbrella and I do, so this is my opportunity to finally break the ice. I know Tré would shake his head if he was here right now, but I couldn't care less.

Asking me to turn down an opportunity to be kind is like asking me to implode. I can't let what happened with Jen discourage me from being myself. Of course, I need to remember boundaries, but there has to be a reason this girl has been on my mind and in my prayers since the first day I set eyes on her. I'm going for it.

"Excuse me." I touch her elbow gently and she turns around before taking off her headphones. Her fruity scent dances around my nostrils, pulling me closer as I almost forget my next few words. "It's raining heavily out there. Do you need an umbrella?" I hand her the solution to her current problem, but she only glances at it briefly before returning her gaze to my face.

"Oh, no I'm fine, thank you. I'll just wait," she says with a small smile before turning her back to me and pulling her backpack close to her body.

Wow, so much for the famous meet cute, huh? Lord, is this it? Really?

I glance at my watch, before prepping myself to try again because if I don't wrap this up soon, I'll be late for my livestream with my membership community. I can't take two Ls in one day. *Lord, please, help me out here.*

Taking a deep breath in, I lean forward again. "My name is Jevaun, by the way. I've seen you working at The Buzz Café. I work there too." I pause, hoping she would say she has also looked up from her laptop and seen me working across from her. But when confusion remains etched on her facial features, I pull my final card. "I'm a writer."

And just as I thought, my last sentence draws the reaction I knew would come. Her eyes light up and a smile breaks forth as she turns her body around to face me.

"A writer?" she asks, before adjusting her backpack strap over her shoulder.

"Yeah, I'm a Christian writer. Like I said, I work at the Buzz most days of the week and I've seen you there twice now."

"Yeah, erm...I'm also...I'm working on a little something too, I guess," she stutters and fiddles with her nails.

"That's great," I say simply, because she doesn't need to know I've been eavesdropping on her phone conversations and know that she's also working on a novel.

Lightning strikes in the distance, followed by the loud row of thunder, and then the wind blows cold showers toward us, so we retreat inside the station. She doesn't seem to be in a hurry, so this would've been the perfect opportunity to get the answers to some of my burning questions.

But if I don't leave now, I'll face the consequences later when I get endless emails from my loyal community members complaining about my tardiness. "The rain isn't easing up. Are you sure you don't want my umbrella?" I offer it to her again.

"Erm..." She glances at the gloomy weather outside before turning to me. "Well, I only need to walk five minutes down the road to check out a new bookstore I saw the other day. It's not a big deal."

Ah, she's a writer and a reader too. How much more of an answered prayer can this be?

"Well, if you're going to buy books, it'd definitely be a big deal. Can't risk getting them wet now, can you?"

A smile tugs on the corner of her lips as she shakes her head. "Okay, fine. I guess the umbrella will be helpful."

"There you go," I say while mentally convincing myself not to break into a dance or pump my fist.

"But what are you going to use?" She glances at the rain once more.

"*Eh.*" I shrug. "Don't worry about me. I don't mind getting a little wet, but your hair looks too nice to be ruined by the rain today."

The sparkle in her eyes spreads to her cheeks as her smile grows even wider. "Thank you. But how will you get your umbrella back?"

"Well." I take retreating steps. "As long as you keep coming back to work on that *little something* of yours, I'll be right there, sitting next to the balcony." I point to The Buzz Café.

"Thank you." She brings the umbrella close to her chest and the sight of her waving me goodbye with that beautiful smile of hers convinces me that my day can't get any better.

"The pleasure's all mine." I nod at her before turning around and making a run for my train.

8

BEX

The spicy aroma that hits my nostrils as I walk into Rachel and Rhoda's flat is the perfect welcome hug I need today. My first week unemployed wasn't as scary as I thought it'd be. But all of that writing can be draining, so this sleepover is going to refuel my energy.

"Hey, big sis," Rachel calls out as I walk into the kitchen, both of her hands deep in oven mitts as she takes the chicken out of the oven.

The sizzling, golden-brown chicken in the oven tray, which is the source of the aroma, catches my attention and I almost forget to respond. "Hey, hun." I give her a hug when her hands are free. "Sorry I'm late, but as always, I've brought reinforcements." I place the plastic bags on the kitchen counter with our favourite drinks—*SuperMalt* for me, tropical juice for Rhoda's sweet-tooth, and ginger beer for Rachel, who is obsessed with the spicy-sweet flavour.

I take off my jacket and hang it on the coat hanger, before placing my shoes on the shoe rack in the hallway and joining Rachel again in the open-plan kitchen.

London is known for its smaller houses, but Rachel and

Rhoda have managed the space so well they were even able to fit a dining table in the living room space. One thing I love about the open-plan kitchen is that we can cook and watch TV at the same time. It's the best of both worlds.

"Where's the *last coco*?" I ask, but before Rachel can speak, the toilet flushes, giving me the answer to my question.

"Hey, Sissy." A squeal escapes Rhoda's loud mouth as she skips across the room and wraps her arms around my neck in a tight hug. "I'm so glad we could all make this one. I'm so excited and so hungry."

"You're always hungry." Rachel looks up from the pot she's stirring. "Come and taste."

Rhoda flies past me and stands next to Rachel, who sends her a questioning look first before giving her a piece of the plantain from the pot.

As Rachel promised, she has made *poulet DG*, which literally means 'chicken for the Director General.' It's an unbeatable combination of chicken, fried ripe plantains, and vegetables in a flavourful tomato sauce. Rachel has also made her signature fried rice and, of course, I can't wait to get it all into my belly.

"Hmm, this is so good." Rhoda moans before taking a bite of the chicken, too. "Can we eat already?"

"Yes, *Ma*. As soon as you help me set up the table." I nod at Rhoda and we both set up the dining table while Rachel wipes down the kitchen counter. "Where's the dessert?"

"In the fridge," Rhoda responds. "I made cheesecake, chocolate brownies, and there's ice cream too."

"Nice. Enjoyment galore." I rub my belly.

Fifteen minutes later, we're all sitting at the table with everyone's plates filled with food, and a side of salad. Just when we're about to open the drinks, Rachel pulls out a large bottle of *Djino* fruit cocktail from the fridge, surprising us all.

"Whoa, where did you find this?" Rhoda's eyes sparkle as we all stare at our favourite Cameroonian soft drink.

"I discovered an African store in Mitcham on my way home from work the other day. The guy mostly sells Nigerian cooking ingredients, so you can imagine my joy when I saw this in their fridge. I told him if he brings more Cameroonian food and ingredients, he'll be my number one grocery store from now on."

"Well, what are we waiting for? Let's dig in." Rhoda raises her glass and Rachel pours out the pink drink for us, which is like orange *Fanta* in its sweetness, but it also has a mix of guava, pineapple, citrus and mango too. A real palette explosion.

"Hmm, this brings back so many memories." I close my eyes, conjuring up the memories I hold dear to my heart about Cameroon. Leaving when we were so young and never getting to experience what it's like to be there as a teenager or an adult means we can easily forget. But we never want to forget. That's why we put in the effort every day to keep those memories alive.

"The food is so good, Rach. Your husband will bask in premium enjoyment," Rhoda adds, swallowing before picking up the last bit of chicken on her plate with her hands.

"Honestly, I can't wait for the day you finally open up that Cameroonian restaurant," I concur. "It'll be epic."

"Thanks, girls. Your encouragement means a lot." Rachel sighs before taking a sip of her drink and tucking a loose braid strand behind her ear. "It's just what I needed right now, because things are getting a little overwhelming."

"Aww, what happened?" I ask, putting down my fork and giving her my undivided attention.

"Well, since I launched the website last month, I've found it a lot easier to standardise getting all the orders through there. But I wasn't prepared to get double my number of orders."

Rhoda and I both smile at her.

"That's a good problem, though, right?" I ask.

"Yeah, I guess. But the new school year has started, and I don't have the time to cook and fulfil those orders on my own. I'll crash and burn."

"God forbid. You won't." I put my arm over my head before clicking it—a gesture I watched my parents do a thousand times while growing up. "What about setting an order time window, so you can turn things on and off if the orders are getting too many?"

Rachel tilts her head. "Yeah, that's a good idea."

"Or you could reduce your hours at the school to give room for the business to grow," Rhoda suggests.

"Yeah, I've been praying and thinking about that. But I'm scared. My income from my job is stable. I don't know how I feel about the monthly income inconsistencies that come with running a business." Rachel sighs.

"Yeah, I feel you, hun." I squeeze her shoulder. "Just take it one step at a time. Do what you can for now. Ask God for direction. We know he wants you to open up that restaurant, so you just need to ask Him how He's going to help you get there. Alright?"

Rachel nods and when we are done with our meal, Rhoda brings out dessert from the fridge. "Okay, remember I'm still learning, so if you don't like it, pretend you do because my poor heart won't be able to take any criticism right now."

"Are you kidding? This is so good," Rachel says after biting into her slice of cheesecake.

"The brownie bangs too," I add, before scooping out some vanilla ice cream onto my plate.

"Really? Aww, thank you. Dan bought me a recipe book, and it has helped a lot. I enjoy baking so much and it's a real stress reliever after long hours of uni."

"Dan, huh?" Rachel and I chuckle as we look at each other.

"Yes, *Dan*. What's that smile about?" Rhoda raises her eyebrows at us, as if she doesn't know what we're implying.

"Dan, your best friend, or Dan, your boyfriend?" I tease and Rachel joins me in laughing while Rhoda rolls her eyes.

"Oh, come on. Can you both drop it already? Stop forcing what's not there. We're best friends and that's it."

"*We're best friends and that's it*," Rachel mimics. "Sure you are!"

"You guys are too cute not to be a couple," I add. "On your wedding day, we'll be more than happy to remind you we knew all along."

"Whatever." Rhoda leaves us at the table while she finds us a movie to watch. We always leave this part to her because no matter how much Rachel and I hate to admit it, Rhoda picks the best movies.

I join Rhoda on the sofa, and after throwing us bags of popcorn, Rachel joins us, too. After one rom com and a thriller, we air out our grievances with the plot and characters of the movie.

"No, but seriously, how stupid does one have to be not to see the signs of an abuser?" Rhoda rolls her eyes as she points to the TV.

"Well, when you grow up and actually get into a relationship, you'll see for yourself that people can do stupid things for love," Rachel responds.

"Not stupid enough to almost get yourself killed," Rhoda protests and something shifts inside me, building up a mix of emotions in my chest as my mind fills up with unpleasant memories of that night.

I try to join in the conversation as Rachel and Rhoda go back and forth, bickering about the realities of physical abuse within relationships, but each time, my words elude me, and a lump builds in my throat.

Then the palpitations start, my hands trembling, my breath hitching, and my vision becoming blurry. Determined not to let my sisters pick up on what's going on with me, I push myself up from the sofa and hide my hands behind my back. "I need some water," I say before dashing out of the living room.

Opening the fridge, I hide behind the door and take deep breaths in and out, waiting for my heart rate to slow down as the girls' voices fade in the background. This is the first time I've had a panic attack inside the house. What is happening to me? I can't let the girls see me like this. *Lord, please help me.*

When my hands finally stop shaking, I grab a bottle of water from the fridge and gulp half of it, the cold temperature instantly resetting my brain.

"Okay, Bex. Come on, you can do this," I whisper before closing the fridge door and walking back out to the girls. "Okay, enough of your bickering, please can we change the subject?"

"Yeah, Rachel, change the subject." Rhoda sticks her tongue out at Rachel, who throws a pillow at her.

"Oh, by the way, Bex, how are you really feeling about the way the conversation went with Mum and Dad earlier this week?" Rachel asks.

I sigh and shake my head, grateful for the change to a subject I actually don't mind talking about. "Listen, it was scary standing there and watching you all looking at me, but now that it's over, I feel relieved and I can't wait until this book is finished."

"Who would've thought that losing your job would be a blessing?" Rhoda asks.

"I know right and such an unexpected blessing. The first step is to write the book, but at the end of the year, I'm hoping to also prove to Dad that it's possible to have a lucrative business as a creative entrepreneur."

"Yeah, and I wish African parents would let their children

explore their creative sides more. Honey, spread your wings and fly." Rachel clicks her fingers.

"Yes, honey, and even if Mum and Dad disown you, we'll stand behind you because we know they can't disown all three of us, as they won't have any bride price money," Rhoda says and we all laugh before sipping on our drinks.

"But seriously though, if only you knew a successful author in real life, they could be your mentor and show you how to actually turn that book into a lucrative business," Rachel adds and then the lightbulb moment hits me. I can't believe I hadn't thought about it.

"Hang on a minute." I gasp as I turn to my sisters. "I already met a writer in real life. A Christian writer."

"You did?" Rachel and Rhoda say in unison.

"Yes, some guy at a coffee shop at Waterloo Station."

"Ooh, a guy, huh?" Rhoda wiggles her eyebrows at me and I throw a pillow at her.

"No, I'm serious. He lent me his umbrella when it was raining, as I wanted to get to a new bookstore I saw."

"Oh, so he's the one who owns the small black umbrella in your bag?" Rhoda points to my bag lying on the floor next to me. "I was shocked to actually see an umbrella in your bag, as you're always losing yours and borrowing mine."

I reach behind me for another pillow to throw at Rhoda, but I've run out, so I smack her arm instead.

"Oh, I beg you, please tell us more about him." Rachel is the one pushing for information now. My sisters thrive on gist like this. *So nosy.*

"What? There's nothing to tell."

"Okay, what's his name?" Rhoda asks.

"I think he said it was Jevaun," I respond.

"Oooh, Jevaun. Sounds like it'll belong to someone really

handsome, am I right?" Rachel grins and leans forward as I suppress a smile.

"Yeah, well, I guess I could say he's not...bad-looking."

"Hmm, I knew it. He's handsome." Rachel and Rhoda give each other high fives and I roll my eyes at them. "So tell us exactly what happened, how you ended up with his umbrella, and please don't leave out any details," Rachel cautions.

"You two are jokers, you know that, right?"

"Whatever, please spill." Rhoda's voice is getting all high-pitched now.

"Okay, okay, calm down, mate." I pause before telling them everything that happened. "As I said, I wanted to check out the bookstore, but it started raining, so I was waiting outside the entrance to the station for the rain to ease up. Then someone touched my elbow, and I turned around to find this random stranger offering me his umbrella.

"To be fair, I was a little freaked out because I didn't know him and my introverted brain was struggling to figure out why he was talking to me, smiling at me, and being so nice to me. So I declined, and that's when he told me he is a writer and he works at The Buzz Café on most days, so he has seen me working there before."

"Sounds like he might actually be a full time writer if he does his writing at the coffee shop most days," Rhoda interjects and I side eye her.

"*Madam*, do you want to finish the story?"

"I'm sorry, *Ma*." Rhoda pinches her lips together and they both listen again in silence as I narrate the rest of our encounter.

"Aww, it's the fact that he cared about you not getting your hair wet. It's giving true Christian gentleman vibes and I love it." Rhoda grins.

"Yeah, it's definitely giving boyfriend material," Rachel follows suit.

"May I remind you, *Cupid*, that I've only met this guy once. This is London, and he could be dangerous."

"Oh, come, we know deep down you don't believe that." Rachel raises a brow and I shake my head before sighing.

"Girls, you know I'm not looking for a relationship right now. What happened with Ayo scarred me and I just want to take things slow."

"*Ugh*, Rebecca Ayuk, you and Ayo broke up four years ago and this new guy sounds nothing like Ayo. Maybe this is a new start for you?" Rhoda blinks her pleading eyes.

New. It's that word again. That same word God has been sending my way. *Lord, is this stranger part of the new plan or am I overthinking this?*

I shake my head to push Rhoda's words out. "Listen, I'm sorry to disappoint you, but on Monday I'm just going back to the coffee shop to return his umbrella and that's it."

"Aww." Rhoda pouts. "Fine, whatever. Since my own sisters don't want me to experience real-life romance through them, I guess we'll be sticking to movies."

"Yes, please," Rachel says as Rhoda picks up the remote again and soon, we're back on the sofa, blanket over our legs, lights off, more bags of popcorn, and watching yet another cheesy romantic comedy.

But only thirty minutes in, my two meddling sisters drift off to sleep, so I cover them up with a blanket before taking out my laptop from my bag and sitting at the dining table. All this talk about writing, business, and Jevaun has given me new inspiration tonight and, as usual, I must fan the flames and let the words out.

· · ·

Medical school lectures didn't come with any surprises for Vanessa. It was either the lecturers were taking it real easy on them or she had done herself a huge favour by studying the material ahead during the summer break. Studying about the human body couldn't get any more exciting. But she silently prayed that when clinical years arrived in the third year, she would also find putting her knowledge into practice as exciting.

Either way, she was enjoying how well she was settling into her routine. Uni life was pretty simple, and she liked when everything went according to plan. The hardest part was getting herself out of bed in the morning to make lectures on time, but Anne helped her with that. They kept each other accountable and made sure there was no slacking.

But as the weeks passed, lectures weren't the only thing occupying Vanessa's thoughts. She didn't know how his voice slowly became the thing she looked forward to hearing all day, or what it was about his good morning text messages that instantly lifted her mood every time she saw them. All she knew was that the more she got to know him, the more she wanted to be with him.

"Are you sure this guy is genuine?" Anne asked one day as they walked back from their late evening study session at the library.

Vanessa looked at her friend. "Of course he is. What makes you think he isn't?"

"Well, because you've only known each other for a month and he's already told you he has feelings for you? It's a bit too soon, don't you think?" Anne raised her eyebrows, waiting for Vanessa's response.

Vanessa sighed and gave it some thought as they continued walking. "Well, I see where you're coming from. But just because we haven't known each other for that long doesn't mean his feelings for me aren't genuine. I know we've only been on one date so far, but he was so gentle with me, so kind, and so thoughtful. You should see the way he opens the doors for me, how he holds my hand, and how safe he makes me feel. It's like I'm living in a real life romance novel."

"Not gonna lie. That sounds dreamy, still." Anne smiled for a second before her frown returned. "Look, Nessa, all I'm saying is that you should be careful. You don't want to get served breakfast now, do you?"

Vanessa shook her head vigorously. "God forbid. I don't even want to think about that."

Anne moved her head back. "Have you ever prayed about it?"

"Of course I have." It was Vanessa's turn to frown. "Every day since I met him. I know what I'm doing, trust me."

At that, Anne nodded. "Okay. If you say so."

When they got back to halls, Vanessa had a shower, had her Bible study at nine PM, and then called her mum.

"How are you doing today, my princess?"

"I'm fine, Mummy. I just missed you, that's all." She threw herself on the bed and brought the phone up to her ear.

"Aww, I miss you too every day." Diana's voice broke as sniffles came through the other end of the line. "But I know God is with you, and I know you will always make me proud."

"Yes, Mummy. Please, don't cry. I'll always make you proud."

"I was praying for you today, and God laid it heavily on my heart to pray against distractions."

Vanessa sat up in bed before asking. "Distractions?"

"Yes, please, my daughter, focus on your studies, okay? Don't let anything or anyone try to derail you from this path that God has put you on. Do you hear me?"

"Yes, Mum. You have nothing to worry about. God is with me."

"That's right. I love you so much, my princess."

"I love you, Mummy."

As Vanessa lay in bed, thinking about what her mum had said, she only came to the conclusion that her mum was worried about her, as any other mother would. He wasn't a distraction, and he has never felt like one to her.

Anne had never been in a relationship, so she didn't understand that it didn't always have to end in tears. Vanessa was a hopeless romantic, forever an optimist, and still believed in true love. Nothing could discourage her from thinking that her story would not have a happy ending.

9

JEVAUN

I never wake up before my alarm, but for the past five days, I have been. Where was this instinct all throughout medical school when I struggled to get myself to lectures or hospital placements on time?

Who would've thought that the prospect of meeting a complete stranger would fuel my motivation for writing again? What is it about this girl whose name I don't even know, that makes me want to be so productive each day, so I can have enough time to run back to the coffee shop?

I didn't mind watching or admiring her from a distance, but boy, speaking to her up close last week and breaking the ice felt like I'd won an Olympic gold medal. Even though that high fell flat when she didn't come to the coffee shop again for the rest of last week, I'm still weirdly optimistic that I'll see her again. Maybe even today.

"Hey, *Lexi*, what upcoming appointments do I have today?" I shout across my office as the digital assistant device chimes from the top of my bookshelf.

"You have the Faith Writers in-person meeting today at 4 PM,"

the voice responds and I walk up to my corkboard and add it to my to-do-list before crossing off the first two things on the list.

After my Bible study this morning, I edited and scheduled the two videos going up on my YouTube channel later this week. The first one is a reading vlog and book review of a Christian fantasy novel by a new-to-me author. The second is my bookshelf tour and sharing my entire book collection—a video my subscribers have been expecting since I rearranged my office three months ago.

My phone buzzes on my desk and it's a text notification on the Faith Writers' group chat. It's Tom—the founder of the group—reminding us about the meeting later today. Since London is so big and most group members live all over the city, we have one monthly in-person meeting in Stratford, but also a monthly virtual meeting to give an opportunity for the members who can't make the in-person event.

Today, I'll be sharing the synopsis of my new fantasy novel with the group to get some feedback before I start working on the first draft. My ghost writing client finished reviewing the outline I sent to him last week. He sent me an email last night telling me how much he loves the outline, so I'll start working on that story at the coffee shop today.

After packing up my backpack with all the essentials I need for the day—my laptop, laptop charger, phone, phone charger, bottle of water, snacks and my wallet—I take one last look at myself in the mirror in my bathroom.

My barber deserves an award because how he can always get me from a 0 to 100 is a fine art. It definitely explains why I don't mind travelling all the way to Lewisham every month to get my haircut. When you find a barber that's this good, you'd be crazy to let anyone else touch your hair.

I brush my hair and beard before almost suffocating myself with excess body spray. Her scent was so captivating, so I think I have to step up my game. "Okay, calm down, Jevaun," I say out loud, pointing at myself in the mirror. "You've only spoken to this girl once, so just get your umbrella back and don't freak her out, please."

But even my reflection can't be deceived because it's general knowledge that the real reason I want to see her again has nothing to do with that umbrella. With one last sigh and sending a prayer to God for guidance and protection for the day, I finally step out of the house.

The shortcut to the train station cuts through a park and since God has blessed us with a slice of sunshine today, the typical Brits have flocked outside, trying to make the most of the warmth before the cold weather sets in again.

At the playground, there are parents pushing their babies in strollers while dogs are running back and forth across the grass, chasing balls or sticks thrown by their owners. I admire the dogs from afar, making sure not to get too close because I don't trust dogs I don't know. This is London, after all.

When I get out of the tube and make my way to Waterloo Station, I walk past a busker perched in the corner just before the escalator. I've seen him here a few times over the last few months, and I always stop to listen to his cover of contemporary Christian worship songs. He's the type of person I would love to speak to one day, but for today, I drop a fiver in his guitar case, alongside the other one and two pound coins, and then I make my way to The Buzz Café.

If disappointment was a person, I would be that person right now, as I scan the entire coffee shop twice and don't find her. With every step I take to my usual table next to the balcony, I'm fighting one thousand doubts in my head about how our last encounter went.

It can only be in the movies where two people meet once and then struggle to meet again because they didn't get each other's contact details. But this is a different scenario because she knows where to find me.

I crane my neck over the balcony, staring at the exact spot where I spoke to her last week. I was so sure I had broken the ice and left her with a good impression. But maybe I was just being delusional and scared her away and she'll never be coming back to this coffee shop again.

I blow out a breath before taking a seat at the table facing the front entrance of the coffee shop. The big clock at the centre of the station strikes eleven AM and I open my laptop to work on my client's manuscript.

Every so often, I take a break to glance at the front entrance of the coffee shop again, wondering whether the next person coming up the escalator might be her. I do that at least five more times until finally, at two PM, she emerges into view like a sunrise and immediately brightens up my day.

Instead of walking up to her, I stay seated, soaking in her beauty as she walks toward the shop. She swings her backpack over her shoulder, her gaze darting around as if she's looking for something...or someone.

She stops in her tracks, bows her head, takes deep breaths in and out, and closes her eyes as if she's praying. Then, when she opens her eyes again and lifts her head, she locks eyes with me. The smile I've been suppressing finally bursts forth as I waste no time raising my hand and beckoning her over.

10

BEX

For someone I've only met once in my life, this mystery guy is giving my heart way too much trouble. I've only been looking at him for two seconds and my heart is already working overtime, pounding and thumping as if it'll pop out any second if I give it the chance.

That's what my body does in crowded spaces. It tries to make me believe that I'm not coping and that the worst will happen. So just two seconds in and the perspiration is building under my arms, my hands are trembling, my throat is closing up, and my chest tightening.

What if everything goes wrong? What if he turns out to be a serial killer and whips out a machete before chasing me down Waterloo Station until my sad story ends up all over the news? What if he turns out to be another Ayomide Bankole—the old version of him that enticed me with his sweet words until I stupidly fell head-over-heels in love before he showed his true colours?

Or what if he's just...him—the nice guy who saw that I was in need, and went out of his way to help me? He could just be the nice guy who didn't have to, but complimented my hair and made me feel really beautiful that day. It can't always be the worst-case scenario. God still has His children walking the face of this earth who are genuinely looking for opportunities to show kindness.

Refusing to let my spiralling thoughts get the best of me, I bow my head in prayer, yes in the middle of a busy coffee shop, silently repeating 2 Corinthians 10:5-6 and determined to take these disabling thoughts captive and make them obedient to Christ.

God has given me the spirit of boldness and a sound mind.

The repeated declarations over my mind slow down my fast heart rate and shaking hands. Coupled with a few deep breaths, the pain in my chest slowly resolves as I lift my head again and lock eyes with him.

Ignoring the questioning looks from the other patrons in the coffee shop, I focus on his smile as he raises his hand and beckons me over. *Boldness and a sound mind.* My feet carry me step after step, meandering my way through the tables as I double-check my backpack again to make sure his umbrella didn't fall off on the train.

"Hello, stranger." His smile is now so wide you would think he has just met his destiny helper. "I was starting to think I would never see you again."

I respond with a sheepish smile, guilty as charged. "Sorry, I actually meant to come last week, but you know... the rain."

"Say no more. I totally understand." He pulls out the chair next to him. "Please, have a seat."

"Erm..." I look over my shoulder at my usual seat at the other end of the coffee shop, and his gaze follows mine.

"Oh, would you like us to move to the corner you're familiar with?"

I open my mouth to agree, but then stop myself. There's

nothing wrong with being out of my comfort zone. *Come on, Bex. It's just a seat. You're not going to die.*

"Actually, no, that's okay. I'm fine here." I occupy the chair next to him before taking out his umbrella from my bag and handing it to him. "Here you go."

He looks at the object in my hand before shaking his head. "No, it's okay. You can keep it."

I raise my eyebrows and it's my turn to shake my head. "Keep it?" Confusion wraps around my voice. "But you said I can give it back to you when next I see you, right?"

"Yeah, but I don't need it. I have more than one." He lifts his backpack, showing me another umbrella tucked in the side pocket, which looks exactly like the one in my hand.

"And you're happy for me to keep this?" I ask.

"Well, do you have an umbrella?"

I chuckle. "No, I don't."

"Then it's all yours. No strings attached, I promise." He laughs, his caramel skin tone brightening up even more, and for the first time, I can take in all his physical features. His beard looks more trimmed than when I last saw him and even with him sitting down, I'm reminded of just how much taller he is than me. But my favourite thing about this stranger is the big smile he has on that always reveals his perfect dentition.

"What? Do I have something on my teeth?" He snaps me out of my thoughts, embarrassment washing over me.

Oh, for goodness' sake. Keep it together, Bex.

"Oh, no, I'm sorry, I..." I shut my eyes tight, trying to make up a lie and then throw my hands up before laying it all bare. "Fine, you caught me. It's just that you have a really nice smile." I lower my voice, hoping he didn't hear me, but also wondering what gave me the boldness to voice out my thoughts like that. This guy could have a girlfriend, so what would she think about me gawking at her man like this?

He smiles. "Thank you so much. That's a very kind thing to say."

"You're welcome." I shrug, my posture becoming more relaxed. "I thought I'd return the favour since you complimented me the other day."

Wow, Bex. Your mouth is on fire today. Look at you keeping a conversation going with a stranger without feeling awkward about it.

"Oh, yeah." His gaze slides up to my hair again as if I hadn't already caught him looking at it earlier. "And I'd still say the same for today. Beautiful."

"Thank you." I straighten my back, my hand subconsciously going up to my hair. Here's the moment where I thank myself for putting in the effort to blow dry my hair and do a crown braid and low puff before leaving the house.

Let's hope he hasn't noticed the eye bags I'm carrying because I stayed up late last night, trying to outline that dreaded scene in my book. But I'll push all that to the back of my mind now since I can still get the word 'beautiful' out of the mouth of a complete stranger.

"So, what would you like to eat?" His question catches me off-guard, as what I thought would be a quick hand-off has now turned into an impromptu date? But I'm going with the flow because everyone needs a friendly, approachable, kind-hearted friend. Plus, he's a Christian writer. God just knows how to put me on the path of the people I need.

"Erm... I like to keep it simple and go for a croissant and Earl Grey tea."

"Really simple, huh?" he says before pulling the menu from a stack at the corner of the table. "Well, I like to try something new every time, so I think I'll go for the egg, bacon, and cheese on brioche."

"Sounds lovely, but...with a recent diagnosis of irritable bowel syndrome, I better not try anything new in a public place." We share a laugh before he leaves me on the table and walks up to the counter to place our order.

Ten minutes later, he's back with our food and I pour out the tea from the small tea pot into my mug. My mouth waters as I watch him try the brioche, savouring each bite as if he's a judge at a food contest.

"Hmm. It's so good." He turns to me when he has swallowed. "It's a shame you can't have any."

"Don't worry. I'm sure there'll be plenty of opportunities to try, and then I can tell you whether it's really as good as you're making it sound." I sip on my tea.

"Really?" He raises one brow. "Is that a seal of approval for this friendship?"

"Well, it depends." I interlock my fingers on the table, surprising myself as my playful side springs forth.

"On what, exactly? That I prove to you I'm not a serial killer?"

We both share a laugh, but mine is definitely filled with nerves as I cast my mind back to my anxious thoughts earlier.

"Don't worry, I'm not a serial killer, I can assure you. Like I said before, I'm Jevaun and I write Christian fantasy novels. I'm hoping to find a literary agent and eventually a publisher for my first novel. I'm working on my second novel now and I also do some ghostwriting. I have a YouTube channel where I talk all about Christian fantasy books, and that recently expanded to an online paid membership community made up of enthusiastic Christian fantasy readers."

"Wow," is the only word I can utter after listening to all his credentials. "So you're like a proper writer doing some serious stuff out here. I didn't even know Christian fantasy was a genre."

"Yeah, I get that a lot, but you'd be amazed at how many amazing books are out there in that genre." He smiles before leaning back. "And what do you mean by proper writer? Anyone who writes is a writer."

I shrug. "Nah, there are levels to this, you know? You're like all those YouTubers I watch who write full time. I never thought I would ever meet any of them in real life. This is so cool." And now I have evidence when Mum and Dad come at me with their doubting questions.

"Wow, it's refreshing to see someone's interest so piqued when I talk about my job. There's usually a lot of skepticism from people like my dad and..." He sighs before his voice trails off. He shakes his head and even though I know nothing about his situation, I already feel like I can relate to his unspoken words.

"I'm new to this, but I think I get what you mean. I'm not sure about you, but my traditional Cameroonian parents don't think I can have a lucrative career as a writer."

"Well, my dad still thinks the same, even though I've been doing this full time for five years. I've lived in the UK most of my life, but I was born in Jamaica, so perhaps it's an Afro-Caribbean cultural myth?"

"Yes, but even outside the Afro-Caribbean culture too, people still look down on creatives for whatever reason. A lot of work needs to be done to break that myth."

"Definitely." He nods. "So what kind of writing do you do, then?"

My body freezes for a second as I realise the attention is now on me. "Erm...well, I just started working on a novel. My first novel actually, so I'm pretty new to this."

"Well, congrats. You're already a step further than so many people."

I frown. "Really? How so?"

"You're among the top three percent of people who actually

write a book and not just think about it. So you're doing better than you think."

"Aww, are you sure you don't want to be my coach?" I say jokingly, but his vigorous nod is the response I never knew I needed.

"Count me in." He takes the last bite of his brioche. "But you know, at some point, I'm going to have to know the name of my client."

My cheeks warm up as I cover my face with my hands, suppressing a laugh. "I can't believe I've been spilling out my guts to you and I never mentioned my name."

"It's not too late. Now I'm *very* excited." He leans his head on cupped hands, as if he's waiting for me to bring out gold for him.

"Oh, it's nothing unique. My name is Rebecca Ayuk. But everyone, apart from my parents, calls me Bex."

"Ooh, we've even reached a place in this friendship where we can share government names. That means you trust me now?"

I chuckle. "Well, you come across as a trustworthy person. I have the spirit of discernment, you know?"

"Come on, now." He clicks his fingers. "Thank God for the Holy Spirit, who is on my side." His laugh matches mine as he keeps his eyes on me, starting a fluttering sensation in my chest. "It's lovely to meet you, Bex, and, for the third time—I'm Jevaun. Jevaun Watson."

"The pleasure is all mine, Jevaun."

After finishing our meals, we spend a bit of time working on our stories, Jevaun working on the ghostwriting project for his new client, while I watch some YouTube writing vlogs to get more inspiration, so I can outline that dreaded scene in my book.

As his hands fly over his laptop keys next to me, I can't help but steal subtle glances at him, first admiring the handsomeness he exudes, but also letting myself dream about the possibility of one day being in his shoes.

This, right here, is proof that God can do it for me, too. I would've never thought that I would receive this answered prayer only a short walk into my journey, but God is truly doing something new and He's going to blow my mind.

An hour later, he closes his laptop and my heart sinks as I watch him pack up his stuff into his backpack. "Time to go?" I ask, hoping he'll say otherwise.

"Yeah. I have a meeting with my faith writing group in an hour. It's in Stratford, so I have to leave now, so I make it on time."

"Well, it seems like you did a lot of work today, so you've earned the break." I smile to hide my disappointment.

"Yeah, I finished writing the first chapter of the ghostwriting project."

"Wow, in just one hour? I have so much to learn."

He smiles. "Don't worry about it. I'm now your coach, remember?" He places his backpack on his lap and then his hand on the table as it brushes mine. "You're going to finish writing that story God has given you, got it?"

My words elude me as I stare into his deep brown eyes, so I nod as he stands up and turns to go.

"Oh, and before I forget." He sits back down again. "I don't know about you, but I really enjoyed this." He gestures between us. "It was so easy talking to you and I feel like we haven't even scratched the surface of our conversation yet. So, if it won't be too much trouble, I'd love to get your number, so we can plan our dates."

My eyes widen. "Dates?"

He laughs. "Yeah, our writing dates."

"Sure." I smile at him before handing my phone over. After entering my number into his phone, we swap phones again. "For the record, I really enjoyed talking to you, too. I can't wait for us to do this again."

"Me neither." He stands there for almost five seconds as silence passes between us. "Well, I hope you enjoy the rest of your day and hope you get home safe."

"You too. Have fun."

"Thanks." He turns around. "Good bye, Bex."

"Bye, Jevaun."

I stare at him as he walks out of the coffee shop and when he gets to the escalator, he turns around and looks at me with one last big smile and waves before he disappears from my sight.

I sit there for a few seconds, absolutely perplexed by what just happened. How did I just so easily make friends with someone as outgoing and confident as Jevaun? It's like I'm a completely different person when I'm talking to him. I can't believe I was so worried and anxious about this meeting and I forgot that God never stops working miracles.

I sigh as my thoughts drift into a daydream about the day when Jevaun's lifestyle would be the norm for me. But until that day, I have to finish writing this book first.

After lectures, Vanessa and Anne always spent a few hours in the library, either sorting out their notes from the lectures of the day or preparing for the lectures of the next day. On the days when they stayed late in the library, they ordered takeaway or bought food from the nearby shops. But when they went home early, they made dinner together in their communal kitchen.

The girls loved anything that was quick to make, so if it

wasn't fried rice, then it was some sort of pasta or noodles or, better still, toast or porridge. At uni, nobody cared whether they had cereal for breakfast, lunch and dinner because everyone was just trying to get through each day.

"Hmm, that was so good." Anne dropped her spoon and leaned back in her chair as she rubbed her belly. "I could have pasta every day."

"Me too." Vanessa answered absentmindedly, her attention on her phone as her thumbs typed quickly, before swiping and locking it.

"Hmm." Anne stared at her friend. "Dare I ask who you are texting and why you're smiling so hard?"

"I don't know what you're talking about." Vanessa got up and took their plates to the sink. After washing and placing them on the drying rack, she drank a glass of water and turned to Anne. "I'm exhausted, so I think I'm going to bed now."

"Okay, then. If you say so. Good night, bestie." Anne said, and even though Vanessa could hear the sarcasm in her voice, she ignored it.

"Good night." Vanessa made her way to her room, locked the door, and threw herself on her bed as she opened her messages again and scrolled through their exchanges throughout the day.

He promised to call her that evening when he got back from placement, but he hadn't for some reason. Vanessa knew he eventually would, and didn't want to be with Anne when he called because she didn't want to hear any more of Anne's skeptical comments.

It was almost nine PM, almost time for her Bible study, but she didn't mind pushing back her Bible study for a few minutes, just so she could see that face and hear that voice she had missed all day.

Vanessa had always thought she would find her husband after she graduated from med school. Or maybe it was just her mum's voice ringing in her ears about why it's important to wait that long for a relationship. But if God had smiled on her and brought him early, she couldn't say no.

She knew her values, and she would not give herself away to anyone that wasn't her husband. But being a hopeless romantic, she also longed to be loved and swept off her feet—the same way she had seen in the thousands of romantic comedies she had watched.

"Hey beautiful." The deep husk of his voice sent butterflies flying around in her belly as she lay on her bed.

"Hey, handsome," she responded. "I thought you wouldn't call."

"I'm sorry I'm late, but you know I always keep my promises. Speaking to you is my favourite part of the day."

"Aww." She kicked her feet in the air and rolled over, trying hard to control her emotions. "How was placement?"

"Let's just say I very much prefer talking to you than running around on the wards speaking to patients."

"Oh, come on. You're in your final year, and you'll be a doctor soon. You know I'll be in your shoes in five years' time, so at least sell it to me." She smiled.

"Nah, the only thing I want to sell to you right now is a birthday party on Thursday."

"Oh?" She frowned and sat up. "Whose party?"

"One of my mates. It'll be at his house. There'll be lots of my friends there. It'll be nice to show you off officially as my girlfriend."

An unsettling feeling rested in Vanessa's chest as she stood in the middle of her room, biting her nails.

"Come on, it'll be nice to meet my friends. They've heard so much about you and they'll love to meet you."

"Really?"

"Yeah," he said. "Don't you want to meet them?"

"I do, but..." She paused. "I usually go to the CU meetings on Thursdays."

"Oh, okay, we can drop in only for a bit to meet my friends and then we'll make our way to CU after. How about that?"

Her smile returned as she sat on the edge of her bed again. "Okay, then. That sounds good."

And that's all he needed to say to convince her, but even after ending the call, Vanessa still couldn't shake off the unsettling feeling in her chest and she couldn't explain why.

11

BEX

"Hey, Mum. Hey, Dad." I grin as I walk up to my parents in the kitchen, interrupting their husband and wife gossip session. A cosy evening for both of them always includes Mum wearing one of her *kabas* and Dad wearing one of his white cotton vests and shorts.

One thing I've noticed for the past twenty-seven years of my life, living with my parents, is that they don't play about spending quality time with each other. Whenever Mum is cooking, if Dad isn't doing something important, he'll be right there in the kitchen, sitting on a stool by the counter and gisting with her, even if the only thing he's doing is peeling onions. They're just the cutest.

"Hmm. That smells delicious, Mum." I inhale the lovely aroma of *eru*, a classic Cameroonian dish, which is a flavourful mixture of leafy greens, assorted meat, and palm oil. My mouth waters as I imagine the vegetable soup in my mouth with pounded yam. "You didn't wait for me? I thought we were going to cook together."

"Don't worry, my dear. We didn't know when you would be back from your...new work. So we decided not to stress you."

I smile at the way she hesitated before saying new work. You would think she was trying to swallow shards of glass. "Aww, that's so thoughtful of you. Will you at least let me make the pounded yam?" In Cameroon, we typically have *eru* with *water fufu*[1], but as that's harder to find here, pounded yam is a good alternative.

"No, that's okay. I have that covered. Please go and shower and get ready for dinner." Dad responds.

"Okay." My gaze darts between the two of them and although I want to figure out why they're acting suspicious today, I'm too hungry to protest, so I heed to their advice and run upstairs.

After showering and changing into my own *kaba*, I descend the stairs, almost tripping over my feet as I make my way to the dining table where Mum and Dad are already sitting.

My stomach rumbles at the sight of the food in serving dishes, and my parents give me another look as I take a seat. The anxiety I was feeling about meeting Jevaun today messed with my brain and I forgot to pack a proper lunch.

The croissant and tea only clamped down my hunger pangs for a few hours, and it took a lot of strength not to try Jevaun's brioche. "Sorry, I haven't eaten much today." I send them a sheepish smile.

"Don't apologise. I suppose it's because you were working hard, right?" Mum asks, smiling before looking at Dad, who looks like he doesn't share the same sentiment.

"Yup. That's right."

Dad shakes his head, but says nothing until Mum asks him to pray over the food.

Mum and Dad dish out their food first and they allow me to unwrap my pounded yam and have a few good swallows before Dad pesters me with the questions I've been expecting.

"So, what exactly did you do today?" He looks up from his plate, his eyes boring into mine.

"I did some writing, but it was mostly research today," I say simply, another mound of the pounded yam and *eru* going into my mouth.

"Research," Dad repeats.

"Research is part of writing, Dad." I let out a sigh, my appetite slowly fading away. "Writing is not as easy as you think. I'm stuck with a particular scene in my book, so I've been watching some videos to inspire me."

"So, what you're saying is that you spent the entire afternoon watching videos?"

"Erm...darling, please," Mum cuts him short, just as my appetite completely dissolves. "Didn't you hear her say she did some writing, too? I'm sure she has had a long day. Please let her eat so she can rest."

"Don't worry. I've lost my appetite. Good night, Mum. Good night, Dad." I wash my hands in the bowl of water at the centre of the table before carrying my plate and walking out of the living room.

"Rebecca, please, wait. Don't be angry, please," Mum calls out, but I don't look back.

I cover my food and put it in the fridge because good food can't go to waste. Then I gulp a glass of water and take deep breaths before walking out of the kitchen and heading toward the stairs.

"I thought we agreed you would not bring this up during dinner," Mum's voice comes through the corner and I wait at the bottom of the stairs for Dad's response.

"I'm just trying to understand why she has chosen this path, that's all," his answer finally comes. "It doesn't make sense to me."

"It doesn't have to make sense because you're not her. She says God has given her the vision to write this book, so why don't you at least show some support as her father?"

"Have I not always been a supportive father? Why would you blame me for having reservations about something that doesn't make sense?"

"Just because it doesn't make sense to you doesn't mean it's not valid or important." Mum's voice is the last thing I hear before deciding I've heard enough.

Upstairs in my room, I shut the door behind me, a lump building in my throat as my eyes water. After pacing the length of my room, I swipe the tears from my eyes before sitting at my desk and staring at the blinking cursor on my laptop screen. I thought this feeling would go away once I finally started writing this book, but now it feels like I've taken a step forward and two steps back.

Lord, help me, please. I scroll through the entire document, reading parts of what I wrote today and trying to get over whatever this feeling is and just write the next scene.

Mum and Dad's voices fade in the background as I tap my fingers on the keyboard, begging the words to come out of my brain. But the more I try to concentrate, the more empty my brain feels. So I give up and close my laptop.

Maybe Dad is right. Maybe I'm wasting my time. The tears return as I throw myself on my bed, sobbing into my pillow until my nine PM alarm rings, reminding me about the commitment I made to God four years ago.

After the roller coaster ride of emotions that has been today, opening my Bible and praying is the last thing I want to do. I'm not in the mood, and how do I even focus my thoughts when they are filled with all this pent-up frustration?

But emotions are temporary and I won't let them be the reason I decide not to speak to my Maker—the same One who rescued me from depression when the world knew nothing about what I was going through. God was there for me four years ago, fresh from my breakup with Ayo, but also still struggling with the aftermath of my university trauma.

To this day, no one truly knows how broken I was—not even my sisters. No one truly knows how close I was to giving up on life, but God does. He was right there. He stepped in at the right time, shined His light on me, and gave me a reason to live again. So, no. I refuse to let a bad day stop me from spending time with my Heavenly Father.

I push myself up from my bed and sit at my desk again before grabbing my Bible and journal from the bookshelf above my desk. Half an hour later, I'm feeling much more encouraged after reading Psalm 61. The lyrics of the popular song from the psalm impress into my heart until I sing them out loud—repeating the last line of the chorus which says: *when my heart is overwhelmed, lead me to the Rock that is higher than I.*

"Help me, Heavenly Father. No one knows the depth of my heart like You do. I know without a doubt that this assignment is from You, but I've also never felt pressure like this in my entire life. Please take away the burden and show me the way. In Jesus' name I've prayed. Amen."

With my foul mood finally lifted, I change into my pyjamas and put on my satin bonnet, getting ready for an early night, when my phone vibrates continuously, alerting me to a video call from Rhoda.

"*Ugh*, this girl never sleeps," I mutter under my breath before picking up the phone.

"Hey, Sissy. What you saying?" The smile that creeps up Rhoda's face is enough to let me know she's on to something mischievous.

"I'm just trying to get some sleep." I lift my phone above me to show her my pyjamas.

"Oh, so I caught you at the perfect time, then. Rach is going to join in a minute," Rhoda says before adjusting her own bonnet as she throws herself on her bed.

"Huh? Why? I didn't know we were going to have a conference call tonight."

"It was an impromptu one because we can't wait to hear the gist," Rachel announces herself, her voice muffled for a bit as she balances the phone, showing us a partial view of the bathroom. The two girls live together, but they are always in different parts of their flat whenever they call me.

"Yeah, we reckoned you'd be done with your Bible study by ten-thirty, and we were right. So, spill, girl," Rhoda orders.

Aww, my sisters can be so annoying, but it's the little things they do that reaffirm each day that they love me. They have it ingrained in their memory that I always have my quiet time with God at nine PM, so they've never tried to call me at that time unless it's an emergency.

"How was the meeting with our handsome author friend today?" Rachel asks as she washes her face over the sink.

"Jevaun, Rach. His name is Jevaun," Rhoda butts in. "We're past vague name references now, aren't we?"

I laugh before nodding. "Yes, Madam. You're right. His name is Jevaun Watson. He's thirty years old. He was born in Jamaica and I'm pleased to say he's not a serial killer."

"Yay!" Rachel and Rhoda squeal simultaneously and I laugh, shaking my head.

"Okay, and?" Rhoda asks.

"And we got to talking. I found out he's a full-time author and a content creator as well. He offers ghostwriting services, and he also has a YouTube channel."

Rhoda gasps as her eyes widen. "No way. What's his channel name? I have to find him right now."

"Well, I didn't get the chance to ask because—"

"Is that him?" Rhoda cuts me short as she sends a link to a YouTube video on our group chat.

I click on the link with the speed of lightning. "Oh, wow. Yes, that's him." My voice comes out more squeaky than I'd like. "Jevaun Talks Books. Thirty thousand subscribers."

"Whoa." Rachel's mouth drops. "That's a lot. He must be so good at what he does to have this as his full-time income."

"Yeah, he's so professional," I say absentmindedly as I watch one of his videos muted on my laptop.

"And we were right. He is *very* handsome." Rachel wiggles her eyebrows before dabbing her face with a towel.

"You know, he offered to be my coach?" I say, strangely determined to tell the girls just how amazing Jevaun is, even though I've only spoken to him twice.

"Aww, that's so cool. Who says God doesn't answer prayers?" Rachel claps her hands.

"I know, right? One day you're watching countless authors online, wishing you knew someone in real life and the next day, God sends you a real-life role model," Rhoda adds.

"Yeah, I know God is in this." That's why I won't even waste my breath telling the girls about the little encounter I had with Dad this evening. Little bumps like that on the road are expected, but I refuse to let it distract me from focusing on the bigger picture.

"So, when next are you guys meeting?" Rachel asks.

"Probably tomorrow, but I'm not sure what time."

"Oh, please tell me you exchanged numbers at least?" Rhoda raises an eyebrow at me.

"Of course. He was the one who asked for mine."

"Yes, sharp guy." Rhoda shakes her shoulders and we all laugh.

"Okay, now that you've heard the gist, can you all let me sleep now?"

"Yeah, I think we've had our bellies filled. Tomorrow is another day to pester you," Rhoda says and I roll my eyes.

"Okay, thanks for the heads up. I'm not picking up any calls from you."

"Oh, you know you'll be the one calling to share the good news," Rachel says, and we bid each other good night, sharing air kisses before I end the call.

After turning off the light and going under my duvet cover, I navigate my way back to Jevaun Talks Books and end up watching his most recent video, which is part of a series of him exploring different bookshops in London and checking whether they have any Christian fantasy books.

He also documents the outcome of the conversations he has with the bookshop owners about stocking Christian fiction books to diversify the literature people can find in bookstores. The man is literally doing the Lord's work out on these streets and he is killing it. You can tell how passionate he is about what he does from the way he talks about books.

Even when he reviews other author's books, he is so respectful in his discussion about what he didn't like about the books. It seems not only are there many Christian fantasy authors out there, but there are also so many readers who love the genre from the hundreds of comments he gets on each video.

My fingers take me to the description box of his YouTube video and I click on the link to his social media pages. The bookish aesthetic he has is so eye-catching, I don't even realise when I hit the follow button.

Immediately regretting my decision, and not wanting to come across as desperate, I'm about to unfollow him when a notification pops up on my phone saying @JevaunTalksBooks has followed me back.

I let out a squeal before clamping my mouth shut, as I'm not ready for another line of questioning from my parents tonight. As I'm still staring at the screen, one, two, and three more notifications pop up saying @JevaunTalksBooks has liked my photos.

Unlike Jevaun's professional-looking page, mine only has a few photos of me—mainly from the times when Rhoda forced me to take a photo—and a caption sharing what God has been teaching me lately. As I'm still getting acquainted with his photos, a text message notification pops up on my phone from him.

Jevaun: Hi, Bex 🙂 I wanted to message you tomorrow as I wasn't sure if you had fallen asleep already, but now that I know you're still awake, I thought I'd check in and make sure you're okay?

Warmth spreads across my cheeks as I sit up in bed and after reading the message five more times and smiling like a fool, I finally send a reply.

Me: Hi, Jevaun. That's so kind of you. Yes, I'm okay. Thanks for checking on me. I got home safe. 😊

Jevaun: That's great to hear. 😊

Looking at the emoji at the end of his message reminds me about his warm smile in person and makes me less nervous to keep the conversation going.

. . .

Me: How was the session with your writing group?

Jevaun: It was good. I got to share the synopsis of my second novel for the first time and the feedback I got was very encouraging.

Me: Wow, that's amazing. Congratulations 😊

Jevaun: Thanks. But even though I loved being around everyone there, I kept wishing I was still talking to a certain girl at The Buzz Café. 🙈

A fluttering sensation erupts in my tummy as I bite my bottom lip, reading the message again. He loves talking to me and I love talking to him, so armed with a new form of boldness, I send another reply.

Me: You can stop wishing then. Should we pick up that conversation tomorrow at 10am?

Jevaun: Sounds perfect. Have a good night, Bex, and see you tomorrow, by God's grace.

Me: Good night, Jevaun 😌

12

JEVAUN

By the time Bex arrives for our second writing date, I'm almost done with my English breakfast. When she said she was going to be ten minutes late, I actually believed her and placed our order, so it'd be ready by the time she arrived. I didn't realise ten minutes was some sort of code for one hour.

"I'm so sorry." She sets her backpack on the floor before pulling a chair, her flustered state making her look even cuter. Today, she's wearing another white t-shirt, which has the word 'beloved' written on it.

"I overslept because I didn't hear my alarm go off and then my mum asked me to run an impromptu errand for her as I was about to leave the house. I'm so sorry." She forms a prayer pose with both hands, drawing a smile from me.

"That's okay. You came, and that's all that matters," I say before putting the last piece of bacon and baked beans in my mouth.

"Oh wow, you even placed our order already?" She uses the back of her hand to feel the teapot of her now lukewarm tea.

"I'll get another one for you."

"Aww, no, no, I was late. I'll get it," she protests, but I reach for her hand and she pauses, her eyes locking with mine.

"Please...allow me. It's my treat."

"Okay, then. If you insist." She relaxes in her seat before taking a bite of her croissant. "Thank you, Jevaun."

"You're welcome." I carry the teapot and head to the counter.

"Hey, Jen," I greet as she turns to me. "I'd like to get some more Earl Grey tea, please. This one's gone cold."

"Sure." She takes the teapot from me. "So, is that your girlfriend?" She nods at Bex, who is now half-way through her croissant.

I smile. "No, she's my new friend and writing partner. She's quite new to it all, so I'm coaching her."

"Right. Is she a Christian too?" Jen tilts her head.

"As a matter of fact, she is. Why do you ask?"

She shrugs. "Well, because it's obvious you have a thing for her. She seems like a nice girl too, so ask her out soon before she friend zones you."

I'll be honest and say I'm surprised that Jen is giving me this kind of advice given what has transpired between us recently, but I appreciate her kind gesture. "Thanks, Jen. Trust me, I'm working on it."

"Good luck."

I don't need luck. I stop the words from coming out of my mouth as I take the teapot from her, before carrying it back to Bex. "There you go."

"Aww, thank you." She pours some tea into her mug, stirs with her spoon, and then takes a sip.

"So, I see you found me on social media then?" I lean back in my seat, watching her chew on her croissant.

She covers her mouth, waiting to swallow the last bite before answering. "Yeah, I did. You were quick to follow me back, too."

I laugh. "Yeah, I was actually replying to some comments

when I saw the notification that you had followed me. The name was familiar, so when I realised it was you, I had to follow you back before the notification got buried in the hundreds I get every day."

"Wow, you are one busy man." She rests her elbows on the table. "I love your YouTube channel, too."

"Really?" I lean forward and she nods.

"Yeah, I watched a few of your recent videos and the community you have there is so supportive. I didn't realise that so many people loved Christian fiction."

"Yes, the rate at which the community grew took me by surprise. It's one way God showed me He was truly in this for me. All I did was do my research and put out the content. I don't know where the people came from."

"Well, you definitely have a new subscriber."

"Thanks, Bex. I really appreciate it," I say as she sips on her tea again.

"So, I'm curious. What exactly is your novel about?" she asks. "I know you're querying and technically you're not allowed to share the details publicly, but I hoped that since I'm your new coaching client, I'll get special insider information?"

"Of course." I take out my phone and open my photo album. I've pitched my book to so many people over the last five years, but the idea of pitching it to Bex gives me a jittery sensation in my chest.

"This is my science fiction fantasy novel, *Parallels*." I gauge her reaction as I show her the aesthetics I've made.

"Oooh. *Parallels*. I love that title. I'm intrigued." She leans closer and scrolls through the mood board.

"It's set in Jamaica and it explores the human quest for control and perfection. When presented with an opportunity to go through a portal into a parallel universe where they can control the outcome of their lives, families and friendships are divided as some choose to go in while others prefer to stay in their current world with a lot of unknowns, but trusting the known God.

"The main characters are a married couple and scientists—Aaron and Hannah Brown, whose marriage is on the rocks after losing their daughter in a car accident. Aaron was driving, and he blames himself for what happened and God for allowing it to happen. With his faith being tested, he takes the offer of a parallel universe without hesitation, wishing to abandon the world of suffering and pain behind. But what he doesn't know is that the forces that control this parallel universe have dark secrets that will lead their inhabitants to a place of no return."

"Wow." Bex's jaw drops as she stares at me and I wait for her to say more, but she doesn't.

"Is that...is that a good *wow*?"

"Of course it is. Wow! That sounds amazing, Jevaun. I've never read a science fiction or a fantasy novel before, but after hearing that, I want to read it right now."

"Aww, it means a lot to hear you say that." She has no idea how much she has just boosted my confidence.

"I've always admired fantasy and science fiction authors. I'm struggling to write about our world, but you are out here making up parallel universes while still talking about relatable topics like grief and faith. Wow." She claps her hands. "I'm so impressed."

"Thank you. Sometimes I wish I was a contemporary writer, though. Writing sci-fi and fantasy is a lot of work."

"True, but the hard work always pays off when you see how much your readers eat the stories up, right?"

I nod. "Right. They're such a loyal bunch."

"You don't have to tell me. How did you even get the idea for a wonderful story like this?" She rests her head on cupped hands.

I shrug, scratching the back of my head. "Well, God gave me this idea while I was studying the book of Job five years ago. We always complain when life doesn't go according to our plan. So I thought about exploring a story idea where the characters had the power to choose an outcome for their lives and face the consequences of their decisions. Kinda like playing God for themselves, but the difference is that they're not omniscient or omnipresent or omnipotent, so they soon learn about their limitations when they can't turn back."

"Wow, I want to reach that kind of place where I can get story ideas too from reading the Bible." She leans back in her seat. "That's so cool."

"Thank you, but enough about me, though. What's your story about? If you don't mind me asking."

"Erm." Her smile fades, and her gaze drops to her fidgety hands on the table. "Let's just say, I don't have a pitch like you do and, erm...I'm actually really struggling to write a particular scene at the moment."

"Oh?" I frown, my heart overwhelmed by a sudden urge to take away all her struggles. "What is it about the scene that's making you struggle?"

She looks up at me, still fidgeting with her hands. "Erm...it's to do with a very sensitive topic and I just want to make it perfect, you know?"

"Hmm. Yes, I understand." I nod. "But first drafts don't have to be perfect, you know? That's why they're called *first* drafts. Most writers have to write and rewrite scenes to make it better, and perfection is subjective. It's the way art works. Perfection is an illusion. There's a time for drafting and a time for refining and editing to make the work the best it can be. You just have to keep relying on God to give you the wisdom to navigate this sensitive topic."

"Yes, you're right." She sighs. "I need to stop being so hard on myself. I'm putting myself through so much pressure and it's not healthy when I'm just at the beginning of this."

"Exactly." I smile, relieved that she is coming to this realisation. "I also think being around more writers will help you see that you're not alone."

She frowns and tilts her head. "But I'm already around you."

I laugh. "Yeah, I know that, but being around even more writers can help you find a community. Remember the writing group I mentioned I was going to yesterday?"

She hesitates before responding. "Erm...yeah?"

"Well, we have a mix of virtual sessions and in-person sessions every month. It's made up of only Christian writers in various stages of their writing career. I think there are some newbie writers there who you'll be able to relate to. They have another session coming up in two weeks and you can come with me, if you want."

"Oh, erm...I'm not too sure about that. See, I don't do very well in...groups or crowded places."

"Sure." I knew she had reservations, but I'm glad I still asked. "I understand. If you ever change your mind, you'll let me know, right?"

She flashes me a smile. "Of course. Thank you for listening to me. I really appreciate it."

I lean forward, holding her hand on the table. "It's always my pleasure." We stare into each other's eyes for a few seconds before she removes her hand from under mine, clearing her throat.

"Well, we should probably do some writing today, shouldn't we?" She laughs and I join her.

"Yeah, we should." We bring out our laptops and she puts on her headphones. But as we both focus on our projects, I steal subtle glances at her, grateful for this friendship that is a breath of fresh air.

13

BEX

I'm not sure what came over me when I agreed to come to this writing group session, but it's too late to turn back now. When Jevaun first invited me two weeks ago, the alarm bells going off in my head clouded my sound judgment then.

All I could think about was having a panic attack in a room full of strangers and embarrassing myself and Jevaun. But when I went back home that evening, a simple moment of prayer made me realise those weren't alarm bells going off in my head —they were just the voices of my fears and doubts.

If I truly believe that God has helped me overcome anxiety, I can't keep letting the thought of what *could* happen limit me from walking in my purpose and calling. I refuse to stay bound to the 'what if' mentality because it doesn't matter if I'm scared. The only thing God cares about is my obedience, so I'll do it scared.

When Jevaun mentioned last night while we were on the phone that he wouldn't be able to come to The Buzz Café because he would go to Stratford straight from his house, I acted on the leading of the Holy Spirit and asked if I could go with him. It was so out of character for me to offer to leave my house without being prompted.

But Jevaun is right. Community is important as a writer. Knowing that someone out there can relate to my struggles makes it much more bearable. To top it off, seeing someone like Jevaun achieve so much already without a published book has opened my mind to all the things I can do with my author career.

The more I think about it, the more excited I become, but my excitement only does so much to calm my shaking hands as Jevaun and I walk out of Stratford train station. I've been to the East London town before with Rachel and Rhoda on our quest to find new social things to do.

Rhoda dragged us to the Westfield shopping centre and after a much needed splurge, we took a nice relaxing walk along the Stratford Waterfront on the Eastbank. Rhoda almost convinced Rachel and me to go on a ride down the ArcelorMittal Orbit, the tallest metal structure in the United Kingdom. But I had to put my foot down that day because I wasn't trying to put a death wish over our heads.

"Are you okay?" Jevaun's voice pulls me out of my thoughts as we wait for the light at the pedestrian crossing to turn green.

"Yeah, I'm good." I smile at him. He must have noticed me doing my breathing exercises on the train because he has asked if I'm okay five times in the last half hour. "Thank you for inviting me."

"No, thank you for coming." He smiles back and when the light turns green, we walk across the road, following the road down for another ten minutes until we reach a community centre.

Jevaun mentioned earlier that the writers' group has been active for over a decade, so they always use the same venue for the monthly in-person sessions. With October here and autumn in full swing, I mutter a prayer of gratitude when the warmer air in the building envelopes us.

There's a seven-foot banner in the reception area giving directions to the room where the meeting is taking place. As we approach the room, the music and chattering get louder with every step we take.

Just before entering the room, Jevaun pauses before turning to me. "Okay, I know you said you don't do well in crowded spaces, but I wanted to say I'm so proud of you for putting yourself out there. I've been part of this group for years and I know they're all good people. They're very chatty, so they'll probably come at you with many questions as they do for every newbie, because they like to get to know everyone."

"But," he places both hands on my shoulders and looks me in the eye, "if you ever feel uncomfortable or overwhelmed and you want to leave, just give me a sign and we'll leave, okay?"

I'm taken aback by the care in his voice. It doesn't make sense that he barely knows me, but could pick up so much from a sentence I made in passing. It's endearing and also scary that he can read me so much.

"Jevaun, anyone listening to the seriousness in your voice would think you're talking about something important and not a silly girl like me who just needs to stop being a crybaby and toughen up." I laugh to lighten the mood, but he doesn't do the same, so my smile fades. "Okay, fine. The sign would be me nodding toward the door."

"Got it." He finally smiles and puts his hands down. "You ready?"

"Now I am."

I follow his lead as he turns right into the room and the warm atmosphere immediately hits me in the face, mostly because I wasn't expecting thirty people to be spread across the room in groups of five, chatting and laughing with each other.

There's a table at the front with lots of snacks, including crisps, apples, bananas, chocolates, biscuits, and even a tea and coffee station.

"Jevaun." A voice from the right turns both our heads to meet a tall, balding Caucasian man with the brightest smile I've ever seen. "Good to see you, mate." He hugs Jevaun briefly before turning to me. "And who have you brought with you today?"

Jevaun places his hand on the small of my back, a sense of comfort washing over me as he introduces me to Tom, the founder of the group.

"It's very nice to meet you, Tom." I shake his hand and smile. Now I just need to do that at least twenty-nine more times if I'm going to speak to everyone here today.

"It's so lovely to have you here with us, Bex," Tom says. "Jevaun tells me you're a new writer."

"Yes." My voice starts off small and then I clear my throat before speaking louder over the worship music playing from the speaker. "Yes, I'm working on my first novel."

"That's great. What genre?"

"Oh, it's...erm...contemporary fiction."

"That's excellent. We have a few contemporary writers here too, and I'm sure you'll fit right in," he says before turning to the snacks table. "Please help yourself to some nibbles, as we'll be starting in five minutes."

"Thank you," Jevaun and I respond in unison as he guides me to the snacks table.

"Anything you fancy?" he asks as I look around.

"Hmm, an apple would be good, thank you," I respond, and he reaches for two apples and places them on a plate for me.

Then he picks up a packet of crisps and a bar of chocolate, with a cup of orange juice, and we find a seat.

Tom and a dark-haired middle-aged woman go to the front as the music stops playing.

"Good evening, everyone. Welcome to October's session of the Faith Writers group. My name is Tom, and this is my beautiful wife, Siobhán. We founded this group twelve years ago because we wanted to bring together Christian writers all across London, so we can help each other along the journey to putting our much-needed stories out into the world. We are a relatively small group, but we keep growing and, in fact, we now have a new member who joined us today. Let's give a massive welcome to Bex." Tom points to me and Jevaun at the back of the room, and my heart literally stops for a second...or two.

Oh no. I freeze in my spot as all heads turn toward us, clapping and smiling. Jevaun must have seen the panic on my face because he places his arm around my shoulder and squeezes gently, his smile warming me out of my frozen state as I wave back at everyone.

Tom continues his speech and everyone turns back to look at him, giving me time to let out a sigh of relief. Jevaun, who is also paying close attention to what Tom is saying, still has his arm around my shoulder—not in a possessive way, but in a "I got you always" kind of way.

"Thank you," I whisper, and he looks down at me.

"I got you, always." The words come out of his mouth as if he was reading my thoughts and the emotions that well up inside me are unexplainable. I'm not sure what God is doing, but with each passing day, I'm convinced that I'm exactly where I need to be in this season of my life.

"And now, for the exciting part." Tom claps his hands, getting my attention again. "It's time to get into our groups, where all the fun stuff happens."

My eyes widen as I turn to Jevaun. "Groups? What groups?"

"Oh, yeah, I forgot to say that Tom usually splits us into

smaller groups based on our genre, as the members get more out of the group that way. There's contemporary, historical, fantasy/science fiction, and non-fiction."

"Aww." My shoulders drop in disappointment when realisation dawns on me. "That means we won't be sitting together, right?"

He nods slowly. "But all the ladies in your group are cool, and I'm sure you'll have a great time."

"Okay." I smile as Jevaun points me in the right direction. "See you later." I watch him join his group of fantasy authors, laughing and high-fiving the other men and women, and it leaves me questioning whether I'll ever get to that level of comfort around strangers.

"Look at your sisters playing. Do they have two heads?" Mum's voice pops into my head from all the years in my childhood, where she reminded me about how reserved I am. Every birthday party I ever went to with my sisters ended up with the same lecture from Mum about how I needed to play with other children instead of clinging to her side the whole time.

It's crazy how Mum's voice has now turned into my own—in my head—chastising me about why I can't make this process easier. But it's so much easier said than done. Coming with Jevaun has helped a lot, or I could've been dealing with palpitations, sweat patches and shaky hands.

Lord, please, help me get through this meeting in one piece.

"Welcome, Bex." A cheery voice forces me out of my thoughts as I take in the sight of the five women sitting around me, their smiles so bright I can almost feel the warmth on my skin.

Say something, Bex. I'm sure they won't bite.

"Hi, everyone." I send them a small wave before shuffling to the edge of my seat, hoping they didn't hear me. But they did, and now that all their eyes are pinned on me, it feels like I should say something else. "Thank you for having me."

"We're so excited to have you here with us. I'm Demi." The biracial woman with the cheery voice speaks again. "I'm thirty and I'm a nanny by day, and a writer of adult romance books by night," she says with a smile as she tucks a strand of her honey-blonde curly hair behind her ear.

"Nice to meet you, Demi," I say, relaxing in my seat as the other women introduce themselves.

"Hi Bex, I'm Lena. Twenty-five, and I write young adult romance novels. I'm currently doing a Master's in creative writing and publishing," the next woman says, her long, black wig grazing her thighs.

"Hi Bex, I'm Rosie." A middle-aged woman speaks next. "I'm forty-five and I write women's fiction. Tom is my brother."

"That's so cool," I respond, imagining what it was like for her growing up with siblings who are also writers.

"Hi Bex, I'm Sienna, twenty-two." A Caucasian girl speaks next as I admire her wavy brown hair. "I just finished uni and I'm looking for a job. But I also write Christian romance books."

"Nice to meet you," I say, casting my mind back to when I was in Sienna's position a few years ago. It's inspiring to see that she's still pursuing her passion while waiting on God.

"Hi Bex, I'm Mia." The last woman waves at me. "I'm thirty-three. I've been writing clean and wholesome romance books full-time now for two years and I recently landed a traditional publishing deal."

"Wow, that's amazing." I restrain myself from firing questions at Mia, but I'm sure my answers will come with time. "As you all know, my name is Bex. I used to work as an investment banker until recently, when I was let go. But now I'm discovering my love for writing Christian fiction."

"That's great," Demi speaks again as she chairs the rest of the session. I sit back and listen as the women give an update on what they've been up to in the last two weeks. Then Demi shares a five-minute encouragement about drawing strength from God when we're at cross roads. It's hard to believe that I'm only meeting her for the first time because God used her words to speak to me.

Lena, Rosie, and Mia share pieces of their writing, reading it out loud to the group and everyone gives feedback. Well, everyone except me. At the end of the feedback session, the ladies quickly share their goals for the next two weeks until we meet again.

"Anything to share, Bex?" Demi asks as everyone looks at me.

"Oh...erm." I fidget with my hands before nodding. "Yeah, I'm currently experiencing some writer's block, so with the very inspiring message shared today by Demi, I'm hoping to draw strength from God so he can help me overcome it."

The ladies all nod and smile at me.

"Definitely, and we'll be praying for you, Bex." Rosie says.

"Thank you so much, everyone." My heart is so full when the session ends and I don't think I've ever been so happy to meet new people. Demi takes my number, so she can add me to the group chat and all the ladies hug me before we make our way slowly toward the snacks table.

"So? How did it go?" Jevaun asks as Tom joins us.

"Amazing," is the only word I can think of. "The ladies are so lovely and I'm so grateful."

"I hope you're not just saying that because I'm here," Tom says, and we all laugh.

"No, seriously. You'll be seeing me again for sure."

"That's what we like to hear," Tom says before turning to Jevaun. "Okay, I have to leave you now, as I've been up since five AM this morning, so it's time to rest."

"Yes, please. I don't want you passing out here, Tom." Jevaun pats his back.

"Well, at least you're a doctor, so I'm in good hands, eh?" Tom laughs and hugs Jevaun and me before leaving.

"Hang on a minute." I squint at Jevaun as we join the queue for the snacks. "You're a doctor?"

"*Was.*" He tilts his head and raises his palm. "I quit my job five years ago and moved to London to pursue writing full time."

I stop in my tracks, my mouth open as I stare at him walking ahead of me.

He turns around. "What?"

"Wow, I just realised you and I have more in common than I thought." We walk again as the queue moves along.

"Really? How so? You quit your job too?"

"*Pfft*, no. I'm not that brave. You should know that by now. But I was made redundant at my investment banking job, and that's how God redirected me to take writing seriously."

"Wow, imagine if that didn't happen. You probably wouldn't be here."

"And I would never have met you."

"You're so right." Jevaun pauses as he looks into my eyes, his unspoken appreciation for my words written all over his face. "You have no idea how grateful I am that He brought you to me."

14

BEX

It wouldn't be a Friday night in London if there weren't intoxicated girls and boys singing, laughing, and making noise on the tube, either on their way to or back from their night out.

From the corner of the train carriage where Jevaun and I are sitting as spectators, bottles are clinking, heads are rolling with laughter and one of them is even showing off how much upper body strength he has by doing pushups on the overhead handrails.

It has always amazed me how much being intoxicated can change your personality. It can make the shy ones seem more extroverted and the reserved ones more free and talkative. It would be interesting to know what *Spider Man* here is really like on a daily basis when he is not under the influence of alcohol.

As we continue watching our entertainers, unwanted images from that night flash into my mind again—a night that started a little like this, but ended up with so much heartbreak and pain. A pain still too raw for me to talk about, but one I know I will heal from—some day.

Jevaun and I watch without a word, his protective arm going

122

around my shoulders when one boy gets too close to our seat, slurring at me before walking away and laughing at his own joke.

I lean into Jevaun without hesitation, his Cedarwood scent teasing my nostrils and a tingling sensation going up my arms as my shoulder presses gently against his chest.

There's something about being here, being with him, that feels safe and feels right. I don't understand why I don't have more reservations, why I don't feel the need to run and why I feel so much peace when I'm with him.

It's because he's not Ayo. And he's definitely not Jason.

The laughter and chatter dies down when the train stops, the doors open and the crowd of noisy passengers gets off the train to wherever their destination is. The silence in the carriage is music to our ears as Jevaun lets out a loud sigh.

"Finally," he says, pulling me out of my thoughts.

"I know, right." I straighten my back, turning my body to face him squarely.

He smiles down at me as if he's trying to decide whether he should say something.

"What?" I ask, tilting my head.

"Well, I'm not sure if we've known each other long enough for this not to come across as creepy, but you smell really nice, Bex."

For the umpteenth time tonight, my cheeks warm up again as I bite my bottom lip to suppress the wide grin appearing on my face. "Thank you. I mix two perfumes; one of them is fruity, and the other is aromatic. That's how I make sure nobody steals my scent."

"That's so clever."

"Thank you. You smell really nice too, you know?"

"Really?" He raises his brows.

"Yeah." As if to prove my point, I lean in closer and sniff on his neck and he turns his face down at the same time, his lips only a few inches away from mine and his warm breath brushing gently against my skin.

We stay in that position for a few seconds, my mind wondering for a moment what it would be like if his lips touched mine, but before letting it wander further, I pull away and sit up straight. "Yeah, I really like your scent."

"Thanks, Bex." He takes his arm away from my shoulders and we stay in silence for a few moments. I'm not sure how much time passes before he breaks the silence. "What's on your mind?"

I tilt my head. "How do you know there's something on my mind?"

He shrugs. "You just have that look." He laughs. "It's obvious you were deep in thought. Care to share?" The train doors close and it starts moving again.

"Well," I start, picking my brain to see what would be worth sharing with him this time. "I was thinking about how inspiring it was for me to listen to the other girls talk about their stories so confidently today." I pause before continuing. "So, I'd like to share a bit about my story with you, if you don't mind."

"Really?" Jevaun's eyes widen. "Of course, I don't mind. I'm excited to hear it."

"Okay." I take a deep breath and exhale before rambling. "I don't have a title like you, but it's about a girl from a Cameroonian family who goes off to university to study medicine in London. She falls in love with the wrong guy, who sexually assaults her, and the story shows the aftermath of that single event, how it affects her relationship with her family and her faith in God."

"Wow," Jevaun says. "Now I understand why you said you were dealing with sensitive topics."

"Yeah, and I still haven't written that troublesome scene yet."

"I assume it's the scene where she..." His words trail off.

"Yup, that's the one." I nod, a lump building in my throat out of nowhere. Why am I emotional? If this is how I'm going to get every time I talk about this story, then we're going to have a problem.

"Can I ask what inspired you to write this story?" Jevaun's words rescue me as I blink back the tears.

"Oh, well, it was inspired by a girl I met in my first year of university who was part of our Christian union. I wasn't close with her or anything, but when I didn't see her after the first semester, I learnt she stopped coming because a guy from the Christian union sexually abused her. For years, I couldn't stop thinking about her and to this day, I wonder what happened to her. So when God inspired me to write a story, I knew I had to do it for all the girls out there like her. Someone needs to remind them that there is hope and there's no one God can't heal."

"Wow, Bex, that's such a beautiful message," Jevaun responds. "I can already tell it will bless the lives of so many women and men alike who are dealing with the same situation. You are so brave for doing this, you know that, right?"

"Well, I wouldn't exactly call myself brave, but—"

"No, I mean it, Bex." He takes my hand in his and my words elude me as he stares into my eyes. "The message God has given you is so powerful and you have to trust Him to birth this story. He chose you because He knew you could do it. He will equip you, so don't think about your current weaknesses or lack of experience. It might seem like a scary undertaking, but do it anyway. Just obey."

Just obey. The words reverberate in my mind as tears wet my eyes again. These are the same words God used to convict me earlier today. If God could help me face my fear of stepping out of my comfort zone and coming to the writing group today, then truly, what more would I be able to do if I stop being afraid?

"Thank you so much, Jevaun." I sniffle.

"Do you mind if I pray with you, Bex? I just feel the urge to do so. Is that okay?" he asks, already reaching for my other hand.

"Of course." I squeeze his hands tight, not caring about the questioning eyes of other passengers sitting on the other side of the train carriage.

"Heavenly Father, thank You for Bex's life and for the incredible story You've put in her heart. You know the height and depth of her current struggles, Lord. So we pray You empower her with strength that only comes from You. Give her the wisdom and the inspiration to write the story You want. Breathe life into her words and help her birth the story that will impact the world for Your glory. In Jesus' name. Amen."

"Amen." Tears are spilling out of my eyes now and Jevaun catches one with his thumb before pulling me in for a hug. I'm not sure how long I'm in his embrace for, but when we part ways at Waterloo Station, the labour pains begin.

So, as soon as I get home, coat and shoes off, I run up the stairs, plant my butt on my desk chair, open my laptop, and birth that scene. Slowly, painfully, and fearfully, but birthing it anyway.

*   *   *

Nothing could've ruined that day for Vanessa...or so she thought. Not only did she have eight hours of sleep the night before, but she woke up early enough to have breakfast, she got to her lectures on time, didn't feel sleepy at all, found out she got a seventy percent on one of her assessments and had a productive study session at the library afterwards.

She was riding on cloud nine, feeling like no one could dampen her mood, especially since she had read her favourite psalm—the ninety-first psalm—and handed her date into God's hands before leaving the house. She hoped it would be the perfect way to end her perfect day.

"You look like a ball of sunshine," he told her as she approached him standing outside her university halls of residence. It was five PM, and he had kept to his word and picked her up early so they could still make the Christian union meeting at seven.

"I feel like a ball of sunshine." She did a spin, her floral yellow dress twirling with her before she leapt into his arms.

Anne's words of caution still lingered in her thoughts, but she pushed them to the back of her mind because Anne worried too much. Vanessa was the one who had been dating him for two months and she knew him better than anyone else...or so she thought.

"Hey, beautiful," he said, before planting a kiss on her lips and hugging her. "I missed you today."

"I missed you too." She clung to his hand as they walked to the train station. "I'm sorry I had reservations about this party before. I think it's so sweet you want me to meet your friends."

"Nah, don't worry about it, babe." He shrugged, pulling her close to him. "I'm just glad you're coming."

The journey was quick. One stop on the tube and a five-minute walk later, they were standing in front of the house. The music blasting from inside could be heard through the closed front door and when he rang the doorbell, a tall, bearded brown skin guy opened it two minutes later.

"Yo, my guy." He hugged the other guy briefly before giving him a wrapped present. "Happy birthday, bro."

"Appreciate it, man," the birthday celebrant said before his eyes turned to Vanessa.

"Meet Vanessa, my girlfriend, innit? Vanessa, this is Omar."

"*Aye*, you're a sweet one, still," Omar said after letting his gaze wander from Vanessa's head to her toes. "Nice to meet you, Vanessa."

"Nice to meet you too, Omar. Happy birthday and thank you for inviting me to your party," Vanessa said as they walked into the house, embracing the warm atmosphere and the smell of food.

"You lot are early, so grab some food and drinks while we wait for the rest of the *mandem*[1]," Omar said, pointing to the food table, which had chicken wings, sausage rolls, pizza rolls, and so much more.

"Thanks, bro." He pulled Vanessa close to him again and placed his hand on the small of her back, as he always did, to remind her she was safe with him. But the more time she spent in that house, the harder it was for her to shake off the uneasy feeling in her chest.

Omar must have seen how much Vanessa winced and covered her ears, because he reduced the volume of the drill music slightly, but it was still too loud for her.

"Would you like something to eat?" he asked, caressing her cheek with his thumb.

She nodded and took a sip of her tropical juice, letting the sweet drink wet her dry mouth as she sat on the edge of the sofa, admiring the shared living space and counting down the minutes until six-thirty PM, when he promised they would leave.

Vanessa and Anne had talked a lot about where they would live in their second year. They had planned to get a two-bedroom house with a shared kitchen and bathroom, and a living room for their movie nights. Vanessa made mental notes of the photo frames on the walls and the artsy decor on the staircase, so she could tell Anne all about it when she got back to halls.

Half an hour later, the doorbell rang just as Vanessa bit into a chicken wing and a sigh of relief escaped her lips as Omar opened the door, welcoming the rest of the party. A single file of five more guys and three girls streamed into the house, wishing Omar a happy birthday and placing their wrapped presents on the table next to all the food.

He took Vanessa's hand in his, going round the group and making more introductions. By the time she met all of them, including another one of his close friends, Jeremiah, and his girlfriend, Natalie, she was exhausted and didn't want to speak to anyone else.

Omar's girlfriend Lakeisha brought out the birthday cake, and after singing happy birthday and blowing out the candles, they ramped up the music again, this time switching to bashment—the dancehall music reverberating through the walls of the house. Vanessa couldn't help but wonder what their neighbours thought of the noise they were making.

She tapped on her phone screen—thirty minutes until it was time to leave, but she couldn't stay any longer. The music was giving her a headache, and everything about being there only made her feel more uneasy.

She turned to him, thinking he might feel the same way, but he was bopping his head, screaming and shouting at the top of his voice like the other guys, while she waited in the corner.

When she finally pulled him away from the crowd, his breath reeked of alcohol and she choked on her words as she tried to explain that she wanted to leave.

"Come on, baby, fifteen more minutes. I already promised Omar I'd stay till six-thirty. I can't just leave."

"That's fine. You don't have to, but I'm going, so I guess I'll see you later." She stepped forward, but he held her arm.

"Okay, fine. I'll come with you. How about one more drink before we leave?"

She scoffed. "Really? Don't you think you've had enough? I didn't even know you drank alcohol."

He gritted his teeth, and she stepped away from him, holding her cross-body bag tight. "Okay, I'm sorry. We'll leave now, but I need your help with something first."

She frowned. "What's that?"

"Come with me upstairs, please. I need your help." He grabbed her wrist, leaving her no time to protest as he dragged her up the stairs and into one of the bedrooms.

"What do you need help with? We need to leave soon if not..." She paused when he locked the door with the key and put it in the back pocket of his jeans.

"What are you doing?" She stepped forward, but he blocked her way. "Open the door and let me out right now."

"You must think you're some self-righteous, perfect little princess, don't you? Is that what gives you the right to judge me for my choices?" He took a step forward, gritting his teeth and balling his hands into a fist, the man standing in front of her becoming totally unrecognisable.

"Get out of my way." She stepped forward again, but he did the same.

"You've been frowning and giving me looks of disapproval all evening. What? You don't approve of my friends, or my choice of music, or what I drink?"

"You don't need my approval for anything. Please, just let me go." Tears stung Vanessa's eyes as her breaths became shallow.

"Well, Vanessa. I've got bad news for you. You're not leaving here until I get what I want."

"Excuse me?" She sniffled, her heart dropping as she stared wide-eyed at him.

He stepped forward and grabbed her by the neck, pressing

hard as she struggled under his grip. "I said you're not leaving until I get what I want."

When he lifted her up and slammed her body against the bed, all her strength left her, and that was the moment Vanessa knew that her muffled screams and her struggles against his muscles would all be in vain. That day, he did, in fact, get what he wanted and left her in pain—unbearable, insurmountable, and totally paralysing pain.

15

JEVAUN

"So, what you're saying is that you got yourself a girlfriend now?" Tré's voice comes through from my phone on the kitchen counter as I make myself some spaghetti Bolognese for dinner.

Video calls with Tré while making dinner used to be more frequent when he was still in med school and had a bit more time for himself on the weekends. Now, these calls are a luxury because of his hectic work schedule, which he's still trying to get a hang of.

I'm so grateful that we're still able to sustain the closeness in our relationship, even with the distance and our different schedules. Mum would be so proud of how far we've come if she was with us now, but she would also give me an earful about how I left things with Dad.

I've been the happiest the last four weeks since keeping my distance from the people that stress me and investing in the relationships that build me. That's how it should be in life. However, I brought this bother upon myself when I looked into Mum's eyes and made that promise. I know at some point I'll have to confront Dad again. I'm just hoping it won't be anytime soon.

"Bro, did you even listen to anything I said?" I turn off the heat on the hob and continue stirring the spaghetti into the mince mix.

"Yes, I did. You've been spending a lot of time with this girl, you clearly care about her and she's letting you take care of her, so it's obvious you two have something going on. I don't understand why you haven't asked her out on an official date yet."

I cover the pot to let the food simmer before leaning against my kitchen counter in front of my phone screen. "You remember what happened with Jen, the girl at the coffee shop, right?"

"Yeah, but this is different," Tré cuts me off, adjusting the durag on his head as he sits up in his bed.

"Yes, I know, but I don't want to jump the gun and scare her away. I've been enjoying getting to know her the last few weeks and I like that things are progressing naturally. When it's time to ask her out, it'll happen naturally, too." I push myself away from the counter and grab a plate from the cupboard.

"Okay, then. If you say so. You must really like this girl, though. You haven't stopped talking about her all week."

"Yeah, did I tell you she was an answered prayer?" I ask, and Tré frowns.

"What do you mean?"

"Hang on a sec." I dish out some food and pour myself orange juice from the fridge before carrying my plate to the dining table.

"So, after that argument between me and Dad last time, I was very discouraged about...everything."

"Really? You?" Tré raises his brows.

"Yeah." I nod. "His words can be very hurtful, Tré. You can't relate because you're the golden child and that's great for you, but if you were in my shoes, years of non-stop discouragement eventually gets to you."

"Wow. I didn't realise it affected you that much."

"Hmm." I pull my plate close to me and say a quick prayer before taking my first bite.

I hate to be the person who paints our father in a bad light because I know Tré will always take his side. The man can do no wrong in Tré's eyes and the last thing I want to do is let Dad ruin my relationship with Tré. All I can hope for is that someday, Tré will find out everything I know and finally see our father for who he truly is.

I swallow my food, savouring the spicy taste of the mince before continuing. "So, after that encounter, I was ready to give up on everything. I didn't see the point of continuing, you know? Then one morning before I left the house, I prayed for God to help me and later that day, He sent Bex my way."

"Okay, but what was it about meeting her that made it an answered prayer?" Tré makes air quotes as he says the words, answered prayer—the sarcasm evident in his voice.

"So, I eavesdropped on a phone call Bex was having with her sister and her excitement about starting the first chapter of her novel reminded me about why our stories are important. God used her to remind me about my why. I don't live my life on someone else's terms. I live my life on God's terms and there's always a beautiful reward that comes with obeying God."

"Hmm." Tré sighs and scratches the back of his head. "Bro, I can't lie. I was a little shocked when you announced you were going to quit your job. I was worried about you, you know? But after seeing your success, I'm glad you followed your heart."

"Hmm, hmm." I shake my head, swallowing another forkful of spaghetti. "I didn't follow my heart. I followed God, who has brought me all the success. I owe it all to Him."

"Yeah, yeah, whatever. You know I'm not all about that, but I'm happy for you all the same." Tré waves a dismissive hand and another knot of disappointment pulls at my heartstrings.

Every time I slip God into our conversations like this, I hope that I'll see some progress, or something to show that the words are sparking some interest in his heart. But until that day comes, I'll keep praying.

"Don't worry about Dad, though," Tré says, pulling me out of my thoughts. "Eventually, he's going to have to accept that you have chosen this path. There's nothing he can do about that. You don't even have to keep going to see him. I won't blame you for that."

I wish it was that easy, the words slip to the tip of my tongue, but I hold them back. Tré also knows nothing about the promise I made to Mum. It's not his problem, so no need to bother him with all that.

"Thanks for having my back, but enough about me." I sip on my orange juice before changing the subject. "How's work?"

Tré groans and rubs his eyes with his palms before looking at me again.

"Okay, actions speak louder than words."

"It's just...mad. That's the only word I can use. I feel like I'm constantly drowning. I'm struggling to keep my head above the water. There's no work-life balance and I don't know if I can even survive the next three months."

My heart aches for him because I remember just how much I struggled the first few months of my foundation training. It's not something you can fully understand until you experience it.

"Please, tell me it gets easier." His eyes beg for some type of hopeful response from me.

"Well, it got better. Once I found a community and also different ways to destress, the work became manageable."

"Okay, good. I'll take that for now. I've made a lot of wonderful friends in my cohort. We have a group chat and I'm looking forward to our first night out. Medics sure know how to destress."

"I'm glad you're making friends. I always keep you in my prayers."

Tré tilts his head and frowns. "Really? I didn't realise God cared about little things like this."

"Oh, He cares *especially* about the little things."

"Hmm, so it's not just about feeding five thousand people, walking on water, or turning water to wine, huh?"

I smile, my heart grateful for that comment. It's another reminder from God that He is working right now, even when I don't see it.

"No, it's not just about the big things, Tré. It's also about the times when you're alone in the sluice room, with pee stains or blood on your scrubs, about to have your fourth breakdown after being pushed around all day by a grumpy consultant."

"Stop! That has actually happened to me." Tré and I burst out laughing for a few minutes before quieting down again.

"Well, you should get an early night because the madness continues tomorrow. Remember, I'm only a phone call away, yeah?"

"Of course. I know that. Good night, bro."

I end the call and say a prayer for Tré before finishing my food and tidying up the kitchen. It always feels weird opening up to others about all the thoughts in my head, but I'm glad I could speak to him today about God. If the only thing my strained relationship with Dad does is to point to my relationship with God, then I'll talk about Him any day, anytime.

I need to have an early night so I wake up refreshed for church tomorrow. After taking a shower, I turn on the night lights in my room, cosying up under the duvet with a book, as the October showers announce themselves outside, with hundreds of raindrops trickling down my window.

The cold and wet weather is perfect for reading, so I better make my way through my book club read for this month, but not before reading through my messages again from earlier in the day.

Me: I can't believe you sent me a voice note at 2am squealing. I hope you didn't wake up your parents. 😊

Bex: Haha, I'm so sorry. I was just so excited I wanted to share it with someone. 😅 You're the first person I thought of.

Me: No, don't be sorry. I actually feel honoured you thought of me first. 😌 Congratulations on writing that troublesome scene. I'm so proud of you.

Bex: 😊 Thank you so much. You have no idea how much your prayer helped. It's like I could physically feel God breaking down all the barriers around me. The ideas just kept flowing, and I had to force myself to fall asleep last night because my brain would not turn off.

Me: Wow, look at God.

Bex: Honestly. I can't wait to finish this story because celebrations are in order.

Me: I can't wait to celebrate with you. Got any plans for today?

Bex: Yeah, I have to do some grocery shopping with my mum, some laundry, and then I'll be meeting my sisters in the evening. We're going to check out this new dessert place in Euston. It's called Shakes and Cakes. Have you heard of it?

Me: Oh yeah, I've heard of it. The waffles on their menu look great. It's a shame I'm left out of this one. I have a real sweet tooth; you know?

Bex: Aww, if it's good, then maybe you and I can go there later?

Me: Ooh yes, I like the sound of that.

16

BEX

There's nothing funnier than watching Rhoda stare at the food she has convinced herself not to eat because she's waiting for everyone else's order to arrive. Her red velvet cake with cream cheese frosting looks and smells divine. But she won't touch it or her chocolate milkshake because she just has to take photos and videos of our food together. After all, it's the only way to prove we actually went out, right?

"White chocolate cookie dough topped with white chocolate sauce and Oreos?" the server calls out and when Rachel raises her hand, he places the plate in front of her.

"Waffles and ice cream?" He finally turns to me and I nod.

"Yes, please." The sweet aroma from the plate wafts into my nostrils and waters my mouth. It looks like they don't play about their presentation in this place.

The carefully-thought-out placement of the waffles, the drizzle of the caramel sauce, and the mound of ice cream with the sprinkles make me want to stuff my face and get everything into my belly all at once.

For a new dessert place, the long queue of people waiting to order is a testament to the fantastic food and the cosy vibe. Rachel and I have been bopping our heads to the old school R&B songs playing from the overhead speakers since we walked in.

Rhoda whips out her phone and after taking a couple of photos, she takes videos of our food, first in slow motion, and then as a boomerang. Rachel and I both roll our eyes at our younger sister and when she's done, we pick up our cutlery and start digging in.

"Hmm. This is so good," I say, grateful that I took Jevaun's advice and tried the waffles. I need to get the photos from Rhoda later so I can send them to him.

"You can say that again." Rhoda sips on her milkshake before turning to Rachel. "How's your cookie dough?"

"Very sweet," she responds. "But I like it."

"Great. That's all that matters." Rhoda clicks her fingers before wiggling her eyebrows at me.

Rachel—our gym-obsessed, health conscious sister—uses every opportunity to tell us off about our unhealthy lifestyle choices. But today is her cheat day, so she's letting us off, even though we all know she'll be hitting the gym hard next week to burn off all the calories.

"So, what's up with everyone?" Rhoda places her arms on the table, but doesn't even wait for an answer before she starts ranting. She just started doing her Master's in clinical nutrition and dietetics and she also works part-time at a bookstore, so her schedule is busy.

"I'll go first. My week was so hectic." Rhoda blows out a breath. "I need to submit my proposal in two weeks, and I've still got a lot of work to do. There's no day I don't wake up questioning my decisions. Why didn't I get a job after uni like everyone else? Why did I have to love this field so much that I put myself through this stress? Who literally sent me to do this

Master's?" She throws her arms up in the air, her gaze darting between Rachel and me as if she expects us to give her an answer.

"*Weh, big mami*[1], you sent yourself." Rachel chuckles and I have to cover my mouth to stop the food from flying out as I suppress my laughter. I think the dictionary needs to be updated to put Rhoda's photo next to the definition of *dramatic.*

"Aww, isn't your *boyfriend* helping you destress?" I tease, and Rhoda sends me a death stare.

"Honestly, Bex, now is not the time." She raises her hand at me before her smile breaks through. "I'm trying to rant and you lot are ruining my moment. You're ruining it."

"*Weh, ashia*[2]. I'm sorry you feel stressed, hun." I take another bite of my waffle before squeezing Rhoda's hand. "Have you talked it through with someone?"

"Not yet." She sighs. "Dan keeps encouraging me to, but I gave myself a challenge to figure it out on my own. The research topic isn't completely clear in my head and that's why I'm struggling."

"Maybe you should listen to the *boyfriend,* then," Rachel mutters under her breath and Rhoda kisses her teeth. "Okay, okay, I'll stop. Calm down." Rachel raises her hands in surrender. "All I'm saying is that figuring it out on your own is not working. So maybe you should listen to your *best friend* and ask for help." She lays emphasis on the word *best friend* before chuckling.

"Don't mind her." I turn Rhoda's head toward me. "Rachel is right. You're running out of time. Please ask for help this week?"

Rhoda pauses for a few moments before she sighs. "Okay, fine. Dan will gloat when I tell him that you lot are on his side." She shakes her head before turning back to Rachel. "So, how's the new school year going so far?"

Rachel dabs the corner of her mouth with a napkin before

responding. "It's not bad, actually. So far, my students are well behaved compared to last year's cohort. Maybe they'll show their true colours soon, but I'll consider it as a blessing for now. I also figured out how to put a cap on the number of orders I receive every day on my website, so I've been enjoying cooking in my spare time."

"Aww, I'm glad you found your balance, sis." I place my arm around Rachel's shoulders. "I knew you could do it."

"Thanks, girls. Your kind words last time really encouraged me. Half-term is in a few weeks, so I'll have more time to cook. What about you, Bex? How are things going with the handsome author?" Rachel wiggles her brows at me and it's my turn to kiss my teeth, but I can't hide my smile.

"Okay, start spilling, Sissy. Are you in love yet?" Rhoda props her head on her cupped hands, her ears standing at attention to receive all the gist.

"Why is my love life always under investigation?" I ask, and of course, Rhoda is quick to throw an answer back at me.

"Because if you haven't already noticed, Rachel's love life is non-existent, as she is too picky and too proper to let any guy into her life."

"Hey, I'm actually offended." Rachel pouts, but Rhoda ignores her and carries on.

"And according to you lot, I can't find love because I'm in love with my best friend, which I'm clearly not, by the way." She wags her finger at both of us before continuing. "So, as you can see, we're living vicariously through you now. Don't deprive us of that joy, please, Sissy."

"Okay, fine, stop whining already." I laugh and shake my head before outlining everything Jevaun has done for me the last few weeks, leaving out the part where we almost kissed on the tube because I don't want them to burst my eardrums with their screaming. "He's such a good friend and when I'm with him, I'm not afraid to be myself. Honestly, he's so kind, so cool and so...different."

"That's a good thing, right?" Rachel asks and I nod.

"Very good. I like him a lot and I think God is showing me that not all men are the same." My sisters nod, their facial expressions telling me they know what I mean.

They were right there with me when I was healing from the disaster that was my relationship with Ayo. They also were the same ones who prayed with me and encouraged me to believe that the right man was somewhere out there for me. If things keep going the way they are, then this might be their answered prayer.

"So, if he asks you out on a date right now, what will you say?" Rhoda asks, grinning from ear to ear.

I shrug before sipping on some water. "I have no idea. I'm still praying about it, so I guess we'll have to wait and see." I wink at them before we continue eating our food.

Wait and see. I like the sound of that. This new season God is bringing me into is full of so many surprises. It's like peeling an onion—so many wonderful surprises packaged for me, and I'm very happy to wait and see this new thing unravel.

♥ ♥ ♥

When Vanessa's name popped up on the screen, her heart sank and the palpitations started again, her chest tightening, the saliva drying from her mouth, and her hands shaking as she gripped the edges of her seat.

It was her first doctor's appointment since starting university, and she had been sitting in the waiting room for half an hour because the doctor was running late. One by one, she had watched the names of others pop up on the screen, her ears already familiar with the sound. But it wasn't just the sight of her own name that kept her glued to her chair, it was the sense of impending doom that she couldn't shake off.

She couldn't remember how long she lay on that bed after he left her. She couldn't remember how many hours she cried as the laughter and music continued in the living room downstairs.

She couldn't even remember how she got the strength to carry the broken pieces of her heart and herself out of that bedroom, down the stairs, out of the house, into the tube and back to halls.

Back in her room, she had locked her door and gone straight into the shower, almost peeling her skin off as she scrubbed with her loofah a million times, her tears mixed with the hot water that ran down her body.

Then, sitting on her bed with her back against the wall and staring at her reflection in the mirror, she had waited patiently for someone to pinch her out of the nightmare she was in. But nobody did, and so she wallowed in her sorrows alone.

The tears didn't stop when Anne returned from the CU meeting and knocked on her door several times, asking if she was okay. They didn't stop when her alarm went off at nine PM, reminding her it was time for her Bible study. They didn't stop when her phone vibrated for several minutes, letting her know it was her mum doing her weekly check-in. It didn't matter what the disruption was because Vanessa didn't budge.

Her eyelids twitched from the lack of sleep, her eyes burned from the endless tears that had soaked her sheets, and her throat hurt from all the sobbing she did until the early hours of the morning.

"Vanessa Molua?" The voice of a young woman with glasses, a name badge around her neck, and blonde hair tied up in a ponytail came from the other end of the waiting room, pulling Vanessa out of her thoughts as she flinched. "Vanessa Molua?" the woman repeated, looking straight at her, and that was when Vanessa realised she was the only one in the waiting room and it was too late to run.

"Yes?" Her voice was low and croaky as she stood up, taking one hesitant step after the other toward the stranger. She had specifically asked for a female doctor, hoping to make things easier for her to talk, but nothing about telling a stranger about what happened to her felt easy.

"Hi, I'm Dr. Ella Green. Thank you for waiting. Please come with me." The warm smile on the woman's face did nothing to ease Vanessa's anxiety. Her hands trembled as she followed closely behind the doctor and she was about to turn around and run out of there when the doctor opened the door and turned to her. "Please come in and take a seat."

Vanessa walked into the warm consultation room, a contrast to the freezing temperatures outside. She took a seat next to the desk while the doctor settled in her own chair in front of the computer.

"So, Vanessa. How can I help today?" the doctor asked, her whole body angling toward Vanessa.

Vanessa opened her mouth to speak, but a lump lodged in her throat, blocking her words. Then the memories came flashing back and before she knew it, the tears burst forth again. "I'm sorry," she said, "I'm so sorry." She couldn't stop herself and was about to stand up to leave when the doctor handed her a tissue and pulled her chair close.

"Don't apologise, Vanessa," the doctor said, not saying anything else, but patting her shoulder and waiting until she stopped crying. "You're my last patient, so there's no rush. Take your time until you're ready to talk."

The truth was, Vanessa didn't know if she'd ever be ready.

She had booked the appointment as a cry for help because she didn't know what to do or who to turn to. But how could she get help if she had no idea how to even articulate herself?

"I was..." she stuttered as the tears trickled down her cheeks. "I mean... I..." she sniffled, finally pulling herself together. "I had...unprotected sex last night, and I wanted to ask for advice about what I should do."

"Okay?" the doctor responded, as if waiting for her to keep on talking, but that was as far as Vanessa could go. Vanessa didn't think the doctor had all the time in the world to watch her break down ten more times, so she kept the rest of the story to herself.

After asking more questions about Vanessa's menstrual cycle, symptoms, and questions about who Vanessa had been intimate with, Dr. Green finally asked, "Was it consensual?"

The silence that broke through the room was enough to make the unspoken words plain. But Vanessa didn't have it in her to share anymore, so she took the easy way out...or so she thought. "Yes, it was."

Dr. Green waited for a few seconds, perhaps hoping that Vanessa would change her mind and say out loud what was already clear. "Are you sure? Please remember, any information you share with me is confidential."

Vanessa looked into the woman's kind eyes. She seemed like someone Vanessa could trust, but it was too painful to recount everything, and Vanessa just wanted to forget.

"Vanessa, I can..."

"I said it was consensual, okay?" She averted her gaze, hoping Dr. Green wouldn't push anymore because she was so close to running out the door again.

"Okay," the doctor said before talking through the emergency contraception options and writing out a prescription for Vanessa.

Dr. Green also offered to examine Vanessa, but when she declined, she gave Vanessa some self-swabs and blood test forms to bring back a few weeks later so they could check for sexually transmitted infections. Vanessa took everything and thanked the doctor before heading for the door.

"Vanessa?" The doctor's voice came again as Vanessa held the door handle.

She turned around slowly, hoping that the doctor would hold her peace and let her be. "Yes?"

"If you need any more help, please come straight back. Just ask for me—Dr. Green. I work Mondays to Wednesdays, okay?" she said as Vanessa's eyes welled with tears again.

All Vanessa had the strength to do was nod, and as soon as she collected the prescription from the pharmacy downstairs, she ran out of the building, into the cold air, with no intention of ever coming back.

17

———

JEVAUN

If there's one voice that sounds like music to my ears or one I look forward to hearing every single day, then it'd be that of the girl whose eyes I'm looking into right now. We've been on a video call for the last half hour and I'm almost embarrassed to say that my mind has wandered off once or twice, just admiring how beautiful she is.

I had no problem with the way I used to spend my evenings before. It usually consisted of me relaxing alone in my flat after my home-cooked dinner, with some worship music playing in the background while I got some words in, or laying on the sofa while watching author vlogs for inspiration or any action movie that tickles my fancy.

But since this beauty walked into my life, I can't imagine going back to that. While I enjoy my own company very much, sharing my day with someone else and talking about everything and anything has shown me a new side to the word peace.

One downside of being a full-time entrepreneur is that you can end up working twenty-four-seven. I used to do that a lot during my first three years because I was afraid of not hitting my monthly income target and falling behind on my rent and bills.

But when I reached a stage of burnout, my business wasn't growing. I lost passion for it and had to go back to the drawing board. After weeks of praying and asking God for direction, He told me to hire a business coach who taught me about the importance of rest.

I could be running around my flat right now trying to cross off the million and one things on my to-do list, but I'd rather be here, listening to Bex describe to me about how her evening with her sisters went yesterday and how dramatic her sister Rhoda can be.

"Sounds like you've got yourself a handful." I smile, bringing myself back into the conversation.

"Trust me, we've all had a handful since the day she was born." She shakes her head and laughs before adjusting the satin bonnet on her head.

"I can't wait to meet them." I rest my hand on my jaw.

"Oh, they've already been bugging me to set up a meeting. Rhoda might have even resorted to threats. The girl has got some nerve. But I love her anyway." She chuckles.

"Well, you just tell me when this meeting will be and I'll be there."

"Got it. Anyway, enough about me. How was your day?"

I shrug. "It was good. Church was great, as always. I had a nap in the afternoon. I woke up and did some reading, had dinner, and then called you."

"Wow, living alone sounds so chilled. Don't get me wrong, I love living with my parents, but being the only child at home means I'm their go-to for errands. I love helping my parents, but sometimes I just want to have a day exactly like you described."

I smile. "When this season of your life is over, I'm sure you'll enjoy days like mine, too."

"Yup, the word *season* is very important." She nods. "What

about your querying process? Any news from the full requests you sent?"

My heart sinks a little, as I hoped that topic wouldn't come up tonight. "Well." I sigh. "Yes, I've heard back from one of the three agents and it was a rejection." I rub my temple, trying to tame my facial expression so it doesn't relay the disappointment I felt as I read that email last night.

"Aww, I'm sorry to hear. Did they say why?"

I shrug. "Nothing specific. She said she really enjoyed the story, but couldn't take it on at this time."

"Wow, that's a shame. I must imagine the hundreds of authors who send emails to them every month. To sit down and look through all these query letters while picking only a few to commit to sounds like a chore. I don't envy their job at all."

"Me neither," I say, and as if she might have picked up the shift in my mood, she continues.

"But of course, none of that matters because you're going to find the best agent for your book." She smiles at me and I can't help but smile back.

"Why are you so sure of that?"

"Umm, *duh*, because you're an amazing writer."

I tilt my head. "Again, why are you so sure of that? I could be getting all these rejections because of how dreadful my writing is."

To this, she lets out a laugh before saying with all confidence. "Jevaun Watson, you're an amazing writer. I know that because I've read your work."

Confused, I sit up straight on my sofa. "You have? When? Where? How?"

She lowers her gaze first before suppressing her smile. "Okay, I might have had a sneak peek at your laptop last week at the coffee shop when you went to the loo."

"Wow." I burst out laughing.

"I didn't mean to, but the words were just sitting there staring at me. I made the mistake of reading one line and then I got sucked in. The way you describe the *Parallels* universe and your characters is so satisfyingly gripping, I couldn't help myself. I don't even read fantasy and yet, you had me hooked. That's what great writing does."

"You know, you could've just asked me to read it, right?"

"I didn't know whether you are like me, who doesn't want anyone to lay eyes on my manuscript."

"Well, I *was* like you when I was writing my first draft. But I've been working on this story for years. The more people read it and give me feedback, the better."

Her eyes widen as she leans forward, grinning from ear to ear. "So, are you saying you're going to let me read the whole thing?"

I lean forward too, mimicking her actions. "It would be my pleasure."

"No, trust me, the pleasure is all mine. I'll just need to remember this moment when you're famous. It'll be my claim to fame. You see that best-selling novel on the shelf, yeah I know the author personally and I actually read the early manuscript."

"Okay, carry on like that and my head won't be able to fit through my doors." I laugh before looking into her eyes again. "Honestly, thank you so much."

"For what, exactly?" She raises her brows, as if she doesn't know what she's done.

"For not letting me doubt myself. Even a self-proclaimed coach can have bad days, too." I'm surprised at how easily I can admit that to her. The more vulnerable I am with her, the closer I feel to her, and the closer I want to get to her. "You're awesome."

"Aww, as much as I'd like to take credit, I'm only returning a favour. You have literally helped me so much in the last few weeks, and I just have to do the same for you. You're awesome."

A moment of silence passes between us as we stare at each other, taking in the moment until I break the silence.

"Bex?" I glance at the time on the top left-hand corner of my phone screen. It's ten minutes until we say good night, so she can do her Bible study. I knew I was going to arrive at this junction eventually, but I didn't think it would be so soon.

"Yeah?"

I pause for a moment, pushing away any feelings of doubt before spilling my guts. "I've really enjoyed getting to know you these last few weeks, and I think it'll only be fair if I'm honest about my feelings."

I look her in the eye, and when she doesn't say anything, I continue. "I like you a lot, Bex. I think you're so cool and at the expense of me getting rejected, I just have to put it out there and see if you feel the same way. Would you like to go out to dinner with me sometime?"

She straightens her back as she sits up in her desk chair. "What?" For a moment, I'm not sure what to make of her facial expression, but then a smile breaks through. "Dinner with me?"

"Yes, I know we've spent a lot of time at The Buzz, but I'd like to take it up a notch, so I'm offering a cosy restaurant, delicious food, a breathtaking view, and good company. I have a feeling you might fancy that, too."

"Well, when you paint a picture like that." She smiles again before biting her bottom lip. "It's hard for me to say no."

The relief that washes over me is indescribable, but I have to keep myself seated, so I don't immediately burst into dancing. "That's awesome. Can you do tomorrow? Let's say five PM?"

"Erm…" She scrolls through her phone screen for a few seconds before shaking her head. "Can we make it Thursday instead?"

"Of course. Send me your address. I'll pick you up."

She tilts her head. "Are you sure?"

"Of course, if it's okay with you."

She's silent for a few seconds. "Hmm, actually, I think it'll be better if we meet somewhere. You don't have to come all the way to Croydon just for me."

"I really don't mind." She could tell me to fly up to the moon and back and I'll just start researching how to do that right away.

"Yeah, but I do," she responds. "I'll meet you at Waterloo Station."

"Alright, then. As you wish. I just can't wait."

"Me neither. Good night, Jevaun."

"Night, Bex." Her smile is the last thing I see before her face disappears from my screen. I push myself up from my sofa, dancing around my flat from room to room, before sending a message to Tré to tell him the good news.

18

BEX

I turn my face from side to side, admiring my winged eyeliner in the mirror as I mentally pat myself on the back for acing it. I usually do the bare minimum when it comes to makeup, but today, I'm putting in all the effort because I feel like it. Rachel would be so proud of me when I tell her I achieved my makeup look in just half an hour.

The last date I had was with Ayo, and that was the day I broke up with him. I remember how apathetic I felt while I was getting ready for that date because I knew it was going to be our last. But this time around, I couldn't be happier. I wasn't expecting Jevaun to ask me out so soon, but I had a feeling it would happen eventually.

I washed my hair last night and blow-dried it before putting the flexi rods in. God heard the prayer I said before I took the flexi rods down half an hour ago, because my curls are giving.

I apply my favourite pink lipstick before shaking my setting spray bottle, but before I can spray it on, my bedroom door swings open and the bottle goes flying out of my hands.

"My goodness! Mum, you scared me." I press my hand against my chest before picking up the bottle from the floor.

"I'm sorry, my darling," she says, but a cheeky smile forms on the corners of her lips as she tucks the loose ends of her *kaba* between her legs. She loves getting her giggles. "I came to ask whether you can redo my *bakala* for me." She points to the old set of cornrows I did for her a month ago. "But with all this *nyanga* [1] you are making, it seems you're on your way out. You look so beautiful."

"Thanks, Mum," I respond, before bracing myself for her line of questioning.

"So, what's the occasion, *Mami nyanga*[2]?" Mum asks as she sits on the edge of my bed. "Is there a fine man waiting outside that your father and I should be questioning?" Her voice is filled with humour, but I know she's serious.

Being the eldest daughter, Mum has always drummed into my head from the moment we stepped into this country about how important it is to get a good education and set a good example for my sisters. We never spoke about boyfriends or let alone boys until I graduated from uni and then she started asking subtle questions about whether I was seeing anyone.

Only Rachel and Rhoda know about my past relationships, so in my parents' eyes, I've never dated anyone. Given how disastrous my last relationships ended, I'm so glad I didn't tell them. Jevaun is my clean slate, my palate cleanser, if you could call it that, but I plan on taking my time before introducing him to them.

With Dad still warming up to my decision to take writing seriously, I'm not sure how he would feel about me dating someone who quit their job as a doctor to become a full-time author and content creator.

"There's no one outside, Mum. But I'm going on a date," I finally respond to her question and she breaks into a smile that is wider than earth itself.

"Really? Hey, Thank You, Jesus." She jumps to her feet

before dancing from one end of my room to the other, swaying the hem of her *kaba* from side to side. "*Praise the Lord. Oh, sing. Oh, sing ooooh. Praise the Lord.*"

I laugh and shake my head because I won't be the one to burst her bubble and tell her she's singing the lyrics of that song wrong.

After finishing her display of many dance moves, Mum wraps her arms around my shoulders, squeezing me into a tight hug. "I'm so happy for you." She releases me before turning my chair around so I can face her. "Tell me all about him. Is he a Christian? What does he do? Does he live in London?"

"Mum, calm down." I place both my hands on her shoulders. "Yes, he is a Christian and yes, he lives in London, but that's all I'm going to share with you right now." I've learnt the hard way how well Mum and Dad communicate with each other. Whatever I tell her will reach his ears one way or the other.

Her shoulders drop as she stands up and lets me finally apply the setting spray. "Where is he taking you?" she presses.

I shrug. "I actually don't know. It's a surprise, but we're meeting at Waterloo Station." Under the four-sided clock, to be precise. It doesn't matter that this has been a popular romantic meeting place since the early 1920s. It's part of our story and I think it's very cute.

"That's nice." Mum's voice pulls me out of my thoughts. "I will wait for you, so you can tell me how it goes."

I shake my head before standing up. "No, that won't be necessary, Mum." I already have Rachel and Rhoda breathing down my neck and waiting for updates when I get back, so I don't want to deal with Mum, too.

After Jevaun asked me out on a date on Sunday, I sent a message to the girls' group chat, thinking they wouldn't see it until after I'd finished my Bible study, so I turned my phone on silent.

When I picked my phone up again an hour later, there were a hundred notifications on the group chat with Rachel already planning our wedding and Rhoda threatening to kill me if I didn't give all the details as soon as possible. I'm trying to reduce the amount of drama in my life right now.

Mum places her hand on her hip before tilting her head. "So this is how you're going to leave your own mother hanging without even showing me his picture?"

I shake my head and chuckle before looking at my reflection in my full-length mirror. "Yes, Mum. That's exactly how we're rolling today."

"*Weh*. Please tell me, *nah*," she pleads and when I shake my head again, she claps her hands and turns her head away before crossing her arms against her chest. It's in times like this that I don't blame Rhoda for being the drama queen she is. The apple, they say, doesn't fall far from the tree.

I adjust the long sleeves of my fitted green dress, which has textured fabric and an asymmetrical neckline. Rachel gave it to me for my birthday last year and I always knew it was meant for a special occasion.

After slipping on my ankle-heeled boots and wearing my cross body bag, I pick up my jacket and kiss mum on the cheek before heading out of the house, ignoring her protests.

I walk to the train station, inhaling the chilly air and realising that the bundle of nerves that tightened my chest earlier today has disappeared. That can only mean one thing—it's all going to go well.

As a girl who grew up in London, there are a few places I've wanted to go to that I believe will help me get the full London experience. One of these places is The Shard, the seventy-two-storey skyscraper that is dominating the London skyline.

But I never imagined coming here with anyone other than my sisters, as we have made it our quest to tick off our never-ending list of places to visit. I'm sure it would've been a blast to come here with Rachel and Rhoda, but it feels even better standing here with someone I've come to admire so much in such a short space of time.

Jevaun holds out his hand for me as we step out of the lift, the cold air on my skin sending chills up my back. It's a good thing I'm wearing long sleeves today, because he doesn't need to see all the goosebumps on my arms every time he says or looks at me in a way that tickles my nerves.

"So, what do you think?" he asks as we walk into a restaurant on level thirty-one of the building.

"This is so beautiful." My jaw drops when we're directed to a window table. "How did you reserve a table for us so quickly?" I stand at the window, admiring the panoramic view of the London night skyline.

"Well, let's just say, when God is in it, He just makes a way, innit?" We share a laugh as he helps me take off my jacket and pulls out a chair for me. "They had a cancellation, so it all worked out."

After settling down in his own chair across the table, we scan through the menu together before Jevaun speaks. "Bex, you look so beautiful." He reaches for my free hand on the table and when I don't pull away, he covers it with his.

"Thank you." I smile and flip my hair over my shoulder. "You look handsome too." There's something about the way he's rocking the simple blue long-sleeved button-down collar shirt and black trousers that my brain and eyes like. *Would it be too much to ask him to dress like this every day?*

"So, British cuisine." He returns his gaze to the menu in front of him, pulling me out of my thoughts. "Made up your mind yet?"

"Erm...yeah." I close the menu and smile at him.

"Still going simple?" He raises his brow.

"Yup, less is more."

"As you wish." He waves over one of the servers and we place our order before handing the menus back.

While we wait, the server brings over our lemonade and pineapple juice, while I admire the decor in the restaurant. The dimly lit space with hanging lanterns and soft music makes the atmosphere really cosy.

"You know, my sister would like to open her own restaurant one day," I say, sipping on my juice.

"Really? Is that Rachel or Rhoda?"

"Rachel. She's a science teacher at the moment, but her dream is to one day open a Cameroonian restaurant in London. We don't have very many of those around. Rachel is very passionate about that and we're all rooting for her."

"That's so cool. I don't think I've ever had Cameroonian cuisine."

"Well, good thing you know me, then. I'm sure you'll have some very soon."

"I can't wait." He tilts his head. "Are you and your sisters close?"

"Yeah, we are. Moving from Cameroon to the UK when we were so young helped our relationship, as we had to look out for each other. They are my best friends."

"Yeah, I can relate." He leans forward. "My younger brother, Tréjon, is also my best friend. He works as a doctor in Nottingham."

"Oh, a doctor too, huh? Is he also thinking about quitting that for entrepreneurship?" I tease, and Jevaun chuckles.

"Oh, my dad will kill me if that ever happens," he says before lowering his gaze, as if he wished he hadn't said it.

"What about your parents?" I ask softly, and he pauses before responding.

"My mum died five years ago. She had breast cancer."

"Oh, Jevaun. I'm so sorry." It's my turn to hold his hand while he takes a moment of silence.

"It's okay." He takes a deep breath and exhales. "She was in remission for two years and it was a real shock to us all when it came back much more aggressive the second time around. But she was so brave and she fought hard until her last breath. She was such a blessing, and I can't thank God enough for the time we got to spend with her."

He stares at our hands on the table before clearing his throat. "*Whew*, okay, this is not how I planned for this to start, but there you go." His smile is back and relief washes over me when the server arrives with our starters.

Jevaun's smoked duck breast with parsley sauce, capers, and mayonnaise looks inviting. But I'm still playing it safe with my grilled Scottish mackerel served with Yorkshire rhubarb, cucumber chutney, and Dorset wasabi. My gut has never had a problem with seafood and I hope today is not the day it disgraces me.

"So, how is it?" he asks after taking the first bite of his duck.

I cover my mouth and raise a finger at him as he smiles and waits for me to finish chewing. "It's not bad at all," I respond, swallowing the last bits of fish. "But..."

"Salt and pepper?" he interjects.

"You got that right." We both chuckle as he hands me the salt and pepper shakers, waiting for me to use them before adding the seasoning to his own food.

As soon as we're done with our starters, our mains are ready and again, my pumpkin and sage ravioli looks nowhere near as delicious as Jevaun's corn-fed chicken served with sautéed rainbow chard, crispy bacon, butternut squash purée, apricot farce, and rosemary jus.

"You like what you see?" The corner of his mouth lifts into a smile when he catches me staring at his food.

My cheeks warm up as embarrassment creeps over me. "I just love the effort of the presentation. Rachel always says when food looks good, the job is already half done."

"Rachel is a wise girl. You want to try some?" He pushes his plate towards me and I shake my head.

"No, don't worry."

"Please?" He insists. "Not gonna lie. Your ravioli smells so good."

"Okay, fine." I smile. "I'll trade you some of my ravioli for your chicken."

"The deal's done."

After taking a bite of my ravioli, he says, "Hmm. This tastes really good. Nothing compared to my chicken."

"I have to agree with you on this one." We both laugh.

"So, Demi mentioned she added you to the Faith Writers' contemporary group chat. Hope they're not bombarding your phone with too many messages."

I shake my head. "Actually, I love being part of the group. At first, I didn't say much, but I've started asking questions and the girls have been so helpful. I also join the Thursday prayer meetings and Friday night livestreams when I can. Everyone is so nice, and it has made me more confident in talking about my story. I even shared a snippet of a scene I wrote on the group chat yesterday."

Jevaun's jaw drops. "Really? That's great, Bex. Well done."

"Thank you."

"Although, now I'm kinda jealous that the girls get a snippet first." He sticks out his bottom lip in a fake pout and I laugh.

"Don't worry. They only get a snippet, but you'll get the full thing when I'm ready."

He tilts his head. "Is that a promise?"

I nod, staring into his eyes. "Yup, it's definitely a promise."

As the night continues, our conversation switches between family, business, and church and I end up inviting Jevaun to our next worship night, which is going to be culture day too. It'll be the perfect opportunity to meet Mum, Dad, and the girls.

For dessert, we unanimously decide to share an apple tart with caramel and vanilla and to end the evening, the server brings us a bottle of non-alcoholic coconut and pineapple flavoured wine.

After pouring the drink out for us, Jevaun raises his glass and encourages me to do the same. "I want to make a toast to new friendships, new beginnings, new adventures, long-lasting connections, and for the opportunity to share this experience with a very beautiful woman."

The smile that radiates from me must be so bright because Jevaun reciprocates with a wide grin before he clinks my glass and we sip on our drinks.

At nine-thirty PM, it's time to leave the restaurant, but that doesn't stop us from continuing our conversation. I can't even say what we've been talking about all evening, but I know I absolutely love spending time with this man.

"So, are you happy I brought you here rather than Shakes and Cakes?" Jevaun asks, holding my hand as we walk into London Bridge station. He only has a fifteen-minute bus ride back home, but he refused to let me walk to the station by myself.

"For the view, yes, it was definitely worth it. But you're not getting out of taking me on a date to Shakes and Cakes. It's not a fair comparison." We stop walking and turn to face each other.

"So." He smiles down at me, as our fingers intertwine and stay locked in place as if we both don't have homes to go to.

"So," I repeat, smiling back at him. "What are you thinking?"

"You really want to know?" He takes a step closer, his eyes wandering from my eyes to my lips.

"I think I do, yes." The warmth of his body close to mine feels so good, and I never want him to let go.

"I'm thinking about how much fun I had with you today and...how much I really want to kiss you right now. But I'm not sure if you'll let me because we're in a public place and I know you don't like crowded places. I'm thinking I don't even know if you want to kiss me too, or if you think I'm weird for telling you this, but—"

"Try me." I wrap my arms around his neck and pull him close to me before he can finish his sentence. His lips are only an inch away from mine now, and I'm not sure what has happened to the shy Bex, who would usually be worried about what other people at the station think about this public display of affection. But I know whenever I'm looking into this man's eyes, I forget about everything happening around me.

"Really?" His smile reaches his eyes as I nod.

With that, he places his hands on my lower back and pulls me the rest of the way until our lips touch. I melt into him, savouring the softness and warmth of his lips as he caresses my back. The moment is so magical and if we were in one of those cheesy rom-coms, this would be the time when the fireworks pop off in the background.

When he lets go, he wraps his arms around me and we stay in that position, hugging tight before we let go. "I guess one of us has to be strong enough to say good night," he says, and I smack his arm gently.

"Okay, then I'm leaving." I turn around, but he pulls my arm, bringing me right back to where I started. It feels good to be shown affection like this. Loving affection with no strings attached.

He kisses me again, softly and slowly, his palm pressed softly against my face, and then he lets me go. "Good night, Bex."

"Good night." I exhale before walking backwards as he smiles at me, his hands tucked into his jacket pocket.

I tap my oyster card and walk through the ticket gate, but before hopping on the train, I turn around to wave my final goodbye. Not only does he wave back, but he blows me a kiss as well, and that's when my heart completely melts in my chest.

♥ ♥ ♥

Back at halls, Vanessa tiptoed through the corridor, hoping that whoever was in the kitchen would be so engrossed in their conversation that they wouldn't notice the jingling of her keys, the squeaking of her door, and the same door slamming shut moments later.

When Anne had knocked on Vanessa's door earlier that morning on her way to uni, Vanessa had not opened, but she had responded to Anne's text messages from the night before, explaining that she had severe period cramps so was going to skip lectures for the day. Anne had offered to buy Vanessa some ibuprofen or some food, but she had declined it all.

The lie had bought Vanessa some time, but she still wondered whether the weekend was enough for her to process her thoughts. What if Monday came, and she still wasn't ready to leave her room? What would happen then? She knew she couldn't stay in her room forever, but she preferred to do that, than pretend everything was okay in front of everyone when her world was slipping away like sand in between her fingers.

The knock on her door jostled Vanessa out of her thoughts, and her hand flew to her chest. "Who is it?" she asked without thinking.

"Nessa, it's me." Anne's voice came through the closed door, and Vanessa immediately chastised her mouth for betraying her. "Can I come in?"

She could say no, but how long could she continue to ignore Anne before she figured out that something was up with her? "Erm...okay." Vanessa slipped her feet into her soft, furry slippers and dragged herself to the door. Letting out a loud sigh, she opened the door slightly and leaned against the door frame.

She didn't need to say a word because as soon as Anne's gaze landed on her, the girl's smile disappeared like an evaporating smoke. "My goodness! Are you okay?" A frown appeared on Anne's face as she lowered the plastic bag she was holding.

Vanessa cleared her throat before crossing her arms against her chest. "Of course I am. Why do you ask?" She followed Anne's gaze as it scanned her from head to toe. Now she wished she had looked at herself in the mirror before opening the door.

"Oh, okay. I know you said I shouldn't, but I bought you a self-care package." Anne raised the plastic bag again. "My older sister used to have terrible period cramps, and she always loved one of these."

Vanessa took the bag from her friend and smiled at the contents—pain relief tablets, a hot water bottle, chocolate, and herbal tea. "Thank you," she said, but it didn't take long for her smile to turn into sniffles and sniffles into sobs. The same way her life had turned from a fairy tale into a nightmare.

"Aww, Nessa, what's wrong?" Anne stepped forward, but Vanessa didn't open the door for her. "When you didn't come to the CU meeting last night like you said you would after your date, I knew something was wrong. What happened?" She lowered her voice.

Anne paused her questioning and then, as if realisation dawned on her, her gaze darkened as she covered her mouth. "Oh, no." She shook her head and took a step back before asking. "What did he do to you?"

Vanessa looked up at her friend, the worry and anger in her eyes, too much for her to handle, too much for her to face. How could she explain what had happened? How could she ever bring herself to tell someone else how foolish she had been? How she didn't listen and didn't pick up the signs and the red flags that were right there in front of her.

"Please, talk to me, Nessa." Anne pressed one more time, but Vanessa couldn't bring herself to get past the sobbing. So she slammed the door shut and threw herself on her bed, sobbing into her pillow again, her chest tightening, and the sense of impending doom hanging over her again like a dark cloud.

19

JEVAUN

Pure bliss is how I would describe my experience from the last three weeks of dating Bex. This reaffirms my decision to wait for the right person and not jump into senseless relationships all throughout my school and uni days.

I've needed to make some adjustments to my schedule to ensure I make time for Bex every single day. It has stretched my organisational skills because this is the first time I'm having to juggle content creating, ghost writing, querying, and a relationship.

It's a new but exciting challenge for me. It's been a long time since I've had to factor in another person in my life other than Tré and Dad. But I have to make it work because Bex needs to know how special she is to me and how much I love spending time with her.

"I'm loving the t-shirt." Bex smiles at me as I hug her at her church's front entrance. She pulls me to the side as we lean next to a parked car, away from the upbeat music coming from the church.

Today is their monthly worship night and culture day, so I had to represent. The only thing I could find in my closet that represents Jamaica is the t-shirt I'm wearing, which my mum bought for Tré and me years ago.

The vibrant green, yellow, and black colours, which represent the Jamaican flag, couldn't be more different from the colours of my regular clothes, which is why I only wear this t-shirt on special occasions like this.

"Thank you. I'm shocked that it still fits. I've had it for so long." I smile and take a moment to admire Bex's outfit.

She has waist-length grey single-strand braids, and she's wearing a black velvet knee-length dress, which has red, yellow, orange, and white embroidered patterns around the neckline, the waist, and the hem.

"Wow, you look so beautiful." I draw a smile from her and she tilts her head, her matching red earrings dangling from side to side.

"Thank you," she says. "This outfit is called the *toghu*, from the North-West region of Cameroon, but many Cameroonians wear it."

"It's beautiful, and so is the queen wearing it." I wink at her and I'm about to pull her in for another hug when two ladies step out of the church building and start walking towards us. They're also wearing similar dresses and judging from the wide smile on their faces, I can only assume they are Bex's sisters.

"Hi, Jevaun." One of the girls waves at me before bouncing on her feet.

"Hi." I wave back and Bex makes the introductions.

"Jevaun, this is Rhoda," she says, sending me a knowing smile. "And this is Rachel." She points to the quieter sister with glasses. "Girls, I'm sure you already know who this is."

"It's so lovely to finally meet you." Rhoda sticks out her hand and shakes mine with a firm grip.

"We've heard so much about you," Rachel says as I shake her hand.

"Really? Good things, I hope?" I ask, looking at Bex, who leans into me as I wrap my arm around her waist.

"Of course, and so sorry our parents couldn't be here today. They had to visit a family friend and their new baby," Rachel says.

"Yeah, Bex told me all about it. Don't worry," I respond.

"It's probably good they're not here today, because they would've been grilling you," Rhoda adds and the girls all laugh.

"Girls, be serious, please. We should go inside before the church members start grilling us," Bex says and we make our way inside the church.

The music grows louder as we walk down the corridor and into the main auditorium, plunging me into a scene I've missed so much. Unlike the conservative Baptist church I attend in Shoreditch, Bex's church reminds me of the Nigerian church I attended while I was working in Preston.

I spot a few waving Jamaican flags from the people dancing in the space at the back of the auditorium, and the ushers greet us at the door as we are directed to our seats.

With the wonderful music the drums, guitar, saxophone, piano, and choristers are making, it's impossible not to join in the dancing. I can't dance to save my life, but when Bex and her sisters show me a few simple dance moves, I join in the groove.

Soon I find myself jumping, shouting, and cheering at the top of my voice as the choir sings songs from different countries. When it's Jamaica's turn, I'm dragged to the front by the other Jamaicans as we dance to Donnie McClurkin's "I've Got My Mind Made Up" medley.

The evening is over in the blink of an eye because time, they say, flies by when you're having fun and it's so fun to praise God with other like-minded believers. One thing I've noticed being here is how free Bex is with the people she knows, and I feel so honoured to be among the people she can share her beautiful smile with.

After greeting a few people, Bex and I make our way towards the exit when an older woman stops us. "Rebecca, darling. How are you?"

"Aunty Vivian." Bex hugs her. "I'm good, thank you."

"That's good to hear. Your mum told me about your job. It's their loss, you know? I'm sure God will work everything out in your favour."

Bex smiles and responds. "Thanks, Aunty. I believe He already has."

The older woman's gaze slides over to me and then she smiles, as if waiting for Bex to make the introductions.

"Oh, Aunty, this is Jevaun. I invited him for the worship night."

"Very nice to meet you, young man. Did you enjoy the service?"

I nod and smile at her. "Yes, it was amazing."

"That's what we like to hear. Have a good evening, and please look after my dear Rebecca for me, will you?"

"You have nothing to worry about." I return her warm smile and when she walks away, Bex looks at me.

"Do you think she knows we're dating?" Bex asks and I shrug.

"Well, I wouldn't put anything past these aunties." I laugh just as Rhoda and Rachel join us, their hands filled with food.

"There you go." Rhoda hands Bex and I our own Tupperware with *puff puff*[1], chicken and *jollof* rice. The aroma is already teasing my nostrils and I can't wait to dig in.

"Thank you so much," I say as we head out of the building.

"Yo, B?" a deep voice stops us in our tracks and we turn around.

"Hi, Ayo," Bex says as we step aside to make way for the other people leaving the church.

The other guy, who I recognise as one of the pianists who played today, has high-top dreadlocks and his wide grin at Bex shifts something inside of me. The more he talks to her, the more I have to resist the urge to wrap my arm around Bex's waist in order to make a statement.

"Seems like I can only keep catching you outside, innit?" He scratches his head before turning to me. "Hi. I'm Ayo."

"Nice to meet you. I'm Jevaun. I really enjoyed today's service. You and your team made us all jump for joy."

"Really?" His smile broadens. "I appreciate the kind words. All glory to God," he says before turning to Bex again. "B, do you mind if I have a quick word in private?"

She looks at me and I'm about to step away when she holds my hand. "Actually, feel free to say whatever you want here." She pauses before continuing. "Jevaun is my boyfriend."

This isn't new information, but hearing her say the words out loud and then leaning close to me dispels the unfamiliar feeling I had a few minutes ago. "It's okay. I'll just wait over there."

She looks at me again, her brows furrowing this time. "You sure?"

"Yeah, of course." I kiss her forehead and nod at Ayo. "Take care, man." I turn around and walk toward Rachel and Rhoda, who are in the car park.

"Jevaun? Where's Bex?" Rachel asks before looking over my shoulder.

"Oh, erm...Ayo wanted to speak to her."

"Ayo?" Rhoda pushes herself away from the car before looking at Rachel. "What does he want with her?" She takes a step forward, but Rachel holds her back.

"Rhoda, chill," Rachel says. "Sometimes, I wish you'd

remember that Bex is an adult and can take care of herself," she whispers, but not low enough for me not to hear. When Rhoda takes a step back, Rachel turns to me. "Sorry, Jevaun. Rhoda loves making mountains out of molehills."

I smile. "Nothing to be sorry about." One part of me would like to prod them more and I'm sure they wouldn't mind telling me who exactly this Ayo guy is, but I'd prefer to hear it from Bex herself—whenever she's ready.

"Sorry about that." Bex wraps her arm around me when she returns ten minutes later.

"Are you okay?" Rhoda asks Bex, worry lines creasing her forehead.

"Of course, I'm okay," Bex responds, her eyes darting between her sisters. "What made you think I wasn't?"

"Never mind." Rhoda waves a dismissive hand. "Are you guys ready to go home now?"

Bex steps back and stands next to me again. "Actually." She holds my hand. "Jevaun and I are going to make a quick detour before I go home."

Last week, when brainstorming places to check out in London, I suggested Tower Bridge and Bex jumped at the opportunity, as she was interested in seeing what it looks like at night.

Rhoda raises her brows. "Okay, love birds. You know I would've offered to be a third wheel if I didn't have a meeting with my supervisor at nine AM tomorrow morning."

"Yeah, and I've got work tomorrow, so enjoy," Rachel says before looking at me. "It was so lovely to meet you, Jevaun."

"The pleasure is all mine." I hug the girls good night before Bex and I head toward East Croydon train station.

❧

After getting off at London Bridge, Bex and I walk hand in hand for a few minutes past many coffee shops and through a walkway in between skyscrapers until Tower Bridge comes into full view.

It's the first week of November, but we're still enjoying cool temperatures of ten degrees Celsius. It's cold enough to wear thick jackets, but not enough to deter us from sitting out here.

"It's so beautiful," Bex says, her eyes fixed on the lit-up Tower Bridge, standing tall in all its glory. The eight-hundred feet bridge—often mistaken for London Bridge—is between two towers built on piers and is one of London's iconic landmarks.

"Told you you would love it." I smirk and she drives her elbow into my side before walking away and shaking her head.

We meander through the crowd of people before leaning against the balcony, as our gaze wanders across the River Thames, which reflects all the lights from the bridge and the skyscrapers around.

My stomach rumbles, cutting across the silence, and Bex chuckles. "Well, someone is hungry."

"Indeed I am. I lost track of time while drafting my new ghostwriting project, so I only had a few minutes to leave the house to catch the train. I didn't have dinner before leaving because I didn't want to be late."

"Aww, you're so sweet." She turns her body to face me. "The more you hang around Africans, the more you'll realise that it's okay to be late sometimes."

"Yup, that was one of the first things you taught me." I laugh.

"Hey, you'll get used to it, trust me."

I shake my head. "I don't know about that. People always say being punctual is one of my good qualities."

She takes a step back and places her hand on her hip before raising her brows. "So, are you saying I'm a bad influence?" she asks, suppressing a smile.

"Oh dear. I feel like I just dug a hole for myself."

"Nah, nah, say it with your full chest, mate." She chuckles.

"Okay, fine. I guess sometimes it's okay to be a *little* late."

She bursts out laughing before placing her hands on my chest. "I can't believe you caved in. I don't give *mean girl* vibes, do I?"

"No, you don't. But the truth is, that pose you struck just now tickled my brain in a way that made me forget my argument."

Her smile spreads across her face as she plays with one strand of her braid. "Hmm. You have a way with your words, don't you, Dr. Watson?"

I smirk. "It's no wonder I quit my job to write full time."

She leans in and plants a soft kiss on my lips. "Come on." She nods toward one of the seating areas nearby. "I don't know about you, but I'm starving."

"Yeah, me too." We take the food out of our backpacks before taking the lids off our Tupperware and inhaling the sweet aroma of the *jollof* rice. "That smells divine." I hold her hand and say a quick prayer before we dig in.

"That's so good." I say, as I bite into the *puff puff*—the soft, sweet dough melting in my mouth.

"You can say that again," she responds before putting a spoon of the spicy yellow rice into her mouth.

When we're done eating, I clean the oil off my hands with a paper towel before clearing my throat. Now seems like a good time to tell Bex about what has been on my mind all day.

If we're going to let each other into our lives, then I want her to know all about me. The last thing I want is for her to be taken by surprise when she eventually finds out about the complexities of my family dynamics. "Bex?"

She looks up from the last bits of her chicken. "Yeah?"

"There's something I need to tell you."

"Oh, okay." She puts the Tupperware back into the plastic bag and wipes her hands. "Everything alright?"

I nod. "Yeah, I just thought I should tell you a bit more about my dad."

"Okay?" She inches close.

I take a deep breath before continuing. "My relationship with him hasn't been great since I became a Christian. It was my housemate in my second year of med school who first shared the gospel with me. He was an international student from China. His name is Victor, and I lived with him for a year before he moved to the US to complete the last two years of his med degree.

"When my dad heard about my decision, he was furious. He claims to be spiritual, but is only interested in following what our ancestors used to believe in. Every conversation I've had with him about God has ended in a full-blown argument." I sigh. "When I moved out of the house and my mum got sick again, she refused to go into a hospice and wanted to stay at home. My dad only allowed me to visit her on one condition—that I won't mention God, Jesus, or the Bible while I was at the house."

I lower my head before continuing. "A few hours before my mum passed away, I was sitting next to her bed holding her hand. She hadn't spoken for a long time and she was getting weaker by the minute. Then she turned her head and looked at me before squeezing my hand back and calling my name.

"I knelt down next to her, thinking God had worked out the miracle I'd been praying for. I thought she would sit up and ask for food. You know, like the story of Jairus' daughter, whom Jesus raised from the dead?" I smile as Bex nods. "But she pressed her hand against the side of my face and told me to promise her that no matter what happened, I would make peace with my dad."

"I gave her my word that day, and every time I close my eyes, every time I remember just how bad my relationship is with my dad, I see my mum's eyes begging and pleading with me to try even harder. It was the last thing she asked of me and I can't even do it." A tear rolls down my cheek and Bex wipes it away.

"Aww, Jevaun." She pulls me in for a hug and I rest my head on her shoulder. After planting a kiss on my cheek, she holds my chin up so I can look at her. "You can't blame yourself for the actions of others. It takes two people to make a relationship work. You and your dad see the world from different perspectives, but that is not your fault."

"I know that, but for Tré's sake, I just wish there was some function in the family, you know?"

"Tré is an adult and I'm sure he also understands that it's not your fault." She kisses my fingers before looking up at me again. "You're doing so well, Jevaun. It breaks my heart to see you be so hard on yourself. God will work it all out, you'll see. I'll definitely keep praying for you, for Tré, and for your dad, too. Okay?"

"Thanks, Bex." I smile, the tears finally drying up. "You have no idea how much that means to me."

"Well, I was serious when I said I'm here to help you too in any way I can."

I wrap my arm around her waist and pull her close to me, drawing a giggle from her lips. "You know, accepting to be my girlfriend alone is already a huge help to me, right?"

She gives me a half-nod before her smile fades and she tucks a strand of her braids behind her ear as she looks into my eyes. "Yeah, but since we're being vulnerable tonight, I think it's only fair to tell you about Ayo."

20

BEX

I'm not sure why I opened my mouth to say I wanted to tell Jevaun about Ayo, but I've already put it out there and I have to follow through with it. He has shared a lot with me tonight and I'm ready to tell him a bit more about me, too.

"Okay?" His voice pulls me out of the spiral of my thoughts and when I look at him again, his soft gaze melts away my hesitation. "I'm listening."

I take a deep breath and start. "Ayo is my ex-boyfriend." I pause, as I'm not sure what I'm expecting his reaction to be, but when he nods, I continue.

"We broke up five years ago because he cheated on me with one of the girls in the choir."

"Wow." Jevaun doesn't need to say anymore for me to pick out the judgement in his tone.

"When the girl found out that I knew, she left the church and I finally got the courage to break up with him." I exhale before straightening my back, preparing myself to dive deep into my unpleasant memories.

"I was in a horrible place at that time, mentally, spiritually, and emotionally. I had just graduated from uni and moved back in with my parents while juggling my post grad job at the bank. My uni experience was...hard, and I was in a bit of a vulnerable state when I left. I'm not sure why I thought jumping into a relationship would help me heal, but it did the complete opposite." Tears blur my vision and a lump builds in my throat.

"That relationship absolutely broke me, Jevaun. Ayo was emotionally abusive, he was manipulative, and he constantly criticised everything I did. My sisters warned me about him, but I had a lot of insecurities back then, and even though Ayo was a walking red flag, I kept making excuses for him." I wipe my tears and sniffle.

"Did he hit you?" Jevaun's jaw tightens as he leans closer and wipes a tear rolling down my cheek.

"No, he didn't." I place my hand against his chest, my words reassuring him enough to relax his jaw.

"That's the one thing I'm grateful he didn't do." I lower my gaze to our intertwined hands.

"So, why did he want to talk to you tonight?"

I shrug. "Well, a few weeks ago he apologised for how he treated me and said God had convicted him about his previous lifestyle, so he is now a changed person."

"Hmm." Jevaun grunts. "So, he wants you back?"

"Yes, but I told him the same thing I told him a few weeks ago. He's not the man for me. God had made it clear to me years ago, so that ship has sailed. I don't love him, I don't have any feelings for him and I made that clear again today." I wait for Jevaun to say something, but when he doesn't, I continue.

"You probably think I was stupid for going out with him in the first place, but here's a truth I've never told anyone before." I stare into his eyes. "The real reason I stayed with him was because I thought if I let him go, no one else was going to love me." Another tear slips down my face and Jevaun wipes it away.

"Bex, I'm so sorry you had to go through all that." His gaze softens. "I can't even imagine what that situation did to you. But I thank God for giving you the courage to leave. I thank God for helping you realise you are beautiful and precious in His eyes." He moves a strand of my braid away from my face before kissing my forehead.

"I just want you to know that you can trust me. I'm not perfect, but I will try my best to make you happy. Your beautiful heart has captivated mine in ways I could have never imagined. I've never felt like this for anyone before. I care a lot about you, and even though we're going to have challenges and fight like every couple does, I want you to know that I'm here for you. Always."

The tears are now rolling down my cheeks with no break. Jevaun pulls me in for a hug and the warmth of his embrace becomes my comfort. He kisses my temple and rubs my back until my sobs quiet down. He doesn't need to say anything else for me to believe him.

I'm not crying because of how sweet his words are, but I'm crying because of how faithful God is. I still remember the prayer I wrote in my journal the night I broke up with Ayo. The response God gave me that night was to wait on Him. To wait for the right person He would send my way.

So being here, in Jevaun's arms, is an answered prayer. Proof that God not only cares about me, but that He is always true to His word. Bex of five years ago won't believe it if I told her that God actually came through. She wouldn't even believe she would get the courage to share her story with others like this.

Today was about Ayo and sharing that part of my life. It's a step in the right direction, but I've still got a long way to go on my journey. Maybe someday, God will also give me the courage to talk about Jason. But that day is not today.

Six weeks passed, and he never called Vanessa, never texted her, and he certainly never came to any CU events ever again. The shock of Vanessa's new reality hadn't worn off because she still couldn't bring herself to understand how gullible she had been.

For six weeks, she woke up every morning, forced herself to go to lectures, acted like she was okay in front of Anne and her other course mates, and then she came back home every evening to cry herself to sleep.

Flashbacks from her move-in day into university pierced into her memory as she stared at her reflection in the mirror. Her mum's prayer was the only thing she could hear ringing in her head. The same prayer Vanessa believed had fallen on deaf ears.

Earlier that day she had had a follow up telephone call with Dr. Green who had explained that all her swab results had come back negative for infection. But even though the news brought some form of relief, it wasn't enough to lift Vanessa's spirits.

Her phone vibrated when her mum sent her a text message asking her how she was doing. Whenever she didn't pick up her mum's phone calls, the excuse was that she was in the library because the last thing she wanted was to break down in front of her mum.

An hour later, her phone vibrated again to tell her it was time for her Bible study, but she turned the alarm off and glanced at her Bible on her desk. The dust that covered its cover was testament to how long it had been since she touched it.

"Nessa, would you like anything to eat?" Anne's voice was faint in the background and Vanessa didn't even notice when her friend entered her room and sat next to her on the bed. "Hey, are you okay?"

That was the opportunity Vanessa had been looking for. An opportunity to rant about how much God had wronged her, and she took it without thinking twice.

"It's not fair," Vanessa voiced out her thoughts in between sniffles and Anne shuffled closer. "It's not fair that he pretended to be something he was not, just so he could take advantage of me. It's not fair that he can go about his life like nothing happened while I sit here and suffer the consequences of his cruel actions. It's not fair that I prayed for protection before I left this room, but felt like I was all alone on the battlefield, fighting for my life with no one to protect me."

Vanessa's sobs grew louder, but she didn't stop until she said the words she never believed she would say. "It's not fair that I've devoted my whole life to a God who let this injustice happen to me. He can't say He loves me and then still let this happen. What kind of cruel love is that?"

"Aww, Nessa." Anne wrapped her arms around her friend and let her cry on her shoulder. Vanessa had prepared her mind for all the responses she would throw at Anne if she tried to defend God, but Anne said nothing. She gave no answers, made no statements, and explained nothing. All she did was sit there, in the stillness of the room, giving Vanessa a shoulder to cry on.

21

JEVAUN

"No! No! No!" Tré slams his game console on the centre table before throwing himself backwards on the sofa and covering his face. It's a good thing the console is sturdy and he doesn't have a glass table, because he would've regretted that action.

Laughter erupts from my mouth and not even Tré's side-eye stops me. It's been so long since I played video games with him and I forgot how good it felt to beat him. "You really thought you stood a chance, didn't you?"

"I'm actually really good. That was a fluke. I'm calling for a rematch." He sits up and I tap his shoulder.

"Yeah, that's how losers talk, mate."

Tré's eyebrows shoot up. "So, you don't think I can beat you?"

"How about you stop talking and *actually* show me?"

"Bring it on, then." He picks up his game console again.

"Oh, hang on, tiger. I'm hungry." I walk around the sofa to the open plan kitchen.

Tré sighs. "Excuses, excuses."

I shake my head before opening the cupboard and taking out a box of Rice Krispies.

"Nah, I need the energy to beat you again, mate." I laugh as Tré joins me in the kitchen and takes out a box of porridge from the cupboard. "I thought you weren't hungry." It's my turn to side-eye him.

"Nah, fam, I'm not letting you beat me again just because you were more energised." He pours the porridge oats and milk into a bowl before putting it in the microwave.

This is my first time visiting Tré in Nottingham since he started his foundation programme. He took five days off work, so I'll be hanging around till the end of the week. This is one pro I love about working for myself—me not having to ask for permission to spend time with my brother.

I took the train from St. Pancras International to Nottingham last night, straight after church, and we ordered chips and chicken before having an early night. Today, we had a lie-in, and after my Bible study and a one-hour video call with Bex, Tré challenged me to a game of FIFA and we forgot about breakfast.

I also sent my manuscript to Bex last night and woke up to several voice messages of her live commentary as she finished each chapter. It was a mixture of her squealing, groaning, gibberish, and run-on sentences that my book-loving heart could totally relate to. I'm already on cloud nine and the day is still so young.

"I love what you've done with this place." I wave my hand across the living room as I shift my mind temporarily from thinking about Bex.

"Yeah? Is it obvious that I was trying so hard to make it a man cave?" The microwave beeps, so Tré takes out the bowl and stirs some sugar into his porridge.

"Yes, but it's *your* man cave, and I was actually shocked when I didn't walk into socks hanging on the doors and shoes littered around the kitchen."

Tré snorts as he cuts up some bananas into his bowl of porridge. "Hey, what do you think I am? A pig?"

"Nah, nah, I'm just saying I'm pleasantly surprised. Might be the only compliment you get from me all week, so you better take it." I pour some milk and add sugar to my bowl of Rice Krispies before we migrate back to the living room.

"So, how are things going at the hospital?" I crunch on the cereal in my mouth.

Tré swallows his food before responding. "Last week wasn't bad at all, you know?" he says. "Maybe it's because I haven't had many night shifts in a while. I want to say that I've got used to the chaos, but it's still not a rotation I enjoy. I'm just counting down the days until I can move on to the next adventure."

"You said it's general surgery next, right?" I ask, and Tré nods. "Boy, that's an entirely different world. I hope you enjoy it better."

"I hope so too." He puts the last spoon of porridge into his mouth before changing the subject. "Oh, that reminds me." He places his empty bowl on the centre table before picking up a notepad and a pen from the pile of stationery in the compartment below the TV stand. "Dad's sixtieth birthday is coming up, and I was thinking we could throw him a surprise party."

I choke on the last bits of Rice Krispies struggling to go down my throat. Tré hands me a glass of water from the kitchen as I bang on my chest. I guess even the Rice Krispies tensed up at the mention of Dad.

"You okay?" Tré's eyebrows crease up as he looks at me.

"Yeah." I wipe my watery eyes before clearing my throat. "So, a sixtieth birthday party, huh?"

"Yes, I thought it'd be good to do something nice for him. We used to celebrate each other's birthdays all the time and we haven't done that since Mum died." Tré pauses and I swallow whatever protest I'd prepared to give him when he mentions Mum.

I can see how much he longs for things to be the way they were when Mum was alive. But she was the glue that kept this family together. I'll never know if she knew what Dad was truly up to. Some days, I wish I had told her before she died. But what kind of son would that have made me, given the physical pain she was already going through?

I admire Tré's ignorance about the whole situation. I wish I could turn back the clock to the time when I didn't know the truth, the time when my father was still my hero too. I hate to be the one to open Tré's eyes to the ugly reality.

"You're right," I respond. "It'll be good to do something nice for him. After all, not everyone lives to the age of sixty, so it's something to celebrate."

"Cool. I'm glad you agree." He writes the words 'guest list' at the top of the notepad and then looks at me. "So, I was thinking of inviting his business partners, too. You know the nice ladies who attended Mum's funeral and who used to drop by the house?"

My jaw tenses. "Hmm, you sure you want to invite them?" Would he change his mind if I just tell him those women are more than just his business partners? "I thought it was just close family and friends?"

"Yeah, but then that would be five people altogether, including Aunty Fiona and her husband. I thought we'd mix it up a bit. You know Dad doesn't have a lot of friends."

He would make more friends if he didn't spend his time making more girlfriends. "Okay, then." I guess I'd just have to stay out of their way the whole time.

"Do you have their contact details?" Tré looks at me and I frown.

"Why would I have their contact details? You know Dad and

I are not on speaking terms, right? You're the one who speaks to him every week, so you can figure out a way to get their contact details the next time you visit him. I haven't spoken to him in two months. In fact, I think you should remove my name from the guest list."

"Whoa, whoa, slow down. You don't have to get all worked up about it." Tré moves the notepad away from my reach. "You're still his son, remember? He's not going to flip out because his son attended his birthday party, will he?"

You really don't know what he's capable of, do you? The words slip to the edge of my tongue, but as I can already feel my muscles tensing up the more we talk about this, I agree, just so we can change the subject and move on.

My phone chimes and a text message notification slides in. The tightness in my chest immediately resolves, and a smile appears on my face as I swipe left to respond. It's the cutest photo of Bex sitting alone at our usual spot at the Buzz with her cup of tea and croissant with a message underneath that simply says,

> It's not the same without you ☹

"Okay, lover boy. Things are going good, huh?" Tré's voice stops my mind from wandering again.

"Yeah, sorry. That was rude of me." I put away my phone after sending a quick response to let Bex know I miss her, too.

"Yes, things are going great. Like I told you before, she's an amazing woman and it feels like I've known her my whole life. As every day passes, my feelings for her grow stronger and I've never felt like this ever. "

"Wow, someone is in love." Tré squeezes my shoulder, giving me a moment to think about his statement.

"Yeah, I guess you could say that. I may not have any other

experience to compare this to, but I'm certain about how I feel about her."

"I'm sure Dad would be delighted to meet his future daughter-in-law." He writes something down on his notepad.

"Oh, no." I shake my head. "Keep her out of this." I walk to the kitchen and place our bowls in the sink.

"So, you won't bring her to the party?" Tré follows me and leans against the kitchen island as I run the tap water and wash the bowls and spoons.

"Why would I? He doesn't know I'm dating and I think we should keep that knowledge to ourselves for now." I place the bowls and spoons on the drying rack before turning around to face him. There's no way I'll be exposing Bex to any of Dad's negativity any time soon.

"Alright, then. If you say so." He crosses off something on his list and then scribbles some more before placing the notepad and pen on the kitchen island. "Okay, I think we have a guest list. Are you now ready for that rematch?"

"Mate, I was born ready." I smirk. "You know I can never turn down an opportunity to show you who's boss." I laugh as we make our way back to the living room.

22

BEX

"Hun, you look so good." Neha wraps her arms around me in a tight hug at our meeting point outside Clapham Junction train station. We've been checking in on each other every week since we lost our jobs, but we've really wanted to catch up in person. I'm so glad this girl's day out finally made it out of our text messages.

"Oh, don't even start. Look at you. You're glowing." I throw a compliment back at her, holding her at arm's length and admiring her perfectly pencilled eyebrows, contoured face, and rose-coloured cheeks.

This might be the first time I've ever seen Neha wearing a full face of make-up. She always complained about how she never had the time for it and between running after her toddler and making sure she double checked everything her husband did, it was just easier for her to go for a natural look when getting ready in the morning.

"Stop it." She pushes my shoulder gently. "You're just saying that because you're my friend."

"No, I'm serious. Your hair is fuller, your worry lines are gone, and your skin is glowing. Seriously, tell me your secret." I link my arm with hers as we walk toward the traffic light, meandering past the power-walking Londoners.

"Well, I have a lot to fill you in on. But first, what do you fancy eating?" she asks when we're on the other side of the road. We both scan the line of coffee shops and restaurants before she speaks again. "I didn't have breakfast or lunch, so I'm pretty hungry."

I glance at the time on my phone and even though I had my usual croissant and tea at the Buzz two hours ago, my stomach is rumbling like I haven't eaten in days. "Cool. Should we try that new pizza place?" I point to the newest restaurant at the end of the road.

"You're speaking my language." Neha grins as we make our way there. My friendship with Neha is probably the biggest blessing that came out of me working at the bank. I miss seeing her beautiful face every morning and having someone to rant to about the ups and down of the corporate world. Even though things won't be the same as it was before, I'm grateful I still have her in my life.

After placing our order, we grab a window seat and take off our coats as the rain trickles outside, sending a gust of cold air into the restaurant every time someone opens the door. Now is when I pat myself on the back for asking Rachel to do these braids for me. My hair needs to be tucked well away from this miserable weather.

"So, how have you been?" I lean forward and support my head with my cupped hands.

"Hmm, where do I even start?" Neha lets out a sigh.

"From the very beginning. Or have you forgotten I'm unemployed and don't have anywhere to be at two PM?"

We both laugh before Neha says, "I'm not gonna lie. At first, things were tough. I spent the first two weeks feeling really sorry for myself. I just couldn't shake the feeling that I had failed.

Arjun and I had a plan. We were working towards a savings goal as a family to get a mortgage within the next two years and all of that just went down the drain." She lets out a breath before continuing.

"I also thought I had failed as a wife because I didn't want the financial strain to be on my husband alone. Arjun is so hard-working and seeing him work twice as hard while I stayed at home doing nothing broke my heart. I also thought I had failed as a mum because I kept worrying about not being able to provide a financially stable environment for Jai. I don't want him to ever experience what I experienced growing up."

Neha and I have bonded over a lot of things over the years, one of them being the fact that we both migrated to the UK when we were young. Neha's mum raised Neha and her brother in the UK all on her own until three years ago, when she finally went back to India to join her husband.

"Yeah, I see why you would think that, but you know you're an amazing mum and wife, right?" I tilt my head, looking into my friend's eyes to check that she understands how truthful my statement is.

"Yeah, I do." She smiles. "Arjun has done a good job of reminding me so many times in the last few months."

"Yes. Go, Arjun." I pump my fist, drawing a smile from her lips.

"Honestly, he has been so supportive, and he has not let me doubt myself. His words of affirmation have been so comforting, and even though he also has a lot on his plate, he always makes sure that Jai and I are comfortable."

"Aww, he's a good man, Neha." I reach out and squeeze her hands.

"A good man, for sure. The best part of this entire experience is that I've had more time to reflect on the blessings I have now rather than worrying about the future and what I can't control.

Jai now goes to nursery two days a week instead of five, so spending time with him the rest of the days has made us form a closer bond. I've come to cherish the blessing it is to be his mum and to be there for Arjun in more ways than I thought possible. I have more time to look after myself and I've been sleeping more. It's just been great."

"Wow, I knew something had changed. Aww, I'm so proud of how far you've come. I know you'll find your balance soon." My heart swells with gratitude for my friend because I know just how much she struggled with the work-life balance. "And what about the job? You said you were going to apply for another one?"

Neha shrugs as the server comes in and places our plates of pizza in front of us. "I have applied for a few, some rejections and some I haven't heard from." She takes a sip of water. "But I'm not in a rush to find anything new. I actually started experimenting with e-commerce and digital marketing. If I can find a niche and build something, then I'd like to continue growing that. One thing losing our jobs taught me was that I'd like to build something for myself too, so that my financial future would not be in the hands of another person. I now manage all our household finances, so I've been budgeting, cutting down our expenses, and making sure we're still saving."

She pauses and looks me in the eye before cracking a smile. "We really need it, since we're expecting baby number two soon."

"*Eeeeeek!!!*" I squeal before standing up and hugging her. "Girl, I knew this skin glow wasn't ordinary. Congratulations. I'm so happy for you."

We sit down again. "Thank you so much, Bex. It was so unexpected, but I've clearly been having too much fun and I even forgot we were trying. When I first found out, I was anxious about bringing another baby into this world while I'm unemployed, but after speaking to Arjun, I've changed my mindset about the whole situation now. I'm embracing this blessing and I intend to enjoy every single stage of this pregnancy without stressing myself about the things I can't control."

"You're preaching right now." I click my fingers. "I totally agree with that and again, I'm so happy for you."

"Thank you so much. But enough about me, though. How are you? Have you also been applying for a job?"

I shake my head. "Nope. I'm taking a break from the corporate world for a year to..." I pause before letting the words out, "to finish writing my book."

Neha's eyebrows shoot up as she places her glass of water back on the table. "You're what now?"

I nod vigorously, unable to stop the grin forming on my face. "Yes, you heard that, right? I'm writing a book." Just as Neha has been doing some reflecting and changing her mindset about how she lives her life, I've also been doing some reflecting. I'm done hiding my lamp under the bed. I'm a city set on a hill that can't be hidden, so I'm in the era of embracing all the gifts that God has given me.

"Wow, I had no idea you were ever thinking of writing one. Hun, what have I missed? Fill me in on all the details." She pushes her food to the side, and that's all I need to know that she's invested in this.

"I've actually been working on this story for a few years—the outline, that is. But I never found the right time to start writing the book because the corporate world just drained me."

"Hmm, I hear you." Neha nods.

"I finally started writing and," I pause, struggling to suppress my smile. "I have a boyfriend, too."

Neha's jaw drops as she squeals in her seat. "You what? How? Where? When?"

I chuckle at the shock on her face. "We met at a coffee

shop at Waterloo Station. He's also a writer, and he has taken me under his wing and showed me the ropes. He introduced me to a writing group, and he has been so supportive of my journey. He's the sweetest person ever, and I like him a lot."

"Aww, that's so great. I'm happy for you, Bex." She leans forward and holds my hand.

Every time Neha asked about my previous relationships, I just told her I had been in 'situationships' which I didn't really want to go into. So this is the first time we're getting to talk about this.

"Thank you. God has been so good to me for the last few months. I've grown stronger in my faith, I'm more confident in my gifts, and I have a clearer picture of my purpose."

Neha nods and even though she and her entire family are Hindu, we have had many cordial conversations before about faith, identity, and purpose. We agreed to disagree from the very beginning about which God we serve, but we both share similar values.

"I'm so proud of you, Bex. I can't believe it. I closed my eyes for one second and you're on your way to becoming a best-selling author and soon-to-be married."

"Whoa, slow down there for a second. We've only been officially dating for a month, and let me finish writing the book first."

"But that's a start, isn't it?" She tilts her head.

I smile. "Yes, you're right."

We finish eating our pizza and when we're done, we walk into the bookstore next door after Neha admits that our talk about books has made her want to check out the popular romance books she has been seeing on social media.

We spend forty minutes navigating through the bookstore and when I walk over to the Christian fiction section, disappointment sags at my heart by the very small handful of books staring at me.

To be honest, I'm grateful I even found a Christian fiction section, as it is a rare occurrence in British bookstores. I can't wait to tell Jevaun all about it. Maybe he can interview the owner for his YouTube series.

I run my hands over the amazing cover arts, flip through the book pages, and sniff them until my toes tingle. Some day, God willing, my books will be on these shelves too. Some day, God willing.

23

BEX

The longest week of my life has finally come to an end because I get to see Jevaun's handsome face again. Okay, maybe I'm being dramatic because he video called me every morning before I left the house and also every night before my Bible study. But nothing beats seeing and holding him in person.

He makes me feel special when he's here and even when he's away. Not being near him this past week has shown just how strong my feelings are for him. That is both scary and exciting.

Scary because I have to constantly push back the negative thoughts in my head based on my previous experiences. Exciting because even though I'm scared, God continues to renew my hope in love again.

As Jevaun walks through the ticket gate at Waterloo, excitement rushes through me as I stretch my arms out towards him.

"Hey, beautiful." He wraps his arms around my waist and lifts me up before spinning me around as I release giggles.

I'm enjoying his firm hold so much that I don't want him to let go. But he can't keep spinning me around at the very centre of Waterloo Station forever.

After putting me down, he plants a kiss on my lips and I inhale his sweet scent, but restrain myself from sniffing his beard the way I was sniffing the pages of those books yesterday. "I missed you so much."

"I missed you too. Maybe I should take trips more often if I'm going to come back to this kind of reception."

"Oh, don't start." I roll my eyes and smack his arm gently.

"I have a gift for you." He smiles and holds my hand as we walk to the escalator.

"Ooh, what is it?" I bounce on my feet as the escalator takes us up to The Buzz Café.

"You wait and see." He winks at me, making my heart melt and when we're seated at our favourite corner of the coffee shop he says, "First of all, what did you think of the end of the story?"

"Ooh, I loved it." I chuckle when I realise how high-pitched my voice was. He finally sent me his manuscript before he travelled to Nottingham, and I couldn't stop myself once I started reading. "It kept me up until five AM last night."

"Really?" His eyes widen. "I don't know how you do that."

"Yeah, I just had to finish it because your writing is so beautiful and it sucked me right in. I didn't realise I loved reading so much. Neha and I went to a bookstore yesterday, and I bought some more books from the Christian fiction section."

"Wow, so that means my gift to you is timely, then." He smirks, testing my patience.

"Oh, stop torturing me. What did you get me?"

"Okay fine, I'll tell you. When Tré and I were walking to the train station yesterday, I came across this Christian bookstore which had amazing bookish products. When I saw these, I thought of you, so here you go." He takes out a small plastic bag from his backpack and hands it to me.

I waste no time in opening it up to find a cute bookmark with the word 'chosen' written on it and also some highlighters and pastel-coloured sticky notes. "Aww, these are so cute." I shift my gaze from the cute items I'm holding to his handsome face. "You're feeding my bookish addiction and I feel like I've hit a jackpot by bagging myself a boyfriend who also loves books."

"I have to agree with you there." He smiles and I cup his face, pulling him close to me. "Thank you so much for always thinking of me." I lean forward and kiss him.

"You're very welcome."

"So, tell me about your trip." I place the items in my back-pack before giving him my undivided attention.

"It was really good. Tré and I talked for hours, played lots of video games, and explored Nottingham. Tré is also planning a sixtieth birthday party for my dad in the new year."

"Aww, that's amazing. Are you going?" I tilt my head, knowing well now how touchy this subject is for him.

"I actually don't know yet. I have to think and pray about it."

"Of course." I rub his arm and change the subject. "And did you get any writing done when you were there?"

"Nah, but I received an exciting email last night." His face beams. "One of the agents who requested to read the full manuscript has asked to jump on a call with me."

"Oh, wow. That's exciting." I clap my hands. "You just need the one and this could be it. When is the call?"

"Next week."

"It'll go well and we'll be praying about it."

"Amen. Thanks so much." He kisses my hands. "And what about you? How's writing going?"

"Really good, actually. After writing that tricky scene, I've just been powering through."

"Yes, that's what I like to hear. I'm so proud of you." Seeing him smile at me makes my heart all kinds of jittery. "My offer is still on the table if you want me to read it when you're ready."

"Yeah, I don't even have to think about that. I would love for you to read it...some day."

"Yes, I'll take that. Are you hungry?" He stands, and after I nod, he makes his way to the counter to order our usual.

As he waits in the queue to order our food, I watch him intently, trying to wrap my head around how blessed I am. A month ago, I would never have thought I'd be here, so I have everything to be grateful for. I know it can only go up from here and I can't wait to see what God does.

When Jevaun gets to the front of the queue, the man who has just paid for his food turns around and walks towards me and my heart stops when I see his face. My breath catches in my throat as he walks closer, carrying a cup of coffee and a sandwich.

I freeze as my eyes follow him to the table across from me. When he takes off his jacket and his backpack, I ball my hands into a fist, my jaw tightening as my eyes water.

Mixed emotions rise in my chest, my heart rate quickening and the muscles in my chest spasming as the unpleasant memories come rushing back, transporting me into a place I never want to find myself in. It doesn't matter that nine years have passed, or that he now has a beard, but I can never forget the face of the man who brought me down to rock bottom.

Jason.

"Bex?" Jevaun's voice tears my gaze away from Jason as I swipe away the tears streaming down my face. "Are you okay?" he asks, placing our food on the table before turning his head to look at Jason.

Unable to get the words out of my mouth, I stand up, wheezing as I pick up my backpack. "I have to go."

"What? What happened?" Jevaun asks, turning his head again to look at Jason, who is now staring back at me.

He freezes with his sandwich midway to his mouth, and the

recognition in his eyes sends a burning sensation up my chest and into my throat.

"I'm sorry, I can't stay here. I really have to go." I pick up my belongings and make my way across the coffee shop.

"Bex?" Jason shouts after me, but I'm focused on the door and I don't stop walking until I'm out of there.

Jevaun calls after me too, trying to catch up, but I run down the stairs and make my way toward the ticket gate, just before the tears gush out of me again.

Eight weeks had passed since Vanessa heard his voice, and for one moment, she thought she was beginning to forget the way he smelled, the way the lines on his mouth formed when he smiled, the way he tilted his head to look at her when he complimented her, and the way she felt safe and warm every time he hugged her.

Being back at home for the Christmas holidays, she had started embracing the blessing of time, because time, they said, was meant to heal all wounds. She hoped that one day, she would forget everything about him she had grown to love and everything about him that had caused hatred to make a home in her heart. She couldn't wait to embrace that reality again, but little did she know she was still very far from it.

"Vanessa, wake up." Her mom burst into her room one Sunday morning at six AM, jolting her out of her sleep. "Wake up. I had a dream about you."

Vanessa's heart sank deep into the pit of her stomach as she pushed herself up, sleep disappearing from her eyes. "A dream?" Her croaky voice came out. "What dream?"

"You were on fire, Vanessa. On fire." Diana paced the length of her daughter's room before sitting on the edge of the bed. "I was standing right outside of this house, screaming and begging you to come out, but you just stood there, crying and refusing to listen to me." Diana's voice shook.

"I called out to you so many times, but you..." She sniffled as tears ran down her cheeks. "You told me it was better to leave you in the house. Why would I ever do that? Why would you tell me to leave you in the fire, Vanessa? What is going on with you?"

"Mum, I..." The words caught in Vanessa's throat as she glanced at the door multiple times, expecting her younger brother Victor to come rushing in. Then she remembered he was away at the church's youth retreat that weekend.

"What is this fire you want to kill you?" Diana demanded. "Tell me, please."

"Mum, there's nothing—"

"Don't lie to me, Vanessa Enjema Molua." She raised her voice and Vanessa flinched. "I carried you in my womb for nine months. I have raised you for eighteen years and I know you, my daughter. Please, don't lie to me."

"Mum, I don't want—"

"Don't lie to me."

"Mum!!!"

"I said, don't lie to me."

"I was raped!!!" The shock of Vanessa's words kept Diana in a frozen state as silence sliced through the room. Indeed, you could hear a pin drop until Vanessa's sobs returned.

"I was raped, Mum. Now you know the truth, are you happy?" Vanessa sniffled as the floodgate of tears opened up while her mum stood there for a few more minutes, against the wall, her widened gaze pinned on her daughter, before her body sank to the floor next to Vanessa's bed.

Diana didn't say anything as her gaze swept through the room. Then, just as Vanessa expected, her mum's wailing broke through.

Vanessa covered her head with her pillow and sobbed too because she knew from her mum's reaction that there was nothing she could do or say that would take away the pain she had brought upon her family.

24

JEVAUN

To say that I'm worried about Bex would be the most understated thing I could say right now. I don't understand how we got here. I've replayed the scene a million times in my mind, and I have no idea what happened.

One minute, Bex and I were fine, and the next minute, she was running out of the coffee shop as if someone was trying to kill her. I've never seen so much fear in her eyes before, and I can't shake off the feeling that it had everything to do with that man.

I've never seen him before, but he clearly knows Bex because of the way he was looking at her. He even called out her name, and that's why she bolted out of the coffee shop without looking back. She had already hopped on the train by the time I got down the escalator and when I went back to the coffee shop, the man was gone.

Who is he? Why did Bex look so terrified of him? Has he hurt her before?

I shake my head to push away the spiralling thoughts before leaning forward on my desk and rubbing my temples. I've been sitting here for the last two hours, telling myself I'm watching videos to prepare for the call I have with the agent this afternoon. But the truth is, I've been sitting here making up the worst-case scenario about what happened at the coffee shop.

The moving pictures on my screen mean nothing because all I can think about is Bex, who has refused to respond to my messages or pick up my calls for the last week. It doesn't help that she has been reading my messages and has been online, but hasn't responded. I woke up six times last night checking my phone to see if she had responded to the last message I sent her.

> Me: Hey, Bex. I appreciate you don't want to talk, but please, can you at least let me know you're okay?

My phone vibrates and I pick it up, hoping to finally see a response from Bex, but it's just a new comment on one of my social media pages. I place the phone face down and push myself away from the desk before taking a deep breath and pacing the length of my living room.

The thumping of my feet across my hardwood floor all morning must be driving my downstairs neighbours crazy. I won't be surprised if I received a message on the building group chat asking me to stop the noise.

In order to stop the silence from doing my head in, I put on my hoodie before grabbing my keys and heading out of my flat. It's one of those good days where there's no one to share the lift with me, so I have quiet time for myself.

The cold air that hits my face as I approach the park next to my house already takes my mind off momentarily from Bex. But as soon as I lower myself on a bench, my phone vibrates again.

This time it's a response from Bex...finally. I've never swiped open a message so fast.

> Bex: Hi, Jevaun. I'm so sorry for my silence this past week. I'm okay.

Phew. Thank God she's okay. Proof of life should be enough for me right now, but I'm still staring at my phone screen, hoping she'll tell me more.

> Me: I'm glad you're okay. Do you want to talk about it?

> Bex is typing...

> Me: You know you can tell me anything, right?

> Bex is typing...

> Me: I promise, I just want to help. I'm really worried about you.

Fifteen minutes pass, and she's still typing. She must be dealing with a lot right now if she can't even think of the right words to say.

> Bex: I just need some space, please. I'll let you know when I'm ready to talk.

. . .

My shoulders drop as I lean back on the bench and let out a loud sigh. I rub my palms across my face before lifting my head and staring at the scene in front of me. A woman is pushing her giggling toddler on a swing nearby and a couple walk past me with their bulldog on a leash.

It's not the first time I've sat here, watching people go about their lives and using their interactions as fuel for my creative brain. But nothing about this scene excites me because all parts of my brain are engaged worrying about Bex. I wish she would just talk to me. But if she's not ready, then I have to respect that.

Picking up my phone again, I swipe through my contacts and click on Rhoda's number before sending her a message. I'm not sure how Bex would feel about me bringing her sisters into this, but I just need to know she's really okay.

Rhoda: Hey, Jevaun. You alright?

Me: Yeah, I'm good, thanks. Sorry to bother you, but have you spoken to Bex today?

My phone vibrates and Rhoda's name flashes on the screen. I pick up the call and place the phone against my ear. "Hello?"

"Hey, sorry. I thought it would be easier to call you," she says and a door slams shut in the background. "You asked about Bex?"

"Yeah, I just wondered whether you've spoken to her today."

"No, not yet. We've all had a hectic week, and she hasn't responded to any of our messages on the group chat, but I spoke to her briefly two days ago and she said she was busy writing." She pauses. "Have you not spoken to her today?"

I sigh, wrestling with how much I should say. *Lord, please help me.* "Yes, I have. But I have a feeling something is wrong. I might be overthinking, but if it won't be too much trouble, could you swing by the house and check if she's okay?"

"Of course. That shouldn't be a problem. Rachel and I will go there after church tomorrow."

"You're a star. Thank you so much." I end the call with Rhoda and even though it's not the most desired outcome, it puts my mind at ease. Now I have to push this to the back of my mind and prepare for my agent call in an hour.

I head back toward my building, saying a silent prayer in my heart as I go. *Lord, please help Bex overcome whatever it is she's going through. And please, help me be patient and to be a good friend to her during this time. Amen.*

I rub my palms together and blow out a breath, adjusting the collar of my shirt before logging on to the video call at exactly four PM. Sam—my potential agent, who seems to be not much older than me—is already there waiting for me, and he greets me with a wide smile.

"Hi, Jevaun. Can you hear me?" he says and I nod, still trying to convince myself that this is actually happening.

"Yes, hi. I can hear you perfectly." I've read so many horror stories about other authors' experiences with 'the call,' but I'm choosing to stay hopeful that this will be the one.

"Amazing. Well, thank you for agreeing to meet with me. As you know from the email I sent, I really enjoyed reading your manuscript. This is just going to be an informal chat, so we can get to know a bit more about each other and confirm whether we have the same vision for it."

"Of course. I understand." I smile because in my heart, there's no possible way that this could go wrong. *Lord, please help me.*

"So tell me a bit more about you and your writing journey."

"Yeah, sure." I clear my throat. "My love for writing actually stemmed from my love of reading books. When I was younger, my mum used to take my younger brother and me to the library every week to pick out a book. I usually read my books within two days and soon a book a week became two, and then three, and now as an adult I could read fifty to a hundred books a year.

"As a teenager, I loved escaping into the imaginative world of fantasy and science fiction and I always found it fascinating how people could make up worlds like that in their head and put it down on paper. Then one day, I got the idea to write my first book when I was sixteen and I never looked back.

"The actual story didn't become clear to me until my faith journey began during my second year of university. You would notice that the book has very strong themes of faith and God's sovereignty and that is entirely what it is about. The more I leaned on God, the more He showed me what the story is and now that it's done, I can't wait to share it with the world."

"Wow, that is an amazing journey and I love that you didn't give up on the story, even when it wasn't clear to you. I think you are a great writer, and I would love to represent you."

My eyes widen as I freeze for a moment. "Really?"

Why do I feel a 'but' coming?

"Yes, I would, but..."

There it is.

"It comes with a condition."

I let out a breath. "Okay." Surely, there couldn't be any condition that would make me turn down the offer.

"I love the characters you have created. Your world is so captivating and I know readers are going to love reading your book. But you also make it...too obvious that you've written it from a Christian worldview. I would love to represent you if you can revise it and trim that aspect of the story."

My heart sinks and words elude me as I stare at my screen. Of all the things he could've asked me to do, this was the last thing I thought. "But the book is Christian fantasy. The genre was clearly stated in my query letter. The Christian worldview is what makes the story. Remove that and the story will lose its flavour."

Sam shakes his head. "I actually beg to differ. Like I said, you've got amazing characters and brilliant world building. All you need to do is make one of your subplots the main plot instead and your current main plot a tiny subplot."

"Erm..." I stutter, my brain unable to find the right words. "But I thought you represent Christian authors and authors who write Christian fiction."

"Yes, of course I do. But I also want to sell this for you. I've been in this business long enough to know that the more subtle you are with the faith elements, the more you will reach a wider audience and the more likely we'll be able to sell it to the big publishers and get a really good deal out of it."

I pause for a few minutes because I'm really struggling to wrap my head around the point he is trying to make. "Erm.. I...I"

"Listen—" He cuts me short. "I don't expect you to decide right now. I can tell this story means a lot to you and you've been working on it for many years. I'd like to give you some time to think about it. "

I lean forward and rub my temple. "Okay, I appreciate that. How much time do I have?"

He shrugs. "As much time as you need. I'll email you the notes I have, so when you've made the revisions, just send me an email and if I'm happy with the changes, we'll work on the contract details."

I rub my forehead and let out a sigh, but there's nothing left for me to say. "Okay, thanks, Sam. I'll be in touch."

Sam ends the call, and I remain seated, staring at my reflection on the screen, my thoughts running at a hundred miles an hour.

Does this journey ever get easier? Could this day get any worse?

25

BEX

I must keep writing. The words swirl around in my brain as my fingers fly across the keyboard, typing word after word without stopping. I ignore the shooting pains in my wrists, the ache in my eyes, and the tension squeezing around my head. I must write faster because the entire world needs to know that I've overcome this.

I've been doing so well and prodding along for the past nine years. I refuse to let some ghost of the past walk into my life and ruin it. Out of all the people I could've bumped into, why did it have to be Jason?

Out of all the places to bump into him again, why did it have to be The Buzz Café? Things have been going so well and it feels like my world is about to slip right through my fingers.

But I'm not giving in to these feelings of self-hate again—the feelings God helped me overcome. I'm not going back to that dark place where everything felt hopeless. I refuse to be dragged back there. Not now. Not ever.

An aching lump builds in my throat and I swipe the tears away from my eyes, ignoring the drops on my keyboard. I can't stop. I won't stop. This can't break me. I've come too far to go back. I must keep writing.

A knock on the door drags me out of my thoughts, and I pause before turning my head away from my laptop. Clearing my throat, I wipe my tear-stained face again with the sleeve of my hoodie before closing my laptop.

After church today, my parents and I had lunch in silence and I retreated to my room straight after. Mum poked her head in earlier and asked if I was okay. Even though she didn't sound convinced when I told her I was fine, she accepted my answer before going to have dinner with Dad. She last knocked on my door half an hour ago, saying she was going to bed as she had a headache while Dad was watching TV in the living room.

Dad rarely knocks on my door. If he wants to speak to me, he just calls me on my phone and summons me downstairs. Most times it is to figure out a technical issue with either his phone or the TV, but occasionally it is about some concerns he has about something I said or did. I just hope tonight isn't one of those nights for him to tell me off because, honestly, I'm not in the mood.

"Come in." I straighten my back.

"Hey, Sissy." The door shrieks open as Rhoda and Rachel poke their heads in and I relax in my seat.

"Hey, what are you doing here?" I hug them both before lowering myself onto my bed, the pain in my lower back reminding me about how long I've been sitting at the desk.

"You weren't responding to any of our messages and you haven't been picking our calls," Rhoda responds, taking a seat at my desk chair.

"Yeah, we came to check on you." Rachel pushes her glasses closer to her face as her eyebrows knit together in a frown. "Bex, are you okay?" She lowers herself next to me on the bed, both of them staring at me and waiting for my response.

"I told you already. I've been writing." I nod toward my closed laptop at my desk. The girls follow my gaze before looking at each other and then back at me.

"What?" It's my turn to frown. "Why are you both looking at me as if you don't believe me?"

"Well," Rhoda speaks up as usual. "I spoke to Jevaun yesterday."

"Jevaun?" My breath hitches in my throat. He couldn't have said anything because I didn't tell him anything. "What did he say?"

Rhoda shrugs. "He just said to come check on you because he was worried about you."

"Did he say why?"

Rhoda shakes her head. "Are you going to tell us why?"

"Guys, I've been writing." I let out a sigh, frustration building in my chest. I push myself up and pace the room. "I also had an IBS flare up. A really bad one, so I've been resting." This lie should hopefully squash this. I can't bring myself to talk about it. I refuse to shine light on it. It's in my past and it will remain there.

"Oh." Rachel stands. "I'm sorry, sis."

I shake my head. "No, it's okay. Thank you for checking on me."

"Yeah, but can you also reassure Jevaun so he can stop worrying?" Rhoda hands me my phone and they all watch as I open my messages. Guilt cinches my chest as I scroll through all the messages he sent me over the past week.

I don't know why I thought ignoring him would be a good idea. Pretending everything was okay and trying to control my emotions would've been a better solution. All I've done is make everyone I love worry about me. What excuse will I give Jevaun to explain my behaviour without telling him the truth?

> Me: Hey. Can we meet?

I chew on my bottom lip as I wait for his response. I hope he's not mad at me now.

> Jevaun: You know I can't say no to that. I have missed your beautiful smile.

An unconscious smile settles on my lips as I read his message again. How could he always be so sensitive to my needs? He didn't deserve the cold shoulder at all. He did nothing wrong. I pray I can fix this.

"So, does that smile mean everything is rosy now in *love-landia*?" Rhoda wiggles her eyebrows at me before we chuckle.

"I guess you can say that," I respond.

"Aww, thank God." Rachel gives me a hug. "You know you can let us know if anything is wrong, though, right?" She cups my face and looks into my eyes, almost as if she can see through me.

I nod. "Yeah, sure. Everything is okay. Don't worry." The words are more for me than they are for her.

"Okay, can we please go have dinner now? I'm hungry, and that *ndolé*[1] in the kitchen is calling my name," Rhoda whines as she pushes Rachel and me towards the door.

"How did you know we have *ndolé*? Did you go into the kitchen as soon as you entered this house?" My eyes widen at Rhoda.

"You should know your sister by now," Rachel says before

turning to Rhoda. "At this point, your middle name should be food." We all laugh as we walk out of the room and down the stairs into the kitchen to share a meal of delicious *ndolé* and boiled ripe plantains while Dad catches us up on world news.

I'm grateful for the break away from my computer. Burying myself in writing and hiding away in my house won't solve the problem. I hope seeing Jason again last week was just a one time occurrence. If that's the case, then there shouldn't be a reason I wouldn't get over this hurdle. It's not worth sabotaging my relationship with Jevaun.

It had been two days since Vanessa told her mum about what he did to her. Two days since she had felt her heart rip out of her chest as she watched her mum weep and roll on the floor, crying out to God for justice and mercy.

Nothing she did made her mum feel better. She didn't even get the chance to explain the full details, but Vanessa didn't know if she could explain if she was asked. The weight of emotions on her chest grew heavier with each passing day, and she had thought about leaving multiple times.

Many times, she had packed up the suitcase she had brought with her from uni. Then unpacked it and packed it again in the middle of the night, convincing herself that it would be better for her mum to wake up in the morning and for her not to be there.

Of course, it had to be easier for her mum if she was not there. What kind of daughter brought that much pain to the woman who birthed her? Children were blessings from God, and Vanessa felt more like a curse that had plagued her entire household.

Victor was totally oblivious to everything going on because he was either too sucked into his video games or his phone screen, making the most of his two-week break from school before he went straight back to write his GCSEs. He didn't know about the tension at home, and she loved that for him.

Vanessa's heart ached as she imagined what her father would've thought if he were still alive. Would he have listened, asked more questions, tried to understand what happened? Or would he have jumped to conclusions and assumed she was at fault? But she knew she would never get the answers to any of those questions.

"Vanessa?" Her mum's voice forced her to open her eyes, and she sat up in her bed as her mum entered her room. Diana's red and puffy eyes were evidence of the sleepless nights she had had. Vanessa had heard her crying and praying and wondered if she had had any sleep at all. "Take a shower and put on your clothes, because we're going out."

Vanessa frowned. "Where are we going?"

"To see Pastor Kemi. She is free to see us this afternoon, so please get ready."

Vanessa's heart rate increased and her chest tightened as she tried to make sense of what was going on. The pastor's wife was a lovely woman, but Vanessa didn't understand why her mum was bringing her up now.

"Why are we going to see Pastor Kemi?" Vanessa asked and her mum looked at her as if she had just asked the most ridiculous question.

"To seek godly counsel, of course. We need godly counsel about how we can handle this situation."

I shake my head before opening my mouth to speak again. "Mum, please don't tell me you told her."

"Of course I told her, so she would know the urgency of the situation. Please, put on your clothes so we're not late for the appointment with her this afternoon."

"Mum, I don't want to go." Vanessa's voice cracked as tears blurred her vision. "She's a stranger and I don't want to—"

"This is exactly what my dream was about." Diana raised her voice, tears filling her eyes as she lifted both hands to her head. "This is the fire the dream was talking about. I'm trying to help you, but you're refusing help."

"No, Mum, I'm just saying I don't want to–"

"You don't want help, Vanessa? How can you not want help when you are clearly not dealing with this the right way? You are letting it eat you up and you won't let me help you?"

"Okay, fine, I'll go." Vanessa gave in, just because Victor was home this time and the last thing she wanted was for him to start asking questions and suspecting that something was wrong with her.

An hour later, Vanessa was sitting in Pastor Kemi's office with her mum by her side, holding her hand. After exchanging pleasantries, the elderly woman on the other side of the desk wasted no time in jumping into the heart of the matter.

"Vanessa?" She leaned forward on her desk and interlaced her fingers, looking at Vanessa straight in the eye. "How are you?"

Vanessa didn't expect that simple question to stir up that many emotions inside of her because, although she wanted to say that she was fine, the reality of the matter was that she was very far from fine.

When Vanessa didn't respond, the pastor continued. "Your mum told me what happened, and I just wanted to say that I'm so sorry. I want you to please remember that it was not your fault. Nobody is judging you here and your mum and I just want to help you. Is that okay?" She reached for Vanessa's hand, but Vanessa retreated.

Her mum nudged her, but Vanessa's gaze dropped to the floor as she shifted in her seat, begging for the woman to stop talking.

"Please, Vanessa, you have to engage in this conversation," her mum whispered and squeezed her hand. "If you don't talk, we won't be able to help you."

"I don't..." Vanessa sniffled. "I don't want this..." The tears streamed down her face because no one could erase the shame and guilt she felt. She was just another case, another statistic, and another girl who would never get justice. There was no point sitting there and having fruitless conversations when all it did was remind her of the night she wanted to forget.

"You have to let us help you," her mum spoke again and at that point, Vanessa had had enough.

So, without saying another word, Vanessa stood up and ran out of the office without looking back.

26

BEX

It's 12:10 PM when I arrive at Regent's Park and after following the live location Jevaun sent me, I finally spot him sitting on a bench nearby. Our planned meeting time was twelve PM, and I actually left the house on time, but the train waited at East Croydon Station for ten minutes for no reason, which delayed my journey.

I even rushed up the stairs, taking them two at a time like a typical Londoner, but none of that matters because I'm here now and I owe Jevaun an apology.

My heeled boots crunch the orange autumn leaves that have fallen from the trees flanking the concrete path. The beautiful sight brings a smile to my face as I embrace the sun's warm rays against my skin. I love the colour orange and autumn is my favourite season, so God definitely wanted me to smile today.

With my hands still tucked into my jacket pockets, I blow out an icy breath and lower myself on the bench next to Jevaun.

"Hey." He smiles at me and even though I don't deserve his warm welcome right now, that smile is my only hope that this conversation will go well.

"Hey." I return his smile. "Sorry I'm late. There was a train delay."

He shrugs and angles his body towards me. "You're here now and that's all that matters."

I lower my gaze before placing my phone on the bench in the space between us. "I missed you."

"Did you now?" he says and guilt stabs at my chest, but relief returns when I lift my head to find him smirking at me.

"Yes, I did."

He leans forward and kisses my forehead. "Well, I'm sure you already know I missed you too, because I've been blowing up your phone all week." We both laugh and the familiar feeling of sharing a joyful moment with him fills my heart with joy.

"How did the meeting with your agent go on Saturday?" I make my first move by steering the conversation away from what happened at the coffee shop. It'll be great if it never comes up, but I know that's just wishful thinking.

He lets out a sigh and shakes his head. "Well, Sam loves the book and wants to represent me."

"Really?" I gasp and squeeze him into a tight hug. "That's good news, right?" I ask when he forces a smile.

"Yeah, but only if I take the faith element out."

"Oh." My shoulders drop. "Why would he ask you to do that?"

Jevaun shrugs. "So that it appeals to the general market and so that it'll be easy for us to sell the book."

I frown. "Doesn't he represent Christian fiction?"

"That's what I thought too, so I'm a little confused by what he's asking me to do."

I shake my head and scratch my scalp before flipping my braids to the back. "So, what are you going to do?"

"Well, he said I can take as much time as I need to think about it and make the revisions. So I've been praying about it.

God brought me this far, so he's going to help me get over this hurdle."

I nod and hold his hand. "Yes, that's right. I'm sure whatever the outcome is, it'll be favourable for you."

"Yeah." He turns to look at me. "What about you? How's writing going?"

"I've been trudging along. I'm writing a bunch of sad scenes at the moment, so I've been channelling all my sad emotions from last week into the book." And that's all I needed to say to open the can of worms.

Why did I have to say that? How do I get myself out of this hole now?

"Hmm." He turns to face the front again. The tension in the air is so palpable you could cut it with a knife.

"Jevaun, I'm really sorry for shutting you out. I...I just..."

"It's okay." He places his gloved hands on my thigh as his deep brown eyes stare into mine. "I just want to know if it's something I did that made you sad."

"No." I shake my head vigorously. "Absolutely not. You've been nothing but kind to me from the moment we met."

"Okay." He shifts in his seat as a couple walks past us holding hands and laughing. "Was it about the man at the coffee shop, then?"

A sinking feeling pinches my chest. "What?" My voice comes out in a whisper.

"The man at the coffee shop who called out your name just before you ran out."

Oh, no.

"Is he the reason you had to take some time out for yourself? The reason you were sad?"

"Erm..." Even though my answers don't come, Jevaun carries on.

"Bex, who is he? Did he hurt you?" He holds my elbow gently, the sobs already building up in my chest.

"Please, can we talk about something else?" I whisper.

"Bex..."

"Please, Jevaun. Can we change the subject?" I lift my head to look at him, my voice firmer this time, as tears slide down my cheeks. I can't believe I came here to explain, and now I can't even bring myself to say a word without choking up with tears.

What is wrong with me?

Jevaun pauses, the concern in his eyes making me sick to my stomach. He opens his mouth to say something, but we're both interrupted by three pings from my phone.

We both look down at it on the bench at the same time, watching the notifications slide in. It only takes a few seconds to read the words, and those few seconds ruin everything for me. I reach for the phone and turn it off, but it's too late now.

"Is that him?"

"I can't do this." I stand up, placing the phone in my pocket and taking retreating steps while shaking my head. "I'm sorry, Jevaun, but I can't do this."

"Bex, I'm only trying to help. Please talk to me." He takes a few steps towards me, but I turn around and make a run for it.

***

"I told you this wasn't a good idea, but you don't listen." Vanessa walked into her room and slammed the door shut before throwing herself on the bed and sobbing into her pillow.

Diana walked in shortly after, taking a seat on the bed next to her daughter. "My darling, I was only trying to help you," she said, tears streaming down her face. "What do you want me to do? You won't speak to me, you won't speak to Pastor Kemi, you won't speak to anybody about it. What do you want me to do?"

"Nothing, Mum." Vanessa sat up and wiped her eyes. "I don't want you to do anything. Just stop making a big deal out of nothing. I don't like telling people my business, so stop telling them, please. I told you I'm fine, so can we just stop talking about it?"

"Are you sure?"

"Yes, I'm fine. I'm not the first person and I won't be the last. I've learnt from my mistakes. Now please, just let it go."

Diana was silent for a moment, and then she sighed. "But what about the boy who did this to you? Aren't you going to report him to the university or the police? How can a rapist become a doctor?"

"Mum, please, stop." Vanessa's voice cracks. "I said I want to let it all go. I just want to focus on getting better." She sniffled as her mum stared into her eyes.

Diana reached for Vanessa's face and wiped her daughter's tears before saying, "Okay, then. If you say so."

Diana never brought up the matter again for the rest of the Christmas break, as Vanessa had requested. But only Vanessa knew the whole truth. She was not fine. As much as she wished she was. As much as she wished she could erase the imprints of his hands on her body and his face in her dreams, she knew she was far from fine.

But nobody else needed to know that. She was determined to live through the pain and find herself again. God might have abandoned her when she needed Him the most, but she was determined to pick herself back up again.

Christmas celebrations weren't the same. Vanessa remembered how sad it was for the family when they had the first Christmas without her dad. But the sadness she felt then was only a blip. It couldn't stand in comparison to her current sadness.

But Vanessa had no choice. She had to push through. She had told her mum she was okay, so she needed to be okay. Even if it meant withdrawing herself from her relatives who had come to spend Christmas day with them. But at least she didn't need to worry about bursting into tears in front of her cousins, aunties, and uncles.

Vanessa had promised her mum she was okay, so she had to be okay. Even if it meant forcing the *jollof* rice and chicken down her throat, even though she had no hint of an appetite. She couldn't remember the last time she enjoyed food.

Vanessa had promised her mum she was okay, that's why when the nightmares woke her up from sleep, and knocked the air out of her lungs, she had to use her pillow to muffle her sobs, because there was no way her mum or her brother could find out that she had been waking up every hour during the night for the last ten weeks.

So she persevered until they celebrated the new year. Soon, it was time to go back to uni and even though Vanessa couldn't shake away the impending sense of doom, she trudged along, because she had a point to prove. She was absolutely fine.

"Nessa, have you picked your outfit for church tomorrow?" Anne poked her head into her room, carrying a green long-sleeved top.

"No," Vanessa responded without looking up as she focused on unpacking her suitcase.

"Okay, what do you think of this top? I've never worn it before and I want to try it tomorrow." Anne placed the green top across her body and struck a pose.

"It's okay. You should wear it," Vanessa said, her back still bent over her suitcase as she took out her clothes really slowly.

First her t-shirts, then her jeans, and then the other pair of shoes she took home with her.

"Nessa?" Anne sat on her bed. "How can I help? Do you want us to go for a walk? Should we watch a movie together? Should I get you the Thai food from the market that you love so much?"

Vanessa shook her head and sighed. "There's nothing you can do, Anne. I just...I just need to be left alone."

Anne nodded before standing up. "Understood." She walked to the door before turning back to look at her friend. "What about a prayer request?"

At this question, Vanessa lifted her head and looked at Anne. If she had asked her this eleven weeks ago, she would have jumped at the opportunity because she indeed believed in the immovable power of prayer.

But she didn't want to give herself false hope again. What was the point of praying when she never stood a chance at winning? Besides, pity was the last thing she needed in her life. She had already given herself enough pity. She didn't need anyone else adding to that. She was fine, after all. This was just a season that would pass. She just needed to wait for the night to be over.

"No, I'm good," Vanessa responded before going back to folding her clothes. She felt Anne's confused gaze on her, but there was nothing left to say. No one else understood what she was going through.

"Okay, then." Anne let out a sigh. "Good night, Nessa." She shut the door again, leaving Vanessa to her wandering thoughts.

Even though her train of dark thoughts surprised her, she welcomed them with each passing day. What was the true way out for someone like her? Someone who had to deal with the stigma, the regret and also the unerasable memory of that night.

What was the true way out of the endless cycle of shame,

guilt, and pain that had made a permanent home in her heart and her mind? How did one ever win against a battle like that?

She placed her shower bag down on her bed and lifted her head to look at herself in the mirror. She caught sight of her Bible again on her desk and, for a moment, she desperately wanted to hold on to the familiar part of her that once felt the peace that came from resting in God's arms.

But how could she go back to Him when she felt betrayed, abandoned, and handed over to the hands of her adversary? How could she even explain just how much anger was eating her up every single day?

She didn't want to be disappointed again, so she averted her gaze from the Bible, and swallowed the urge to open it and read from the ninety-first psalm. Because nothing about her situation felt like she could call God her refuge and her fortress.

27

JEVAUN

I press the doorbell outside Rachel and Rhoda's flat and tuck my hands back into my coat pocket to keep them away from the freezing temperatures. The light comes on from the inside, followed by the sound of footsteps, and then the door opens.

"Hi, Jevaun." Rhoda opens the door and lets me in. "Rachel is in the living room." I place my coat on the cloth hook and leave my shoes in the hallway before following Rhoda's lead.

"Hi, Rachel. Thanks for letting me come over on such short notice," I say as she gestures for me to sit down. Rhoda takes a seat next to her sister on the sofa opposite from me.

"That's okay. You sounded really worried over the phone yesterday and it's about our sister, so of course we're going to do everything possible to help."

"Thanks, I appreciate it." I lean forward before getting straight to the point. "I'm really worried about Bex and I just wanted to ask if she said anything when you spoke to her last week?"

The girls look at each other briefly before Rachel speaks.

"Well, she just said she had an IBS flare up and she was also busy writing, so she took the week off to rest."

"Okay, did she say anything else?" I ask.

"No, but did something happen?" Rhoda frowns before shuffling to the edge of her seat.

I take a deep breath in and exhale. I didn't want it to come to this. I didn't want to have to divulge personal information to her sisters, but given that I'm literally worried about her safety, I hope Bex will forgive me for doing this.

"Bex and I met up two Saturdays ago, as usual, for our writing date. She seemed absolutely fine when we talked and I went to order us some food. On my way back, I found her packing up her stuff, getting ready to leave, and she looked very shaken up. I asked her what was wrong, but she just told me she had to go. I was so confused and while I was trying to figure out what was happening, there was this man sitting at a table close to us, and he called out her name. As soon as he did that, Bex bolted out of the coffee shop."

"A man?" Rhoda asks.

"Yes, I don't know him and I've never seen him before. I ran after Bex because I wanted to make sure she was okay, but I couldn't catch up with her. When I went back to the coffee shop to get my things, the man was gone."

"Do you remember what this man looks like?" Rachel asks.

I rub my temples, trying to picture the scene in my head again. "Yeah, he was tall, dark-skinned, and had some stubble on his cheeks. That's all I remember."

The girls shake their heads.

"Hmm, any hint of a name?" Rhoda asks.

"Well, okay, here's where I think I might be on to something." I pause before continuing. "When Bex and I met up yesterday at Regent's Park, she seemed very uncomfortable when I brought up the man at the coffee shop and she begged me to change the subject. I was going to let it go because I saw how physically distressed the conversation was making her. Then, while we were talking, three notifications came through on her phone."

"Did you see what they said?" Rhoda cuts in.

"I only read the first message, and it was from one of her social media platforms. The message said something about talking about what happened between them in the past. I didn't catch the full username of the sender, but I know it had the name Jason in it."

"Jason?" Rhoda stands and walks to the back of the sofa before leaning her arms forward and repeating the name to herself.

"I don't think we know any Jason," Rachel says.

"Yeah, we do." Rhoda's eyes widen before picking up her phone from the centre table.

"We do?" Rachel turns to her younger sister, who is now frantically scrolling through her phone.

"Yes, remember her first boyfriend? The guy she dated when she was in her first year of uni?"

Realisation dawns on Rachel as she rushes to Rhoda's side. "Oh, that Jason."

"Yeah, she never spoke about him much, but it seems like she really liked him. That's why we were both shocked when she told us they had broken up and he had left the university. We forgot about him after that," Rhoda says. "It was a long time ago, but I'm pretty sure she sent us a screenshot of one of his photos and also a photo of them on their first date." She pauses. "*Aha*, I found it. Is that him?"

I take the phone from Rhoda and, without even having to look at the photo twice, I nod. The sight of his arm around Bex, and them sitting so close to each other, leaves a sour taste in my mouth. "Yes, that's him. Like I said, he has a stubble now, but still pretty much looks the same."

"Wow, okay. So she saw her ex again at the coffee shop, and he messaged her, but that doesn't explain her reaction," Rachel says, walking back to the sofa and sitting down.

"I hope I'm wrong about this, but I just have a feeling he did something really terrible to her." My gaze moves between Rachel and Rhoda as the next few words are heavy in my mouth. "Maybe he was physically abusive, maybe he..."

"Okay, I think we should speak to Bex about this." Rachel stands again and walks up to me. "I know you're worried about her, but I'm sure we'll get to the bottom of this and everything will be fine."

"Yeah, you're right. Everything will be fine." Of course it will. God is in control.

"Rachel and I can go back to the house tomorrow to speak to her again," Rhoda says, but I shake my head.

"Actually, if you don't mind, I'd like to speak to her." I cross my arms against my chest. "She doesn't know I've told you about this Jason guy, and since I know about him and the messages, maybe she'll be able to open up to me if I speak to her again. But I need your help because she hasn't been responding to my text messages or picking up my calls since yesterday."

"Yeah, okay, that's fine," Rachel says.

"But are you prepared to meet our parents? There's a high chance they'll both be home tomorrow." Rhoda places her hand on her hip, a smile tugging on the corner of her lips. "If you do, you'll definitely be getting a grilling."

"Don't worry, I think I can deal with that." I crack a smile.

"Okay, future brother-in-law. We're loving the confidence." Rachel claps her hands and for the first time, we can share a light-hearted laugh together.

"I just want to say, we really appreciate how much you care about Bex," Rachel says, and Rhoda nods in agreement. "I'm not sure how much she told you about her last relationship, but it was a disaster. You are everything Ayo was not and I love that for Bex. She's clearly going through a lot right now from the looks of things and if you didn't bring it up, we probably would've missed it. Bex doesn't like bothering others with her problems, so it usually takes a lot of prodding and poking to get her to share."

"Yeah, she definitely cares about you, too," Rhoda adds. "But please be patient with her as she processes this. She only withdraws like this when she is feeling overwhelmed. That's how she has always been."

"Of course, I understand." I reassure them. "Your sister is very special to me and I'll do everything I can to support her. Thank you, girls, so much for helping me."

I walk out of their flat, feeling a little lighter than when I first came in. But there are still so many unanswered questions, and I can only hope that the meeting with Bex goes well tomorrow. Hopefully, we can get one step closer to figuring out the mystery about this Jason guy.

28

BEX

loud sound pulls me out of my slumber and my eyes flicker open. The last thing I remember was sitting at my desk trying to finish writing the chapter I was working on. But I only had four hours of sleep last night and I was up at four AM with no hope of any sleep returning.

I thought I could pour all my energy into writing, but the fatigue finally caught up with me. I'm not sure how long I've been sleeping for and the fact that it's dark outside literally means nothing. It could be as early as four PM or as late as eleven PM.

Reaching for my phone on my bedside table, I tap on the screen to check the time. It's six PM, so there's still time to have dinner, take a shower, do some more writing, and then call it a night.

The doorbell rings again as I sit up and rub my eyes, trying to adjust to the light in my room that I forgot to turn off when I fell asleep. I thought I was dreaming the first time I heard the bell ring, but the sound of muffled voices coming from the living room downstairs confirms someone was actually at the door.

Pushing myself up from the bed, I slip my feet into my warm, fluffy slippers, and put my dressing gown on to hide the fact that I've been wearing my pyjamas all day. I open the door and walk down the stairs, my whole body aching with every step I take. Who would have thought that sitting and sleeping all day could make you feel so tired?

The voices get louder as I approach the bottom of the stairs, but my brain's still too foggy to make out the owner of the voice. Laughter erupts from the living room round the corner, and here's where I'm grateful I can slip in and out of the kitchen without anyone seeing me.

"Rebecca?" Mum calls out and I pause midway through opening the kitchen door.

I'm not really in the mood to meet anyone today—no aunty, no uncle, and no family friend. I just want to eat, write and sleep. Is that too much to ask?

"Rebecca?"

"Yes, Mum. I'm coming." I stomp my feet silently against the kitchen floor, before making my way towards the living room, opening the door, and then freezing when my eyes land on him.

They all turn their heads to look at me, Mum, Dad, and Jevaun. What I really want to do is close that door, run back up the stairs, lock myself up in my room and never come out. But my legs stay rooted in place, my whole body too paralysed from embarrassment to move.

"Jevaun? What are you doing here?" My hands fly up to my silk bonnet as I try to remember if I've even brushed my teeth or washed my face today.

Why would they ambush me like this?

"Oh, that's no way to greet your visitor, Rebecca." Mum beckons on me to come inside. "We were just telling him how you've been under the weather because you've been locked up in your room all week."

I think he already knows that, but thanks for reminding me again, Mum.

"You didn't tell us this was the young man you went out on a date with last month," Dad chimes in and here's the point where I wish the ground would open up and swallow me.

"You refused to show us his photo, but who knew he would turn up at our doorstep? He is very handsome o. A handsome young man." Mum sends Jevaun a big smile, and even though I had prayed for my parents to love him, this is definitely not how I pictured them meeting.

"Hi," I say, tightening my robe around my waist.

"Hey." He smiles at me, and the awkward silence that crosses the room sends tingles crawling up my spine.

We both look at my parents, who are now staring at us as if they've never seen us before, the grin on their faces making me cringe even harder. Here's the time where you hope they'll get the hint and leave, but not my parents.

I clear my throat and nod toward the door, and they spring to their feet.

"Well, I guess that's our cue to leave," Mum says, pulling Dad up with her. After a silent protest from Dad, he finally yields and follows Mum out of the room. "We'll be upstairs, darling. Just let us know if you need anything."

"Yeah, thanks, Mum." I keep the smile on my face until she shuts the door and then I turn to Jevaun. "What are you doing here?" I whisper, my smile completely gone. "Are you trying to get me in trouble?"

"Bex, I'm sorry. I just really wanted to talk to you."

"Then you call me instead of just showing up at my house unannounced." I want to be mad at him, but I really can't. I haven't been responding to his messages and I sure wouldn't have picked his calls, so what am I even on about?

"Bex, I'm sorry." He touches my elbow gently before closing the gap between us, and the annoyance in my chest disappears.

"Please, I just want us to talk." He looks down at me with his warm gaze and there's no way I can say no to that. If I were in his shoes, I probably would've done the same.

"Okay, fine." I walk past him, heading for the door. "This way." He follows me outside, and I shut the front door to ensure none of our conversation is overheard. Good thing is the front door light comes on, so we can at least see each other's faces in the darkness.

The cold air wraps around my exposed legs, and goose-bumps rush up my body. I really didn't think this through, but I'm just going to have to deal with it. "I'm here. What do you want to talk about?"

He raises his brows and shakes his head. "Really? Is this the game we're playing now?"

"Do I look like I'm playing games? Why did you have to come all the way here?"

"Well, because." He raises his voice, stops himself and lowers it again. "Bex, I'm worried about you. Something is going on and you don't want to tell me. I'm worried that you're in danger and this Jason guy is right in the middle of it."

"What?" My eyes widen and I take a step back. "How did you know his name? Have you been...have you been digging up about me?"

"No, I spoke to Rhoda and Rachel and they—"

"You spoke to...oh, my goodness," I turn around and place my hands on my head, mixed emotions welling up in my chest as my eyes become wet with tears. "I told you to let it be. I wanted to deal with this on my own, but you just had to get my family involved, didn't you?"

"Bex...no, I'm just trying to help."

"Well, you're making things worse, can't you see?" Tears

escape my eyes. "You're making it worse by forcing me to relive the memories I want to forget."

I wipe the corner of my eyes and sniffle. "You have to go, Jevaun, please. I need to get back to writing."

"Bex, please." He holds my wrist. "I know you're hurting, but you can't throw yourself into writing and hope the problem will go away. You have to deal with it head on or it'll keep coming back to haunt you."

"You know nothing about my pain." I pull my hand away. "You know nothing about what I've been through. God is literally using this book to heal me and..."

"But, Bex, it's not about the book."

"Yes, it's all about the book."

"Why?"

"Because Vanessa is me, okay?" The words come out of my mouth in frustration before I can even stop myself. My sobs fill the silence as Jevaun stares at me.

"What?" The shock in his voice is clear.

"You wanted the truth, right?" I sniffle. "Well, there you go. Vanessa is me. It was never about some girl I knew in my first year of uni. She is me, but the only difference is that Vanessa had the courage to tell people about her pain earlier in her journey. I kept it to myself for nine years. Nobody knows what I went through. I dealt with the pain, and the guilt, and the shame without telling anyone else. It was just me and God and it was out of that pain that this book was born.

"It has everything to do with the book because women in my shoes need to know that they can learn to speak up when someone else hurts them. It was something I was too afraid to do, but now I can share the lessons through Vanessa's story. So there you go. You wanted the truth and now you have it."

"Bex, I'm so sorry." He leans forward and reaches for my face, but I step back.

"Please, stop. I don't want your pity." I tighten the belt of my robe around my waist as a gust of wind passes by. "Why do you care so much, anyway?"

"Why do I care?" He frowns, looking at me as if I've asked the most ridiculous question ever.

"Yeah, why are you going through so much trouble for me?"

He drops his shoulders and lets out a sigh. "Because I love you, Bex."

His confession knocks the air out of my lungs as I stand there, staring at him, absolutely speechless. "What?"

"My heart smiles every time you smile, and it breaks into a thousand pieces every time I see you cry. I haven't been able to sleep at all for the last week because even though I didn't know the full story, I could tell you're hurting so much." His eyes glisten with tears as he takes a step forward, closing the gap between us.

"Yes, I'll never understand your pain, and I'm not claiming that I do. I don't even have any answers for you right now, but I have hope in God that we'll figure it out...together." He reaches for the side of my face and wipes a tear away. "Bex, no one has a perfect life and everyone comes with baggage, but God is still Jehovah Rapha and He is able to heal you."

My tears return as I look him in the eye, letting my guard down as I let him take my hand in his.

"I'll do anything you want me to do. If space is what you want, then I promise I'll respect that and give it to you. If you want me around, then I promise I'll always be there for you. I love you, Bex, and nothing about your past changes how I feel about you. I don't expect you to feel the same way about me, but I just want you to know that at this moment, I'd love to be the shoulder you cry on."

He leans his forehead on mine and I let him hold me. His strong arms wrap around my waist and he pulls me closer, before planting soft kisses on my temple. In that moment, I let myself come completely undone in his arms and he strokes my back as I sob on his chest.

If there was ever a perfect definition of rock bottom, then Vanessa was sure her life was it. It had to be, because there was no way things could get any worse. The trouble was, she didn't understand how people picked themselves up from a place like that.

The taste of misery was bitter, but the more she was in it, the more she wanted to stay in it. She had given up and there was no longer any will left in her to fight. What was the point of fighting when her life would never be the same?

She was never going to forget, so there was no point in continuing. She couldn't remember the last time she showered, and every time Anne knocked on her door to ask her if she would eat, she just told her she wasn't hungry.

It had been four days since being back at uni and she hadn't stepped out of her room. She couldn't tell what the time was, what day of the week it was, or what she was meant to be doing that day. All she wanted to do was lay on her bed and sleep for hours on end, so the pain would stop. But it didn't.

When Anne knocked on her door again at the end of the day, Vanessa was at the end of her tether. If it wouldn't stop, then she was going to make it stop. So with every strength she had left in her, she dragged herself out of bed and stood up, a dizzy spell overwhelming her before she steadied herself.

Opening the door, Anne's smiling face appeared in her view

as she brought out a plate of spicy *jollof* rice. "Look what I cooked."

The aroma filled Vanessa's nostrils, but even that was not enough to stop the determination in her mind. She walked past Anne and dragged her feet toward the kitchen without responding.

"There's also some salad in the fridge if you want," Anne said and followed Vanessa into the kitchen. Anne placed the plate on the kitchen table and opened the fridge.

Vanessa walked over to the kitchen sink and scanned the dishes lying in it and even the ones drying on the rack, but she couldn't find what she was looking for.

Anne's voice faded in the background as she rummaged through the fridge, her back towards Vanessa. One by one, she took out all the food items she thought Vanessa would fancy, but Vanessa continued her mission by opening the cupboard.

One by one, Vanessa moved the cutlery around, until her eyes landed on the perfect one that would do the job. Her mind never wavered from how sharp and shiny the knife looked lying there. All she wanted was some relief, that the pain would stop and that she would be free from the thoughts that plagued her mind and robbed her of her peace.

So even as the tears ran down her cheeks, Vanessa picked up the knife and turned around, holding out her left arm as her other hand shook.

At that moment, Anne turned around and froze at the sight of her friend. The bottle of SuperMalt dropped from her hand and by the time she could run across the kitchen to where Vanessa was, it was too late. The knife had done its job and the last thing Vanessa saw was the blood gushing out of her wrist before everything went black.

<h1 style="text-align:center">29</h1>

<h1 style="text-align:center">JEVAUN</h1>

I thought I'd experienced a few hard seasons in my life and come out of the other side in one piece, but this has been one of the hardest things I've ever had to do.

For the last two weeks, every time I sit at my desk with my Bible open in front of me, praying for Bex, I still get flashbacks of the pain in her voice when she told me what happened to her.

It has taken a lot of self-control not to hunt Jason down on social media, figure out where he lives, and then show up there to give him a piece of my mind. I'd never understand why some people can be so cruel.

I thought for a moment I was going to lose her, but I'm so grateful she was vulnerable with me. We have a long road ahead of us, but at least I know all hope is not lost.

Today's challenge is to smile and pretend to enjoy being in the company of my dad and his many girlfriends while praying I don't get in their way. Tré did a wonderful job hiring the decorators, caterers, and getting everyone here on time.

Moving the furniture around has made the living room more spacious and the blue sixtieth birthday banner and balloons have given the space some colour. The caterers perched in the corner are serving starters of spiced fried plantain, jerk spice wings, and also some drinks. There are old Jamaican tunes playing in the background, just like my dad loves. Tré and I are even wearing matching suits today, so I hope this will be enough to make Dad happy.

There are a total of fifteen guests, including Dad's two brothers and his sister. Tré told me he reached out to Mum's younger sister—Aunt Noelle who lives in Leeds with her family, but she said she was busy and couldn't make it. It's a shame because apart from the occasional video calls, we haven't seen Aunt Noelle since Mum died. Our busy schedules have made things so difficult.

"Wow, I have to admit that I was a little skeptical when you told me to leave all the planning to you." I turn to Tré, who picks up a glass of wine from the table.

"Really?" He smirks. "Why is that?"

"I just didn't see you pulling it off, but this is brilliant. I'm glad I didn't intervene, because I would have messed everything up."

"Yeah, you definitely would've. But the most important thing is that you're here. Thanks for coming, man." He squeezes my shoulder and smiles at me.

I have no other option but to smile back, sending a silent prayer to God that this event finishes without any fights or arguments. At least I owe it to Tré.

"So what's Dad's ETA?" I ask, and Tré looks at his watch before tapping on his phone screen.

"They should be here any minute now."

"Cool."

"Everyone, shh!!!" Tré shushes and closes the door to the living room. "They're here. Turn off the music and the lights."

The room plunges into darkness as everyone stays still in

their positions. The front door creaks open and Dad's voice comes through, followed by female giggles.

I roll my eyes and shake my head, grateful that we're in darkness and no one can see me. *Lord, please make the time fly by because I don't know how long I can take this for.*

As soon as Dad opens the door and turns on the light, everyone shouts out, "Surprise!"

Dad gasps as he takes a step back and laughs. Confetti goes up in the air and cheers erupt from the guests.

"Wow." He turns to his mistress next to him. "You did all this?"

"No, not me." The woman shakes her head and pulls her shawl over her shoulders before caressing his arm. "It was your sons." She points in our direction and Dad's gaze follows her finger.

Dad approaches both of us, his shoes leading the way. His shiny suit is the object of everyone's attention as he takes off his hat and places it over his chest. "Thank you so much." He opens up his arms wide, inviting us in for a hug.

Tré hugs him back without hesitation, while my hug comes with a bit more stiffness. But Dad taps both our backs before letting us go. "I'm so proud of you," he says, looking at Tré only before turning around to the rest of the crowd. "What a way to make their old man feel special, eh?"

Everyone cheers as the music returns and Dad goes off to greet everyone else who has come to celebrate with him. Now I can take a deep breath that the worst part is over. All that is left is for me to stay in my lane, and in an hour, when we've cut the cake and taken the photos, I can be on my way.

"Okay, give me a big smile." Joshua, the photographer Tré hired, brings his camera up in our faces and I wrap my arm over Tré's shoulders as we pose for the camera. "Brilliant, look at that." He leans over and shows us his brilliant shots.

"Wow, that's cool. Tré, please make sure you send these to me when they're ready."

"Of course."

An announcement goes out that it's time for more food, so after letting Dad go first, it's our turn, then the rest of the guests. The evening goes by slowly and I'm so in my head that I can't even fully appreciate how good the curry goat is.

I glance at my watch and it's half an hour until I can be on my way, so I find Tré and let him know so he can move things along. Tré announces it's time for Dad to make his speech, so everyone claps as he stands and walks to the centre of the living room space.

"Thank you all for coming. I don't think people realise just how much of a blessing it is to be this old and still look this good." He laughs, and the crowd joins him. Everyone except me. "It's a blessing I don't take for granted."

Of course you don't.

"But I'm very grateful to all of you. Thank you for taking out time in your day to make me feel special. And to my sons." He turns around to look at us. "Thank you for your brilliant minds. You know I'm always going to be proud. I love you," he says, and for the first time all evening, he actually looks at me. His gaze lingers for a bit before he turns to the crowd again and ends his speech.

If I didn't know Dad well, I would have actually joined the crowd to fall for his lies. But what if he actually meant those words? I shake away the thoughts and excuse myself before heading upstairs to use the bathroom. I release my tie around my neck before washing my hands and drying them on a paper towel.

Looking at myself in the mirror, I take a deep breath and exhale before looking at my watch again. Fifteen more minutes and then I can go. *Lord, please help me.*

I open the door to find Dad standing right outside the hallway, his hand in his pocket. "Hello, son."

Oh, no.

This is what I've been trying to avoid, and that's exactly what I've got myself into. "Hey, Dad."

"If I didn't know you well enough, I would've thought you were avoiding me all evening." The sarcasm in his voice is sickening. "I have to say, I was surprised to see you today."

"Why? You're still my father."

"Ah, I see. I'm glad your God still teaches you about giving respect to whom respect is due."

I bite down the response I want to give because that's what he wants. To keep pushing my buttons until I explode. I will not be doing that today.

"So, how's work? Or shall I say, how's the business?"

I frown. "Why do you ask? I thought you didn't care about that part of my life."

He laughs and shakes his shoulders, causing annoyance to bubble up in my chest. "Come on, what kind of father do you think I am?"

Once again, I hold myself from answering that question because I'm sure he's not interested in my answers.

"Business has been great."

"That's good." He rubs his hands and takes steps towards me. "Tréjon mentioned you were trying to get an agent to represent you. I was shocked because I thought you already had an agent and were publishing books. It's been five years, Jevaun. What's taking you so long?"

Here's where the mockery starts and from experience, it just gets worse from here, so I could walk away, but not without letting him know God is actually answering my prayers. "Actually, I had a call with an agent a few weeks ago, and he will represent me."

"Oh, that's fantastic." He claps his hands. "So why do I hear a *but* coming?"

"He would like me to think about cutting out the faith element of the book," I say before realising how I've just willingly given him another opportunity to taunt me.

"So why do you look all torn up about it? Does it really matter whether you talk about your God in the book? Take Him out and you'll see how the money will flow. Isn't that what you want?"

"No, Dad. It's always about the impact first and the purpose behind why I write. I write to show others about the power and glory of God, not just to have money."

He shakes his head and chuckles. "You see, this is where I marvel at just how brainwashed you always sound. Does that make any sense to you at all? Giving up an amazing opportunity like this, all for what? A God who doesn't care about you?"

"Okay, it was nice talking to you as always, Dad." I take a step aside and walk towards the stairs.

"Oh, but didn't your Bible say you should always be ready to give a reason for the hope that you have? Why are you walking away from this brilliant opportunity to prove me wrong?"

"It's not my job to prove you wrong, Dad." I turn back to him, knowing fully well I should continue walking. "God will do that Himself when He exposes you for all the horrible things you've done." He wants the truth, so I think it's time I tell him.

"Oh, I didn't know you had it in you to fight back. Go ahead and tell me what a wicked and despicable person I am. Aren't you the only righteous one? Tell me what sin I've committed now and how much fire and brimstone await me in hell."

"You have no shame." My nose flares as I look at him, wondering just what Mum saw in him that made her choose him every day until the day she took her last breath. "Mum loved you with everything she had, but we all know she deserved better. You couldn't even wait for her to die before you went about desecrating your marital vows by sleeping with your so-called business partners. I'm done having this conversation with you, but all I'll say is that it's time for you to repent of your sins and turn to God before it's too late.

"I love you, Dad, but," I gesture between us. "This relationship will never work unless you admit that you've wronged your dead wife *and* your sons. So when you're ready to have that conversation, you know where to find me."

I turn around to walk down the stairs, but pause in my tracks when I find Tré standing on the landing. Pain and confusion flash through his eyes as his gaze darts between me and Dad, and then he walks away.

I turn around to look at Dad again, who is still standing tall, with no sense of remorse in his features, and that's when I realise that it's truly time to move on.

BEX

Sniffles fill the air as Rachel and Rhoda sit on either side of me on my bed, their arms around my shoulders. The reason I kept what happened between Jason and me a secret was because I was scared of judgement—even from my own sisters.

I didn't know how they would see me, if they would think differently of me. The pressure of being the eldest child in an African home is that you have to live up to high expectations and always set good examples; well, at least that's what my parents have always told me from the moment I learnt I was going to be a big sister.

I couldn't tell them what happened to me. It wasn't their cross to bear. It wasn't their job to worry about me. I was the one who they had to run to for help and not the other way around.

"I'm so sorry you had to deal with all that alone." Rachel takes off her glasses and dabs the corners of her eyes.

Mum and Dad went to visit Aunty Vivian and her husband after church and they usually spend hours over there, so we have enough time to cry our eyes out before they return.

"I wish you had said something because we would've

supported you in taking Jason down. I can't believe he got away with it."

I shake my head and smile at the passion on Rhoda's face. I've always known my sisters would have my back, so I can't believe I entertained the thought of them judging me. It would have been a lot easier if I had their shoulders to cry on when I was in the thick of it.

"Yeah, and to think he had the nerve to reach out to you after everything he did?" Rachel lets out a frustrated groan. "I think he needs someone to give him a good punch."

I raise my eyebrows at her, because that's usually what Rhoda would say. "Yeah, I don't think it'll be a good idea to send someone who can't even hurt a fly to defend me."

Rachel elbows me. "Oh, come on, sis, you know what I mean." She sighs. "I hate that he did this to you."

"Well, let's look on the bright side of this. I've come a long way and things aren't as bad as they were at the beginning. But," I pause before my gaze focuses on my Bible, my journal and my laptop on my desk, "I think I still have a lot of healing to do."

I stand and walk up to my desk before pulling the chair out and taking a seat. I open my desk drawers and pick up a stack of my old journals, my fingers running through the spines until I find the exact one I'm looking for.

The purple leather-bound notebook was my first journal while I was in my first year of uni. When I first started journaling, I used to spend a lot of time decorating my journal pages with colourful stickers and washi tape while I listened to worship music in my room.

I used to dedicate a good portion of my Saturday mornings doing this and even though I don't do that anymore, it was important during that season of my life to keep me sane and to keep me soaked in God's presence.

It felt like having a date with God, every Saturday, with my cup of coffee, the music, my Bible and then a creative art expression before I poured out my heart to Him with my words.

Even after everything that happened with Jason, I still carried on. Even on the days when I didn't feel like opening my Bible, when the doubts came and the anxiety was at its peak, I would sit at that desk still, crying and letting my tears fall on the pages as I increased the volume of the music to drown out my sobs.

As the years passed, my priorities shifted because not only did I not have enough time to spend hours drawing in my journal, I also realised that what mattered more were the words. So now, it's just me, my notebook, and my colourful gel pens.

I flip the journal to a page dated three months after the incident with Jason, when I had had enough time to process everything and had finally stopped crying myself to sleep every night.

I run my fingers through the page, as they go over the dent caused by my tears. Then I smile and turn the page around to show the girls. "This has been my prayer for the last nine years."

They take the book from me and as they read through the page silently, I recite the prayer in my head, too.

My heart hurts and I've lost all my words.
I don't know what I'm supposed to do.
I don't know how I'm supposed to get through this.
But I know who You are and who You have shown Yourself to be.
So reveal Yourself to me, even in this painful situation.
Show me every day that You are still good and still kind.

Heal me, Lord, from the inside and out.
Heal me so I can have a reason to testify.

"Wow," the girls say at the same time before looking at me.

"Yeah." I nod and take the journal back from them. "I believe God has worked on my heart and I have made significant progress in my healing journey. But seeing Jason again triggered some very unsettling emotions inside me. So after speaking to Jevaun two weeks ago, I took some time out to pray and even though it's not something I ever considered before, I've decided that I'd like to try therapy."

Rachel nods while Rhoda scrunches up her nose.

"Sissy, are you sure?" Rhoda asks. "You really want to let a stranger into your business?"

"Hey." Rachel smacks Rhoda's arm before turning to me again. "I actually support this idea, sis. I'm glad that you've finally got to this point where you can talk about it. We'll definitely be praying for you, too. But yes, if there are trained professionals out there who can give you the strategies to help you unpack these emotions, then it's a bonus. I think you should try it."

"I will. In fact, I already saw my GP, and she was lovely. She sent me a list of some charities that provide counselling for women like me." I take the leaflets out of my bag and hand it to them. "They have one-to-one sessions and also group therapy sessions."

"Oh wow, so you have the option of telling even more people about your personal business all at once," Rhoda says, flipping the leaflet over and Rachel smacks her arm again. "*Ouch*, you've got to stop doing that."

I smile and respond to Rhoda. "Yes, I think I'm going to try the group therapy option first. It's a shorter waiting time and although it will put me out of my comfort zone, I think it will do me some good to know that I'm not alone. I mean, I know you girls will always be here for me and support me, but it's different when I can speak to others who actually relate, you know?"

They both nod.

"Yeah, that makes sense, I guess," Rhoda finally concurs. "You know we'll support whatever you want to do. We love you."

"Aww, I love you girls too." I hug both of them. "Oh, and, erm...can we just say this is also one of those things we keep Mum and Dad out of?"

"Of course," Rachel says.

"So, are you ready to tell us how your talk with Jevaun went?" Rhoda places a pillow on her thighs and leans on it.

"Yeah, you promised you'd give us the full gist," Rachel adds and I roll my eyes.

These girls never forget any promises. Why did I make yet another one?

"Okay, fine." I smile before letting out a breath. "He told me he loves me."

Rhoda squeals and a bright smile appears on Rachel's face as they both start talking over each other and throwing a hundred questions at me at a speed that makes it difficult to understand what they're saying.

"Girls, girls. Breathe." I raise my hands at them. "You have to talk one at a time."

"How did that happen?" Rachel speaks first.

I shrug as a smile forms on my lips. "Well, he came over, as you both know, since you didn't stop him."

"Listen, I tried to warn him." Rhoda raises a hand.

"Yeah, that's true. Rhoda tried, but the guy didn't even care. He's daring and we love it."

"Of course, he wouldn't care. He's in love." Rhoda shrieks again and I have to cover my ears this time.

"Okay, can you stop with your weird noises so I can finish my story?"

"Sorry." She covers her mouth with her hand.

"I gave him a hard time at first, because I didn't feel comfortable being that vulnerable with him. But I'd been vulnerable with him before and he was so supportive and encouraging when I told him about Ayo. He was just worried about me and wanted to make sure I was okay. If I was in his shoes, I'd be worried about me too. Even when I told him what happened, he didn't pressure me for the details. He said he loves me and wants to be there for me in any way I want."

"Wow, I actually believe him, you know?" Rhoda says.

"Yeah, it's obvious from his actions. I believe him too. I think he's a keeper. He's a good man, Bex. A good man."

"Yeah, I know." Another smile crosses my lips. "I'm so grateful that God brought him into my life, and if this relationship is going to work, then I have to work through these emotions. I don't want to project any of my past hurt on Jevaun. He doesn't deserve that. I need to work through it so that our relationship can be as healthy as possible."

"So, are you going to tell him the full details soon?" Rachel asks and I nod.

"Yeah, as soon as he recovers from his dad's sixtieth birthday party, which was yesterday. He and his brother have had a busy week planning it, so when he has had some rest, we'll meet later this week to have a chat."

"Cool, and what about your book? How's the story coming?" Rachel does her weekly check in on my progress.

"Well, I've decided to take a little break from that, actually. I'm eighty percent done, but I have to ask God for some direction for the last part of the book. I want to make sure that the lessons and the themes are clear, but I need to ask God first."

"Of course. I'm so proud of you, Bex. I can't believe you only have twenty percent left. Our sis is going to be an author." Rachel gives Rhoda a high five as if they just won some tickets to see a celebrity.

"Erm, calm down, please. Let me write the book first."

"The book is already written, as far as I'm concerned," Rhoda says.

"Amen," we say in unison.

"And then you can let me read it first, please. Like you promised." Rachel grins.

It seems like I've been making way too many promises lately.

"Actually, I promised Jevaun he'd read the book when it's done."

Rachel feigns a gasp. "Wow, I thought they said blood is thicker than water."

I chuckle. "Well, he'll be my critique partner and he'll help me make the book much better. So you'll be getting a better version."

"Okay, fine. If you say so." Rachel smiles.

"What about me? I want to read the book too," Rhoda says and Rachel and I burst out laughing.

"Since when did you start reading?" I ask and Rhoda squints at me.

"Excuse me, have you seen the number of papers I have to read to write my dissertation?"

Rachel cocks her head. "Sis, sorry to burst your bubble. But just because you have no choice but to read a bunch of papers for your thesis doesn't mean you like reading for fun."

"Oh, whatever." Rhoda rolls her eyes. "I just don't want to be left out of the loop."

"Don't worry, I'll narrate the story to you as I read it. How about that?" Rachel taps Rhoda's shoulder and her smile returns.

"That sounds like a plan." Rhoda grins. "So, who's hungry?"

JEVAUN

The silence in my living room right now tells you a lot about where my head is at the moment. I like to have music or a video playing in the background because I hate silence. But after the events of last night, I need the silence to help me process my thoughts.

The two things I feared the most happened last night. First was having another confrontation with Dad, and the other was Tré not only witnessing another one of our arguments but also finding out the truth.

Tré left the party early and when I asked him where he was going, he said he wanted to cool off. I haven't spoken to him since and he hasn't responded to my text messages or phone calls. I know he took the entire week off from work and he was supposed to be spending the rest of the week at my place, but now I'm not sure if he'll come over.

I should've just kept my mouth shut and walked away. I knew that was the right thing to do, but I chose otherwise. What was I trying to prove? Who was I trying to impress? I know better than to get into fruitless arguments with Dad. He only ever speaks about God to mock me. So why did I think yesterday's conversation was going to go any differently?

"I can't keep doing this to myself." I let my head fall in my hands as a heavy feeling settles in my chest. "Mum, I know I made a promise, but I'm sorry. I can't keep doing this."

I pick up the bowl of my half-eaten porridge and place it on the kitchen counter before walking into my office and sitting at my desk. I haven't done any writing at all in the last few days. First, it was because I was too busy worrying about what would happen at the party to concentrate on any writing.

Now I can't write because I've been worrying about Tré and all the ways our relationship could be ruined because of last night's events. I should've never gone back to that house. The last time I had an argument with Dad three months ago, I came so close to giving up on writing. If God didn't send Bex my way to remind me about my purpose, I don't know what would've happened.

Three months later, I'm back at the same spot, feeling so discouraged it has affected my creative routine. If I'm going to make progress in my career, I need to surround myself with people who believe in me. It's not that I need anyone's permission to fulfil my calling, but I need to do this to protect my heart.

My phone rings and my pastor's name flashes on my screen. I've been at Grace House for five years and every time I haven't been to church, Pastor John has always called or texted me to make sure I'm okay.

I pick up the call and bring the phone up to my ear. "Hello, Pastor John?"

"Hi, Jevaun. How are you?"

"I'm good, thank you." I lean back in my chair.

"That's great to hear. I was just calling to check on you. I remembered you mentioned about visiting your dad this weekend?"

"Yes, yes, you're right. It was his sixtieth birthday surprise party yesterday."

"Oh, that's amazing. I hope he loved the surprise. Your brother came down from Nottingham, right?"

"Yes, he did, and my dad loved the surprise." I rub my temple and close my eyes, hoping the conversation can end so I don't have to talk about Dad anymore.

"Okay, great." He pauses before speaking again. "Are you okay, though?"

I open my eyes again and straighten my back. "Erm...yeah, of course I am."

"Okay. I only ask because I had this tugging in my heart to pray for you today. God instructed me to pray about people who were feeling discouraged and immediately you came to my mind. I'm not sure why. Are you sure you're okay, Jevaun?"

I let out a heavy sigh and at that moment, the realisation hit me about how much this has been weighing on me. I open my mouth to speak and instead, tears roll out of my eyes. "Erm...no, not really." I sniffle and wipe my eyes before clearing my throat.

"I...uh...I guess you could say I've been experiencing some sort of persecution for my belief in God by a...close family member for the last five years. I thought I could brush it off because I love them and really want them to be in my life, but constantly being mocked for my faith in God is very discouraging."

"Hmm. I'm so sorry you've been going through that, Jevaun. It always gets complicated when it comes to family members or people that we love, doesn't it?"

"Yeah, for sure." I laugh, trying to stop more tears from falling.

"But it's important to guard your heart, Jevaun," he says. "Surround yourself with people who speak life into you and who encourage you to draw closer to God. Distance yourself from people who will remind you of pain and hurt. The last thing you want to do is to open your heart up to bitterness and hate. That'll only put you in a vulnerable place where the enemy can easily strike. Do you remember what Jesus taught in Matthew chapter five?"

"Yes, I do." I nod as he continues.

"He said those who are persecuted for righteousness are blessed and their reward is in heaven. He also encouraged us to keep praying for those who persecute us and let the joy of God continue to fill our hearts. God is proud of you, Jevaun. That's all that matters."

Pastor John's reminder strengthens my heart and my mind, and all that is left for me to do is confidently walk in that powerful promise that is in God's word. With God helping me, I can successfully overcome this and focus on God's calling over my life without worrying so much about what my dad thinks.

Three hours later, my doorbell rings and I push myself off the sofa, where I had settled in to watch some writing vlogs. I figured if I'm not in the mood to write, then maybe watching other authors meeting their goals will motivate me too.

I'm not expecting anyone and it can't be the mailman because I haven't ordered anything online. *Or have I?* I sigh and drag my feet toward the door as the doorbell rings again.

Looking through the peephole, relief washes over me and I take a step back before opening the door for Tré, my eyes dropping to the suitcase by his side. He's wearing a thick black coat with his hood up to protect his head from the pouring rain. I didn't even realise it was raining this hard.

"Come in." I step aside, letting him in and closing the door as a bolt of lightning flashes outside.

Tré takes off his wet coat and shoes and makes his way to the living room, before lowering himself on one end of the sofa. After putting his suitcase away, I join him on the sofa as he wipes the water from his face with the sleeve of his hoodie.

There's a lot to say, and I don't know where to start, so I let him take his time. I'm not sure if he has already spoken to Dad, and what Dad has told him about me, but the fact that he's here gives me hope.

Tré clears his throat and leans forward. "So...I spoke to Dad." His voice dispels the silence as thunder rumbles outside.

"You did?"

He nods.

"What did he say?" I ask, mentally preparing myself to spend the rest of our conversation defending myself.

Tré shrugs. "He didn't deny it." He sniffles and wipes his nose. "I confronted him about everything you said, and he didn't deny any of it." He turns to look at me, his eyes glassy with tears.

Emotions twist inside my chest as I notice the pain and hurt in Tré's eyes. This is exactly what I'd hoped wouldn't happen. At least I've known about this for years, and it took me a while to process my thoughts. But finding out the way Tré did must have been shocking for him. How will he ever come to terms with the fact that the man he has looked up to as his role model his whole life is actually not who he says he is?

"I couldn't believe it at first." He leans forward and rests his arms on his thighs. "So I called Aunt Noelle last night after the party."

I raise my eyebrows. "You did?" He actually beat me to it. I've been putting off that difficult conversation with Aunt Noelle for a long time and now that Tré has the answer, I'm not sure if I want to know.

"What did she say?" I brace myself for what I think is coming.

"She confirmed all the things you said and," he pauses and looks at me again. "She said Mum knew about Dad's extramarital affairs. She said it had been going on for years and Mum blamed herself for it because she was sick and couldn't look after her family properly."

"Wow." The revelation hits my chest like a ton of bricks. I push myself up and walk the length of the living room. Now I understand why Aunt Noelle stopped coming to the house after Mum died. She just couldn't bear to face Dad after everything he did to her sister. "I can't believe Mum knew about his affairs and didn't say or do anything." I shake my head in disbelief.

"Yeah, and the way she looked at him, with so much love in her eyes, even on her deathbed." Tears are rolling down Tré's eyes now. "How did she ever make peace with what he did? How did she find it in her heart to forgive him?"

I walk back to the sofa and sit next to my brother, putting my arm around his shoulders. "Tré, I'm really sorry you had to find out this way. I know this situation seems really messy right now, and of course, Mum isn't here to answer all our questions. But one thing I want to assure you is that she was very selfless and the legacy she left on this earth was her kind heart."

"Yeah, I know, and Dad took advantage of her." He wipes the corners of his eyes. "He has no idea how good a woman she was."

"You know, shortly before Mum died, she made me promise that I would make peace with Dad, no matter what."

"Of course she did." Tré shakes his head and smiles. "She was so optimistic, but she needs to see you both now. You two can barely stand each other, so how's that going to work?"

"Yeah, I asked myself that same question too for five years. That's why I kept coming back, even though Dad's words made me feel worthless. I kept showing up, hoping and praying that I'd see things through Mum's eyes."

Tré looks up at me. "But that's not going to happen, is it?"

I shake my head. "I'm definitely going to keep praying for him and for us, but I need to stay away for my own sanity. For my own peace of mind."

"See, I don't blame you for that. Knowing what I know now, I'm struggling to decide if I even want to go back there. I admire you for wanting to keep your promise to Mum, but if she was here, she'd understand that you've tried your best. Even God would understand that you've tried your best."

At Tré's mention of God, I smile and tilt my head. "Yes, you're right about that."

"You know, in a way, I feel some sense of closure. Even though it's a messy situation to be in, I've thought about everything and one thing I'm grateful for is how close you and I have become over the years. Having you in my life has been the greatest blessing, so it's not all bad." Tré taps my shoulder and smiles.

"Wow. You have no idea how happy that makes me, Tré. I was so worried about how you'd take all this. I'm grateful for you too and you know I love you, right, bro?"

"Of course I do." He wraps his arms around me, and we pat each other's backs before he lets go. "Okay, then. That has to do it for one night. What have you been watching?" He picks up the remote and presses a button to wake up my dormant TV.

"Oh, by the way, Aunt Noelle invited us to spend Christmas with her in Leeds. It'll be nice to catch up with our cousins, right?" Tré asks.

"That would be so much fun. I think we should video call them tomorrow too. It's about time I catch up with her too."

"Yeah, no worries."

The vlog I was watching earlier starts playing again on the TV with an ASMR clip of the author's fingers typing on their fluorescent keyboard.

Tré turns his head slowly to look at me. "Please, don't tell me this is what you've been watching all evening?"

"Come on, you don't like the sound of the tapping keys? It's so soothing."

"You're such a geek."

I laugh. "What? No, this is just part of the vlog. Trust me, it was more action-packed before you walked in. The author was narrating the story about how she lost her manuscript because she forgot to back up her files."

"Oh, you're such a geek," he repeats and I smack his shoulder. "How about we play some FIFA, huh?"

"Say less, bro." I pump his fist and grab the remote while he sets up the Xbox. This day couldn't have turned out any better. They say you win some and lose some. But in this case, like Tré said, I'm only choosing to count my blessings. I still have the people I care about in my life, and that's all that matters to me.

32

BEX

I smile at Jevaun, who is sitting next to me on the sofa, holding my hand while Rachel makes dinner behind us. We both offered to help her, but she forbade us from coming into the kitchen because after surviving another stressful term at school, spending some alone time cooking is what she needs to destress.

Now that she's on her two-week Christmas break, she'll have more time to accommodate more orders on her website. There's something about chopping, peeling, seasoning, and stirring that makes Rachel so happy, and you just have to let her get lost in her own little world.

I haven't had the courage to go back to The Buzz Café because I can't shake the feeling that Jason will be waiting for me there. I know I'm being a little paranoid, as I'm sure the guy has better things to do with his life, but I never responded to his messages and I think he might try to find me in person again.

I'm not sure how I feel about seeing him in person, so for now, I've decided to lay low. Not gonna lie, it feels like I'm taking ten steps backwards because I was finally getting out of my shell and overcoming my anxiety about going out. But I'm trying to see this season as temporary and one that is necessary for my healing journey.

Mum and Dad don't know about Jason, so for now, Jevaun and I agreed to meet at Rachel and Rhoda's flat, so I can tell him the full details. Rhoda is staying late at uni today and Rachel is the perfect chaperone because she's always cooking and I can never say no to a good meal.

"Is Tréjon back in Nottingham now?"

Jevaun shakes his head. "No, he'll be leaving this evening. I'll take him to the train station."

"Oh, okay. How did your dad's party go last week? You didn't say much about it."

Rachel pours some onions into her pot of hot oil and the aroma diffuses into the atmosphere as she stirs.

He sighs and looks at me. "Yeah, it was a lot, for lack of a better description."

I frown and lower my head so my gaze meets his. "What happened? Did you and your dad argue?"

He nods and tells me everything that went down at the party, his dad's affairs, the revelation his aunt told Tréjon about his mum and the conversation he had with Tréjon a few days ago.

"Wow, I'm glad Tréjon has made peace with the whole situation."

"Yeah, that's what I'm most grateful for. I don't know what I would've done if this situation had severed our relationship."

"Your mum was a true peacemaker, wasn't she?" I wrap my arm around his and lean my chin against his shoulder.

He smiles. "Yeah, she was."

"But you know, she would've been proud of you if she was here, right?"

Again, he nods. "Yes, I know."

"I'm proud of you, too, babe." He turns his head to look at me, his face so close I can feel his warm breath against my face.

My gaze wanders from his eyes to his nose and then down to his lips, only a few inches away from mine.

"That means a lot." He closes the gap between us and covers my lips with his. I've missed the softness of his lips, and the way he holds my face with so much tender-loving care when he kisses me.

Rachel clears her throat from the kitchen and bangs the wooden spoon against the pot. "Guys, you better be careful. I'm still here."

We all laugh as we break the kiss. "Yes, *Ma*."

A moment of silence passes between us before Jevaun speaks again. "So, how have you been, really?"

I shrug. "I've been better. But I'm not at my worst." I straighten my back and scratch my temple. Now is not the time for my scalp to play up. I took off my braids last night, but didn't have the strength to wash my hair, so I tucked it all underneath an orange turban today.

"I think I'm ready to tell you everything now."

"Okay." He adjusts in his seat.

I take a deep breath and exhale, hoping that I won't end up in tears like I did when I told Rachel and Rhoda last week.

"Jason and I met in my first year of uni. We were both studying our BSc in accounting and finance and on our first day of lectures, we sat next to each other in the lecture theatre. Being the introverted person that I am, I was quiet throughout the lecture because I was too scared to say the wrong thing or make the wrong impression. I hadn't made any friends because I didn't really attend many freshers' events and all I did was stay in my room and watch movies.

"Jason was the first person who ever tried to be friends with me. That day after the lecture, he commented on how bored he was because of the lecturer's monotonous voice and the way he said it was so funny, I surprised myself when I laughed out loud.

He then introduced himself and the more we talked, the more we realised how much we had in common.

"He is also the eldest child in his family, and he has two brothers and a sister. But he was nineteen then because he had taken a gap year before uni. His family is from Zimbabwe, so he could relate to some of my struggles growing up in an African household. We spent the first few months getting to know each other while adjusting to uni life. He said he was a Christian, but we never really talked about God and I never asked because I was too busy falling for him to question his beliefs and convictions.

"He treated me well, so I fell for his charms. He officially asked me to be his girlfriend after the Christmas break and, of course, I said yes because I was in love with him. I even remember when we went on our first date at a Mexican restaurant. He took a photo of the two of us and that's the one I sent to the girls. He respected my decision for us to wait until marriage before having sex, and that was a huge green flag for me. Everything was going great until it wasn't." I shake my head and swallow the lump building in my throat as I recall the next part of the story.

"He changed. Suddenly. He became very controlling of everything I did. When I started making friends with other people in the course or at church, he became very angry. He would shout at me and tell me I was a horrible girlfriend because I didn't make him my priority. He constantly commented on what I ate, who I hung out with, and where I went."

Jevaun shakes his head and closes his eyes, his jaws tightening as he asks, "Did he hit you?"

"Not at first. But he threatened that if I left him, he was going to hit me. I felt so ashamed to tell anyone about what he was doing to me because I had hyped him up so much to my sisters and I hadn't really made any other close friends to rant to. I wasn't active in my uni church at the time and even though different people tried to form relationships with me, I pushed them away because I was scared of what Jason would think."

I adjust in my seat and blink back the tears. "Just before we went on our Easter break, I went to visit him at his flat and he was in a very bad mood. He had just had an argument with his dad over the phone, but when I tried to ask what the situation was, he just kept shouting at me. His flatmates had gone out, and I was uncomfortable staying there with the mood he was in, so I offered to leave...but he didn't let me.

"He accused me of being self-righteous and said I was leaving because I thought he was a sinner for arguing with his dad. Everything happened so quickly, because I remember I was so uncomfortable I actually wanted to run out of the room, but he overpowered me, slapped me a few times and next thing I knew, I was back on his bed, and..." The tears are rolling out of my eyes now as the words catch in my throat.

"It's okay, babe." Jevaun pulls me close and kisses my temple. "I'm so sorry you had to go through that. I'm sorry."

The warmth of his embrace soothes my sobs as he strokes my back. He waits for me to go quiet before planting another kiss on my forehead. "You okay?"

I nod.

"Are you sure you want to keep talking about this?"

I breathe out a sigh and nod. "Yeah."

"Okay." He holds my hand again as I continue the story.

"That entire experience broke me, Jevaun. I couldn't tell anyone because I was ashamed and still in shock about how I had let myself get into that. When I went back to uni after the Easter break, Jason was gone. I found out weeks later from one of his friends that he left the university because he got an admission to study medicine in Malta. That's what his dad had always wanted him to do, so maybe that's what they were arguing about over the phone.

"For years, I blamed myself for what happened and bottled up those emotions inside me. I knew he was the only one in his flat that day, but I still went to see him. It affected the way I saw myself, and that's why I tolerated Ayo's actions for so long. I just didn't think I had any worth left after what Jason did to me, so I didn't have the right to pick and choose which men were interested in me. I thought that because I was damaged, I had to accept whoever came my way." I wipe my eyes before lifting my head to look at Jevaun.

"But God helped me break out of that mindset and he taught me about finding my worth in Him, regardless of my past traumas. Now He wants me to deal with those traumas head on, instead of running away from them like I've been doing for the past nine years. So next month, I'm going to be starting group therapy. I already had my initial assessment and my first session has been scheduled for the first week of January. I've been holding on to these emotions for too long and now I want to let them out and deal with them."

"I'm so proud of you." Jevaun leans his forehead on mine. "I think you're so brave and I know God will help you get through this. I know this must have been so hard for you to do, but I appreciate you being vulnerable with me."

"Thank you for always encouraging me to be the best version of myself." I run my hands over his cheeks and play with his beard. "Even when you didn't know the full story, you always made me believe in the woman God has called me to be. I love you, Jevaun."

A wide grin appears on his face as he raises his brows. "Hang on a minute. Did you just say you love me?"

"Yeah, she did." Rachel responds for me and I chuckle. I

thought she was listening to music the whole time with those headphones over her ears.

"Yes, I love you," I repeat. "It might have taken me a while to realise it, but I can't keep denying the fact that what I feel for you is real and stronger than anything I've ever felt for anyone else before."

"Okay, now you're going to get me all emotional." He smiles and I push his shoulder gently. "I love you." He pulls me close again and kisses me, before Rachel makes another interruption to let us know food is ready.

So we stop playing *love birds* and get down to the real business, which is stuffing our bellies, starting with the fish rolls and beef *soya*[1], and followed by delicious chicken stew and white rice.

Vanessa opened her eyes to a dimly lit room, completely disoriented and with no memory of how she got there. But as she pushed herself up, the pain that shot up her left wrist juggled her memory and she groaned.

Laying back down, she let out quick breaths and waited for the pain to subside before bringing her wrist up to inspect. It was covered in a bandage and there was a cannula inserted into the back of her right hand, the IV line running to a beeping machine standing tall next to her bed.

She tugged on the neckline of her hospital gown and turned her head slowly to look outside the window when a woman walked past wearing a blue nurse's uniform. Then two more women walked past in green uniforms.

She pressed the buttons on the bed rail next to her, waiting for the head of the bed to slowly rise as she massaged her forehead to ease the headache. How did she let herself get to that point? Shame took over her as she looked down at her wrist. Why did she do that to herself?

Outside the window, she caught a glimpse of the nurse's station where a tall Caucasian man was talking to someone, and from the blue scrubs and stethoscope around his neck, she assumed he was a doctor.

The doctor turned around and looked toward her room, revealing the person he was talking to, and Vanessa's stomach sank. She froze in her position as her mum's gaze met hers.

As she watched her mum run toward her room, her heart rate increased and if the ground could open up and swallow her whole, then that would've been the perfect time. How was she going to look into her mother's eyes and answer the questions about how she got here?

God, please forgive me.

"Vanessa?" The door swung open and then shut again as Diana walked in, her arms stretched out. "Oh, my daughter. You're awake." She put the bedrail down and sat on the edge of her bed before wrapping her arms around her daughter, the warmth of her hug making Vanessa relax.

"You're awake." Tears streamed down her mum's cheeks as she held Vanessa's face in hers. "I was so worried about you. I thought I'd lost you." She hugged Vannessa again.

"Mum, how did you know I was here?"

"Anne called me last night when you were in the ambulance, so I left work and made my way straight here. Thank God she was there when it all happened."

A lump built in Vanessa's throat as more details of the night before came rushing back to her memory. "But what about Victor?"

"Don't worry about him. He'll be staying with Aunty Veronica from church for a few days."

"Does he know about this?" She looked down at her wrist, the feeling of guilt and shame attacking her again.

"No, he doesn't. But please, darling, there's a doctor outside who would like to speak to you. He said he's from the psychiatry team and they want to talk about what happened last night. Please."

"Mum, I don't..." She started to protest, but stopped herself when she remembered where protesting and refusing help had gotten her. "Okay, fine. But just one meeting."

"Thank you so much. I will let them know and they will come in later when you have eaten and rested."

With her mum's help, Vanessa washed and dressed. Then they removed her IV line and her cannula. Her mum helped her get into the chair and even though she didn't like the sandwich and ice cream the hospital gave her, she was grateful she now had an appetite for food after not caring for weeks.

A knock on the door made Vanessa and her mum lift their heads as a middle-aged South Asian man walked in. "Vanessa Molua?"

"Yes, doctor. Please come in," her mum responded and stood up. "She's the one. My daughter."

"Vanessa, my name is Dr. Raj Kapoor. I'm from the psychiatry team. Do you mind if we have a quick chat?" He rolled the sleeves of his shirt up his elbows before opening the notebook in his hand.

Vanessa nodded and bowed her head while her mum hugged her again.

"I'll be waiting outside, so you can be free to talk to him. Let me know if you need anything, okay?" Her mum stepped outside of the room, leaving Vanessa alone with the doctor.

The man pulled a chair and placed it across from Vanessa's

meal table before taking a seat. "How are you feeling today, Vanessa?"

She shrugged. "Better, I guess. Grateful to be alive."

He makes some scribbles onto the notebook on his lap. "Okay, that's good to know. Do you want to talk about what happened last night?"

Vanessa shook her head and averted her gaze.

"Okay, how about we talk about how you're feeling now? How would you describe your mood at the moment?"

She fiddled with her fingers. "Better than it was last night, for sure."

"Would you be able to rate it for me out of ten?"

She shrugged. "I don't know, maybe three?"

"How long has your mood been low?"

"A few months at least."

He nods. "Have you ever struggled with low mood or anxiety in the past?"

She shook her head.

"Was there any significant life event that affected your mood in the last few months?"

Vanessa paused before looking out the window. She had promised her mum she would engage, so she had to try her best because she didn't want to end up back here. "Yes, I was sexually assaulted, but I'd rather not talk about it in detail, please."

"Okay, that's fine." He looked her in the eye. "I'm sorry that happened to you."

Vanessa only nodded, but said nothing else.

"Have you ever thought about talking therapy to deal with the emotions of that event?"

Vanessa shook her head.

"Is it something you'd like to try?"

"Yes, but for now, I just want to go home." She lifted her head to look at the doctor. "I regret what I did last night. I never want to do that again because I love my mum and brother so much. It was just a moment of weakness and I gave in because I have refused support so far. But I'm ready now, and I don't think being here is helping me either. Please, I want to go home. I'll book an appointment with my GP who knows about my situation. I just don't want to be here, please."

"Okay." The doctor nodded. "We'll get you home as soon as you're given the all-clear. We'll write to your GP as well to update them about what we've talked about and make some recommendations going forward. Is that okay?"

Vanessa nodded and as she watched the doctor leave her room, some level of comfort washed over her. Just knowing that she didn't want to be in that dark place again was enough motivation for her to finally do the right thing and seek help.

God, please forgive me. Please, help me.

33

BEX

Christmas and New Year celebrations are over and while I appreciated the distraction of the decorations, happy music, delicious food, and the warmth of having family celebrating the birth of Jesus, it's time for me to get right down to business and take that significant leap of faith with God. It might scare the living daylights out of me, but that doesn't matter because I'm doing it with God.

I swipe left on my phone screen to read the last few text messages from Jevaun. He has been so determined to ease my anxiety about these group therapy sessions. If it was possible for him to come with me, just so I don't feel alone, then I'm sure he would've jumped at the opportunity. But I need to do this and hopefully by the end of these six weeks, I'll feel less alone fighting this battle.

After opening my Bible app, a sense of peace washes over me because it can't be a coincidence that the verse of the day is 2 Timothy 1:7, reminding me about how God has not given me a spirit of fear, but of boldness and love and a sound mind. I'll never stop being amazed at how intentional God is about me.

I put my phone on silent and place it inside my bag, alongside my journal, a pack of coloured gel pens, a bottle of water, and the small orange wallet which houses my oyster and bank cards.

Looking up at the grey building in front of me, dread settles in my chest, the same feeling I had the first day I went with Jevaun to the writing group session. But that experience turned out to be one of the best decisions I've ever made for my writing career. I need to see this process as the same thing. Just because it's terrifying at face value doesn't mean it'll be a terrible experience.

I walk through the automatic doors at the front entrance, the warm air enveloping me as I follow the signs leading to the Arise charity hub. Taking off my scarf, I unzip my coat before mustering up the courage to speak to the woman sitting at the reception desk.

Breathe, Bex. God is with you.

"Good morning." The woman smiles at me. "How can I help?"

"Morning. I'm here for a group therapy session?"

She lowers her gaze to the computer. "Sure, can I take your name?"

"Rebecca Ayuk," I respond, watching the woman type on the keyboard and scanning the screen.

"Yes, your session is up on the second floor, in the Lily room. Lifts and stairs are down that way." She points to her left. "When you come out of the lift, turn right, and the room is at the far end."

"Thank you so much."

Up on the second floor, I step out of the lift and into the corridor with light green carpet all around. The instant calming scent that teases my nostrils pulls me further down the corridor as I approach the Lily room.

I poke my head into the room and there's a woman inside,

arranging the chairs into a semi-circle and placing sheets of paper and pens on them. "Hello?"

The woman turns around to look at me, her glasses sitting on the bridge of her nose as she pats down her brunette pixie cut. "Hi, are you here for the group therapy session?" she asks and I nod. "Oh, goodness, you're early. My name is Charlotte, the counsellor." She shakes my hand as I introduce myself.

I was half an hour early, but I had to choose between that and arriving twenty minutes late because the bus times were moving mad today. There's no way I would choose to walk in late and have all eyes on me.

"Please take a seat, and hopefully the others will join us soon." She hands me a blank sheet of A4 paper and a pen before carrying on with her task. I fold the paper and put it in my bag before taking out my journal and gel pens instead.

Half an hour later, four more people turn up and occupy the seats around the room with Charlotte at the front and centre, facing us all. While waiting for everyone else to arrive, no one says anything, so I drop my gaze and fiddle with the pages of my journal. I even write the date in the top right-hand corner before breathing out a sigh of relief when the last person walks in.

"Good morning, everyone. Welcome to your very first Arise group therapy session." Charlotte finally breaks the silence, her loud, cheery voice almost jerking me out of my seat. "It's so wonderful to meet you all. My name is Charlotte, and I will be your counsellor for the next six weeks. You have all taken a big step to be here today, and I hope you will find it beneficial when we get to the end."

She crosses her legs and adjusts her flowy dress as the hem hits the carpeted floor. "These sessions will last approximately 1-2 hours and there are few things that will be useful to know. First, everything that happens inside this room is confidential and we need to treat each other with respect. Although you will all get the most out of these sessions if you participate, I want this to be a safe space for everyone, so you don't have to feel pressured to speak or share."

Oh, thank God for that.

Charlotte presses her bright-red lips together before saying, "Now, I'd like for each of you to introduce yourself, and if you don't mind telling us why you have joined us today, that'd be great."

The room plunges back into silence, and once again, I drop my gaze to my open journal, this time underlining the date and even drawing a rectangle around it. It feels like I'm in school again, trying to avoid being picked on by the teacher to answer a question.

"I can start." The voice comes from the woman sitting next to me, who is wearing a hoodie and blue jeans. She introduces herself as Josie, a twenty-eight-year-old who recently got the courage to break up with her boyfriend, who was physically abusing her for two years.

Fatima speaks next, a twenty-six-year-old mother of three, who recently summoned the courage to report her abusive husband, who brought her into the country from India. Thérèse is a thirty-three-year-old Ivorian woman who came into the country four years ago as an asylum seeker, but ended up getting sexually assaulted by a friend who promised to take care of her.

Laura is a thirty-year-old data analyst who was sexually assaulted by her previous employer and is currently undergoing a court case. Then Alice speaks last, and she is a forty-year-old woman who was sexually abused by her father until she was twenty years old.

Listening to all these women share their stories tugs at my heartstrings so much that I don't even realise when it's my turn to share.

"Rebecca?" Charlotte's voice pulls me out of my thoughts. "Would you like to introduce yourself?"

"Erm...yeah, sure. Hi everyone, my name is Rebecca, but you can call me Bex. I'm twenty-seven years old." I take a deep breath before saying the next few words, my previous reservations about telling my business to strangers flying out the window because I know these strangers will definitely understand.

"I was sexually assaulted nine years ago by my first boyfriend during my first year of university. I'm here because..." I pause as the words *new thing* press into my heart, the same words God was whispering to me the morning I got fired from my job. "Well, because after many years of feeling overwhelmed and discouraged by ongoing battles and setbacks, I'm ready to embrace a new start and...a new hope."

They all nod and turn back to Charlotte, who continues to lead the session by throwing another question at us and encouraging us to share our thoughts and feelings. There's no pressure and no rush as we each share whatever is on our minds.

Soon, I'm no longer fidgeting or bouncing my leg or counting the minutes until I leave because of how engrossed I am in all the women's stories. I even surprise myself when I volunteer to share what setbacks I've been experiencing on my healing journey.

When I get home after my first session, I sit at my desk, scribbling all the words that came to me on my train ride home. My new thing for that session is to do a study on how I can find refuge in God's character and promises when I feel overwhelmed and discouraged in my healing journey. After writing out all my key points from Psalm 91 onto sticky notes, I put them up on my wall.

The same thing happens over the next five sessions, where Charlotte alternates between leading the session and letting us talk about whatever we want to. I scribble down notes in my journal whenever a woman says something that makes me think about a character in the Bible or a passage of scripture, reminding myself to study it when I get home.

Through the women's stories, I'm reminded about how God is doing a new thing in helping me embrace my identity in Him, how He is doing a new thing according to His good and perfect will for me, and how He is constantly making things new and actively carrying out His plan in my life despite what season I find myself.

After our last session, apart from the sad feeling of moving on from the women who have provided a safe space for me to share, the one story I can't stop thinking is that of Fatima, who shared today that her biggest progress in the last six weeks was when she looked her ex-husband in the eye and told him she has forgiven him.

How did she ever get to that place where she could genuinely forgive her abuser? The man who caused her so much pain and upended her life and that of her children. The peace and joy was evident in her voice today, and it was so great to see everyone hug her and share encouraging words with her. Why can't I stop thinking about Fatima's story and why can't I stop thinking about Jason?

I sniff the bouquet of roses Jevaun sent ahead of our dinner date. The card it came with says,

Happy Valentine's Day, my love.
It's your last day and I'm so proud of you.
I can't wait to see you tonight.
I love you

After spending a few minutes reading the words over and over again, I place the roses in a vase and pour some water in it.

Back at my desk again, I flip through the dozen pages in my journal filled with words in different colours, reading them out loud to myself before looking at the pink sticky notes on my wall.

"It's true what they say, Lord. You never compel us, but You change our desires so they align with Yours." I exhale, smiling to myself at how crazy it is to even entertain this idea. "Okay, Lord. I'll do it."

The excitement rushing through me inspires the next scene in my book and for the first time this new year, I open my laptop and start writing again.

* * *

"So, how's your hand?" Victor sank into his sister's bed and stared at her bandaged wrist as if he had never seen one before.

She shrugged and dipped her right hand into his bag of popcorn. "It's not too bad, actually."

"I can't believe you tripped and fell and did that much damage. You're so clumsy." He laughed and Vanessa couldn't help but join him. She had no problem accepting that label at all.

"Yeah, you know. Things happen." She put popcorn in her mouth and chewed. "How was school today?" She remembered how stressed she was when she was preparing for her GCSEs. She had promised to check in on Victor regularly during his first term, but she got side-tracked and totally forgot about her promise. Part of her was grateful he didn't mind because he was an amazing brother, but she knew she needed to do better.

"It wasn't too bad. We have a few more exams coming up, so

we'll see how that goes." He rubbed his palm over his high-top hairstyle. "It's so long, though. I can't wait for it to be over." He leaned back on her bed and let out a heavy sigh.

"I know you're absolutely going to smash it, so don't worry." She squeezed his arm.

"You think so?" He sat up, his face begging for some encouragement, and Vanessa knew she had to grab the chance.

"I know so. If I could do it, then you sure can. You work so hard, and God is going to help you, okay?" It felt good for her to say those words out loud again with confidence.

"Victor, it's time for dinner." Her mum walked into the room, carrying a tray of food in one hand.

"Okay." He playfully punched Vanessa's shoulder and left the room, closing the door behind him.

"Mum, you didn't have to." Vanessa took the tray from her mum and sat up straight. At first, she felt guilty about her mum using up her emergency leave at work to look after her. But that guilt soon turned into gratitude for the support system God had blessed her with. She couldn't dare to think what could have happened to her if Anne wasn't there that day.

"This looks so good." She inhaled the aroma of the fried rice and grilled chicken with fried plantains, before covering it up and placing the tray on her desk. "Thank you so much, Mum, for everything."

Her mum sat on the edge of her bed. "You know I would do anything for you. You're my daughter." She lifted Vanessa's chin so she could look into her eyes. "I'll always be here for you. We're in this together, okay?"

Vanessa nodded, her eyes glistening with tears. "Mum, can you please do me a favour?"

"Of course, you know you can ask me anything."

"Please, can you pray for me?"

Diana's gaze softened as she looked down at her daughter.

"I don't want to stay in this dark place anymore. I hate it here." Vanessa sniffled and leaned forward, her hands shaking as she held her mum's arm tight. "Please ask God to save me, Mum. I can't stay here. Please ask Him to forgive me."

"Do you remember what the Bible says, Vanessa?" Diana cupped her daughter's face. "If you confess your sins, then He is faithful and just to forgive you and He will cleanse you from all unrighteousness."

"I already asked Him to forgive me."

"Then believe with your heart that He has forgiven you."

"But what if I never stop feeling this way? What if I never overcome this?"

"Not while my God still sits on the throne." Diana sprung to her feet and Vanessa wrapped her arms around her mum's waist. "Yes, you will go to therapy and do all that is advised medically, but we also serve a God who has the power to heal, to redeem, and to restore.

"The name of the Lord is a strong tower and the righteous run into it and they are saved. His name is above every other name and at the mention of the name of Jesus every knee will bow, in heaven and on earth and under the earth, and every tongue will confess that Jesus Christ is Lord, to the glory of God the Father. So lift up your hands, o ye gates, and be lifted up, you everlasting doors and the King of glory shall come in. Who is this King of glory? It's the Lord who is strong and mighty. The Lord who is mighty in battle. The Lord of hosts. He is the King of glory." Diana's voice cracked and tears streamed down her face, but she didn't stop praying.

"Vanessa, do you not know? Have you not heard? The Lord is the everlasting God, the Creator of the ends of the earth. He never grows tired or weary and no one can fathom His under-standing. For He gives strength to the weary and increases the power of the weak. Even youth grow tired and weary, and young men stumble and fall, but those who hope in the Lord will renew their strength. They will soar on wings like eagles. They will run and not grow weary. They will walk and not faint.

"Vanessa, the enemy thought he had won the battle over your mind, but he forgot that He that is in you, is greater than he that is in the world. Whenever the enemy comes in like a flood, the Spirit of the Lord will lift up a standard against him. Have you forgotten that he who dwells under the shelter of the Most High shall abide under the shadow of the Almighty? A thousand may fall at your side, ten thousand at your right hand, but it will not come near you because you have made the Lord your refuge. You have made the Most High your dwelling place."

Tears streamed down Vanessa's face as her mum referenced her favourite psalm. She cast her mind back to that fateful night that changed her life, and the last time she had put her hope in God. Even though she had no idea the turmoil that lay ahead of her, she remembered how joyful it had been when she trusted God.

She wanted to be back there in the safety of His arms and not to be lost in the darkness of her pain. She didn't want to stay where she was. She wanted to be free and there was only one Person that could give her freedom.

"Thank You, Jesus," Vanessa whispered as Diana continued praying scriptures over her.

"Vanessa, because you have set your love upon the Lord, He will deliver you. He will set you on high because you have known His name."

"Thank You, Jesus."

"Yes, call upon Him because He will answer you. He will be with you in trouble. He will deliver you and honour you. With long life, He will satisfy you and show you His salvation. Vanessa, you have been set free today, and who the Son has set free is free indeed."

"Thank You, Jesus." Vanessa's hands shook as her voice grew louder and louder until her words turned into sobs. Her shoulders shook as her tears soaked through her mum's dress, but she didn't realise when her tears of pain turned into tears of joy, because for the first time in a long time, hope had risen in her heart again.

34

BEX

"Babe, are you sure you still want to do this?" Jevaun asks again for the millionth time and I nod. If he had asked me this last week, I would've said "definitely not," but God changed something in me when I started praying for Jason.

"It's not too late to change your mind." He squeezes my hand and looks into my eyes, concern etched in his features. "I've been doing some research since the day you told me you wanted to do this. It's actually not advisable to meet up with someone like Jason who has caused you so much harm. He's most likely going to be dishonest and manipulative and he could trigger negative emotions for you."

I sigh and lean into him before pressing my hand against the side of his face. "Listen, my love. I know this is a dangerous thing to attempt. I wouldn't recommend anyone do this and trust me, I didn't want to do it either. But I'm certain about what God told me and I know He doesn't make mistakes. The same spirit of God, who gave me a sound mind to survive six weeks of group therapy, will also give me a sound mind when I face Jason. I'm starting to realise there's so much I can do with God if I just say yes and let Him take the lead. Trust me, I wouldn't be here if God hadn't told me to come. Babe, you trust God, don't you?"

He nods. "Of course I do."

"Okay, then watch Him take the lead today, okay?" I know Jevaun wouldn't understand this fully and that's okay.

He sighs and waits a few seconds before responding. "Okay, fine. But if I sense that the guy is moving mad or making you uncomfortable, do I at least have the permission to get you out of here?"

"Yes, sir." I chuckle as we take sips of our caramel lattes. Jevaun recommended the café in the South Bank centre—London's biggest arts centre, which is also home to the Royal Festival Hall and Hayward Gallery.

Although it's a lot busier than the Buzz, I love seeing so many people scattered around, working on their laptops, and the occasional cheering and clapping coming from upstairs.

"Hmm, this tastes good." I savour the sweetness of the hot drink.

"I told you." He grins. "Next time you should try the—"

"Whoa, slow down there, mister. Remember, I said I was only going to take this one step at a time?"

He nods. "Of course. As long as it's not your plain old Earl Grey or green tea, I'll count it as a win."

"Hey, my teas have a lot more health benefits than this pile of sugar, okay? Rachel said so. Plus, you're a doctor, so you should know that too."

Jevaun throws his head back and laughs. "Yeah, but this tastes a thousand times better."

I squint at him before shaking my head. "Fine, you win."

As I turn my head to glance at the door again, I see Jason walking in and my smile disappears. "He's here," I whisper and Jevaun follows my gaze, his arm sliding around my waist as he pulls me close to him.

Jason sees me and starts walking towards us, his tall, muscular frame bringing back so many memories of all the times he towered over me whenever I tried to stand up to him. I shake my head to dispel those thoughts because I need to focus on what God wants me to do.

"Bex." The strain in his voice is clear as he takes a seat on the other side of the table. "Thank you so much for agreeing to meet with me." He puts his hands together in a prayer pose.

Even with his smart casual clothes, it's clear from the puffiness around his eyes and worry lines across his forehead that all is not well with him. Even his beard looks unkempt, very unlike the Jason I used to know—who was so into his looks.

"That's okay. This is Jevaun, my boyfriend."

Jason turns to Jevaun and extends his hand. "Nice to meet you, man."

After staring at the hand for what seems like forever, Jevaun finally shakes it, but doesn't say another word.

"Okay, Jason. You wanted to speak and now I'm here. What do you want?" I cross my arms against my chest, staring straight into his eyes and determined not to let him intimidate me.

Jason opens his mouth as if he wants to say something, then closes it again. He drops his head and sighs. Then after a few seconds, the sniffles start before morphing into full on sobbing.

"Bex, I'm so sorry." He lifts his head to look at me, his eyes red and tears streaming down his face. "I'm sorry for everything I did to you. I'm sorry for the pain I caused you. I have no excuse to justify what I did. It was all my fault and I take full responsibility." His voice is now shaking as he wipes the tears from the corners of his eyes.

I don't think I've ever seen him look so broken, but I keep a straight face, determined not to give in easily. This could be one of his techniques, and like Jevaun said, he could just be trying to manipulate the situation. To manipulate me.

"I'll totally understand if you don't want to forgive me," he continues, breaking into my thoughts. "If you decide to report me to the police, then please go ahead. I deserve it. I deserve all of it. But I just want to let you know how sorry I am."

When I don't say anything, he adds, "Bex, I've had no peace since I left uni." He drops his head. "My life has been an absolute mess and I know it's because of how cruel I was to you."

I frown, wondering what he is going on about. "What do you mean?"

He lifts his head again. "Please, permit me to give you some context, and I don't want you to see this as me trying to make excuses, but please just hear me out." He sniffles.

"That night when you heard me arguing with my dad over the phone, I was so angry because he had made a decision for me and planned out my whole life without my consent. I didn't want to study medicine, and I didn't want to go to Malta, but nothing I did or said mattered to him. Myself and my siblings saw this as we grew up. It was always his way or no way. Whenever my mum tried to stand up to him, he hit her until she stopped fighting back.

"I felt like I didn't have a choice, so I left the university and went to Malta. But I struggled so much to adjust or make new friends or progress on my course that I became depressed and failed my course three times, so I was expelled from the university."

He pauses before continuing. "After returning to the UK, the arguments between me and my dad escalated, and I ended up leaving the house. I stayed with an uncle of mine for years while I tried to pick up the pieces of my life. I got a job at a post office and a call centre and tried to save some money to get my own place and go back to uni. But during that time my dad had a heart attack and died in hospital." Tears well up in his eyes again, but he wipes them away.

"I never got the chance to reconcile with him or to say goodbye because I was still so angry. I thought I hated him for what he did to me, my mum, and my siblings, but his death hit me real hard and I spiralled out of control. I reached an all-time low when I sustained a knee injury while at work that affected my mobility for years. I had to go through a few surgeries and months of physiotherapy to recover. I slipped into depression again and only finally came out of the other side last year, when my physiotherapist introduced Jesus to me.

"I thought I knew Him because I went to church on Sundays and listened to the pastors talk about Him and all the wonderful things He has done. But I only knew of Him. I didn't know Him for myself. Last year, after a battle with myself, I finally surrendered my life to Jesus, and He saved me from the state of hopelessness I was in.

"But the one prayer I couldn't stop praying was for God to give me an opportunity to apologise to you." He raises his head to look at me as tears roll down my cheeks. "I tried looking for you, Bex. But I didn't have your number on my phone anymore because I deleted it. I remembered you had sisters, but I couldn't remember their names or what they looked like. I tried typing your name online a few times, but nothing was helpful until I saw you at Waterloo Station a few months ago. Bex, I'm so sorry." He wipes his nose with the sleeve of his jacket.

Jevaun hands me a tissue and I dab the corners of my eyes, reflecting on Jason's story and just how good God has been to both of us. I had prepared myself to feel anger towards Jason and I thought Jevaun would have to restrain me, so I didn't jump at his throat.

But look at me shedding tears of joy because of how good God is. No one is incapable of being saved by God. Even Jason, the man I used to be so sure deserved a place in hell, next to the devil himself. That's the same man God has saved and chosen to be part of His family.

I could definitely report him to the police, and looking back, I wish I had done so from the very beginning. Jason knows he deserves it and he has confessed, so that should be an easy win for me. But going through that legal process is not what I need at this point in my journey, so I'm choosing to end it here because it's what's best for me.

This step right here is important to me because I want to move on and I want to live my life knowing that I have let go of all the things that could hold me back. So if God could help me forgive Ayo, there's no reason I can't forgive Jason too.

"Jason?" I say as he looks at me, tears still streaming from his eyes. "I forgive you."

He raises his brows and straightens his back. "Really? You forgive me?"

I nod. "God has been preparing my heart for this moment and He was the One who prompted me to finally respond to your message. Seeing you again was the last thing I thought I'd do on this earth, but God is very intentional about both of us and wants us to experience the true joy of the salvation we have found in Him. I won't be able to experience that joy if I hold grudges against you, Jason. So, yes, I forgive you."

"Thank you so much, Bex. You have no idea how happy that makes me. Oh, this is incredible. Thank You, Jesus."

"I have no plans to report you to the police, but I truly hope that you have learnt from your mistakes. I hope that you continue to grow in your faith and knowledge of God and that from here on out, you treat His daughters with the loving care and respect they deserve. Goodbye, Jason." I squeeze his hand briefly and smile at him before nodding to Jevaun, who leads me out of the coffee shop.

The feeling of peace impressing in my heart is nothing I can explain. I guess now I understand what Fatima meant. It feels good to do what God wants, and now I know exactly what the next scene in my book will be.

Vanessa leaned her head against her mum's shoulder as they both sat in the waiting room of the GP surgery. It was packed compared to the last time she had been there, and it was easy to tell the January temperatures had dropped significantly, given the amount of coughing and sneezing going on.

But at least they had some entertainment from the toddler running around the room, chasing his little sister as their mum shouted at them to be careful. Sitting next to Vanessa was a blonde woman comforting her fussy baby, who was dressed in the cutest blue fleece overall Vanessa had ever seen. The baby's beautiful blue gaze rested on Vanessa as his mum cuddled him, his two-toothed smile warming Vanessa's heart, and she couldn't help but smile back.

Vanessa couldn't remember the last time she noticed things or people around her without being absorbed in the spiral of her thoughts. Even though the doctor was running late as usual, she didn't have any fidgeting legs, shaking hands, or nausea in the pit of her stomach like she did the last time. Maybe part of it was to do with her mum being there, but she knew she wasn't the same person who sat in that waiting room a few months ago. Something had shifted and changed inside of her, and she had only God to thank for that.

"Vanessa Molua?" The familiar face of Dr. Ella Green appeared round the corner, as the screens weren't working that day. The doctor's blonde hair was in a half-up, half-down style, and she was wearing a polka dot dress with black tights.

Vanessa sat up straight before turning to her mum. "Are you sure you don't want to come in with me?"

Her mum shook her head. "No, please, I want you to feel free to tell the doctor what you want."

"Okay, mum. Thanks." She squeezed her hand before walking up to the doctor.

Vanessa still remembered her warm smile and, unlike the last time, Vanessa smiled back before following the doctor to her room.

"Thank you so much for waiting. Please, take a seat." She pointed to the chair before sitting in front of her computer. "So, it has been a minute since we last spoke, but I'm glad you're back. How have you been?" She turned her body to give Vanessa her full attention.

Vanessa smiled. "Well, a lot of things have happened since our last appointment. Things got worse, unfortunately, after that, and I became more depressed. I couldn't eat or sleep or focus on my uni work. Then one day I wanted to end the pain, and I wanted some relief. So, I cut myself and ended up passing out." She lifted her left wrist to show the doctor the wound the nurse had dressed after taking out her stitches an hour before.

"I woke up in A&E and I've never felt that much regret ever in my life. It was as if something reset my brain, and seeing the pain and hurt in my mum's eyes and the impact of what I'd done made me want to do better."

Vanessa exhaled. "So, I told the doctors at the hospital I wanted to be better. I promised them I'd follow up with you, so here I am—keeping my promise." She smiled, and was surprised by how she had gone through the whole story without crying.

"Wow, I'm happy to hear that things are getting better. It's also good to see you smiling and being more positive. Have you reached out to the charity yet? Would you consider getting some talking therapy?"

She nodded. "Erm...well I had a look at them, but I decided to go with a private counsellor. She's a pastor in my home church back in Coventry. I had my third one-to-one session with her yesterday and it has been very helpful."

"That's great." The doctor tucked a strand of her hair behind her ear. "What about your support network? Friends? Family?"

"My best friend, Anne, who called the ambulance when I passed out. She has been a huge blessing to me and my mum has also been supportive. We had an argument at the beginning when she first found out what happened to me. But I can see that she was just genuinely trying to help me. She even came here with me, and she's in the waiting room. This experience has brought us closer, and it has also strengthened my faith in God."

"Would you say that your faith in God played a big role in your mindset shift?" Dr. Green asked.

"Yes, and I know the road ahead of me won't be easy. There will be ups and downs, I'm sure. But I have hope that things will get better. That's the one thing I didn't have when I came to see you a few months ago. God has helped me with that."

"You know I'm a Christian too, and I find what you've said right now very inspiring."

"Really?" Vanessa's eyes widened at the revelation, as if she was seeing the doctor in a new light. "Wow, I knew there was something different about you. I just wanted to say thank you so much for your help last time."

The doctor frowned. "My help? I didn't do anything."

"No, you did. You listened to me, you didn't judge me, you didn't pressure me to speak even though you clearly knew I was lying. That's why I could tell the psychiatrist at the hospital I had support from my GP. It was because of how kind you were to me. Thank you, Dr. Green."

"You're welcome, Vanessa. Do you mind if I book you in for a follow-up appointment in a couple of weeks to check in?"

Vanessa nodded and smiled. "Of course. Do you mind if I make a request for you to be my usual doctor?"

"It'd be my pleasure." The doctor smiled back and as Vanessa made her way out, it wasn't shame and guilt she felt like the last time. She felt heard.

35

JEVAUN

"Wow, that is so cool!" Bex exclaims as we walk hand-in-hand through Shoreditch. I've lost count of the number of times she's said that since I picked her up from the train station.

I follow her gaze to yet another vibrant work of art on the wall. I've been hyping up Shoreditch to her for the past six months, so I'm glad she's not underwhelmed. The busy streets made up of creative minds have officially charmed her.

It's Good Friday and Tré is on his way to spend the long weekend with me, so he'll officially be meeting Bex today. But his train doesn't get here until another hour, so I thought I'd take Bex on a tour while we wait.

I have a meeting with Sam on Tuesday to tell him about my final decision about his offer of representation. It has been four months since we had our first call, and even though he told me to take as much time as I need, I didn't expect him to be so responsive after this long.

The events of the last few months have cemented my decision and I think it'll only be fair to tell him, so he knows where

I'm at. But before then, I have a long weekend to spend with Bex and Tré and to celebrate the resurrection of my Saviour.

"You just don't see this in Croydon." Bex wraps her orange scarf around her neck before pointing at another set of mixed media art on a wall across the street.

"Yeah, this one always makes me stop and admire every time I walk past here."

"No wonder your brain is always so creative. You're literally surrounded by creativity." She spins around and I catch her when she loses her balance and almost trips over.

We both laugh as I help her up again, my eyes sliding up to her hair. "The orange highlights look more vibrant today," I comment, admiring her signature style—a high puff with an *Ankara* headband.

"Yeah, I retouched them when I went to the hair salon yesterday. You like what you see?" She looks up at me, wrapping her arms around my waist.

"I *love* what I see. You're so beautiful." I close the gap between us and plant a soft kiss on her lips, her warmth perfectly contrasting the freezing air around us.

After we break the kiss, I glance at my watch. "Okay, if we don't leave now, Tré will end up being grumpy when we keep him waiting."

"That's okay. You can tell him you were late because you were kissing your girlfriend in the middle of the high street." She winks at me and I smile.

"Oh, you're cheeky, you know that, right?"

"Guilty as charged." She zips up her jacket and holds my hand again as we make our way back to Old Street Underground Station, where we take the Northern line to Kings Cross St. Pancras.

Stepping out of the tube, my grip tightens around Bex's hand as we meander through the crowd, making our way to St.

Pancras International. Once we climb up the stairs into the station, the sound of acoustic music fills my ears and I turn right to find the busker I usually see at Waterloo Station.

"Hey, I know him." I point to the young man perched in the corner with his guitar microphone.

I glance at my watch again, and with Tré's train arriving in twenty minutes, we have some time to enjoy some worship music. "Do you mind?" I ask Bex, who shakes her head and follows me as we approach the crowd gathering around the busker.

For the next ten minutes, he takes requests from the crowd and plays a selection of Christian contemporary songs. We go from bouncing and clapping to lifting our hands and singing at the top of our voices as he leads. The experience is so amazing, my heart swells with gratitude for the gift of music that we can use to worship our Maker.

The passersby have no idea what we're doing, and that's okay. The tangible presence of God is here with us, and this was a beautiful reminder for me as we go into celebrating His death and resurrection this weekend.

When the busker finishes, Bex and I walk up to him as he starts packing up his guitar. "Hey, man. My name is Jevaun, and this is my girlfriend, Bex."

The young man, who looks to be in his early twenties, runs his hand over his dark silky hair before shaking our hands. "Nice to meet you both. I'm Chris."

"Thank you for letting God work through you today. That was amazing."

His wide smile broadens. "Thank you so much. I'm glad it blessed you."

"I've seen you a few times at Waterloo Station. I didn't know you came here, too."

"Oh, yeah, I alternate between Waterloo, London Bridge, and

here. I have a schedule with dates on all my social media pages if you want to know where I'll be." He points to the banner behind him and Bex and I take a photo of it so we can follow him later.

"How long have you been doing this?" Bex asks as she leans into me.

"Two years now, and God has been doing amazing things through this ministry."

"Oh, we can definitely testify to that," Bex concurs. "What was your inspiration for doing this?"

"Well, it was after I had a rude awakening and a near death experience after moving with the wrong crowd for so long. I grew up in a loving and functional Christian home, but I wanted a different path for myself. Family and friends warned me, but I thought I knew best. I dropped out of school and started dealing with drugs, and I ended up getting stabbed and in hospital, fighting for my life. When I woke up, I made a promise to God that I would never stop telling the whole world about Him. I've always loved singing since I was a child, so it seemed like an obvious choice to use this talent for God's glory."

"Wow, that's so cool, man. Bex and I are both writers, so we love connecting with other Christian creatives." I wrap my arm around Bex's shoulders.

"Oh, really? That's amazing. We definitely need more of God's children infiltrating that space and spreading the light of God in literature," he says.

"I couldn't agree with you more. It was so nice chatting with you and looking forward to worshiping with you again soon." We shake his hand again and take a photo with him before tapping our phones on his contactless payment system.

As we make our way to the ticket gate to wait for Tré, I send up a prayer of thanksgiving to God for giving me yet another confirmation for my response to Sam.

36

BEX

I'm not sure what I'm expecting when we walk into Jevaun's flat, but I have to say I'm pleasantly surprised. It probably has to do with the fact that I've largely believed the stereotype that girls are a hundred times neater than guys. Or maybe it's because my sisters and I have similar cleaning habits. So imagine my shock when I walk into a sparkling clean flat staring back at me.

"Welcome to my humble abode." Jevaun stretches out his hand in a sweeping motion. "What do you think?"

"It looks good," I say, walking further into his living room and admiring his grey sofa and dining table.

Tréjon plops down on the sofa and turns on the TV, which has a potted plant standing next to it.

"Is that real?" I point to the plant as I approach it, but Tréjon shakes his head.

"My brother here is very good at taking care of humans, but please never trust him with any other living thing, whether it's pets or plants." Tréjon shakes his head before picking up a game console from the centre table.

I laugh and turn to Jevaun. "Is that true?"

"Guilty as charged." He sends me a sheepish smile. "But forget about Tré. He's a hater. Come on, let me show you the rest of the flat." He takes my hand in his and we walk across the living room to his balcony. "I only ever come out here in the summer."

I lean against the balcony's glass barrier and admire the lovely view of the park, the skyscrapers, and the other blocks of flats. You can even hear faint noises from the busy high street. "It's a lovely view."

"I know, right." He takes me back inside to the kitchen. "Here's where I make all the food that keeps me fuelled. Can't wait for you to try what I cooked for you." He winks at me and before I can get used to the delicious aroma, or take a sneak peek into his pots, he pulls me out and back into the hallway.

"Here is bedroom number one." He points through the open door and I catch a glimpse of another potted plant next to his chest of drawers. "And here's bedroom number two, which I use as my office." He opens the door slowly and lets me in. "Here's where all the magic happens."

"Wow." I look around in awe, not knowing what to focus on first. Every piece of furniture or item has been strategically placed. From his writing desk, to his recording studio setup, and his bookshelf. "It's so cool that you have a dedicated office space. If only I could convince my parents to stop using our spare room as a storage space and a home gym, then I could get my own."

Jevaun laughs and places his arm over my shoulders. "Don't worry, one day you'll get your own office space." He kisses my forehead before leading me back into the living room. "So, are you hungry?"

"Yes, I'm starving." Tréjon springs to his feet, abandoning his game console and turning off the video game. "I'm famished."

"I wasn't talking to you, mate." Jevaun points a finger at his brother.

"I know you weren't, but I'm sure Bex doesn't mind me answering the question for her." He raises his eyebrows at me.

"Of course I don't mind. Now, be nice." I touch Jevaun's cheek and he snarls at his brother before asking us to take a seat at the dining table.

"I just wanted to say thank you," Tréjon says, rubbing his beard, which makes him and Jevaun look like twins. "For all you do for him. It's like he's a new person. Even a blind man will tell you how happy he has been for the last seven months. He couldn't stop talking about you from the very first day you met. He says you're his answered prayer."

My cheeks warm up as I suppress a smile. "Aww, he said all that?"

"Yeah, he loves you, Bex. So thank you for making him happy."

"I love him too and he's also my answered prayer." My smile breaks forth anyway and Jevaun walks in, clearing his throat.

"I hope you guys aren't gossiping about me."

"Why would we waste our time doing that?" Tréjon responds before laughing.

"There you go, babe." Jevaun places a plate of food in front of me that gets me salivating instantly. "Jamaican-inspired curry chicken, white rice, and fried plantains."

I lean forward and inhale the spicy aroma. "Hmm. That smells delicious." I take out my phone and take a few photos of the food, and send it quickly to the girls' group chat, so they can see how much enjoyment I'm having. My cheeky caption, 'look what my man made for me,' would get them squealing and kicking their feet in the air for sure.

"It tastes delicious too." It has the right amount of spice from the curry mixed with the perfect amount of sweetness from the plantains and the result is an explosion of flavour in my mouth. "But it's pronounced *plantayne* and not *plantin*."

"*Uh oh.*" Tréjon covers his mouth as he chews his food. "The war's about to start again."

"Oh, please, I pronounce it the same way we pronounce *mountain* and *fountain.* Right, Tré?" He turns to his brother, who lifts both hands up in the air.

"Nah, nah, you will not drag me into your lover's fight." Tréjon shakes his head and focuses on his food.

"See? The woman is always right. So I can't be hearing about this *plantin* business, please." I point my fork at Jevaun.

"Okay, fine. You win this one. But only because I want to live to fight another day." He leans forward and plants a kiss on my lips.

After dinner, Tréjon picks up the game console again and, after my initial hesitation, the boys convince me to try out a game of FIFA. It takes me a good few games before I can get my head around how to even use the game console, but after trying a few characters, I finally win one game.

"Okay, we need to leave soon," Jevaun says after our last game, glancing at his wall clock above the TV. We'll be attending the Good Friday service at his church today, so I can meet his pastor and church family.

"Yeah, sure." I stand up and pick up my bag from the sofa.

"Hey, can I come with you guys?" Tréjon asks and Jevaun retreats backwards from the hallway before poking his head into the living room.

"What did you say?" Jevaun asks, his head tilted to the side as if he didn't hear what Tréjon said.

"I said, can I come with you guys? To the Good Friday service?" he asks again, his gaze darting between Jevaun and I.

Jevaun is so stunned, his words can't even come out of his mouth.

"Yes, of course you can come with us," I respond before

touching Jevaun's arm lightly while he thaws out of his state of unbelief.

"Yeah, sorry, of course. That would be awesome." He walks over to his brother. "How come you want to come with us? Just curious."

Tréjon shrugs. "Well, the short answer is I'll be bored when you guys are gone." He smiles before sighing. "But the long answer is that I don't want to end up like Dad. He was my role model for so many years, but when I found out the truth at the party, it felt like the scales finally fell from my eyes. If Dad's belief system makes him see no wrong in what he's done, then I have to be better. I see so much pain and suffering in the work I do and I have to believe that there is more to life than just working, eating, and sleeping. I'm open to exploring any options that would give me hope to keep going every day despite the challenges."

"Wow, I'm so happy you've decided to do this, Tré. I love you, man." Jevaun hugs his brother, and I know he's trying so hard to keep his emotions in check. This is an answered prayer happening in front of us.

Jevaun pulls me into his office and wraps his arms around me before lifting me off the ground and twirling me around. He puts me back down and plants a kiss on my lips and forehead before breaking out into dance moves that make him look like he's trying not to step on ants.

"Babe, can you see? Can you see what God has done?" he says in a hushed tone while holding my face.

"Yes, my love. I can see. It's amazing and we have to keep praying. Even for your dad."

"Yes, we have to keep praying for my dad. Never stop praying because God is always working."

37

JEVAUN

Once again, I'm sitting in front of my computer in my office, staring at my screen and counting down the seconds until I join the video call with Sam. Last time, I was a bundle of nerves because I just wanted him to tell me he liked me and my book.

The desperation to get one acceptance almost clouded my judgement and made me consider tearing apart my story. But now, I'm more at peace because I've never been so confident in what God wants me to do.

"Hi, Jevaun." Sam's smiling face appears on my screen. "Good to see you again."

"Hi, Sam. Thank you for being patient with me, even though I took so long to get back to you."

Sam waves a dismissive hand. "No worries at all. I think the partnership is worth the wait, anyway. So, I take it you want to talk about the notes I suggested?"

"Yeah...erm." I clear my throat and adjust in my seat. "After giving it a lot of thought and praying about it, I've decided to decline your offer."

Sam's eyebrows shoot up. "Really? Can I ask why?"

"I don't think we have the same vision for the book and I—"

"Hang on," he cuts me short. "You know I wasn't asking you to completely take out the faith elements, right? I just suggested we edit them and make them subtle, as the chances of us selling the book to a major publisher will be higher if we do it that way."

"Yes, I understand and I appreciate that you are trying to help me, but when God gave me the idea for this story five years ago, I knew He wanted to use it to glorify His name. The themes and characters and even the world building were all inspired by God's character. It wouldn't make sense for me to edit that part of the story, so I'm sorry."

"Jevaun, are you really sure you want to do this? It's okay if you want to take some more time to think about it. I'm not pressuring you at all."

I nod and smile. "Yes, Sam. I'm very sure."

Sam shakes his head and lets out a breath. "Okay, then. I totally understand. I was really looking forward to this partnership, though. But I admire you for sticking to your convictions. I'm sure you'll find the right agent and publisher for you. I still think you are a great writer, so if you want to query me again with another book, I'd be open to giving it a look."

"Appreciate it, Sam."

"No worries. Wish you all the best."

We exchange our goodbyes, and I close my laptop, returning to the silence of my office again. I lean back in my chair and stare at the posters on my corkboard on the wall. There are post-it notes on it from back when I was outlining *Parallels* and when I was doing revisions. It has been a long time coming and even though it seems like I've lost a battle, I know in my heart that victory is coming.

I pick up my phone and dial Bex's number. It only rings once and she picks it up before switching it to a video call.

"Hey, that was quick." She moves her phone around, so I can see her in the full frame while she works on twisting her hair in front of the mirror.

I nod. "Yeah, it's all done now and I couldn't be happier."

"Aww, I love your positive attitude towards the whole thing. You're not seeing this as a setback, which is great."

"Yeah, I have a positive attitude because God has actually given me clarity about what to do with this story."

Bex pauses and brings her face closer to the screen, her eyebrows scrunched together. "Wait, you got an offer from another agent?"

I shake my head.

"One of the big five publishers reached out to you?"

"Nope."

"Okay, this could go on forever, so please just tell me."

I laugh before spilling the beans. "I'm going to be publishing the book myself."

"Really? That means you can get the story out sooner than expected, right?"

"Yes, I can even get it out before the end of the year. All I need to do is get a professional editor, a cover designer, and then work out the kinks of getting the book onto the various vendor sites. If others have done it successfully, then I'm sure I can learn the ropes too. God has given me the privilege to build a platform of avid readers who are passionate about not just any kind of book, but fantasy books that give Him glory. I've made amazing connections with these people all around the world, some of which have been supporting me for years. There's not a day that goes by that someone doesn't ask me when my book is coming out and when they can read it."

"I think you should do a surprise announcement then," Bex suggests. "I'm sure they'll be thrilled."

"That's actually a brilliant idea." I glance at the clock. "I can do a pop-up livestream in ten minutes and announce my decision. At least putting it out there will keep me accountable and remind me to get to work, so I can make this dream a reality."

Bex claps her hands. "Oh, I'm so excited for you, I could scream."

"Hey, do you want to do the livestream with me?" I tease, and her eyes widen.

"Please tell me you're joking," she says, one hand still clinging to the twist she's in the middle of braiding.

I throw my head back in laughter before nodding. "Of course I am. But it'll be cool to have you on someday, though?"

She just shrugs and turns away again. "Maybe."

"*Maybe* is a good answer, so I'll take it."

Ten minutes later, I'm in the video recording part of my office, lights on, camera ready and pressing the 'go live' button. I share my publishing plans, the title, and the themes of the story before asking them what they think of it.

Ten minutes after ending the livestream, hundreds of positive comments flood in with so many people expressing their interest in the book and saying they can't wait to read it. They even give me lots of brilliant ideas for the book release, such as crowdfunding and offering special editions for the book with merch and stationery. If all goes well, then that will offset a lot of the publishing costs.

I open my notebook and start scribbling all my thoughts, and after an hour of writing everything down, I have a solid publishing plan, with some ideas for marketing the book and also crowdfunding.

As I open my laptop again to start researching editors and cover designers, my heart swells with joy and gratitude. I can't wait to see God use this story to impact the lives of others, just as He promised He would.

38

BEX

"Whoop! Go, Bex." Everyone cheers as I walk down the stairs with my laptop in hand. Rhoda ran her mouth as usual and told Mum and Dad I only had one chapter left to write in my book, so Mum suggested we celebrate by inviting everyone over, including Jevaun.

"Guys, you know I haven't actually written the last chapter, right?" I shake my head before placing the laptop on the dining table.

"Yes, but we're still going to cheer you on until you finish," Dad says, and I would've believed his enthusiasm if I didn't remember how skeptical he was before.

He might just be happy that it has only taken me seven months to get to this point rather than the one year I initially thought. Whatever his reason is, I'm still grateful for the support.

"Well, I need to write in absolute silence, so you all will need to stop the cheering." I take a seat at the table and open my laptop.

"Okay, guys, we need to migrate to the living room and let our author here do her work," Rachel says.

"Yes, and Rachel and Rhoda need to help me in the kitchen, anyway." Mum beckons on my sisters, who follow her without another word. Mum was up at six AM this morning, cooking, and every time I wanted to come into the kitchen, she shooed me away as if she was cooking up an experiment in there.

"One second," Jevaun says to Rachel before walking up to me. "Hey, do you want me to sit here with you?"

I shake my head. "No, I think I'll be okay."

"Alright. Just remember that you can do this," he says as his loving brown gaze melts my heart.

"Thank you, babe."

"I love you." He kisses my forehead and walks out of the room, closing the door behind him.

After putting on my headphones, I'm able to drown out the chattering coming from the living room and the clanging of pots and pans in the kitchen. Staring at the blinking cursor on my screen, I place my fingers on the keys and say a prayer. *Lord, please help me.*

* * *

It was all done and dusted. Vanessa had stayed up all night worrying about it, but everything had been seamless and she couldn't be more grateful to God. The advocates from the charity she was involved with assured her she didn't need to speak to the police if she didn't want to, but they gave her enough information about her rights, her options, and what she could expect.

Anne wasn't sure if it was a good idea and even Vanessa's mum had asked her to pray about it first. But even after praying, Vanessa remained confident she was doing the right thing. The last time she didn't listen to God, she had to deal with the consequences of her disobedience, so she didn't plan on closing her ears to what He was saying to her this time around.

After Vanessa made her official police statement, it felt like a weight had been lifted off her shoulders. She knew the journey wasn't over, and that the road ahead of her was going to be long and turbulent as the police officially launched the investigation to decide whether the case would be prosecuted.

Vanessa knew it could take months before she heard an update about the case, and she also knew the battle ahead of her was going to be fierce, but she was willing to travel that road because she knew she wasn't travelling alone.

Her phone alarm rang and Anne flew into her room without even knocking. "*It's time.*" She did her best to mimic Mariah Carey, but ended up croaking out the words. Vanessa laughed at her best friend's eagerness to study God's word.

The reason Anne skipped into her room like a gazelle was because they had found their journaling Bibles in their mailboxes earlier that day and they were going to start using them. Even though Vanessa loved the journaling Bibles, her old journal was very precious to her, as it was filled with so many testimonies of what God had done for her, so she decided to keep using it.

Vanessa pressed play on her phone, and worship music filled her room. The two girls both got to work, choosing to start from Psalm one. They read through each of the verses, talked about it, shared insight, and then they journaled their thoughts on the big lined margins of the Bible with their coloured gel pens.

Vanessa was so grateful to be back to her usual routine of meeting with God every day at nine PM, and it was also an added blessing that she could share that experience with a friend—a loyal friend.

Of course it wasn't easy at first. In fact, Vanessa didn't open her Bible until three months into her counselling sessions with Pastor Kemi. She started off slowly, as Pastor Kemi had suggested, with a verse a day. Then she started reading two verses, then three, and then a whole chapter.

Vanessa cried the day she read through the ninety-first psalm again from the beginning to the end. It did take time, but the hope in her heart continued to grow. So when Anne offered to do Bible studies with her, Vanessa jumped at the opportunity as she knew having accountability would help.

"Thank you, Anne," Vanessa said as her friend lifted her head to look at her. She didn't even need to say anything more because Anne knew. "I hope you know just how much I appreciate and love you."

"Aww, hun, I know because you tell me every day." Anne chuckled. "Your journey has inspired me so much, you know?"

Vanessa frowned. "Really? How?"

"Nessa, can't you see? You're proof that God answers prayers. I was praying for you from the moment I knew something was wrong. But look at you glowing again. God really answers prayers and your journey has really strengthened my faith."

"Wow." Vanessa smiled and hugged her friend. Who would've thought that God would use her rock bottom experience to strengthen someone else's faith? He really works in mysterious ways.

Later that week, Vanessa attended the Christian union meeting for the first time since the incident, and the joy of fellowshipping with everyone else, worshiping God and encouraging each other, made her forget everything that reminded her of him.

Many people had told her university years were going to make or break her, and she had definitely had her fair share of brokenness, but she had now entered her healing era and she didn't intend to fall back.

Vanessa had also been granted extenuating circumstances for all her assessments in the first semester, but now that she was back and better, she was determined to finish strong and continue working on her dream of becoming the first medical doctor in her family.

God had taught her so much about who she was—beloved and cared for—no matter what had happened to her. So even though nothing could've prepared Vanessa Molua for those months of turmoil, she still had hope in her heart and she had learned that healing was possible with Jesus.

THE END

"I did it." Tears run down my face as I take off my headphones and look at the last two words in disbelief. "I can't believe this. I finished my book." Sobs escape my mouth as I take in the reality of the wonderful testimony sitting on my laptop. "Thank You, Jesus. Thank You for not giving up on me, Lord."

I stand up and walk to the door before opening it and yelling at the top of my voice, "Guys, I finished writing my book."

The squeal coming from the kitchen lets me know Rhoda has heard, and she is the first person to appear at the scene, throwing her arms around me as she launches in for a hug.

"Congratulations, Bex. I'm so proud of you." Rachel hugs me next, followed by Mum and when it's Dad's turn, my heart drops a bit because I don't want him to ruin the moment by mentioning how I have to go back to finding a job.

"Come, my daughter." He holds my hand and leads me to my

laptop, both of us looking at the last few words on the page. "Wow, fifty thousand words? You wrote all that?"

I nod. "Yes, Dad, I did."

"I'm so proud of you. I know this book will bless so many people in the future." He pulls me in for a hug as everyone choruses an amen.

More tears stream down my face when Dad and I break the hug and he wipes them with his thumb. "I hope those are tears of joy."

"Definitely. Thank you, everyone, for your support." I glance at Jevaun, who is standing behind Mum, waiting for his turn.

The big smile he gives me when he finally gets to the front of the queue warms my cheeks. "I'm so proud of you, Bex." He squeezes both my shoulders and the genuine care in his voice brings up more tears because he's the only one who knows how much I struggled.

I can't believe it was only yesterday we were celebrating him deciding to independently publish his book and today he is celebrating me finishing mine. It's a celebration galore for both of us and I love it.

"I can't believe my first mentee actually finished writing her book."

"I know, right." We both laugh.

"Don't forget, you still have to edit it one hundred times before it's ready for publication." He chuckles and I shake my head. "But of course, I'll be ready to coach you through it as well."

"Thank you so much, Jevaun, for helping our daughter reach this milestone," Mum says. "We can agree that you have been a good influence and blessing since you came into her life. We are grateful."

"Yeah, very grateful," Dad concurs.

"Honestly, it's not a problem. I'd do anything for Bex." He places his hand on the small of my back and looks into my eyes. "I love her," he says, and a smile appears on my lips.

"I love you too."

"Aww," my sisters say before Dad clears his throat and Mum directs us girls to the kitchen, so we can help her set the table.

Twenty minutes later, there's a fine spread of Cameroonian cuisine on the table, ranging from fried rice served with chicken, *poisson braisé*[1], and *miondo*[2] served with the famous Cameroonian green spice and pepper sauces, *koki* beans[3] served with boiled ripe plantains, and of course, the wonderful *water fufu* and *eru*. Rachel also made sure we remembered our five a day, so she made a tray of authentic Cameroonian salad.

"So, Jevaun, now that you've dipped your toes into Cameroonian cuisine, what do you think?" Rachel says from across the table.

"I have to say, I've been sold from the moment you gave me the food the last time. My brother loved the fish rolls, too." He places a spoon of rice into his mouth as I stare at his plate, which has every single food item on it.

Jevaun has always been adventurous when it comes to food, and I love how generous he was with the pepper sauce. I just hope we don't end up having to call the ambulance when the spice kicks in.

As I watch Jevaun describe what he loves about every single food item on his plate, my heart swells with gratitude. Who would've thought that my whole life would change so drastically in seven months?

Back in September, when I lost my job, I had no idea what God had in store for me. I could've never imagined it turning out to be this. Going from constantly feeling burned out to a place where I feel happier, more fulfilled, and on my healing journey is a blessing I can't comprehend.

I have no idea what the next seven months will bring. I may end up going back to work at a corporate job, or find an agent for my book, or even decide to publish it myself. There's still a long road ahead of me I've never travelled before, a continuous journey of experiencing new things with God, and I'm here for all of it.

EPILOGUE
TWO YEARS LATER

"So, for our last question of the evening." Demi's gaze sweeps over the crowd of approximately fifty people sitting in the bookstore, listening to our Q&A session. It's the same bookstore Neha and I found at Clapham Junction two years ago and just like I imagined it, God answered my prayer and put my book on their shelves.

"What would you say is the one lesson you would want readers to take away after reading your book, *Hope Arise*?" Demi brings the book close to her face, her honey-blonde curly hair matching the book cover's colour theme.

I bring the microphone up to my mouth, my mind still getting used to the fact that the name on that beautiful book Demi is holding is mine. The events of the last two years can be summarised as a rollercoaster ride, but God brought me exactly where I needed to be.

After finishing the first draft of *Hope Arise*, I spent six months going through intense edits with Jevaun's help before entering the query trenches. I also applied for a new investment banking job and got one at another bank with much better pay and benefits.

I landed my dream agent, Amy, a year ago, and she loved the vision and themes of the story. Within a few months, we signed a two-book deal with the biggest Christian publisher in the UK.

The last few months have gone by so quickly with Jevaun and I getting engaged and also my publisher organising a last-minute UK book tour for me. When I shared the news with the girls at the Faith Writers group, Demi kindly offered to chair the London session as she has experience doing that for other authors. I dreamt of this moment for years and now that it's here, I still can't believe Vanessa's story is out in the world.

"The lesson I would want everyone to take from this book is the simple but powerful encouragement that healing is possible with Jesus. No matter how careful we are in life, we can't always avoid getting hurt and trust me, I've experienced my fair share of pain. But the depth of your pain doesn't matter to Jesus. His love for us goes deeper than our deepest hurts. So it doesn't matter how broken we are, He is more than capable of loving us back together again."

"Wow, that is so profound. I'm getting a little emotional over here." Demi fans her face and laughter erupts from the crowd. "I got an early copy of this book, so I've read it twice and I have to say that Vanessa's story is beautiful." She places the book on her lap.

"Thank you very much, Demi."

"I know I said that was the last question, but I'm sure everyone is dying to know what we're going to be expecting next from Rebecca Ayuk. Please tell us what your future plans are."

I turn my body to face the crowd, catching a glimpse of all my loved ones in the front-row seats. Mum and Dad are wearing their matching *toghu* outfits today, representing the Cameroonian culture, of course.

Rachel and Rhoda are grinning and waving at me like the proud and supportive sisters they've always been, Neha is waving too and sending me air kisses, and Jevaun—my love and soon-to-be-husband—is sitting there, looking dapper in his suit, and even more handsome than I remember seeing him earlier.

"Well, since I have a two-book contract with my publisher, the next book you'll see from me will be the second instalment of Vanessa's story. We all know book one is about her learning hard lessons about life and love, but in the next book, *Hope Restored*, she'll be finding love again and that's all I'm allowed to say."

"Oooh," Demi says. "I'm sure everyone is excited about that."

"Also, some of you know I got engaged recently." I whip out my hand and showcase the silver rock sparkling on my finger, and the crowd cheers. "My wonderful fiance and I are getting married in six months time and after that, we're going to be co-authoring a few Christian romance novels, with dual points-of-view."

Demi's jaw drops. "You're joking. That's so cool. I'm super excited about that and I cannot wait."

"Thank you." I smile before turning to look at Jevaun again. "I'm excited about it too, because he is an amazing writer. His debut Christian fantasy novel was published two years ago and since then he has published four more books in that series, which have touched the lives of so many people. I'm looking forward to doing business and ministry with him."

Jevaun mouths, "I love you," and the crowd 'awws' again before Demi speaks.

"We are all so excited for you, Bex, and we can't wait for the exciting things God has planned for you." She turns to the crowd. "Thank you all for being so engaging today. We hope you enjoyed the session. Bex will be signing books in the next ten minutes in the corner there and don't forget there are still lots of refreshments at the back. God bless you all and goodnight."

Music comes on and everyone stands, before scattering to different parts of the bookstore, either to the merch table, snacks table, or to purchase a copy of *Hope Arise* at the till.

I hug Demi, Neha, and the other girls from the Faith Writers group who came to support me. Then I walk over to my parents, hugging them tight as they speak more prayers and blessings over me. Rachel and Rhoda can't stop squealing as they shower me with praises about how confident I looked up there.

I didn't sleep at all last night as I was rehearsing the answers to my questions. The funny thing about the way God works is that I didn't even answer any of the questions the way I rehearsed. All I asked God for today before I climbed on that stage was for Him to give me the right words to say, and He did exactly that.

"Hey, beautiful." The deep voice that comes from behind warms my cheeks, and he slips his hand around my waist and pulls me close to him. The warmth of his body against mine sets off the butterfly feeling in my stomach and I turn around to welcome his loving gaze on me.

"Hey, handsome." I place my hand on his chest and fall into his arms, letting his scent tease my nostrils. "Sorry I put you on the spot there. I just can't stop talking about how amazing you are."

"It's okay." His cheeky smile shines through. "I hope you don't mind when I put you on the spot too and tell the world about how amazing you are."

"Oh, no. I just dug a hole for myself, didn't I?" We both laugh as he stares into my eyes.

"You know God is only getting started with us, right?"

I nod. "Yes, and I can't wait for everything He has in store."

"Oh, guess who RSVP'd for the wedding?"

I frown and tilt my head. "Who?"

"My dad."

I gasp. "Really? That's a good thing, right?"

Jevaun and his dad haven't really spoken since his sixtieth birthday party two years ago, but we've never stopped praying for him.

"Yeah, I guess. He'll be in London in a few weeks and he even offered to take us to dinner. He says he would like to meet you before the wedding, but you don't have to accept."

"Babe, I'd love to meet your dad. Who knows, maybe God has been doing something in his heart. I guess we'll have to wait and see."

"Yeah, okay then. I'll speak to Tré and see if he wants to join us too when he is back from Bali." Tréjon took a year out after completing his Foundation Programme to do some locuming and traveling. He'll be going back soon to start his GP training and we're all very pleased for him.

"I can't wait to marry you," Jevaun switches the conversation back to us as his lips inch closer to mine. I glance around to find my parents still engrossed in conversation with the people at the snacks table, so here's the chance to have my kiss before I spend the next hour signing books.

"Me too." I close the gap between us, my lips welcoming his and my hands travelling to the back of his neck. "I love you, Jevaun," I say when we break the kiss.

"I love you too." He winks at me and watches me walk away to the book signing table where Demi has set everything up, ready for me to get to work. But even as I go through the rest of the evening conquering my fear of talking to so many strangers, forming relationships, taking photos, and signing books until my wrists ache, I can't stop thinking about just how amazing God has been to me. My whole life is an answered prayer.

God promised He would do a new thing, and He did. But that leap of faith no longer scares me like it used to. As long as

God is with me, I know it will end in praise and it'll be all for my good.

THE END

(To read a bonus epilogue of Bex and Jevaun's proposal, click here or follow the link: https://dl.bookfunnel.com/28q79a2sx1

A PLEA

Thank you so much for reading this book. I would be very grateful if you could please take some time out to leave a review online by clicking here or following the link: https://books2read.com/u/49GkdX

Reviews are very important for independently published authors like myself. They help the book become more visible to others so they, too, can be blessed by it. Thank you again and God bless you.

GLOSSARY

1. Bex

1. "Ankara" refers to brightly coloured patterned clothes associated with West African fashion.
2. In British English slang, "soz" is an informal abbreviation for the word "sorry." It's usually used in text messages or online to express regret or to apologise, often for something minor.

6. Bex

1. "Chai" is a West African slang used as an exclamation to express surprise or disappointment or grief.
2. "Last coco" is a Cameroonian slang that refers to the last born of the family.
3. "Jollof rice" is a West African rice dish made from rice, tomatoes, chillis, onions, spices and sometimes other vegetables and/or meat in one single pot.
4. "Njangsang" is also known as Ricinodendron heudelotii, and it is a seed commonly used in West and Central African cuisine. It has a nutty flavour and tough exterior and is often used as a thickener and flavouring in various dishes like soups and sauces.
5. "Country Onion" refers to the fruit of the Afrostyrax lepidophyllus tree, a plant native to Cameroon, Gabon, and Ghana. The seeds are dried and used as a spice, often ground and used to flavour dishes like stews, sauces, and pepper soups.
6. "Weh" *is* a Cameroonian slang used to express sadness or disappointment. "Papa God" is Cameroonian Pidgin English for "Father God."
7. "Abeg" is a Pidgin English slang that means "please."

11. Bex

1. "Water fufu" is a Cameroonian starchy dish made from fermented cassava.

14. Bex

1. In British slang, "mandem" means a group of close male friends.

16. Bex

1. "Big Mami" is a Cameroonian pidgin slang which literally means "grand-mother' but can sometimes be used to refer to any woman.
2. "Ashia" is a Cameroonian slang which means sorry.

18. Bex

1. "Nyanga" is a Cameroonian slang that refers to the act of enhancing one's natural beauty or appearance.
2. "Mami Nyanga" is a Cameroonian slang used for a girl who likes to dress up, look cute and show off.

19. Jevaun

1. "Puff puff" are deep fried dough balls and a very popular West African street food.

25. Bex

1. "Ndolé" is a Cameroonian dish which consists of stewed peanuts, bitter leaves, fish or beef and prawns.

32. Bex

1. "Soya" is a popular Cameroonian street food, which is basically marinated beef that is threaded on skewers and grilled. Also known as suya in Nigeria.

38. Bex

1. "Poisson braisé" translates to braised fish in English and it is a popular dish in Cameroon which consists of braising a whole fish in a flavourful marinade often with vegetables and spices.
2. "Miondo" is another Cameroonian staple food made from fermented cassava and wrapped and cooked in thin banana leaves.
3. "Koki beans" is a Cameroonian dish made from blended black-eyed peas, cooked in banana leaves.

BOOK TWO

Rachel and James' story.
A Christian marriage of convenience romance.
(Coming soon)

AUTHOR'S NOTE

The inspiration for this story came to me in 2020 while I was reading a book called *Light On Glass* by Michelle Keener. In this women's fiction book, the main character was a writer and she took some time away from her family to go on a solo writing retreat, so she could finally finish the first draft of her first novel. I remember reading that book and being able to relate to the struggles of a writer that the main character was going through. I also really loved how the author weaved in the story the main character was writing into the main plot of the novel. I finished that book feeling so inspired to also write a book where either one or both of the main characters are writers and that's how the idea for *Love, Scribbles & Other Things* was born.

I didn't initially plan on tackling the heavy topic of sexual assault in this book, but as Bex beautifully described, once God starts tugging on your heartstrings, you can't stop until you birth the story. I knew it was going to be a very sensitive issue to discuss, so I had to rely on God to help me write in such a way that would still point every reader to the redeeming light we have in Christ.

Did you know that in the UK alone, 1 in 4 women have been

raped or sexually assaulted since the age of 16? The sad thing about this statistic is that as of September 2024, less than 2.7% of these cases have been reported to the police. So you see that there are so many women like Bex out there who are suffering in silence with lots of unresolved trauma because they are too scared to speak up.

While Bex decided (with God's guidance) to meet with her abuser face to face, forgive him and not report him to the police, I'd like to stress that this will certainly not apply to everyone. In Vanessa's case (again, with God's guidance), she chose to report her abuser to the police and even though these two women made different decisions, the one thing their stories had in common was that they both realised that their healing was found in God alone.

The key lesson I hope everyone will take from this book is that **there is no pain God's love can't heal. It doesn't matter what our past is and how broken we are. God is able to love us back together again. He is the only one that can make us whole again.**

If you are a victim or know someone whether man, woman or child who is a victim of sexual assault/abuse, then please know that there is help available through the police, medical professionals and also lots of charities who are working to provide the help and support you need. Please don't be ashamed or afraid to seek help. You don't have to go through the pain alone. Healing is very possible with Jesus.

The central Bible verse for this book was taken from **Isaiah 43:18-19** and it says *"Forget the former things; do not dwell on the past. See, I am doing a new thing! Now it springs up; do you not perceive it? I am making a way in the wilderness and streams in the wasteland."* This theme was mainly for Bex as she struggled with a lot of unresolved trauma in this book and needed to go through a lot of emotional healing. The scripture alludes to the fact that some-times we can become comfortable in the place we are in, until God forces us out of our comfort zone, to confront our fears, so that we can finally take that leap of faith with Him and start our healing journey. So if you have been stagnant and afraid to take that leap of faith with God, I hope this story encouraged you to embrace the new thing God is about to do in your life.

The key lesson for Jevaun in this book was that he needed to make the decision to protect his heart from the constant perse-cution he faced for his faith in God. Unfortunately there are a lot of Christians who are experiencing this because they have family members or friends who are either atheists or part of another religion. Jevaun had to learn that there was only so much he could do, actively praying of course, but also keeping a healthy distance, so he didn't become discouraged. I hope his story encouraged you to keep praying for your loved ones who are not saved. **God hears all our prayers and He will work everything out according to His good and perfect will at the right time.**

This is the first book where I was able to share more about my Cameroonian culture and I loved every minute of it. As some of you may know, I was born and raised in Cameroon–a small country in west central Africa. I hope you enjoyed learning a bit more about Cameroon. There's still so much to share and I'm excited to showcase all the amazing things about my home country in future books.

Finally, if you're reading this and you're yet to surrender your life to Jesus Christ as your Lord and Saviour, here's an open invi-tation to do so today. It is not too late. The Lord's open arms are waiting, and He is calling you to come home. Jesus has already paid the price for you. He wants you to abandon your pride today and run to Him. He has loved you from the beginning of time and He always will. If you want to take that bold step today, please say this prayer with me;

Dear Jesus, I come before you today with thanksgiving in my heart. I accept that you are God and I am not. I am a sinner, but You alone are the Forgiver of sins. Please come into my heart today. I surrender my all to you as my Lord and Saviour. Make me clean and teach me how to love and obey you. In Jesus' name I've prayed. Amen.

If you've prayed this prayer of faith and are willing to walk into your new life with Jesus, congratulations. Welcome to God's family. Please get plugged into a local church if you haven't already done so. Commit to studying the Bible with fellow believers and find a spiritual mentor you trust who will help you along the journey. If you would like to share a testimony with me, please reach out to me on social media or using the contact form found on my website: www.joanembola.co.uk.

Until the next book,

Lots of love,

Joan.

ACKNOWLEDGMENTS

Thank You Heavenly Father for giving me the inspiration to write this book, for breathing life into these words and for helping me get to this point. I would have never finished writing this story if You didn't help me. So I dedicate this story back to you, oh Lord. Please use it for Your glory.

To my love and amazing husband, Oladunni. Thank you *onitemi* for your constant support and for always reminding me that with God, I can do hard things. I love you so much.

To my beta readers, Blessing and Naomi. Thank you so much for your amazing feedback and encouragement. You helped me strengthen this story and I am so grateful.

To my editor, Michaela Bush, thank you so much for your amazing feedback as always. Your kind words are a great help to me. I always appreciate you.

To my cover designer, Carelle, thank you so much for bringing my vision to life. I appreciate your talent and hardwork so much. God bless you.

To you reading this book, thank you for giving it a chance. I hope it gave you hope and taught you to believe that there is no pain God can't heal. He loves you very much.

Finally, I'll have to go back to my Heavenly Father—the One who made this possible. My Lord, I started this journey with You and I'm finishing it with You. To You be all the glory, honour and praise forever and ever. Amen.

nhɪial68rz to download *A Promise To Keep,* which follows a Nigerian couple—Dayo and Dara as they navigate the challenges of life while learning about endurance and what it means to experience the goodness of God.

ABOUT THE AUTHOR

Joan Embola is a UK-based Cameroonian-Nigerian Christian author who aims to share God's love one word at a time. She writes books about multicultural characters whose hope-filled stories point to the love and goodness of God in our broken world. She is a qualified Physician Associate and also the founder of Love Qualified, a ministry dedicated to encouraging others to experience the sovereign love of the one true God who has qualified us to be His beloved ones. She is a passionate lover and teacher of God's Word, as shared on her YouTube channel and other social media platforms. When she's not writing or curled up with a book, you'll find her watching movies, YouTube videos, or making memories with her family and friends.

You can connect with her at www.joanembola.co.uk and on instagram, TikTok and YouTube. Subscribe to her newsletter to stay up to date with exclusive behind-the-scenes book news, cover reveals, how to sign up for advanced reader copies, and fun giveaways.

DISCUSSION QUESTIONS

- At the beginning of the book, we see Bex in a place where she is still struggling to deal with unresolved trauma but she is unable to tell anyone about it. Have you ever been in a situation like that where you feel no one will understand your pain, so you choose to go through it alone?

- We also see Jevaun struggling with a promise he made to his mum because he kept putting himself in a position where he was persecuted for his faith. Have you ever experienced persecution because of your faith in God?

- How would you describe the relationship between Bex and her sisters?

- How would you also describe the relationship between Jevaun and Tré?

- How would you describe the relationship between Bex and Olanna? Did they have a good foundation for their friendship?

- Do you know anyone who has experienced sexual assault? In what ways would you be able to support them?

- What roles did the side characters (Bex's parents, sisters and Tré) play in the lives of Bex and Jevaun? How did these people influence them?

- What lesson did Bex have to learn to get her to where God needed her to be?

- What lesson did Jevaun have to learn to get him to where God needed him to be?

- Do you understand the overall theme that the author was trying to portray?